D0467252

Also by Joanne Meschery

In a High Place

A Gentleman's Guide to the Frontier

Truckee: A History

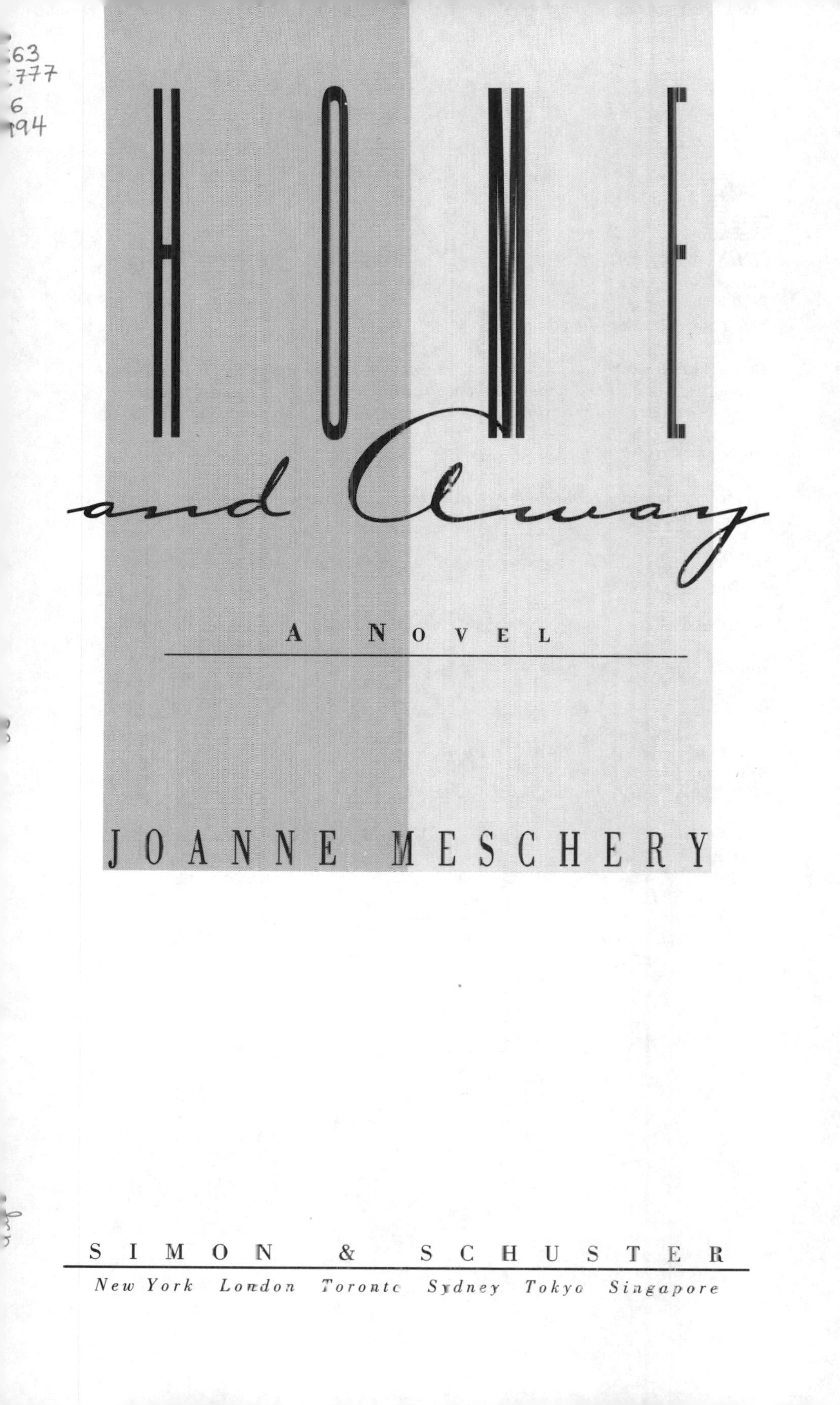

SIMON & SCHUSTER
New York London Toronto Sydney Tokyo Singapore

SIMON & SCHUSTER
Rockefeller Center
1230 Avenue of the Americas
New York, New York 10020

This book is a work of fiction. Names, characters, places and incidents are either products of the author's imagination or are used fictitiously. Any resemblance to actual events or locales or persons, living or dead, is entirely coincidental.

Designed by Bonni Leon

Manufactured in the United States of America

10 9 8 7 6 5 4 3 2 1

Library of Congress Cataloging in Publication Data
Meschery, Joanne, date.
Home and away / Joanne Meschery.
p. cm.
1. Family—California—Fiction. 2. Women—California—Fiction. I. Title.
PS3563.E777H66 1994
813'.54—dc20 *94-915*
CIP

ISBN: 0-671-88419-0

For Janai, Megan, and Matthew,
my children, my old sweethearts

. . . when best we love
We have no reason but to fail
in reason learning as we live
we cannot fail what we forgive.

—John Ciardi from "Song for an Allegorical Play"

It is a poor memory indeed that only works backwards!

—the White Queen to Alice in Wonderland

My daughter Jen got moved up to varsity the day we started bombing Iraq. I was working swing shift at the station when the war news came through on the scanner. Norman Spoon's voice broke against the static. "A few minutes ago, at about three P.M. Pacific Time," Norman says, "the United States and its allies launched air attacks on Baghdad under the code name Operation Desert Storm." And then Norman adds, "God bless America" and "Do you copy?"

Norman is the sheriff's office dispatcher. Now and then, things can get a little slow on the local level, so Norman does his best to provide some fast-breaking filler. He likes to keep himself on the cutting edge. He was 200 miles on the other side of these mountains, sitting out at Candlestick Park watching the Giants and the A's warm up when the big earthquake hit in '89. Somehow Norman made it to a phone before all the lines jammed and called up here to the station. And a good thing he did because we have an average of 11,000 vehicles passing through this place every day and most of that traffic is headed for the San Francisco Bay Area.

I am a wife (regardless of my present situation) and a mother, and a public officer, employed by the California Department of Agriculture. There are moments on the job when I like to think of myself as guardian of the great golden gates. If you are traveling all the way west on Interstate 80, you're bound to be stopped at this spot, just before the highway takes its final pitch up the Sierra's eastern wall. We are a border station, not exactly on the border—the state line falls some fifteen miles back. Still, it's possible I could be the first official representative of the state you meet. This is something I try to bear in mind. First impressions, my mother used to say. And so I am careful.

A few minutes after Norman's war dispatch, my daughter phones in tears. I tell Jen that some people would consider it an honor to be promoted from Girls' J.V. to the Women's Varsity Basketball team.

The leap to "women" is a pure lie for Jen's benefit. There are no adult females on the varsity team, only high school girls. Although you might claim an exception in the case of one top-scoring forward, who looks like she has a hot hand with more than a Wilson regulation basketball.

"Listen, Jen," I say. "Think about when you were a Brownie—the year I was your den mother."

"You were never a den mother," Jen says, with just a trace of accusation in her voice.

I ignore this, relieved to hear my sniffling daughter regaining herself. "You wore a brown uniform and a little brown beret."

"They weren't berets."

"Whatever," I say. It is my experience that a child will nearly always abandon tears for intellectual superiority over a parent. "Anyway, remember when you flew up? There you were—just a Brownie. And then, bingo, you flew up to full-fledged Scouts."

"This isn't the same," Jen answers. "I'm not ready for varsity. And besides, there's another thing—Coach Michaels says she wants to talk to you. I think she needs your permission to move me up."

Right here I get interested. I have only the most remote memory of the last time anyone required my permission.

"You can tell her no, Mom. Just say there isn't any way you'll let me do it." There's a little pause, then Jen adds, "You're my mother, after all."

I hang up, speechless. Jen has taken the words out of my mouth. If I've said it once, I've said it a million times: I *am* your mother, after all.

Outside the office, an Atlas moving van has pulled into the station's turnout. A trucker pushes open the office door and stamps his feet, as if to shake off bad weather. But it's a beautiful January day and there is no rain, snow, or sleet in California. For the fifth straight year, drought is general throughout the golden West. The truth is, this state is in something of a mess. Nobody can balance the budget. Our schools are a shambles; unemployment is on the rise. Still, people keep arriving.

This moving van holds 10,000 pounds of household goods from Chester, Arkansas. Including outdoor furniture, which, as I explain to the driver, presents a problem. I write up a quarantine notice and hand him a copy, along with a yellow slip that reads:

> Welcome to California! Your moving van invoice indicates that you are traveling from an area infested with gypsy moth. Upon reaching your destination, please call your friendly county Agricultural Commissioner and let him know that you are in town. If necessary, he will send a courteous inspector to your new home . . .

"Headaches." The trucker sighs over the slip of paper. Then he takes off his sunglasses and nods across the office counter. After a moment he says, "I've got a Florida orange in the cab of my truck."

"You'll need to leave it here," I tell him. I can see that this man wants me to confiscate something from him for the good of his soul. I follow him out to his truck and he hands me the orange, which is not Florida but Imperial Valley Valencia, simply making a trip back home.

I take the fruit anyway. As he pulls onto the interstate, the trucker waves from his high white cab. A law-abiding citizen. He looks pleased. This is not to say we don't get our share of tough customers. But working here, I have found that deep down, most people want to do the right thing.

We are the leading agricultural state in the nation, which is why we remain so vigilant about pests crossing our borders. Now and again somebody who is stopped forms the erroneous impression that California is a snob state, that we turn up our noses at the Georgia pecan, the Washington apple. But I can tell you, we're not all Hollywood and Silicon Valley. Next time you sit down to supper, think about the food we put on your table. Then consider the medfly, fire ants, apple maggots, pecan weevils, the alarming variety of deadly nematodes, and the sinister curly top virus. I could go on. If you caught just a glimpse of what I've seen in my years on this job, you'd be amazed that anything edible ever survives to cross your lips and travel the slippery, dark corridors of your large and small intestines.

In the lull between trucks I cross the lanes of cars waiting to be allowed through. There are normally four of us on duty here, and we like to rotate from automobiles to trucks, just for the sake of keeping things a little more interesting.

Midge is working the middle auto lane, bent at the window of a beige Chrysler. An elderly woman behind the wheel appears determined to surrender two harmless bananas, which Midge refuses. Midge is a no-

nonsense sort of person. She brooks no foolishness, as my father used to say before his stroke. But for all her cool efficiency on and off the job, Midge cannot drive a boat. If there is any good to come out of this drought, it will be that Steelhead Lake manages to drop another three feet, making it impossible for Midge Stiverson to put her Chris-Craft Avenger into the water.

Except for the deep twilight hours of graveyard shift, vehicles ease steadily through our lanes. There is a rhythm to the stop and go. Cars idle at different speeds. Tight brakes, soft brakes. Car windows are rolled down; I bow to one face after another, speak loud to be heard above the noise: "Good afternoon, where are you coming from, please?" Across the way, eastbound traffic roars toward Nevada, uninterrupted. No one is ever stopped when leaving the golden state.

The sound in my ears is that of a high wind. Midge looks up from the Chrysler and I tell her the war is on. She nods. We glance across the lanes to our shift supervisor, Marshall Painter, who does reserve duty at Mather Air Force Base. We're not really surprised by the war news, either of us. For weeks now, the lines of military convoys have grown longer. I've taken grapes, apples, and pears from the paper bag lunches of reserve privates who call me ma'am. They've been called up. One moment I'm checking freight papers for a truckload of Serta Perfect Sleepers, and the next, here comes a bill of lading for five and a half tons of armaments in a long silver van, unmarked except for a small round symbol and the code "Class A" printed beneath it. These trucks just keep rolling through. Nights on graveyard, come the top-secret loads—eighteen wheelers escorted by Chevrolet Suburbans with dark tinted windows and government plates. Antennas everywhere. The smoky electric window of the lead Suburban hums down. There is an M-16 racked below the dash. I bend to a man in the driver's seat, this man silent as the stars in the cold night sky. I do not ask, "Where are you coming from?" "Where are you going?" "Do you have anything to declare?" I wave the top-secret load up the interstate, over the Sierra into the pitch black climbing to 7,000 feet, then pounding down through the sweet Mother Lode and onto the straightaway that leads to Drake's Bay and the ports of San Francisco, Oakland. Mare Island. This beautiful country.

Then I tell Midge about how Jen is being moved up. My eyes burn from the wind, but there isn't so much as a breeze. Above the station, the stars and stripes and the state flag with its golden bear hang limp in the late afternoon sun. This wind is only a sound in my ears. And my eyes are brimming for no reason I can give. I am generally a very strong person. And my daughter has only been called up to varsity.

Midge lifts her eyebrows at that piece of news. She drops an Idaho potato into my hand, then gives me one of her nervy little smiles, a smile so crooked as to slide from mildly suggestive to outright salacious. "Life goes on," she says. But this isn't Midge talking philosophical—no high-flying sentiment because war has been declared and still these cars and trucks keep coming and a girl will put on the uniform of her school, then push up for the center jump with every hope of getting a piece of the ball.

I am crazy about Midge, but this needs to be said: Midge's mind has a tendency to run in the gutter. If Midge is talking about life, she is—strictly speaking and more often than not—talking about sex. And if she's directing her remarks to me, then you can trust it's in regard to two people. She is referring to my husband, Ward, and to a man named Pink.

Two

Last August after his stroke, my father came to live with us. That's when I added my maiden name, so it's now Hedy Gallagher Castle. I'm trying my best to create a family that counts my father in. Of course, Midge would prefer to see this recent addition to my signature as a reversion: the first step in subtracting Ward Castle from my life.

According to Midge, I have not spent the last half of my thirty-eight years being married to Ward. I've simply been raising him. Which is why, on the day following Ward's most recent departure, Midge's only comment was, "Congratulations, it's just possible your first child has finally left home for good."

This is Midge's opinion. I doubt you'll find another soul in town with a bad word to say about my husband. Locally, I married a legend. If you should ever stop for lunch at our town's popular Pastime Cafe, you'll find yourself dining with a gallery of Ward's trophies and glossy victory photos. There's a table beside a window reserved permanently for him. "Our town's greatest natural asset," the Pastime's grinning proprietor will tell you, nodding not to the spectacular thrust of the Sierra outside that window, but to the place setting and an empty captain's chair signifying my husband.

In this place called Coarsegold, where no gold was ever discovered, Ward Castle is a lightning vein of glitter splitting cold granite. He is St. Elmo's fire exploding from those icy peaks above town. And I saw this happen. There is nothing in the years since, or the time to come, that will ever erase that first winning day.

He stood at the crest of Tinker's Knob, where the rising sun first strikes. Daybreak, and the lower flank still in shadows, the snow packed solid—that slick frigid mountain like glass before the melting rays. He dropped into his demon tuck, shoved off, skis racheting the density of ice—a vibration pricking the soles of his boots, sending a tingle into his feet he claims he still feels to this day. Himself, the centrifugal force causing silver pines to lean aside, as if from a blast of wind. There are moments—I swear this—when mankind does not seem merely mortal. Standing at the bottom, even from a safe distance, I felt the very axle of the Earth snap, the trusses of my heart give way. He came straight down, like a stone, swift to the bottom. My heart flooded. They clocked his descent at 112.80 miles an hour. It was an unofficial record.

Four months later, when summer had melted all but the highest Sierra chutes, he followed the snow into the southern hemisphere. In Portillo, Chile, he made his time official. Ward Castle was the fastest individual ever on skis, ever in the world. A year later we were married. And a year after that he broke his own record in Chervinia, Italy. And the record stood. For five years running, no one had ever lived—nor was alive—who could better that time.

Jennifer was conceived and born into those winning years of muscle and stamina—record years. This may be one reason why I'm feeling that she can make the grade playing varsity. She is listed on the J.V. roster as a center, number 22, 5′11″, sophomore. Her lanky height dismays her. She lives in fear that she'll wake up some morning and discover she's topped six feet. I don't tell her that I continued to grow another inch and a half during my first and only year of college. I was what is called a late bloomer.

Even so, Jen has surpassed me by five inches, her father's height exactly. Her muscles are full of memories, a first dance of chromosomes that split the single cell in two, those two the scientists call daughter cells. She has Ward's quick hands the dense curve of his calf, high cheeks. Her brown eyes are mine—a tentative glance, whereas the body is sure. I am not a competitor. You'll find me sitting in the stands. But I know the game.

She's sleeping by the time I get home from work. I make a cup of instant Swiss mocha, decaf and sugar free, then climb the stairs to her bedroom. My father snores softly across the hall. Since his stroke he is a light sleeper, though he's less wakeful now that he has his little dog. He allows the dog to curl beside him under the blankets. Had you known my father before his illness, it would surprise you that he permits this. Or that a man who once tramped the pine woods with hearty black labs could ever love a quivering Chihuahua mix. He calls the dog Bark, because it is a word he can say. As his speech therapist keeps telling me: This is the person your father is now.

Jen's room is, as usual, clean and neat as a ribbon. There's no risk —even in the darkness—of tripping over her size 10 Adidas. No danger of splashing into a half-full can of soda left on her blue carpet. A mother is safe here; an adult could live in this room. Such adolescent tidiness disturbs me. I do not find anything about it normal.

Every last article of my daughter's clothing is folded away into drawers or hung in her closet. One hundred and two cassette tapes are alphabetized according to artist and catalogued in pale wooden fruit crates Jen pirated from my workplace. On a top bookshelf, her collection of furry miniature mice is arranged by sex and occupation as suggested by wardrobe: bespeckled professor mouse, a distinguished silver-gray male in starched smock and tiny stethoscope, male wearing kilts, lederhosen, hard hat, policeman, fireman, farmer in overalls, jockey. Of female mice, there are four: bride in white, nurse in white, Swan Lake ballerina wearing downy white feathers, and one white-aproned, sharp-nosed grandmother looking closer to the mole family.

"You do know," I said to Jen one afternoon, "that mice aren't really all that cute." According to our border station's official guidelines, only those mice of the domesticated variety are allowed entry.

Jen was sitting across the room, at her desk with the plastic executive organizer holding her school supplies in absolute order. She shut her geometry book and frowned up at me, puzzled.

I waved a hand toward the bookshelf. "I just mean that basically mice are rodents—they're disease-ridden vermin."

"Mother," she said, "you are warped."

Below these mice, one shelf down, stand the stubby troll dolls, singular obsession of Jen's second grade. My daughter is her own fastidious and faithful archivist. She requires no doting mother to lovingly fill scrapbooks and label boxes of mementos to be stored in the attic. It seems nothing belonging to Jen has ever escaped her room. Stand here too long and you may never leave.

Over the past week I've climbed the stairs to her bedroom feeling full of resolve—determined even now to maintain myself in the midst of this room where nothing has ever been lost. To keep my composure, to tell her what I feel in the marrow of my bones to be true. To say,

"Jennifer—about your father. About your dad. I don't think he's coming home this time. I got another letter. I'm pretty sure this time he's gone."

She stirs in her double bed, rolling away from me. I haven't touched her. I could not so much as brush her hand and find a voice for what I've just said.

"What," she mumbles, finally coming awake. "What's going on?"

I shrug, feeling all of a sudden like I should be wearing my sweater. My arms seem so bare, stiff in this green Department of Agriculture regulation shirt. This man's shirt. "Just nothing." I turn from her bed. Stand here too long and you will lose your nerve every time. I pause in the doorway, searching for something more to say. "I mean, I was just wondering if you'd decided about the team. You know . . . moving up."

"Oh that," she says, as if the whole idea had never caused her a second thought, reduced her to tears only hours ago. "I talked to Pink and he said I should do it."

She flops away from me, her weight squeaking the mattress springs. She is a big girl, large-boned. Strong, like her father.

But she still needs my permission.

Safe in that knowledge, I wander downstairs. I pour cold Swiss mocha into the sink. Never mind what Pink says. This man Pink, as everybody knows, is a Minnesotan and short. He is a graduate of Gustavus Adolphus College—an institution whose name puts me in mind of anemic students addicted to cough drops—where he majored in what appears to be bad journalism and played soccer, which is not an American game. And it is on this basis that Pink Lindstrom presumes to write a sports column for the *Coarsegold Register* and advise my daughter as to whether she should or should not move up to varsity basketball.

I sling my clothes over a chair, pull on a flannel nightgown, and shoo Dustin off my bed. Dustin is our ninety-five-pound rottweiler, but not vicious as these dogs are sometimes said to be. "You are developing terrible habits from Bark," I tell him. Although I think if I were seventy years old and alone as my father is alone and unable to call upon all the words I had ever known and exiled from myself without warning and so suddenly as to scarcely comprehend that split second when the full present of my life became the past forever—well, then I think I would sleep with a dog, even an animal the size of Dustin.

Before I turn off the light, I watch a minute of late news—a Day 1 recap of our war in the Gulf. I see a family in Tel Aviv stepping into a sealed room, then fitting gas masks over their heads. Despite the airtight mask, the man of this family is still able to tell the viewing audience about the weight of plastic used to cover windows, how a towel can be wedged at the base of a door.

In the darkness I pray, although I am not necessarily a religious person. Only a creature of habit, a preacher's kid—P.K. The man upstairs, not God but my father. A man of the cloth who ministered all of forty years to the sick and poor, the weak of heart. The person he is now.

I pray for him. And for the war to end, even as it's begun. For the family in gas masks. Bring them safe through the night. For my husband's safe delivery from drought. Set his feet in the deep powder snow. Bless my daughter who still needs my permission. She is only fifteen. Still a child. I rest, safe in the knowledge.

Safe, I sleep.

Three

They are usually awake first. My father was an early riser, even before his stroke. Some days it's still dark outside when I hear him in the kitchen. And Jen never sleeps through her alarm. Every morning, without fail, she eats a well-balanced breakfast. She makes it to the corner way ahead of her school bus. She has not once, so far as I know, neglected to study for an exam or forgotten a homework assignment. With Jen, I sometimes have the feeling there's been a mix-up similar to a delay in the mail. She hasn't yet been notified that she's a teenager.

"Anyway," I tell her as she slips a flawless poached egg onto wheat toast, "the point is that Mr. Lindstrom has no part in this decision."

"You mean Pink," Jen says.

I pour a cup of coffee. "Well, whoever."

It seems our conversation was never interrupted by seven hours of sleep. I've found this to be a feature of family life. It's possible to resume almost exactly where you left off. The topic of conversation is always on the floor and nobody ever needs to read the minutes of the previous meeting. Since I tend to be named to committees and am presently serving on one where nearly all subjects wind up tabled, it's a relief to climb out of bed in the morning and discover that nobody's really had the last word and everything is still open for discussion.

My father pays no attention to our conversation, his head bent over the newspaper. The headline says, WAR WIDENS. It is Day 2 of Operation Desert Storm I don't know how much of the news my father understands, although we've been working on his reading. He runs a finger across the columns, as if following the words, and sometimes he says one aloud in a voice that's perfectly clear. Once—this happened while he was still in the hospital—I sat on his bed turning pages in a *Life* magazine. My father rolled his eyes at a picture of Margaret Thatcher, who was prime minister at the time. Then he tapped his finger on her sharp chin and said "battle-ax," plain as that. So I think there is hope.

"Just what," Jen wants to know, "is the problem? Yesterday you were pushing me to move up." She polishes off her orange juice, rinses her dishes in the sink, then kisses her grandfather's bowed head. "Catch you later, Reverend."

He glances up over his glasses and grins at that old familiar title, a word he knows better than his own name, which is Galen.

"It's just an awfully big jump to varsity," I say. "A lot of pressure." Standing here, I remember that it's not Brownies, but Bluebirds who fly up to be Campfire Girls. And Cub Scouts are the only ones with den mothers. And Jen is altogether too young and far too preoccupied with neatness to ever mix it up under the basket among varsity women. Yes, they are women—forget whatever I've said. And not just women, but amazons, long of limb, broad-backed, with fierce, steaming eyes. As official J.V. scorekeeper, I sometimes stay to watch the varsity team take the floor. So I know whereof I speak.

"Listen," I tell her, "maybe you should give junior varsity one more year, stay where you are. Besides, I thought you needed my permission."

Jen shoots me a look and hauls on her royal blue letterman's jacket with its fleecy white C for Coarsegold. Pinned to that chunky block letter is nearly all the precious metal this town has to offer: gold lyre for band (she plays the trombone), lamp of knowledge for scholarship and her A average, gavel for student government, a shining star for her selection as Student of the Month last October, and one gold basketball the circumference of a marble signifying a game average of 14 points, 11 rebounds, and 5 assists. In this laden jacket, Jen is already a walking autobiography. It worries me how she'll bear the weight of her life by the time she's a senior.

"Maybe you're right," she says. For a minute she hesitates at the door, looking so serious it seems she isn't leaving for school, but going for good—a light traveler with all her credentials crammed on her chest.

She slings her book bag over one shoulder and blows a strand of pale brown hair from her eyes. "The thing is, I am sort of stressed about this. Coach Michaels will want me to play the high post, and I'm so slow—too slow. Plus, my jump shot sucks. And *plus,* there's you and Dad."

I hold myself still a moment, set my coffee cup in the sink. Now I think I should tell her about the letter, about how her father hasn't left this place simply to find snow, but to find himself—he actually wrote this. How he would plant his skis at the top of the hundred-meter run of rigid hard-pack and let go, hit the speed trap streaking 140 miles per hour and break the current record, rise first in the world again, his comeback. To tell Jen now: Your father has this thing he feels he must do. Instead I slide my eyes slow, away from her. "What about me and your dad?"

"I don't know," she says, her voice trailing.

I watch her take a step from the doorway, as if to get out of the bright morning sun. She's grown up with Ward's comings and goings. "It's Daddy's job," I used to explain when she was little. Ward phoned from every race, and I'd hold the receiver to her ear. Sometimes I truly think this was how she learned to talk. "Tell Daddy good luck," I coaxed. "Gaahhh," Jen would garble. And I always translated: "She says good luck . . . She loves you . . ." Until, sooner than I ever thought possible, Jen wasn't just talking, but jabbering, and Ward would laugh when I got on the line and say, "She gives good phone."

It used to be that easy. We never hung up without Jen saying, "When are you coming home?" We shared the telephone—Jen and I. We shared Ward's absences. And every absence seemed to draw the two of us closer, giving us easy freedoms with each other.

But standing here now, I feel my daughter losing courage. She's stopped asking Ward, "When are you coming home?" And she won't ask me. Everything is not open for discussion, after all. Some silent motion has been made to table the subject of a husband and father who's already been gone eight months—since June 9, to be exact.

Right now we need somebody else to step into the room, somebody to tell us that eight months is just a very long time for a person to be searching for snow. Somebody, now. I turn to my own father, stuck on the same page of the newspaper. Since he came to live here, he has not once spoken Ward's name. But then, he's lost so many words. Aphasia, the medical report calls it—an impairment in the use and/or comprehension of spoken and/or written language. My father's "deficit," the doctor says.

Of course, if Midge was present she'd give us to understand in no uncertain terms. Never mind that I've told Midge—as I've also explained to Jen—that the bottom line here is livelihood. I believe it is;

truly, I want to believe. So I could try to make the point once more—ask Jen: How can your father earn a wage in this drought, instill his winning technique with no snow or a streaking white run down a mountain and no beginners, intermediates, or advanced skiers to teach?

But it seems Jen and I are already past this question, way beyond the need for easy answers.

Finally she looks over with a shrug. She tries for a smile. "Pressure," she says. "That's what comes from having a famous dad and a beautiful and intelligent mother. Right?"

"Oh, sure," I mumble. I think there's a laugh intended here, but I can't find it.

"Pink said that part about beautiful, I didn't," she adds. Then quick, she is out the door.

I follow her to the front gate, watch her tramp down the walk in her sharp-pressed jeans. She is the only child I know who enjoys ironing. "There's one thing," I say.

She glances over her shoulder.

"Ask my permission."

"Give it to Coach Michaels," she says, walking on.

"Ask me."

She swings around, hooks her thumbs in her pockets, and tips her chin, as if listening for a sound, the click of a timer counting off seconds. Finally she says, "Mother, may I . . ."

There was a game we used to play . . . Take one baby step, you may take a giant step.

"You may."

Jen nods, then saunters off. But not before I hear her say, "Ditzoid," a term I think she means for me.

I lean against the metal gate. It's so mild for January, Jen scarcely needs her jacket—so mild I'm out here in my nightgown. My hair is longer than it's been since I was seventeen, only because I never seem to get time for a cut. Magazines talk about middle-age acne, which I believe I have. This is hormonal; the rest is a downward pull. Take away my bra, and a straight line can be drawn between my elbows that will precisely intersect the nipples of both breasts. This is not Jen's geometry, but my age.

"And another thing," I call after her, "you can play the high post with the best of them." She's nearly to the corner, the school bus is just slowing curbside—the closest she's ever come to not being there. "Listen to me—the jump shot is yours. You can make that shot with your eyes closed!"

Then she is on the bus, a square of royal blue crammed against a moving window. In public, Jen will sometimes masquerade as a legitimate teenager. She won't wave, because that would not be cool. And I can't say that I was ever, or am now, beautiful. But there will come a day—I guarantee this to happen—one day in a rush out the front door I'll grab her jacket by mistake, the way you do when you're in a hurry and not looking. She'll truly be gone then, somewhere out in the world like her father. But her jacket will still be on a hook in the hallway because, as I've said, nothing of Jen's has ever been moved upstairs to the attic.

So there I'll be, snapped into that jacket, racing down the aisle of the supermarket, looking for oregano, or bay leaves, or whatever little item it is that I've just got to have, when all of a sudden I am stunned by the feeling that this very moment has occurred before. Exactly, as in déjà vu. Which is not to say that a person has had some other life in which this same thing actually happened. Only that there is a life taking place in the mind—an existence moving backward and forward that will not let the school bus simply pull away, but would have me standing in the supermarket, even as I am standing here watching her go. Would have me wander into the aisle marked Baby Needs, where I am known to linger now and then for the lost smell of talcum powder and the sight of all those small colorful jars lined like rows in a vegetable garden. Plant me there, in her jacket I will never grow into. The knit cuffs hang at my knuckles, her gold pins flash loose on my chest. Everything she ever was I wear on my body. Catch me later in her jacket, in the flesh, and I think then I may be beautiful. I can picture this clearly, though I'd give the world to keep that day off the calendar. But as Midge says, Life goes on. Jen is already moving up.

Before leaving for work, I linger over one last cup of coffee. My father has abandoned his newspaper, moving into the other room for a TV recap—"Yesterday in the Gulf." For a minute I study the paper's front page, then I reach for my purse. I open Ward's letter, spreading it flat on the newsprint and read again:

Dear Hedy,

Sorry I haven't written lately, but things have been going downhill very fast over here. (That's Bruno Hall's bad joke—we've been clocking each other in the trap.) Anyway, the skiing's great. We've had almost perfect conditions—no catch to the snow at all. It looks like Dibloc's finally agreed to sponsor. And I'm feeling terrific. Like I told you a couple of weeks ago on the phone, I seem to be at the most unbelievable place in my life right now. It isn't just being on the circuit again. It's more inside me, like I'm on that edge where everything is just about ready to come together. I'm getting so close, Hedy. For the first time in years, I'm feeling almost like my old self. God, I love you—just being able to tell you and know you'll understand exactly what I'm saying, because I can't quit now. I never thought I'd get another chance at this—probably my last chance. I mean, to really find myself, to be 100% who I am. I've got to go with this, sweetheart—no matter how long or wherever it takes me. Otherwise, I'll be no good to you or anybody else, especially myself. Meantime, I'm just damned lucky to have your love and all your strength behind me. . . .

I fold the letter back into my purse and dig for my car keys. I wish I could sit now and write an answer to match Ward's breezy downhill words.

He says conditions are perfect. And even in this drought. I know absolutely what those conditions are. The course is deep and solid, frozen hard—they call this transformed snow. There's no slush to snag and slow the skis. It would be a day without wind, with the temperature hovering at 25 degrees I could fold my hands at the table now and pray, Give us this day . . .

Of course, I have no control—I can't order snow to drift from the clear, frigid sky. But here at home, within these walls, I've tried to keep all the conditions as close to perfect as possible. And until lately—until this most recent letter—I thought I understood what those conditions were. I believe I've wanted Ward to succeed nearly as much as he himself has.

What they say about sports is true—especially at such an excellent and rarified level. It's irresistibly charged, if not thoroughly addictive. Watching Ward race, I've felt that loud straight-on buzz—fear so strong as to be erotic. So many nights, I've lain beside his sore, bruised body and heard him whispering those familiar words, "Winning isn't everything, it's the only thing." And in this high striving Ward has never wavered.

There's something admirable about such intensity of purpose. I've always been aware—even appreciated—that I am not, and never will be, the sole subject of Ward's single-mindedness. This knowledge has been something of a relief. I've never courted anyone's undivided attention, never craved a full spotlight aimed at center stage. For as long as I can remember, I've preferred to remain in the safe middle distance of a person's range of vision.

I've been told that couples are drawn to each other in two ways: love at first sight, or love as a slow process of discovery. And I tend to agree. Either way is fine by me, as long as it all takes place through binoculars. I have never wanted to be too discovered.

If only for this reason, I believe Ward and I were destined to meet. Our paths first crossed on a long ago September night at Coarsegold High. Ward was an upperclassman—an established senior—dancing at the Freshman Welcome Mixer with one of my laughing, buxom classmates. I mention buxom because at that humble, freshman time, I myself remained braless in my Fruit of the Loom undershirt.

I'd attended this mixer with Midge. She explained how the dance was not so much a welcome as an opportunity to taunt and humiliate us underclassmen, heap torment upon us. "Then why are we even here?" I asked as the two of us stepped inside the crepe-papered cafeteria. "We're here because we're virgins," Midge said, her voice barreling loud above the music. "And we're looking for true erections."

Just then the music stopped, interrupting Little Richard in mid-scream. On the dance floor, couples broke apart and lunged to grab fresh partners. It was a get-acquainted ploy—each stop and start of the music forcing students to dance with somebody new. "You're new," Ward said, bumping against my shoulder as I wandered past. I wasn't even dancing at the time, not even playing this get-acquainted game. "We're virgins," Midge quipped, right behind me. (It shouldn't surprise you that in our yearbook, Midge is listed as Class Clown.)

Ward smiled as the music started up again. "I'm Ward Castle," he said to me. I couldn't speak, my cheeks still burning from Midge's announcement. I was a virgin. I was new. I wore my navy trapeze dress that hung shapeless and my hair cut blunt across my forehead, revealing a pale band of skin where the summer sun had never touched. It hurt to look into his bright eyes. Yet somehow I was able to shuffle my feet dancelike until the music stopped and he stepped away. But not before he said, "Are you really one?" I swung around, puzzled. He shrugged. "You know what I mean." I blinked off across the cafeteria, the hot crush of groping, entering freshmen. It was 1967, and everywhere a musky hint of the sexual revolution hung in the air. Finally I turned back to him. "I'm not absolutely one," I said, steadying my prim voice close to his ear. "Just physically."

Maybe it was this remark that first sparked Ward's interest in me. He might've understood even then that there was something chaste about him as well—how he saved himself for speed alone, the next perilous run consuming his whole passion.

I doubt anyone else could've seen what a perfect match we were—aware only of a slight timid girl trailing alongside Coarsegold's rugged, rising star. To those who walked our high school's corridors, Ward Castle was like some earth-shaking event. But for me, Ward represented excitement without chaos. A dramatic but orderly romance—that's what I'd wanted and somehow miraculously found. It was only after he'd left for the University of Colorado that I felt a first sharp panic that I might be losing him for good. But I shouldn't have worried. Ward complained—actually confided to me—that campus co-eds were way too possessive. So he avoided each and every one, along with the Vietnam War. "That's what I love about you," he told me time and again, phoning long distance from his Colorado dorm. "You're always there." I noted that he never once said "here." And across the miles, I adored him all the more, thrilled at the pure luck of creating a relationship without plunging dangerously into the thick of one. Safe at home (except for one brief foray over the mountains to Sacramento State) I remained dreamily in love, my romance thriving in the sunny, agreeable bosom of family.

Yet, when Ward and I announced our plans to marry, my parents appeared surprised. It seemed they never really believed Ward and I were seriously involved. My mother sat me down and gazed at me long and hard. She asked: Are you sure this is what you want? I'd finished only that first year of college, but just then I thought I knew all I needed. Ward had bestowed his educated kisses on me; I'd graduated into his sure arms. On my finger I flashed a two-carat diamond—a ring I've long since locked in a box for safekeeping. The price of this diamond was drastically reduced by our local jeweler's admiration for Ward's racing talents.

This is something I learned early on: exceptional allowances are made for exceptional athletes. We're not all paying the same price. There are those irresistible few, those who by sheer beauty and physical genius appear able to surmount anything—world records and championships, the steepest obstacles, lowliest conventions.

But with Ward, I gladly paid full price. I couldn't deny myself the complete certainty of his smile, his exhilarating strength. His body seemed its own sweet victory. Never mind that the first time Midge watched him race—so sleek in his low tuck, his arms extended, parting the air—she said he reminded her of a hood ornament. Inside that tight, sealed racing suit I knew Ward in the flesh. I traced the pale knobs of his wrists, both wrists broken the fourth year we were married. I braced my hands at his knees, as if to repair the ragged ligaments.

When Ward tore the medial collateral in his left knee the second time, I applied for a Class A position at the border station. I hadn't intended to work for more than that winter. But after I learned that I'd been hired above six others, when I realized just how much faith had been placed in me . . . well, of course, I felt a further obligation. And I found a surprising satisfaction as well. With Jen starting school and Ward racing all over the world, a day seldom passed that I wasn't glad to leave our empty house for work.

My occasional talk about having another baby never seemed to get very far. But then, those conversations usually took place long distance —me here, Ward there. Plus, our finances sometimes presented a worry. Speed skiing isn't what you'd call a steady job. Fortunately, Ward had little trouble attracting sponsors. And we needed them. I would never have guessed how fast a simple article like ski wax can add up to a small fortune.

But somehow we always almost managed. When he wasn't training or racing the circuit, Ward worked part-time at ski areas here or there. And we had my income as well. Then, six years ago, Ward announced his retirement from the sport. It was a surprise announcement—surprising even to me, since Ward was skiing in Vail at the time. He still ranked high—twelfth in World Cup competition. But he explained that he wanted to quit while he was ahead. With some dignity, he said.

Naturally, I felt excited and just slightly beside myself at the prospect of having Ward and his full attention home for good. I opened cookbooks. I regrouted the bathroom shower and bought new sheets, or "bedclothes," as the department store clerk in Sacramento referred to them. For the "Master Bedroom," these sheets of the softest Egyptian cotton and 220 threads per square inch.

Then, not more than a week after Ward had hung up his racing bib, Alpenglo Resort—Coarsegold's biggest—hired him as director of skiing. The position sounded important and permanent, and pregnancy crossed my mind again. But Ward didn't appear at all interested. Plus, by that time I'd been given a Class B promotion in my own job. And of course, I had Jen. Most of all, Jen.

When it comes to my daughter, you won't be surprised to hear that Midge has accused me of classic compensating, a phrase she's been bandying about since 1976. This doesn't bother me in the least. From the day Jen was born—when I first saw her slippery with afterbirth and heaved flopping onto my pale belly—from that moment, I knew that the full price I'd given for love had been prepaid and repaid a million times over. Even as Midge has continued to shove a whole library of Self-Help under my nose, I've persisted in believing. With Jen, I've been wholly compensating and compensated.

But for Ward, it seemed nothing quite amounted to enough—not the carefully boned salmon poached with Walla Walla onions and sun-dried tomatoes. Or the master bedroom bedclothes, with me snug along the curve of his back and those dreamy down pillows under our heads.

Ward had trouble sleeping in his own bed. His new position as ski director turned out to be scarcely more than a title. Two months into the job, he'd accomplished little beyond signing several dozen promotional form letters. By March, he'd ridden a chairlift with Prince Albert of Monaco and provided an afternoon's instruction to executives from Kodak's San Francisco office. Otherwise he skied every run, where he could easily be seen. The sight of Ward shooshing down a slope proved good for business.

Then the drought hit. All around town, resorts opened late in the season and shut down early. Ward still drew his monthly paycheck, but suddenly he was home almost full-time. And his attention was definitely not on me. He stood at our living room window and gazed up at the bare summit. He checked the mantle clock, forever calculating the time in Switzerland, Austria, France.

I'd more or less assumed there'd be a few rough spots after Ward retired. He'd need to do some adjusting. The truth is, home can be such a reality. I think there's a tendency to forget this, particularly among those of us who've been steeped in it for a while—home, that is. But sometimes it seemed Ward and I weren't simply resuming where we'd left off, the way we'd managed all his comings and goings in the past. Instead, it felt as though we were creating a whole new marriage. And with Jen, too—the three of us settling into being together full-time.

And then one night—facing the fourth winter of drought—I woke up shortly after 2:00 A.M. and found Ward waxing his skis. He sat on the sofa in the living room, one Dynamic ski laid across his knees—that ski, 240 centimeters long, the international requirement. His racing skis. He'd drained all the water from my steam iron and was melting a stick of Dibloc up and down the ski's smooth cobalt blue surface. He claimed his old iron—the one he'd always used to heat the wax—had broken. He'd thrown it out. He was using my good iron, with the twelve settings and the misting feature, plus automatic shutoff in case you forgot and left the house with it on, and the wax drizzling down the hot silver flat of it onto his knees with the scars—three very small holes around the kneecaps from orthoscopic surgery, you wouldn't notice unless you'd held his leg across your lap the way I saw him holding that ski—wax trickling over the arm of the sofa, dripping to the carpet. For a minute he sat nodding up at me, telling me, explaining everything. But all I could think to say was how hard, it would just be so hard, to get that wax out of everything if I ever could.

Then Jen heard us and came downstairs. And at that moment, I realized Ward was sitting there naked. But Jen didn't seem aware, even though she was about to turn fifteen and of that age. Thinking back, I believe all either one of us saw was the ski. It was the ski, I think, that made him appear wholly clothed.

So naturally I had no idea I'd been on the verge of tears this entire time until I followed Jen back up the stairs and tried to tuck her into bed, when she told me, "I'm no baby." And then she said, "Is he going? Dad?"

"Not right tonight," I answered, pulling myself together. "But maybe for a while he'll be gone. You know—like before," I said.

And so, in June, he left for a race at Mount Hood. He was still well within the continental United States. But he skied just fast enough to place. And from then on, it seemed almost like before. Ward believed he could reclaim his old spot on the World Cup circuit, even at age forty-two. I had to admit this was possible. Speed skiing doesn't necessarily require the agility of youth—there are no razor turns through the giant slalom's gates. Ward's sport is directly down, straight down, as in the shortest distance between two points, the path of least resistance . . . Twenty seconds and you're at the bottom—twenty seconds tops. Ward contended that whatever he might've lost with age, he could more than compensate with experience. He possessed the strength to hold his tuck against the jolting force of wind and speed. And he remains one of the finest wax technicians in the world.

I found some on the dog, splashed and hardened—wax, pale as moons. There were little drops on the kitchen windowsill. I scraped it off the good sheets. I ran hot water hard to melt it from under my fingertips. I'm still finding it.

Then, on August 17 this past summer, I was seated at my keyhole desk, paying bills, when the phone rang. I heard Dr. Vernon telling me to come to the hospital. My father had suffered a stroke. After that, everything tumbled fast, in a scalding blur of hours. I called my brother Dex from the hospital, and he said he'd be on the first plane. Then I drove to the school and picked up Jen. We stayed at the hospital until my father opened his eyes. That was around one in the afternoon. Jen said she'd wait in the room while I tried to reach Ward. Except I couldn't think where he was. Ever since morning, I'd been frantic to remember, because I knew Ward had told me and it was written down somewhere—I'd written it myself—the name of the hotel and number. I should've known. But it seemed my entire daily life and every detail had vanished right out of my head.

I tore home from the hospital, thinking I only needed to slow down, stay calm, and sort carefully though all the papers strewn across my desk. Fortunately, Midge arrived just as I got started, or I might still be looking. It was Midge who had the presence of mind to pull the credit card statement from the stack of bills I'd been paying. On July 30th, Ward had charged sun block and wax at a ski shop in Argentina —Las Leñas, the statement said.

"Of course," I told Midge, suddenly knowing, recalling exactly what Ward had told me—how he'd been training there for the past three weeks.

I let Midge dial all the numbers. When she finally got Ward on the line, she handed me the phone. But all I could think was how I couldn't speak Spanish and I'd never be able to make myself understood. And then I realized this was Ward saying, "Honey, we've got a bad connection, there's an echo. Can you call me back?"

I shook my head. Ward's voice sounded deeper—husky, as if he'd been asleep. I had no idea what time it could be in Argentina. But I didn't hear any echo. I cleared my throat. "It's Dad," I said.

And then I was rushing, telling Ward everything that had happened, and I knew he would ask, just as he'd asked that time when I got so scared and called him about Jen having the appendicitis attack, which it turned out she wasn't . . .

"Sweetheart—listen," he said. "I'm twenty minutes from the airport. I can probably make it home by tomorrow night." There was a little pause. "Do you want me to come?"

I turned to Midge, as if she could answer. Yes. I wanted Ward home. Now. This wasn't like that other time. My mother had still been alive then. I looked off, thinking maybe if she was here now, my mother—the two of us sitting in that hospital room—then maybe it would be different. I could tell Ward not to worry, we'd keep him posted, and if things got any worse . . .

I swung back to the phone, hearing Ward asking, "Is he awake—your Dad? Is he conscious?"

"Yes," I answered, and I could see my father's eyes blinking open, and his mouth open, too—his whole face wide and utterly still with confusion.

"Well, that's a good sign," Ward said.

"Yes," I whispered. My father's eyes are hazel brown—almost amber. His hair is white, but it looked darker against the hospital pillows. As I'd left his room, a nurse arrived to change the IV. Jen sat clutching her schoolbooks in her lap, as if she might read something while I was gone, put her mind to it. But I knew she'd be worrying, waiting for me.

"I mean, if he's awake and conscious . . ." Ward's words trailed away, as if he was waiting, too.

For a moment I let the silence on the other end stand, refusing to say what it seemed he wanted to hear. Then finally I sighed into the receiver, my voice stammering, my breath stale with coffee. "I think maybe I should just get back there—to the hospital. Maybe if I call you tonight . . . I might know more. Maybe we'll have a better connection."

"Well, if you're sure," Ward said, speaking fast all of a sudden and louder. "All you need to tell me is what you think—what you want."

"I think everything will be all right," I said, though I did not honestly believe that. But some part of me still stood at the base of the mountain, still followed the path of least resistance. There was no drought. My father still commanded the language. He opened his Bible and spoke with the tongues of angels . . . *Love beareth all things, believeth all things, hopeth all things, endureth all things* . . . And Ward would only be gone for a while. Like before.

"Try not to worry," I told him.

"You too," he said. "And tell your dad I'm thinking about him. He's just so lucky, Hedy—lucky you're there."

Five

I'd been at work maybe five minutes when Marshall, our shift supervisor, handed me this:

LEAGUE GAMES 1990–91
Coarsegold Lady Miners Varsity Basketball

DATE	DAY	OPPONENT	TIME	PLACE
Jan.18	Friday	Foothill H.S. SQUEAKER	6:00 P.M.	Home
Jan.25	Friday	Iola H.S. Killer	6:00 P.M.	Away
Jan.29	Tuesday	Seven Persons H.S. Killer	6:30 P.M.	Away
Feb.1	Friday	Meadow H.S. KB	6:00 P.M.	Home
Feb.5	Tuesday	Rich Lake H.S. KB	6:00 P.M.	Away
Feb.8	Friday	Seven Persons H.S.	6:00 P.M.	Home
Feb.19	Tuesday	Meadow H.S.	6:30 P.M.	Away
Feb.22	Friday	Foothill H.S.	6:00 P.M.	Away
Feb.26	Tuesday	Rich Lake H.S.	6:00 P.M.	Home
March1	Friday	Iola H.S.	6:00 P.M.	Home
March 7-8-9	Th.Fri.Sat.	State Tournament Northern Division	TBA	Sacramento Capital Events Center

Head Coach: Grace Michaels
* School Holiday, Feb.11-15 (Ski & Skate Week)

The comments belong to Midge. She had the day off, but made a point of dropping by the station with this schedule so I could begin worrying *now* about tomorrow night's game, which according to Midge will be a Squeaker, followed by a Killer next Friday. K.B., Marshall explained, stands for Kick Butt. He said Midge had been watching the war news. Otherwise the word would be Laugher, meaning the team shouldn't have any trouble getting past those schools.

Midge is probably right about all this. She's an involved parent—member of the Coarsegold Booster Club and chair of the Family Life

Education Committee on which I serve. Midge and her husband have three children and are hosting an exchange student from the island of Martinique. Midge's youngest son Foster plays varsity football—wide receiver—and is a self-described gross person, a quality I appreciate. Occasionally I come downstairs from telling my immaculate daughter goodnight and am filled with an urge to dial Midge's number just to hear again the horrific description of Foster's bedroom—a place where unspeakable filth has caused orange stalagmites to find nourishment on something as utterly dead as Styrofoam. Where, under the bed, a plastic finger splint was found cradling a stillborn mole. How a package of unopened Walnettos, a product last seen in 1950 movie theaters, is believed to have transmigrated to the loamy corner of a window Foster has not opened in over six years.

Midge claims that Foster is the perverse result of a father expert in sewage treatment and a mother charged with pest exclusion. It's your classic story: a doctor's child overdosed on prescription drugs, the preacher's kid sleeping all over town—which I never did—gone wild and rebellious. I wasn't. Although something flickered in me this afternoon when I told Dorothy Bascombe that my father would no longer be attending sacred dance classes on Tuesday nights.

As soon as three o'clock rolled around (I was on day shift) I tore home, changed out of my Department of Agriculture greens, and drove over to the Sugar Pine Senior Citizens Center. I found Dorothy Bascombe with my father in the hobby room. For the past week, the two of them have been working on a latch-hook rug, something that would've held absolutely no interest for my father six months ago. Still, I realize this activity is good for him. I've checked out a library book titled, *Stroke: From Victim to Victor*. This book states that certain stroke victims need practice improving their fine motor skills and their patience. But my father was never a patient man. The instant he spotted me, he pushed from his chair, letting a nest of yarn fall to the floor.

Before he hustled me out the door, I explained to Dorothy that starting next Tuesday she wouldn't need to give my father rides to sacred dance, as he was going to be otherwise occupied.

"Oh, really?" Dorothy said. She turned to my father and gave him a goosey little nudge. "And just what will we be doing on Tuesday nights?"

Since his illness, I've noticed that some people have taken to addressing my father in terms most often reserved for small children or royalty. Dorothy is one of these individuals.

"He'll be helping out at school basketball games, right Dad?"

My father nodded, though it might not have been at the words, but at the sound of the question in my voice, my smile. Sometimes I'm certain he understands, other times there's no way to be sure.

"Jennifer's been moved to the varsity team," I told Dorothy.

"Varsity," she said. Her hand darted up, fluttering at the top button of her pantsuit. Dorothy is partial to browns, this particular shade rounding her like an acorn. She swept her eyes away, looked past me. "I hear they have a new coach this season."

"We do," I said. Some slight edge in Dorothy's voice shifted me squarely into the ranks of Lady Miners. I felt myself making the switch to defense, hurtling to block the unexpected shot. Apart from my daughter, there are nine members of this squad, only one of whom I vaguely know. The coach is first year—fresh to the school and to our committee where she serves in an ad-hoc capacity. Grace Michaels instructs P.E., Driver's Training, and will teach the revised Family Life Education Class if our committee can ever agree on the curriculum. Coach Michaels has her work cut out for her. This season will be an uphill battle. But I'm on board. "We" is for more than children or royalty. Ask me months from now when I myself moved up, and I will mention this day, with Dorothy Bascombe looking mildly distressed, proceeding to tell me in gentle tones that given my father's spiritual calling, sacred dance is an activity far more appropriate than team sports.

"I know you mean well, Hedy," she said. "God knows you're a blessing to your father, taking him in the way you have and all. But maybe we should just ask the reverend which function he would prefer." She touched his chin, as if to get his attention. "We do have a mind of our own, don't we?"

My father nodded.

When he was in the hospital, the neurologist drew me aside. She said, If you could see your father's brain . . . Massive damage to the left lobe, she told me . . . He's been severely injured . . . The pictures show . . . If you could see, you'd be amazed he's making even the slightest progress. She said, He is a miracle. And this was true. He awoke and rose like Lazarus. His paralysis vanished. My brother had arrived from Seattle, leaving an open return, fearing the worst. We sat in his hospital room, watching him slowly swing his legs over the mattress edge and lower himself into a straight chair beside the bed. This was day 1. It seemed the accident in his brain had not reduced, but restored him. He emerged full of astonishing energy and appeared to require no sleep. On day 2, he strode victorious down hallways crammed with wheelchairs and metal walkers—victims weeping into their hands, struggling for just some little progress. My father wanted only to go home. He was, I see now, no victor after all, but the sole walking wounded. The word in war is shell-shocked, the result of a world reduced to chaos, his chaotic mind. Day 3, he spoke his first complete sentence: How do we get out of here? He rattled doors marked Emergency Exit, was discovered leaving by the fire escape. He required constant observation. The unit was understaffed, so they put him in a restraining bed. I found him in this bed, a mattress floor like a toddler's playpen, chest-high vinyl sides. He'd torn off his hospital clothes, but wore his glasses, peering over the quilted vinyl wall. Helen, he said to me. It was my mother's name, a natural mistake, the sounds so close. I told the night nurse, Take him out of there; I'll stay. So they rolled in a cot with a foam pillow and grainy white sheets. I lay facing his bed, keeping an eye out, my overnight case open at the foot of the cot. Sleep, I told him. I slept. I dreamed my father was a little figure molded of soft pewter and pressed so thin I must carry him perfectly flat across both palms to keep him from melting featureless in the sun. When I woke, he was standing at my cot, urinating into my suitcase. In his hospital medical exam, under Genitalia, he is listed as Senescent male, meaning in the state of being old. But that morning by the half-light of dawn, his penis looked to me as it did when I was a child and caught him stepping out of the tub, immodest and brash in the world. Full of laughter, with God on his side. Vainglorious. I listened to his steady stream, thinking this sound alone could prompt the long-inhibited rain clouds to finally just let go. He gave his penis a little shake, then dropped the lid of my suitcase shut. My father has made small considerations a lifetime habit and would never leave a toilet seat up. I watched him fumbling to tuck in a shirt that wasn't there, fasten a snap. The belt should be buckled. Oh Dad, I whispered. For a minute I turned my head away, composing myself. Then I sat up in the cot and hooked my arm around his thin, straight leg. I said, Dad, I believe you are a very confused man. He glanced down at me and for a moment his face gave way and I think just then he did truly comprehend what had befallen him. He sank beside me on the cot. He tapped his hands to his bare chest, as if to explain himself, his dry mouth working hard to make me understand his own choked voice stammering, What happened to me . . . What happened was . . .

I would like to tell Dorothy Bascombe that I have seen a picture of my father's brain, that I know his own mind. That what she is looking at here is a miracle. Say how a blood clot like a modified Scud missile slammed a direct hit, a fire storm, brainstorm. And left a man still standing. But God is not at his side.

I smiled at her. "Thanking you very much," I said, which is not the way I talk, except I was disturbed.

"Hedy, my goodness," Dorothy said. "Goodness, dear." From her pantsuit pocket Dorothy pulled a square of lace that could never in this world have been a handkerchief. She dabbed at my eyes, but I was smiling. I am a smiler. "There, there," she said. "We all understand what a heavy load you have right now. I only wish Ward wasn't out of town again—oh where are these men at the very moment we so need them!"

"It's just that my dad . . ." I turned to him.

"A heartbreak, I know." Dorothy touched my father's cheek. Truly, she is a Christian woman and inordinately fond of my father. Then she looked over, resting her gaze on me. "Good can come of this, Hedy—believe me. Sometimes it takes a broken heart to move a person to lean on the Lord."

But I was leaning on my father. "The team needs him, is all." I nodded against his blue shirt, my chin taking the slight bump of the pacemaker just beneath his skin. "It's basketball," I said.

"Well, if I'd realized how strongly you felt." Dorothy looked off, her voice straggling. "Far be it from me."

"Thank you, Dorothy," I said.

"Besides," she said, her face brightening, "I know our Reverend. Once he's got his mind made up—"

My father grinned. "You bet," he said. Clear as day.

And that is why—if anyone should ask—we are parked out here in the dusty back lot of the high school at the vacant hour of 5:30 P.M. when students, teachers, and administrators have long since fled. Jen isn't with us. She's inside the building—one of those diehards who's remained for varsity practice. In the two-hour wait since classes ended, I'm positive she's completed all of her homework for tomorrow. No dash across the street for a slice of pizza at the Dew Drop Inn. No executing the lambada behind closed doors of the girls' restroom—a dance I understand is physically suggestive, if not flat-out sexual. None of this for Jennifer.

"Anyway," I tell my father, "you and Mom always loved the fox-trot. You could've won a contest. You were that good, remember?"

"Sure," my father says. And I believe he probably does recall. His long-term memory is most reliable—it's what's occurred five minutes ago that sometimes escapes him.

I tap the steering wheel—antsy. I've set the alarm on my father's digital watch for six, when we'll make our appearance in the high school gym. It seems wise to allow a little time, so as not to call attention to ourselves. I wouldn't want to distract or embarrass Jen. Although in spirit I feel we should be punctual, given this is her first workout with the squad. Hence, we are on the grounds, reclining in the bucket seats of our Chevy Blazer 4 X 4. We are not wealthy, but we buy American. I've parked well back of the two other vehicles sitting in this solitary lot. The red Volkswagen Rabbit I imagine belongs to Coach Michaels. The truck—a '79 Ford stepside—would be Pink Lindstrom who's got less business being here than we do, and this bolsters me somewhat, has kept me from driving straight away after only fifteen minutes.

I lean across, patting my father's knee. His little dog Bark is in his lap, but you'd hardly notice. The animal is almost a perfect match against my father's fawn slacks.

"Truth is," I say, "I never could feature you at sacred dance in the first place. Twirling around with those streamers. Dip and glide, dip and glide. Tossing plastic petals here and there. Little bells. They never even let you play tambourine. And you the only male in the bunch. I'm telling you, Dad, were you to appear on that stage next Palm Sunday, I'm certain those men in white coats would be on hand.

We can only thank our lucky stars for varsity." I look over at him, take a deep breath. Sometimes in the company of my father, I will do this —talk fast and too much, racing to hold up both ends. "Not that you weren't graceful, because you were truly outstanding. But let's face it, a person of your stature."

My father shrugs. This is only false modesty. He knows exactly how handsome, his hair thick and silver white, a solid gleam in his brown eyes, the weight of his words. Reverend—a rumble on the tongue, like the sound of distant rolling thunder, a prayer intoned way off on the horizon. That rain will fall. Or his voice from the pulpit saying, "Come unto me all ye that are weak and heavy laden." And I will give you rest, shelter from the storm. I will not let him go out on a dip and a glide, not die, but keep before him the long-term memory of himself, who danced the fox-trot and sang "Down Around the Mountain" and trespassed into the burning Nevada test site, carrying a sign reading PEACE, even as the bomb exploded underground, costing him a hundred-dollar fine and two nights in jail. We know—the both of us—precisely who he was. Do not tell me this failing man, this person he is now—

The alarm sounds. My father taps his watch. The dog's head comes up quick and trembling at the beep. My father performed an inadvertent irony when he named this animal Bark. The dog has never made a noise.

I nod over. "What time is it?"

My father rolls his wristwatch under his eyes and squints, his lips riffling slightly. I watch him counting up from one, relying on the familiar progression of numbers, the words to come. "Six," he says finally. He glances at me, his eyes sharp with knowing. "Six, zero-zero."

"You got it."

Then we are out of the car and across the lot, stepping past Pink Lindstrom's 3/4-ton truck, the darkness falling around its primal gray undercoat condition, still waiting for real paint, and it has been months. I BRAKE FOR ARTESIANS is the peeling bumper message, which tells you nothing at all about the man if not that he is careless and indifferent to appearances. But then, I am sensitive to automotive details, working as I do at the border station. Vehicles, I've found, are a form of body language. For instance, the fluorescent strip on the rear of Midge's '87 Subaru says: SHIT HAPPENS. That's Midge.

We are all the way to the double doors of the gym when I see that my father is carrying Bark against his chest. This is unfortunate because I think there may be regulations about animals. But my father is holding the door open for me, a lifelong practice I'm obliged to accept.

The big steel doors clang shut behind us, echoing through the immense gymnasium awash in its own sounds—the drubbing of basketballs, squealing rubber soles. The gym appears to have grown much larger than I recall from Jen's J.V. career. In the space of twenty-four hours, the raftered ceiling has climbed so high, it seems birds might be glimpsed soaring through the streaking light.

We walk past a bank of bare bleachers, this side where Home fans sit. Today—I think due to nerves—we seat ourselves in the second row of the empty Visitors section, as if we won't be recognized. Which is complete foolishness, because no sooner have we settled here than Pink Lindstrom goes, "Hey, Hedy!"

He is clear across the gym, standing beside Coach Michaels—an indication of exactly what his hollering has entailed just to reach us. So naturally Jen who's on the court, positioned at the dreaded high post, swings her head our direction, thus allowing Tara Simonet to drive directly past her for the basket. And what's worse, my father shouts back at Pink and jiggles Bark's tiny paw in a wave.

Coach Michaels blows her whistle and says, "Take five," because—as can be seen by the muddle under the basket—the concentration of this scrimmage has been entirely lost.

"Well," I say, leaning to my father, "we've made a true spectacle of ourselves. We have jumped straight out of the sacred dance skillet into the fire."

He catches my meaning and screws his face in a grimace. During my one matriculated year in upper education, I was instructed to avoid the use of cliches at all costs, or know the reason why. So here's why: it's these old shop-worn phrases that have survived undamaged and whole in my father's mind. They're automatic as breathing. And for that I am grateful and will not tolerate a disparaging remark to be made against the common cliche.

My father nudges me as Jen strides toward us.

"I'm sorry, Jen," I say before she's even close enough to hear. I see what a mistake—how we've shamed and humiliated her. And this, her first day of varsity. I have dragged my father—a sick man and his dog—into this cold cavernous place for a reason he neither knows nor understands. I myself cannot explain precisely what has brought us.

"We just stopped by for a minute," I tell Jen in a rush. I wave my hand toward the big clock at the gym's north end, those harsh lights glaring down from the rafters.

Jen stands square at the sideline, fanning her crimson face. Flushed with anger?—I can't be sure. She's breathing hard, unable to speak. Her hair, still wavy from the permanent I gave her, curls in damp tendrils along her neck. Her Fishbone T-shirt looks soaked.

"You did say to give Coach Michaels the permission." I glance around, but Grace Michaels seems to have disappeared. "I thought maybe . . ."

"Oh, right," Jen says at last, as if everything makes sudden sense. "Right." She lumbers into the bleachers and scoops Bark up in her wide basketball hands. "Where's Dustin?" she asks. She looks over—does she imagine he should be here, too? One rottweiller—all ninety-five pounds of him, present for practice.

I stare at her. I cannot even begin to fathom this child.

She mops her glistening forehead with the loopy stretched hem of her T-shirt, giving us a glimpse of smooth belly, her solid, state-of-the-art sports bra. Then she turns and takes two rows in one bounding step and sets Bark on the court. Bark prances, skittery, her paws clicking across the slick-sealed hardwood. She isn't much bigger than the ball that Tara Simonet rolls her way. Tara's the hot power forward who is, by reputation, frisky on and off the court, although this evening she's looking a little droopy, her sweatband riding low on her forehead, perky breasts almost pendulous under her cutoff T-shirt. Tara's first name comes from *Gone with the Wind*. Simonet is French, as in Simmonay. I mention this to avoid confusion should you hear Midge pronouncing it Simon et. This is only Midge's lascivious mind talking.

At the other end of the court, Pink Lindstrom appears to be demonstrating free-throw technique for a straggle of slouched players. He releases the ball, giving it just the slightest backspin. His hand is up, then drops loose at the wrist, fingers relaxed after the ball. Relatively speaking, he has an okay follow-through. Otherwise, there's nothing impressive about his form. But regardless, I'm unaware of Coach Michaels speaking to me until she touches my arm.

"Coach," I say, leaping straight up from the bleacher. My father rises to stand beside me.

"It's Grace," she says. "I thought you might need this."

She hands me the league schedule, which Midge has luckily given me, so I'm able to glance at it with an expert nod and mention tomorrow night's Squeaker.

Coach Michaels smiles and says what a relief to have Jen on the team, being that Rachael Pickett is sidelined with a stress fracture. I glance across the court and yes—there's Rachael sitting out practice in her school clothes and looking definitely stressed and gimpy.

Then Coach turns to my father. I rush to introduce them. My father has not taken his eyes from Grace Michaels. And no wonder, because this young woman who will lead the Lady Miners through ten games of near back-to-back Squeakers and Killers, in addition to kicking butt—this woman is hands-down, drop-dead gorgeous. Her hair is the color of clover honey, blunt cut to her firm shoulders, gray-blue eyes, dark lashes. Standing beside my father and me, she is taller than either of us. She carries herself like an athlete, loose-limbed, casual. She is San Francisco Nob Hill, New York Park Avenue. In her name, there's a smile that won't be denied—a sound that leaves the lips parted.

"Grace," my father says as she shakes his hand. Her wristwatch is waterproof, the band navy grosgrain.

Too soon, she's turning away, about to resume practice. Quick, I catch her elbow. "Coach," I say, then correct myself. "Grace," I say. I glance to the blazing steel rafters, my mind scrambling for words. "Grace, my father and I have come to volunteer our services. What with . . . well, the budget cuts, plus recent reduction of staff—which I know to be a hardship—and now of course the war, we would consider it a privilege to do our part. Isn't that right, Dad?" He nods and slings an arm across my back. He has come here on faith, neither knowing nor understanding, but trusting to me. "I have personally one year's experience as official scorekeeper for the girls' junior varsity—"

Just then, Jen pokes her head in the midst of us, plops Bark into my father's arms and says, "Don't worry about my ride home. Pink's going to stick around after practice and help me with my fadeaway jumper."

"Absolutely," I say, not paying the slightest attention, just keeping my gaze steady but kindly on Coach Michaels. "Now, my father has many abilities. His strongest attribute lies in large motor skills." Here, I'm quoting directly from the hospital's physical therapy report dated September 16. I do not add that he was listed as most adept with beanbags. "So you see, we are prepared to help in any and every way possible." I feel my father's arm go tight and hopeful around my shoulders. "Just any little way, anything, we would be happy."

"Well . . ." Coach says hesitantly, and she is blushing, which I consider an odd reaction, and it worries me—this pause with the team clowning on the court behind her, waiting, the diminutive Pink Lindstrom standing perfectly still, a basketball tucked under his arm, eyes squinting our direction.

"We are in need of a statistician," Coach Michaels finally says. I note that she is speaking in my exact tone of voice and fidgeting with the silver whistle around her neck, and I would like to reassure her in some way. A certain expression on her face leads me to believe that she has recently wandered out of a small college dormitory and would be only too glad to stretch her long legs under my kitchen table and drink a cup of Swiss mocha decaf. "The stats," she sighs.

"Oh, the stats," I say. "I can certainly handle those."

"And we could use—." Coach gazes off vaguely toward the bench, pursing her lips. "Well, a ball person. You know, the big canvas bag. We have fourteen basketballs." She turns to my father, speaking a little louder, but he understands this tendency and does not take offense. "More basketballs than players," she says with a jittery laugh. "Reverend Gallagher, would you . . ."

"Wonderful," my father says.

And so it is. Coach Michaels looks overjoyed, if not extremely relieved. She puts the whistle to her mouth and waves the Lady Miners to center court. My father and I head for the big double doors. Behind us, I hear the bump of balls starting in, swelling—more than fourteen—hundreds, sounds thick and rounded, striking all the air in this lofty place. If I ever journey to Venice, Italy—as my father once did—and happen to find myself at St. Mark's Cathedral where, my father has told me, a person will discover the clearest and most achingly pure acoustics known to mankind, sounds traveling as if from the celestial vault itself—if ever I'm there, I will think of this Coarsegold High Gymnasium and early evening with nine girls and fourteen basketballs filling the space of the universe. This sound.

I glance back and see Jen in the air, soaring toward the basket, pale hair flying, arms outstretched for the crosscourt pass.

"Play ball," I say to my father.

Then I hear Pink Lindstrom bellow, "Hey!" And he is between us, fast as that.

"Hay is for horses," I shoot back, and my father lets out a laugh.

Pink gives him a nod. "How you doing, Reverend?"

"He's just fine, thank you very much." I answer, in the vain hope of sparing my father.

For my own part, I cannot even bring myself to so much as look at Pink Lindstrom because he is wearing maroon sweats with a lavender oxford cloth, button-down journalism shirt, plus black high-top Converse athletic shoes of the type worn by Chuck Taylor on the old Celtics team long before my time. And even longer before Pink Lindstrom who has no clothes sense and not one iota of experience in the world, only ideas, such individuals being the most dangerous in my opinion.

He shoves his jet hair off his forehead, darting his cool face like a breeze, smack in front of me. "Your husband still out of town, Hedy?"

"He most certainly is," I say with great force. This is another thing about Pink. He is devoid of social subtlety. Ever since last Labor Day when I first met Pink Lindstrom I have done my utmost to discourage, if not avoid altogether, further contact with the man. But Pink refuses to keep a distance. This makes me extremely nervous. He has gone so far as to tell Midge—Midge of all people—that we share an emotional connection. When in fact I have never, not once, in the several months that Pink has lived in this town, presumed to ask him a single personal question. Never.

Now I glance up and catch him shaking his head. For a moment he stares at me, looking grave for no reason at all. Then he blurts straight out, "Hedy, you are some kind of incredible woman."

I grip my shoulder bag tighter and push my eyes directly past him. For example: I have not sought to discover how a male person acquired the name of Pink. Nor do I care to confirm my suspicions regarding his familial history, which are that he spent his childhood among dairy herds and was raised a Unitarian. I do not ask.

Pink grins. "Well, she is truly something else, isn't she, Reverend?"

"OhGodyes," my father says, stringing the words all together and matter-of-fact, through no fault of his own. Pink Lindstrom possesses a quality that brings out the blasphemous in my father.

Behind us, the team is running half-court sprints, up from the baseline and back. Crushers. The drumming basketballs have stopped. No sound now except the whine of rubber.

Pink tips his smooth chin in that direction. "She needs work on her fadeaway jumper."

"Well, you just go right ahead," I tell him. "Just fade away." And with that, I snatch Bark from my father's arms and move for the door.

Then I hear Pink hollering after us. "See you tomorrow night, six sharp. You're coming to the game—right?"

I hesitate, then let out a sigh and glance to my father. "Is the pope—"

"A Catholic," my father says. He reaches over and flicks Bark's perky ears. Then he checks his watch. "Six . . . three, zero. Sharp."

I swing around, squinting up at the big gymnasium clock.

"See you," Pink calls again, his words drifting through the rumble of Lady Miners.

I stare at the clock. "See you," I say, thinking only of my father now. I sweep my hand through the blazing light, as if to make Jen, Coach Michaels—all of them—see. The time is exactly 6:30. My father has hit pay dirt.

Then I turn, stepping close beside him, and we head out the door. In the darkness of the parking lot, he takes my arm, as he is wont to do. Death will not rob him of this night. As we move across the asphalt, I give my father his short-term life, remind him: You told the time. You stepped onto the court beneath bright lights. There were nine young women. "Girls," I say. "Fourteen basketballs. You spoke well over a dozen words."

He nods at my side. "I saw the high church."

"Yes," I say.

"Drums and angels," he whispers.

"Yes," I tell him, "those too." He opens the car door and I slide behind the wheel.

All that we are in the world depends on memory. My father is walking the comeback trail.

Six

At home games, varsity uniforms are gold with royal blue trim. Jen has managed to keep her old J.V. number. She wears the number front and back, honoring her father who skied to world records in a blur of 22. Jen carries this winning luck. Even so, the Lady Miners are trailing as the buzzer sounds ending the first half of play.

Without a word, I hand the halftime stat sheet to Coach Michaels, then watch her follow the team toward their locker room. Jen straggles behind, apart from the others, as if she isn't really one of them—not a member of this squad. She walks, head down, broad shoulders rolled forward. If my mother were here, she'd rise from these bleachers and tell Jen: Chin up! Walk tall. I would tell Jen. But halftime brings an abrupt silence. On the bench below, my father leans over his big canvas bag and yanks the drawstrings tight, throttling the sound of basketballs.

The gym is almost empty. Down this long bank of bleachers I count only eleven Home fans, including myself, plus Midge who's dragged the Caribbean exchange student along, her own son Foster not about to be caught dead accompanying her. And to a girls' game, besides.

This is basketball on a Friday night, but no pep band blares out the fight song. Cheerleaders do not stir the crowd to a victory chant. And my daughter hasn't played even one minute of the entire half.

Yesterday Jen returned from practice nursing a jammed thumb. It was a mild injury. During the team's scrimmage, she'd made a poor catch off a quick outlet pass. I crushed some ice in a dish towel and wrapped the swollen thumb. "Too bad it's your shooting hand," I said, sliding into a chair at the kitchen table. Across the table, Jen gave a little shrug. "Coach kept me in the scrimmage anyway. She says sometimes it doesn't hurt so much if you just stay in there—she calls it playing to the pain." I smiled over my coffee cup, thinking of how often lately Jen had invoked Grace Michaels' name or quoted some little scrap of her advice. But tonight I wonder—how is Jen supposed to play to the pain if she can't even get into the game?

Beside me, Midge shifts her fireplug weight on a Coarsegold Booster's stadium cushion, then nods down to the vacant bench. "Jen just needs to learn the offense, find a spot for herself. Remember, these girls have been together a while."

"Yes," I say, because I know all this. I read Pink Lindstrom's column in the *Coarsegold Register* and am aware as anybody else that the varsity Lady Miners played eight preseason games without Jen. That prior to Rachael Pickett's stress fracture, the team was ranked right up there in Double A League forecasts.

I'll credit Pink Lindstrom with this much—he covers the Lady Miners, even when nobody else in town appears the slightest bit excited about girls' sports. At least Pink is here tonight, standing at the sidelines with a 35mm camera dangling around his neck. Forget for a moment that his next column is liable to begin: "Friday night's contest against the Foothill Cougarettes found our Lady Miners sleeping soundly on the pines." Or some other such viciousness.

At Midge's left, the Martinique exchange student leans out to me. "We must rally more support for our sisters," he says, flicking one of his dusty, dry dreadlocks.

"Absolutely," I say. This young man's name is Jean Pierre Duval, although he has asked to be called Nekuda Adowa, a request I henceforth intend to honor, if only because he's had the ultimate good sense to come watch the Lady Miners, an activity considered definitely uncool by his peers. Except it seems this boy Nekuda has no peers. He is the only known Rastafarian—let alone black student—enrolled at Coarsegold High. His matted hair hangs at his shoulders, partially obscuring the perfect profile of Emperor Haile Selassie knitted into his sweater. He speaks a lilting King's English, but wears the colors of Mother Africa. Midge will tell you Nekuda Adowa is just a pretense, that Jean Pierre comes from old colonial money and attended the finest boarding schools in Paris. Just another rich kid gone slumming, Midge says. She claims the boy's dense hair is a housing project for gnats. Of course, that's what Midge would think, considering her long tenure with pest exclusion. I tell her never mind. Let this Jean Pierre be Nekuda. When it comes to reforming itself, the world needs to start somewhere.

Midge sits straighter, rearranging herself like a brood hen. She touches my blue-jeaned knee. "He's staring at you," she says.

Midge is referring to Pink. I turn to her, give her a long look. "I am a married woman," I say.

Below us, the teams are back on court. The Foothill Cougarettes take halftime warm-ups, looking confident and casual. At the other end, our Lady Miners run their grapevine, Jen under the basket for the quick pass, now in the air for a lay-up. The ball skims glass, then sloughs off the rim. Like a pro, Jen flexes her legs and glances to the overhead game board for the halftime score she already knows. Down 13 points. I watch her loosening up, shaking out her hands. God, I say to myself, let her get into this game. Let her play, just one minute.

"Seems to me you've got grounds for an annulment," Midge says.

My father stands at the team bench, the empty ball bag folded over one arm, his other arm hooked across Coach Michaels' square shoulders. They appear to be studying the first half stat sheet, although my father isn't all that comfortable yet with numbers. In our workbook at home, he's counted only so far as twelve. "Farmer Roy is delivering a dozen eggs to his neighbor," the workbook reads. "How many eggs are in the carton? A dozen eggs equals _____ ."

But I can count farther than twelve. And on the grounds of sheer numbers, no matter where in the world my husband chooses to find himself, annulment is impossible. With Ward I feel the long stretch of time. And this weight of days seems justifiable grounds for our marriage. There's safety in those numbers.

I touch Midge's arm. "Please let me remind you—I have been united with Ward in the state of holy matrimony for nigh onto nineteen years."

Midge shrugs. "It's not a matter of time we're talking about here. The question is consummation. How long's it been, Hedy?"

"Oh please," I groan, losing all patience. Sometimes it baffles me how—out of a population of nearly 5,000 citizens—a person with Midge's alarming proclivities could've ascended to chair of our Family Life Education Committee.

"Well, there ought to be a statute of limitations when it comes to copulation." This is a word Midge uses liberally, particularly at committee meetings—*copulation*, sometimes preceded by *oral*. I glance two bleachers up to Corrine Simonet, mother of the team's power forward and our committee's recording secretary. To her credit, Corrine has never entered "oral copulation" in her zippy shorthand, nor have these words ever been uttered in the reading of the previous meeting's minutes. I hold with Corrine that this term is not a linchpin of tenth-grade sex education.

"Use it or lose it," Midge says. "As much as Ward's been gone, it's a miracle you ever conceived Jen at all."

I ignore this, turning to a blank stat sheet. Coach Michaels is staying with her five starters to begin the second half. Nothing unusual about that. Except Jen is still on the sidelines, still in her warm-up jacket. I doubt she's even broken a sweat. Her uniform is bench-warmer crisp, not one chestnut curl has escaped her ponytail. "Give this girl a chance," I whisper under my breath.

"Listen to me," Midge says. "Life is just too short."

Nekuda Adowa nods around her, as if in agreement. As if he could know the lightning bolt of years—this slight youth of sixteen. But I have heard the quick clap of thunder that follows the flash. And so I know before Midge speaks precisely what she will say, because this is an old conversation and these words always come next:

"He saved your life." She means Fink again. I look down, and he's aiming his camera for the throw-in at mid-court. The Lady Miners have possession. Our point guard inbounds the ball and the third quarter is underway. Across court, a few Foothill fans call from the Visitors section, "De-fense, De-fense, Take that ball away." And the pass meant for Tara Simonet is intercepted at our free-throw line. I mark the turnover in my stat sheet under the heading: Bad Passes, Ballhandling Losses.

"Not once, but twice." Midge taps my arm. "*Two times* he saved your life."

"I don't believe that for a minute," I answer calmly.

"Well, I was there. I can tell you for a fact—you weren't breathing."

I keep my eyes on the game, my pencil poised over the stat sheet.

"Sometimes I think you've just plain lost your mind," Midge says. "My CPR handbook clearly states that brain damage can result if somebody's without oxygen for even four minutes." She glances over at me. "You were *not* breathing."

"Enough," I whisper into my stat sheet. The score is 31–14. Our speedy point guard, Rita Avent, hustles the ball downcourt, beats the trap, then takes a clanger off the glass. And I'm scribbling the numbers, racing to keep up and thinking of my father sitting beside Coach Michaels, his hands folded, the back of his silvery head moving just slightly, following the direction of the ball. I cannot count those minutes that struck him down, when he stood in his own kitchen with the telephone at his ear and found he couldn't speak, when the phone slipped from his hand and he fell, folding inward on the black and white linoleum floor. How many minutes, how many brain cells lost oxygen just then?

I need no reminder about breathing, about the death of the brain. Whatever Midge says—whatever occurred last Labor Day at Steelhead Lake with Midge behind the wheel of her Chris-Craft Avenger and the motor stalling, stalling, stalling, and me, sinking again and again into the wake of my water skis, me, clutching the towrope, hanging on for dear life because I am not one to ever let go—whatever happened, I did not stop breathing. I felt the rush of air, blood coursing to my brain. Count these bleachers, five rows down. Coach Michaels is calling time out; the team turns from the floor to gather around her. Girls towel off, blowing like racehorses. My father's breath falls soft on those faces. He wears his royal blue V-neck sweater in honor of this team. They break from the huddle. My father rises, claps his hands.

I understand how life is lost; I saw my mother die before any of us had time to save her. Her cancer caught us unawares. But I know better now, and I am on the lookout. Here, every minute on the minute and five bleachers down—here, among the living—stands my constant brush with death.

I nod to Midge. "Labor Day was nothing but an incident—an episode, like when Foster got the double mumps."

Midge lets out a snort. "A person gives you mouth-to-mouth resuscitation. Then not more than an hour later he's performing the Heimlich maneuver on you. And you tell me all that was just some little incident?"

"The Heimlich maneuver was totally uncalled for, and if you had even the slightest shred of an idea as to how to drive a boat—" Tara Simonet penetrates the paint and puts up a little one-hand floater off a bounce pass from Rita Avent. I record the basket and the assist, noting that Tara, our top-scoring forward, has sunk only three of the fourteen shots she's taken.

"Listen to me, Hedy Castle—your face was blue. You turned blue as the sky."

"Tara's game is off," I say, but my mind is on Jen. I realize now she should've stayed with Junior Varsity. At least she'd be playing, would've made the starting lineup, even. Sitting here, I'm sorry I gave her permission to move up. Not that I actually ever did, strictly speaking.

"Ahhh, blue," Nekuda Adowa says, leaning out from the bleacher. "In my mother country of Africa, there is a regal tribe called Tauregs, who are also known as the Blue People. Their robes are only blue. They paint their faces blue and their limbs, also. These are handsome people and every one of them blue. Even the little dykes."

"You mean tykes," Midge says. She turns to me. "English is Jean Pierre's second language—his native tongue is French."

"Of course, French," Nekuda says. He fishes under his Haile Selassie sweater and from his shirt pocket, pulls out a pair of wire-rimmed glasses of the type once worn by certain '60s radicals. "Also," he says, "I speak rap."

Midge pats Nekuda's raggedy wool arm. "Jean Pierre's a reggae rapper."

"That's nice," I say, glad that among Jen's 102 catalogued cassette tapes, no rap musicians appear, only Jimmy Cliff and Bob Marley—plus Ziggy, the late Mr. Marley's son, all three of whom I approve.

In the next few exchanges up and and down the court, I mark a line violation, one reaching-in foul, and a double dribble. Then Tara Simonet travels with the ball. The score is 40–16 with thirty seconds left in the quarter. Tara's shoulders sag as she glances up at the clock. On the very top of her head Tara's blonde curls are gathered in a rubber band, giving her hair what I would call a fountain effect. Gazing at this girl, I'm reminded of "The Flintstones," which, as a parent, I once watched on Saturday mornings with regularity. Tara is a flesh and blood Pebbles—Pebbles being the blue-eyed, button-nosed child of Fred and Wilma. Except Pebbles was simply cute. Tara Simonet possesses a more complicated beauty. And while Pebbles Flintstone might bounce onto the floor as her team's flirt-skirted cheerleader, Tara chooses to bounce the ball. Never mind those who say Tara's game takes place on and off the court. At least she's trying, even now, with the quarter buzzer sounding, her face way too pale, and this contest no Squeaker, as advertised. Only a rout.

The team leans to Coach Michaels. Coach balances a clipboard on her slim knees and dashes diagrams with a felt pen—all business. My father reaches behind the bench for plastic water bottles and hands them around. Not once since this game began has my father given me so much as a glance. But according to my library book on stroke victims, this is all to the good. The book emphasizes the need for recovering victims to feel independent, to retain a sense of themselves as free and viable individuals acting of their own accord—at large in the world. Of course, we all require this to one degree or another, which is something I remind myself when Jen breezes out the door or my thoughts turn to Ward who is going to make his speed skiing comeback. Come hell or high water, as the saying goes. I believe he'll rise in World Cup standings, plus recapture the record. And I intend to write him a letter to this effect, because I have his return address in France folded into my pocket, keeping it with me at all times, just in case the exact, right words should come to me at the random and unexpected moment, such as now, with Midge sitting beside me carefully explaining to Nekuda Adowa that dyke is an alternate spelling of d-i-k-e, meaning a bank of earth controlling the flow of water, as in that boy who jammed his finger into the hole and held off the flood.

"And so the town was saved," Midge says. She sits back a moment, then turns again to Nekuda. "Now, the colloquial usage of the word dyke—and one I consider disparaging, by the way . . ."

I listen to Midge defining lesbian, quoting word for word from the third edition of *Human Sexuality*, a tome she lugs to each and every meeting of our Family Life Education Committee, while Corrine Simonet, Angela Tucker, Penny Bower, and Mae Arnold sit tight-eyed and solemn, Bibles open in their laps. This is not a pretty picture. Our committee has entered its eighteenth month of meetings and we have yet to pass a motion permitting use of the term *masturbation* without the qualifying notation of Genesis 38:9–11.

"Oh yes, lesbian," Nekuda says, his musical voice rising with comprehension, a new day dawning.

I glance up the bleachers to Corrine Simonet, relieved that this conversation doesn't appear to be reaching her. She sits nestled beside her husband, gazing down to the team. She's wearing the knit stirrup pants I like so much, plus her I WAS SAVED TO SAVE sweatshirt. Corrine is a lovely person, really. She once won second runner-up in the Miss Arizona state pageant where her talent was the harp. This is always the first thing you'll hear about Corrine and will always be the first thing, forever, which fills me with so much sadness I can't begin to say. Maybe this has something to do with my own legendary husband and his comeback. Because I could weep—this is the truth—at those rare times I attend Calvary Bible Church and watch Corrine tip her harp into her open arms and strike those melodic chords, her dewy blonde looks blurring to watery, her eyes full of moist memory. And I bow my head at the closing prayer and thank God I've reached the age of thirty-eight and have managed to remain a blank page with the first line of my obituary still a mystery.

Nekuda brushes at his wool tweed pants. I hesitate to mention this, but there is something about this boy that reminds me of a braided rug. "I know these gay people," he says. "I myself once believed I could be such a person."

"Well, that's a completely natural feeling," Midge says, and I nod. It has occurred to me that one day after school I might deposit my daughter on the Stiversons' doorstep in the hope that Midge will discuss with Jen those intimate topics I haven't yet covered, which—when I think about it—amount to nearly every chapter of Midge's book. But then, Jen expresses so little interest. I think in this regard she may resemble me—a late bloomer. In my own high school days, it required a whole month of Ward's concentrated interest to rally me to so much as accept a date to Homecoming—and afterward, a hesitant first kiss at my front door.

Coach Michaels brings Chris Nye off the bench to start at guard for this last quarter. In the opening minutes, the Foothill Cougarettes collect six unanswered points. The Lady Miners' offense has fallen apart, and Jen is still sitting.

Across the court, Pink Lindstrom has stopped taking his newspaper notes and is simply standing there, looking straight up at me. He is fixated on me, according to Midge, because he saved my life—a rescue that is, in itself, debatable. Midge claims Pink's preoccupation is psychological, as in certain kidnapping cases, when a captive forms an attachment to his or her captor. And here's where the whole premise fails, because there is no connection whatsoever between abduction and the incident at Steelhead Lake.

With four minutes left, the game unravels sloppy and slow. Our Lady Miners appear lulled by the Cougarettes' scoring monotony. Or maybe it's just my own spectator lapse. I mark a three-second violation, then drop my pen into the notebook and return Pink Lindstrom's brazen stare. If this were not a basketball court, but a court of law, I'd challenge every version of that September afternoon. I wouldn't blink under the steady gaze—never bend with such close scrutiny—but take the stand and counter each eye witness word for word, in my own words.

Here is what happened: It was the last holiday of summer—Labor Day. Both Midge and I had the afternoon off from work, which is unusual, considering how traffic jams through the station at the close of a long weekend.

We slipped the Chris-Craft into Steelhead Lake, using the public ramp at the west shore. The boat belongs solely to Midge; her husband Walt does not care for bodies of water. But regardless, this started out as a family affair—Midge, Foster, my father, Jen, and I. Then, at the last minute, Midge invited Pink Lindstrom. She said this was only a friendly gesture, considering how Pink had just arrived in town that week and knew next to nobody. However, I guarantee Pink's being hired as sportswriter at the *Coarsegold Register* held some sway, what with football season nearly upon us and Foster in the lineup as wide receiver. Not that Foster needed any promoting.

Foster is a born athlete and possesses infinite patience. His parents believe he is slow, as in "slow learner," but that is often an assumption made about deliberate and forbearing people. I trust Foster, which is why I allowed him to fit my feet into the rubber bindings of his neon orange water skis.

I took hold of the towrope and leaned back into the waist-deep shallows—water that on its best days hovers right around 68 degrees. My submerged knees bent slightly. The tips of Foster's skis broke the smooth surface, with the towline taut between the tips, shimmering and stretching to the idling Chris-Craft.

Until then, I admit, I'd paid almost no attention to Pink Lindstrom. Now I observed him sitting at the back of the boat, holding a small red flag. Then Foster hollered from the shallows, "Hit it!" and Midge gunned the engine, and I was hauled up and out of the water—a sensation I cannot describe except in a memory of release, with my legs splayed wide open and words drifting over me, the doctor saying, She's crowning—that water sheeting off me as I emerged, skis slap-slapping waves, the sizzling texture of sunlight and air streaming everywhere around me, sky rushing to me. The red flag dropped low, signifying: She is up, she is clear. *She is crowning.* Always—always—it is the mother who is delivered at childbirth. And I was skipping like a stone, borne across the bright dappling water.

Then suddenly the Chris-Craft lost speed. The boat faltered. Then it regained power and jolted forward, sending a hard snap through the towline. After a moment the engine slowed again, then surged. And for some time, this stutter and start kept up—until it must've seemed to those on shore that I was performing a cock-eyed aquatic show, one moment plowing half-submerged and torpedo-like behind the wake of that lagging engine, and the next moment jerked bolt straight above the waves. Midge later speculated about water in the fuel line. She mentioned the mixture of oil. I believe she flooded the motor, jammed the throttle—she tends toward excessive.

Pink kept hollering from the boat, yelling for me to release the line. But as I mentioned, I am not one for letting go, particularly in the middle of glacier-fed Steelhead Lake where that dark, deep cold is liable to stop the heart before a person even finds time to crown. Besides which, I was wearing Foster's yellow life vest buckled snug around me. So I was in no danger of drowning when Midge finally cut the engine altogether and Pink Lindstrom took the plunge of his own accord without one word of encouragement from me, such as a cry for help. Throughout everything, I had managed to keep my grip on the towline and was clutching it still as Pink heaved me like a fish into the Chris-Craft.

It's true I had taken on some water. I felt a leaden gushing, which I vaguely assumed to be nothing more than a nosebleed. So for the briefest time, I allowed myself to lie quiet at the stern end, just closing my eyes and drifting off, my body trickling and listing slightly, lapping like bilge at the bottom of Midge's boat.

When momentarily I opened my eyes, it was to Pink Lindstrom's point-blank face blocking out all the sky, plus Midge, and she is not a small person. I blinked into Pink's hazel gaze, then raised myself up a little and stared. Frankly, the man looked a wreck. Except for his face, he appeared extremely pale, even for a Minnesotan. Water spiked his straight dark hair, pricked his bare chest. In place of swimming trunks, he wore gray gym shorts bearing the insignia of Gustavus Adolphus College. He was soaked to the skin and plainly bereft of a jockstrap, this absence sinking him into some lower generation entirely. His breath came hard as if from serious exertion, his face flushed deep, ears crimson. His hands trembled as he helped me onto the boat's cushioned seat.

And so out of common human concern, I said to Pink, "Are you feeling quite all right—is there anything I can do for you?" Whereupon, Pink Lindstrom sank beside me on the cushion and laughed and glanced over at me and chuckled and shook his head and guffawed and stared, until I began to feel naturally uncomfortable.

"My God," Midge said. She started the boat, then swung around to me, looking suddenly tired and far too rattled by this engine trouble. "You're asking *him* if he's all right?" She was close to shouting.

"Well, I am asking him, yes, I am," I said in a snippy tone only Midge can summon in me. I felt at my frigid feet for a beach towel and yanked it around my shoulders. It was then I saw Foster's life vest hanging open over my bathing suit, and not simply unbuckled, but nearly torn off me. And then I noticed Pink Lindstrom's wide grin, or rather his teeth, which it seemed I could literally feel. I put a hand to my mouth, scaring up a rawness, an impression of incisors and molars beneath my swollen lips, the force of teeth and lips that were my own and not my own.

"Hedy Castle, you are one for the books," Midge called over the motor's racket and the thunk of the Chris-Craft crossing its wake as we turned for shore.

Pink stopped grinning. He ran his hand through his blue-black hair, then gave me a solemn look that reminded me of some distant boyhood. It seems adults seldom appear so grave.

"You almost drowned," he said.

"Oh," I said. "Well . . ." I frowned down at myself, fumbled for the life vest straps. I cinched the vest tight at my chest, feeling a low ache there—my lungs, the heart.

"I resuscitated you," he said.

I gathered the beach towel close to my chin. And then I forced my eyes straight ahead and said, "You did not."

Before he could speak, I shifted toward him, returning his swift gaze; I stayed steady, unblinking, catching a flicker of anger at the corner of his mouth. After a moment he glanced to his lap, opened and closed his square hands. "All right, then," he said.

And those were the last words we exchanged until the barbecue and the Heimlich maneuver which was, of course, the final straw insofar as my nonexistent relationship with Pink Lindstrom is concerned.

Just upslope from the boat ramp, Jen and Foster had spread a tablecloth on a picnic table under a stand of yellow pines. I helped Midge unload a watermelon and soft drinks from the cooler, plus her famous German potato salad. There was no mention made of the lake incident, at least not in my presence. Although Foster did launch into an enthusiastic description of a trick ski he thought I might like to try next time out—something called a knee board.

My father and Pink Lindstrom manned the barbecue. I'm not one to comply with the strict distribution of tasks along gender lines. But my father had only recently been released from the hospital's rehabilitation unit. Just that week I'd met with the staff psychologist. Dr. Scott spoke of reestablishing the stroke victim's sexual identity and self-esteem. He described the human psyche, the painful process of finding one's self. And I listened carefully, because at the time, my father's superego, his libido, plus the id appeared to be in general disarray. So it pleased me to see this barbecue being manned.

The livelong, everyday procedure of swallowing food and drink presented another problem for my father. After his stroke, it seemed he'd entirely forgotten how to swallow. It's a common disorder—so common I've since learned of swallowing clinics located all across America. Amazing, but true, what a land of opportunity we have here.

So when the five of us sat down to eat, I purposely sidled onto the picnic bench beside my father. Pink Lindstrom grabbed a place at his other side. These two were still in their manly mode, Pink discussing circular saws, a piece of equipment my father never in his life owned nor, to my knowledge, ever used. But he was paying rapt attention, all the while cramming forkfuls of London broil into his mouth. His cheeks grew lumpy, pouching his otherwise fine chiseled face, until he resembled a chipmunk.

"Dad," I said softly, not wanting to just butt in. "Dad—chew a little, then swallow."

My father ignored me. He leaned farther in Pink's direction and kept stuffing. After a minute I reached over and touched his solid chin. I ran my fingers down the skin of his throat, past his Adam's apple to his collarbone. Then up and down once more. This is a trick I learned from the veterinarian when Dustin refused to take his deworming pills. It gets a swallow every time.

But my father flicked my fingers aside, not even looking over. I watched him cram a bite of Midge's potato salad, for which there was not one iota of room left. Mayonnaise drooled milky from the corner of his mouth. I offered him my paper napkin. He waved it off. Then I made a show of crinkling the napkin, fluttering it as a reminder beside his plate.

And finally my father turned. He stared at me as if I were an imbecile, but it was he who looked the half-wit, his mouth dripping, teeth oozing the pink of rare meat, his eyes suddenly full of lunatic rage. That I would dare to interrupt this talk of the circular saw, that I would cajole him like a house pet, ask him to accept this bitter pill, say: Father swallow, Father chew. Use your napkin. Father please, I wanted to beg just then . . . don't look at me this way.

Across the picnic table, Jen lowered her head as if to hide her eyes. "Grampa . . ." she said. Midge, Foster, Pink—everybody had turned quiet. My father was still staring with such an anger, food dribbling, soiling his white knit shirt. For an instant I believed he would strike me, although in all my childhood I don't recall his ever laying a hand. There was no precedent—not for anything. No precedent in a man's lifetime of Christian labors that he should come to this.

There are these moments when everything hangs in the balance. A long silence falls at a table. It seems if you alter the silence in a certain way—if you release the breath you're holding inside you, if you attempt to smile or speak and hear your voice too high, or cross your legs, if you should blink, allow a tear to come to your eye—split this silence and it may all go wrong.

I looked down at my plate. I crept my hand to my fork, but took no comfort from the familiar feel of that utensil. Slowly I pushed the metal tines under the meat, lifted it to my mouth. Jen watched me, feeling for her own fork. Midge glanced to her food. We would eat this meal.

Take, eat, the Scripture says. And I would set this moment right. For him, I would chew. For him, I would swallow. Only I could not. Just a small piece of red meat, but my throat closed around it.

Carefully I lowered the fork to my plate. I took great pains not to cough, because the silence was such, my father's gaze softening now to curious. I made no sudden movements, I would not call attention, simply pressing my hand to my chest. My mouth, my cramped throat —everything felt parched dry. Except the pressure in my chest, as if a residue of Steelhead Lake were building behind the bulkhead of my ribs, my lungs filling. And I would lose my life, because my father could not swallow. I leaned to him, not caring anymore, only wanting to ask: Where is the logic in this? To say: Tell me if you see any sense —Father, look into my eyes and tell me if you see that I am choking; there is a message here for you. Raise your hand to me, dislodge me. Loose your wrath. Father, get it through your head.

I could not speak. But I believe I was still breathing when Pink Lindstrom took it upon himself to swing his legs from under the table and duck around my father to where I sat. I felt four sharp blows to my back, near the spot where the straps of my bathing suit crossed. I wheezed and glanced to Midge. She nodded, irritated. By now it seemed she'd lost all patience with fear and may have thought I had this coming. Except I did not deserve the Heimlich maneuver, which Pink performed over my objections and those of my father, who by this time had miraculously swallowed everything in his mouth. And that breakthrough amounted to all the rescue I needed.

However, Pink would not be deterred. I was swept up, hauled off the bench and onto my feet. Pink's arms wrapped around me from behind. He locked his hands, tight as a vise, above my waist. I sustained the quick upward thrust of his fist. And then another. I felt his hand might ram all the way through me, shatter my ribs, plow into my heart. I braced myself against his fist twice more. And then I vomited.

When finally I stopped heaving into the dusty, drought-brittle brush, I stood straight, wiped my hand across my sore mouth, and said to Pink Lindstrom, "Well, I hope you're happy."

Pink turned and spoke to my father. Then he trudged to his primal gray pickup and removed a short-handled camp shovel and a plastic bucket. He sifted dirt over my vomitus, while my father stepped to lake's edge and dipped the pail. They moved with all earnestness—

these men at work—two doughboys manning the trenches. Then my father returned with the sloshing bucket, handed it to Pink, who emptied two gallons of lake water over my head. Jen, Foster, and Midge simply stood by as this took place. Midge said later that it was like watching a tableau, except people were moving. I myself felt like a one-woman Red Cross field day—me, the first aid practice dummy, sole recipient of exercises in disaster preparedness.

Pink believed he should drive me home from the lake, as if this was his duty. My father concurred; he stood swallowing—actually *swilling*—a warm beer he'd found on the floor of Pink's truck. As a retired member of the clergy, my father does not drink beer or any other form of alcohol, the occasional glass of celebratory wine being the one exception.

"I'm riding with Midge, thank you very much," I said. I blotted my dripping face with a towel Jen had brought me. Then I turned again to that wretched individual—this person unknown to me heretofore—who had battered, hurled, hauled, and struck me. "*You,*" I said, "You, Pink Lindstrom—if that is indeed your true name—have manhandled me for the last time."

And at this, I saw Pink's eyes flare. "Hah!" he hollered, jamming behind the wheel of his pickup.

It was then I realized that my final words to Pink Lindstrom had placed me in the greatest danger of all. Such silly dramatic words I've used so often with Jen—after a round of gin rummy, when I slap the cards down and say: You have trounced me for the very last time, my hearty! Which is, of course, a challenge. And she will rise to the bait every time. Even as I form this phrase in my mind, she is shrugging out of her warm-up jacket. Without fail, she rises.

"She's been tapped off the bench," Midge says.

Nekuda Adowa reaches across Midge's lap and jiggles my arm. "Look, Mrs. Castle—she is going to play."

"She's reporting to the scorer's table," Midge says. "There goes the substitution buzzer. Now she's got the go-ahead from the officials, they're waving her into the game."

"We are not on the radio," I say in my coolest, unmotherly voice. "I have eyes. We aren't broadcasting the play-by-play."

But my heart is racing and leaping and plummeting, just watching her trot onto the court, and I don't honestly believe I will survive this.

The only mercy shown me appears overhead, red numerals glowing as if from the firmaments, assuring me there's only a minute, forty-three seconds left in this final quarter, and the game is a foregone conclusion —the score reads Visitors: 57, Home: 32. Too late to save the day. I wish I could holler this piece of information to Jen and spare her such panicked anxiety. Tell her, No need to go out there and act like a hero and get yourself killed. Just do the job you've been trained for and with any luck this will be over sooner rather than later and we can all go home, God willing.

Instead I say to nobody except myself, "Don't be nervous." Then the ball's in play, she speeds across mid-court, looking for the pass. "Don't be—"

"Scared shitless," a voice pipes in beside me.

I jump at the sound, glance over. It's only Foster, arriving for the boys' games that will begin shortly, sooner rather than later, God willing. "Don't talk to me," I say. "Can't you see she's playing and I'm supposed to be keeping these stats and we're getting slaughtered and my poor father down there with a bad heart, wearing a pacemaker for Heaven's sake and a war on besides and my own husband not even on hand, I don't care if they are being cautiously optimistic. I mean the Pentagon, it's still the worst, Foster, just so awful I can't even begin to keep track, so please don't talk to me, don't."

Foster nods. "Mark down a basket. She just hit a jumper off a pick and roll."

"Oh, she did not," I say, but I record the points anyway, because Foster has this uncanny ability to make me feel that everything is really all right with the world. "Wait a minute—" I flick my eyes from the stat sheet. "Did you tell me a pick and roll?"

"Court sense," Foster says. "She's got it."

"Of course she has," I say, jamming my gaze right back to the sheet. "Court sense."

"Now she's taking the intentional foul," Foster says.

"Well, I should hope."

"That was a smart foul," Foster says.

I note the infraction after Jen's name, then add "intentional," just in the event Coach Michaels forgets that this was a smart foul taken, because more likely than not, those Foothill Cougarettes have it in mind to run out the game clock, eating up precious seconds, simply dribbling and passing and playing cat and mouse and waiting for the final buzzer and victory.

"She's a selfless player, Mrs. Castle." Foster places the span of his wide receiver fingers on my shoulder, as if to steady me. "See how she grabs the offensive rebound, goes up for the basket, then fakes left and passes off to the open man—I mean, girl. Or woman. That's very unselfish—it shows me something."

I enter Jen's rebound and her assist, just as the final buzzer sounds.

Foster gives my shoulder a pat. "Jen's a class act."

"She played a great game," Midge says, pushing to her feet.

Nekuda Adowa removes his wire-rimmed glasses and nods across to me. "She has the true balls, your daughter."

I let this pass, because Nekuda is one of the original eleven stalwarts to witness this debut and because he is, after all, a sojourner in our town and may not fully understand that balls could be construed as an aspect of male genitalia.

"It was worth sitting here, risking my herniated disk, just to see the last minute and a half," Midge says.

"Isn't that the truth," I answer. And then it occurs to me that I never saw the last part—not even five seconds of it—I only heard the game from Foster, his reassuring voice calming me, telling me, talking me through Jen's performance. When I couldn't bear to look, Foster spared me. He said Jen did just fine.

I start down the bleachers, then glance back at him. "Thank you, Foster."

He smiles, looking a little puzzled. Foster is extremely large and blond and neat in his person, in his woolly football letterman's jacket. On the basis of his appearance, you would never have the first idea about the catastrophic state of his bedroom.

"Catch you at the border," Midge booms. We're both working day shift tomorrow. Marshall our supervisor has rearranged the schedule so I can attend every home game, although I wonder now if I have the heart for spectating. Still, somebody needs to keep these stats.

The team has disappeared for their locker room by the time I reach the bench. I snag one of the J.V. girls, whose game I missed earlier, and ask her to see that Coach Michaels gets the second-half sheet.

"Jen was terrific," the girl remarks before she turns away. "I just knew she could cut it."

"Well, that's very sweet of you to say." I hear the syrup in my voice, my small mind already demoting this spindly girl to mere messenger, understudy of the greats. "You played a good game yourself," I call as she darts off. I haven't the slightest notion if the J.V. team—a squad I followed with such interest just days ago—even won or lost tonight. That's how far I've fallen in Jen's move up.

At the bench my father stoops, collecting basketballs in his canvas bag. He gathers up damp sweaty towels, plastic water bottles. Then he bunches a towel and buffs the length of the bench, giving it a serious polish.

I step beside him and take the towel from his hands. "She was wonderful, Dad, wasn't she."

"Ohwonderfulyes," he says. "Wonderful." His words are slurred, the way they sound at the end of a day, his voice soft and hoarse with fatigue. You come to realize, when you're around someone like my father, how we are all just so much machinery—pumps and hoses and valves—how we are wound perfectly tight and spun out in the world, how we run down and break and can be fixed. But there are still times, as now, when I do not know what keeps my father going on.

"I mean, she didn't play all that long—well, a minute and forty-three seconds, but even so . . ." And I wish that my father could actually carry on this conversation with me, that we could gab all the way out to the car about the game and who did what and my father could fill in those little details I might've missed, and we would feel slightly smug without really saying anything until we stepped through our front door, and then we would be full-out proud and boastful in the privacy of our own home, with a glass of celebratory wine, we'd shout Jen's name to the rafters if we had a mind to, because she did play one heck of a game, while she was out there.

"One hell of a game," Pink Lindstrom is practically yelling into my ear, "a bad loss—we gave it away. But Jen didn't shut down. I guess you saw how she moved on that pick and roll."

"I most certainly did." I step back from Pink's blunt, direct gaze.

"Oldest play in the books, but it still works."

"Like a charm," I answer, heaving a sigh. You can depend on Pink Lindstrom to insert himself into every conversation. When just prior, I was standing here, happily sharing a small family moment with my father.

I glance away, seeing the bleachers filling for the boys' games. A clutch of cheerleaders wag at the gym's doors, flashing blue and gold and sunny as ducks. High in the stands the pep band tunes up. It's as if the night doesn't begin until now—with the boys. Even I feel it, an excitement building to the main event. Just minutes ago the Lady Miners were here, racing, wheeling, leaping for the ball. But their struggle is worse than forgotten by this Friday night crowd. It seems that none of those girls—not one—ever truly got into the game.

I take my father's arm. "Let's go home."

"What about Jen?" Pink says.

"She's getting a ride," I tell him, although this is no concern of his. "She's staying for these—" I gaze around again. The lights appear brighter overhead; the crowd is growing loud, winter-tan cheerleaders shed their brassy Coarsegold jackets. "For this."

"And how about you, Reverend?" Pink drops a loose ball into my father's bag. "You care to hang here with me?"

"Sure," my father says, before I can speak.

I tighten my fingers around his arm. "Dad . . ."

"Hedy," he says.

"You're welcome to stay, too." Pink nods, gives me a smile. I notice he is wearing his black Chuck Taylors, allowing him full freedom of the glossy court.

My father glances down, following my gaze. He squints behind his silver glasses, his mouth working. Finally he says, "Good shoes."

"Dad, I think you're tired—you look tired—are you tired?"

"Converse All-Stars," Pink says. He drops to one knee, and quick —just like that—pulls the lace on his right foot, yanks off a Chuck Taylor, and thumps it smack into my father's hands.

My father eases onto the empty players' bench. He taps the heel of Pink's gym shoe in his palm. For one awful moment I believe my father will trade in his ministerial black Bostonians for this one, reeking, outdated, faded, frayed canvas, flapping shambles of a shoe. And I can bear no more.

"I'm going home," I say. "But I'm waiting up." I turn to Pink, averting my eyes from the hole in his right sports sock, his naked big toe. I tap my own penny loafer on the glossy floor. "I am waiting up, do you understand?"

"Fine," Pink says, with a maddening, agreeable shrug.

"I will leave the porch light on." I tap, keep tapping my foot, aware of my father gazing curiously from the bench and Pink nodding as if to humor me.

"Of course," he says.

He gives me another smile, and I turn away in disgust. I lean at the bench to brush a kiss across my father's cheek. Then I hear Pink's voice.

"Hedy—"

I glance up, seeing him step toward me. Quick, I shake my finger in his face. "Now, listen—the front door will be unlocked. But regardless—" I hesitate, glaring at Pink, infuriated by the sight of my own pale hand. "Regardless, I'll be up." Then I dash for the gym's double doors. "And make no mistake about it," I call, shoving outside, rambling onto the school parking lot, and not caring who hears, just allowing myself this running off at the mouth. "Don't doubt for a minute!"

I fling open the car door, slam myself behind the wheel, and start the engine. I lurch across the parking lot, then hit the brakes. For a moment I gaze up to the glowing windows of that high cement building . . . Jen, Pink Lindstrom, my father within. And me here—my fingers holding tight to the steering wheel and my voice without, still calling, "I will be waiting up . . ."

Seven

January 18, 1991

Dearest Ward,

Tonight Jen played her first game as a member of our Lady Miners Varsity Basketball Team. She scored a basket, was credited with one assist, and committed an intelligent foul. It was a selfless act of no small sacrifice. I think you'd be proud . . .

I read over what I've written so far (this is my fifth attempt), then I let the ballpoint roll from my fingers. I tell myself this is what comes of dropping out of college. A person will never know the words to write a proper letter. Or maybe it's just this new fear I feel at Ward's absence —a fear that has left me uneasy with all the old, comfortable words as well.

I reach for my ballpoint, trying one more time. Then finally I crumple the letter and toss it to Dustin, who's sprawled under the kitchen table. Dustin and I are keeping this vigil, waiting for Pink Lindstrom to deliver my father home safely from the high school gym. The frail-hearted Bark has long since climbed the stairs to bed, having given up all hope.

Not that it's overly late by adult standards. A little past ten by the clock on the stove. And not that my father isn't perfectly capable of functioning without me. He's in and out of this house for hours on end, being picked up and delivered by a host of people, such as Dorothy Bascombe, Ellen Short—even Corrine Simonet, bless her heart. It's just that this is his first time with a man. Well, that's not completely true—there's Herb Renfrow and Alfred Welch. But they're church trustees, devoted members of Calvary Bible. This is only to name a few of an entire congregation who've come to my father's assistance and upon whom I depend, given my other obligations as wife, mother, and public officer charged with preventing pests from crossing our border. And now, on top of everything, my father appears to be taking up with Pink Lindstrom.

After a minute I push from the table. I wander into the living room and turn on the war news, which calms me somewhat. The television screen glows with cautious optimism. Viewing this conflict in the Persian Gulf reminds me of the final one minute, forty-three seconds of tonight's Lady Miners game. I am watching the war, but I'm not seeing it, and what's more, I don't even need to look. Yet I have the impression of observing the entire engagement—I can simply let my head fall back against the sofa and allow the reassuring words to quell my fears as they did only hours ago with Foster beside me. I'm receiving full coverage, I am closing my eyes . . . And then I hear the front door. I leap from the sofa and switch off the TV, catching a glimpse of Field Commander General H. Norman Schwarzkopf before the picture disappears. For just an instant I'm stalled at the screen, struck by the extraordinary resemblance Foster bears to this gentleman, Schwarzkopf.

By the time I reach the door, Jen is already inside. "Oh, it's you," I mumble.

"Just me," she says. She flings off her jacket, her curly hair all ends and crackling from the winter air. "Am I too early, late—what? You want me to walk out and come back in, so we can try this again?"

I touch her cold hand, look up at her. She seems taller tonight, gazing down from the heights of varsity, the basket's lofty rim. But then, I'm in my stocking-feet. "You played so well. I loved watching you." This is not entirely accurate, but I need to say it. "Midge, Foster, everybody thought you were terrific."

"We lost," Jen says. "We were totally thrashed by a team we should've taken." She tramps down the hallway, rattling all the way to the kitchen. "They had no offense, just run and gun, they committed eighteen turnovers, and we still couldn't get into the game."

I follow her to the refrigerator. She swings open the door, slides out a quart of orange juice, chugs it directly from the carton, bumps the refrigerator closed with her hip, flattens the carton in her hand like a beer can, aims for the garbage, scores another basket, makes a fist, knocks at her sweatered chest, and lets out a tremendous belch.

"We had no concentration out there." She turns, heading back through the hall. I trail her up the stairs. "I mean, what were we thinking—where *were* we?"

"I don't know," I say faintly, because I am in shock. I have never observed my daughter in this jacket-flinging, juice-guzzling, chest-thumping, belching state.

"Well, I'll tell you," she says, disappearing into the upstairs bathroom.

I retreat a few steps and wait. She is flushing the toilet, now running water in the sink, opening and closing a cabinet, water still flowing. I estimate she's used twenty-eight gallons by the time she emerges—one child in this drought-ridden west.

"We were in the ozone, that's where." She's donned her pink flannel nightgown, a familiar relief, her scrubbed skin trailing the scent of oatmeal soap as she breezes past.

"Listen," I say, dogging her to the bedroom, "you didn't happen to see your grandfather . . ."

She plops into bed and yanks the blankets up around her ears. "He watched the boys play, then he and Pink went out for pizza."

"Oh, well . . ." I glance around Jen's spotless room, flap a hand. "Pizza."

She asks me to turn off the light, and I move for the wall switch at her door.

"Tara Simonet gave me a ride home," she says. "There was a dance after the game, but I need to get up early."

"Right," I say. Jen spends part of every Saturday morning studying for her SATs. Never mind that she's still over two years away from college. Jen isn't one for procrastinating. If memory serves, she's been cramming for this entrance exam since her preteething days.

"Tara's coming over, too," Jen says. "She took the test last month and needs to raise her score at least a hundred points."

I'm still standing across the room, Jen's voice traveling from the pillows. Tara Simonet is a senior honor student, but an improvement of one hundred points sounds astronomical, like the gameboard high in our Coarsegold gym spewing red numerals all the way to the moon.

"She's applied to Harvard, Berkeley, Brown, and Oral Roberts."

"That's a nice mix," I say, aware how Tara's mother, Corrine, has populated her house with battery-operated radios, so as not to miss one second of the "Oral Roberts Religious Minute."

"Anyway, Tara says she's swearing off men so she can concentrate on her SATs. She's bailing."

I smile in the dim light from the hallway, picturing my daughter and Tara Simonet, an unlikely duo before this night. Teammates, I say to myself, then glance toward Jen. "Well, she's a gorgeous girl, Tara. I bet she has all the boys after her."

"Really, Mom," Jen says, her voice suddenly rising—haughty. "There's a whole lot more to the world than looks."

"I just meant it must be hard sometimes for a girl like Tara." I feel my mouth turning a little dry with this shift in the conversation. "You know—the pressure and all."

"Oh brother," Jen mutters, "Oh God."

"Please do not take the Lord's name in vain." I fold my arms over my chest, clear my throat. "Besides, I think you're beautiful, plus you're extremely intelligent."

"You're my mother," Jen says.

"And you've got very good court sense. Foster said so."

"Foster is a dick."

"Well, he is not," I snap back. And then Jen's words catch up to me. I cross her carpet, feeling the weight of Varsity, a full-court press of upperclasswomen, and this child of mine, not even out of Driver's Training, a girl yet to have what I'd consider a real first date. Five steps and I'm standing at the foot of her bed. "Tell me this. Did you or did you not—just now—say 'dick.' "

Jen shoves up on her elbows. She looks thin all of a sudden, shoulders straight-planed, her face angular. "I did, yes."

"Ay-yi-yi," I say, such nonsense I haven't spoken in years, but I am stunned and deciding how to be—I mean, with Jen. And then I think of Nekuda Adowa, his mix-up with the word *dyke*, followed by *balls*. "Listen, you do know what 'dick' means . . ." For a moment I hear Midge's calm voice explaining to Nekuda. "The colloquial usage," I add.

"It's locker room talk," Jen says.

And suddenly this entire conversation seems somehow easier. "Oh, is that all—locker room talk." It sounds like another form of language altogether. I feel an immense liberty, as if a whole new lexicon has been discovered, extending every boundary of the free world. I ease onto her bed. "What else," I ask after a minute. "What else besides 'dick'?"

She shrugs and I feel her looking at me closely in the half-light. "Just words," she says. And then she whispers, "Short hairs."

"Short *hairs?*" I say. I am incredulous, but only for her benefit. "Are you speaking of dogs, as in dalmatians and dachshunds, as in the short-hair variety? Is this your *short hairs?*"

"Lower your voice," Jen says. She nods toward the hallway. But this house is empty—only the two of us sitting on her white spool bed. She listens a moment, then gives me a slight smile. "I think you might be getting just a little bit hysterical."

"I love you," I say.

"I want you to get me a book," she says. "About . . . well, sex. I mean, like a workbook—I need to study."

"Absolutely yes, you should have a book." Sitting here, I form a mental picture, I see my daughter, every Saturday morning, cramming—preparing for sex and the SAT.

Jen creeps a finger. I feel her shy touch on my arm.

"I think I need to know."

"Well, of course," I mumble, glancing away. Downstairs in my dresser drawer, my ancient pink diaphragm has lain so long its soft rubber has turned brittle and cracked. And more recently, the pills inside my medicine cabinet . . . Those pills I stopped taking on November 1, before the date on the label ever expired. I quit. And now my own daughter appears to be looking to me for advice—all the questionable wisdom of my years.

Casual, I lean back on her bed. I take a deep breath, composing myself. "Ask me," I say, in what I take to be a warm and expansive tone, "anything."

"Kissing."

"*Kissing?*" I am momentarily limp with relief. I blink over at her. "You mean to tell me a kiss isn't covered in locker room talk?"

She shakes her head, then makes a foolish face. And I realize this daughter of mine—this girl—may have moved up to Varsity, but her carnal knowledge has not even reached the J.V. level.

I rest on my elbows and gaze across the room—our only light, that little glow from the hall. Somewhere I hear a sound, the dog padding.

"Dustin," Jen whispers.

"Yes," I answer.

Then I sit straight beside her. I lean to her, take her in my arms. "You are the best," I say, my voice falling along her skin. I feel her wide flannel shoulders, a tremor as if from her young bones. I brush the hair off her cheek. And then I kiss her, holding her trusting face, my mouth to hers, we cling like butterflies. I taste toothpaste, feel the fine, strong shape of her. And I think I will never again know her in such a way. Something is being lost here. So for a moment more I keep her. I hold her to me. "This is the first kiss," I say. "It shouldn't be overly long."

She nods. Then she shifts and turns away, not speaking. Carefully I move from the bed. I worry I've made a mistake, overstepped some boundary, believing a mother could give her daughter a first kiss. I glance down. "Sleep," I tell her. Then I move across the carpet. But at the door I stop, hearing her voice.

"Mom . . ." she calls, her words trailing, hesitant. "Is it always so sad?"

And I answer, "No, it will never be sad again."

Then I start down the stairs. They are standing in the entryway—my father and Pink Lindstrom, side by side and almost exactly the same height. I would never have known. My father grins. Pink Lindstrom says, "We stopped for pizza."

I step to my father. "How were the boys' games?" I ask, holding my eyes only on him.

"Ohfine," my father says with a little nod.

At my father's other side, Pink rocks up on his Chuck Taylor toes—I assume to give himself some advantage. But then, just as I'm leaning to help my father out of his wool overcoat, Pink reaches around. And I feel a residue of cold in that dark wool, and Pink's fingers brushing mine, both of us gathering the coat in our hands, touching.

This takes place in an instant—so quick, I think maybe it didn't happen, because all of a sudden Pink has his hands shoved into his pockets, and my father's coat is right here, folded on my arm.

Pink gives a little cough. "Jen home?"

"She is." I tip my head, frowning over, as if to remember exactly what it was that I just felt.

"Good," Pink says.

My father nods between us. "Good," he says.

"And your dogs?" Pink asks.

I stare at his mouth, the curve of his lower lip. "They are both in for the night, thank you."

"Well, then." Pink takes a step back. "I'd better shove off." He shakes my father's hand. "Thanks for a great time, Reverend."

"Thankyou," my father says.

Then Pink turns to me. "Be seeing you," he says, and before I can utter another word, he is out the door.

I step past my father, onto the porch. Everything has happened so fast, I'm certain my head must be spinning. I watch Pink dash to his pickup. Just now in the hallway, it seemed something . . . but, well, I decide, probably nothing.

I wait for the sound of the truck's engine. Then I move back inside. I switch off the porch light and turn the lock. Probably nothing happened.

"Nice boy," my father says.

I nod, scarcely hearing. I look down, noticing I'm still holding my father's overcoat and somehow this reassures me. I lean into the hall closet for a hanger. "So," I whisper in the closet's darkness. My daughter is upstairs asleep, the dogs are both in for the night. He asked this. I answered that. So whatever else happened, probably didn't. I hang up the coat, aware of my father lingering behind me. He smiles, waiting.

I tap his arm. "Come with me a minute . . ." I hear my voice and feel relieved at how normal I sound. I lead my father into the kitchen and see everything in its rightful place. Nothing happened, nothing's changed.

"Your pills," I say.

They are arranged on the kitchen table; I've set them in a row and can name every one. My memory still serves. Dilantin for his heart, Coumadin to thin his blood, stave off the deadly clots, Theo-Dur to ease his breath, Peri-Colace to move his bowels, Percodan for his rest. All this for him—without these my father would be lost.

I fill a tumbler with water. Then I think of tonight's game and pour two glasses of red wine. Tonight we are celebrating Jen.

My father lowers himself into a kitchen chair, and I scoot close. He reaches for his water, screws his face at the pills before him.

I watch him swallow them one by one.

Then I raise my wine glass. "A toast to Jen."

"Jen," my father says, and we drink to the girl.

There is a little quiet. In these minutes, I am easy with my father's silence. It's not quite midnight, and I'm glad for this light shining in the kitchen of our darkened house, to be sipping red wine, Dustin snoring at my feet.

After a while, I reach over and take my father's hand. "Well," I say softly, "you survived your first date."

My father glances up from his wine, bunching his silvery eyebrows. I watch him working his way through the words. He sits back, then looks over, as if to see me from some distance. And finally he laughs.

"Date," he says and shakes his head and howls until his eyes are brimming. This is so like him now—laughter and tears always hovering at the surface of his face.

"But all you got at the front door was a handshake and good-bye. No kiss," I tell him. I glance away. "No kiss . . ."

"A kiss," my father says. He touches his lips, as if to straighten his crooked mirth. Then he turns, and I see him gazing to the drafty window above the sink, that glass black with night. He is thinking of Helen, his wife. My mother.

He has a long memory; it is coming to him now, stirring him like wind in so many dead fallen leaves. And I am bringing this memory to him, carrying it to him from mother to daughter. I step round his chair, cup his chin in my hand.

"Do you remember your first kiss?"

"Helen," he says.

I bend to his face, his deep eyes. I hold my mouth to his. And there comes to me a late summer day. I feel a sudden draft falling swift at my back, somewhere water is running, and a chill plunges fierce on my lips and seals me, black breath billows me. And I believe on that day my life was saved. This happened.

Eight

Considering the size of this town and the lively interest taken in all residents—an interest which might be construed as gossip inclined particularly toward newcomers—it's surprising that so little is known about Pink Lindstrom. I myself am not one for prying. But in light of the attention Pink's been showing my father and Jen, I've felt obligated, for their sakes, to glean whatever information I can about the company they're keeping. As I explained to Midge, this would understandably ease my mind.

Pink does not attend church. I think I already knew this. However, Midge says he subscribes to the Sunday editions of four newspapers, including *The Christian Science Monitor*. He's a member of The Sierra Club and receives their monthly magazine, in addition to *Sports Illustrated* and the *Gustavus Adolphus Alumni Quarterly*. All of this reading material is stuffed into Pink's box at our post office, otherwise Midge might not even know this much about him. Of course, where it concerns Pink, reading of any kind could be construed as job related. However, he did attend two meetings of the Coarsegold Historical Society, at which I was not present.

I seldom spot Pink passing through our border station. But according to Midge, there's a pattern to his rare crossings. She claims that Pink tends to enter the auto lanes after nightfall, between 7:30 and 11:00 P.M. on the fourth Friday of each month. "Regular as clockwork," Midge says, and I have no reason to doubt this. However, I believe today could be an exception. I'm standing in the station's far lane, on this bitter cold Monday morning, January 21, Day 5 of Operation Desert Storm, and I feel reasonably certain Pink will be rolling through here shortly.

Today, Pink Lindstrom is taking my father to breakfast. This is their second date, Pink having phoned last night and asking to speak directly to my father. I had no opportunity to say so much as "thank you for calling," let alone any expression of indebtedness regarding the Labor Day resuscitation and Heimlich maneuver. Because it has occurred to me that I do owe Mr. Lindstrom the courtesy of a "much obliged," if nothing else. And so, after my father hung up the phone, I hesitated only long enough to gather my thoughts. Then I found Pink's number in the directory and dialed.

When Pink answered I said, "There's a conflict," which seemed the best way to begin, leading with the breakfast topic at hand, then easing on to gratitude. I mentioned that Corrine Simonet would be taking my father to Monday Morning Prayer Circle at Calvary Bible.

"No problem," Pink said. "We'll eat later. Maybe we'll make it brunch instead of breakfast." Here, I heard a slight chuckle on the other end. "Brunch following prayer."

Naturally, this last remark unsettled me. It is difficult to extend one's appreciation to a flippant individual. I glanced up from the receiver, making certain my father had left the room. Then I lowered my voice. "Listen," I said, "you had better not be trifling with my father."

"Hedy—" Pink said.

"Because he may be ill, but he isn't a fool, my father. He stood first —for your information—in his graduating class at Boston University School of Theology, and kind . . . He has never once in his life turned a soul away and tolerant, not a spiteful bone in his body, He loves Mother Teresa and Thurgood Marshall and—"

"I love you," Pink said.

For a moment I stared down at the phone, shocked utterly still. Then, finally, I found my voice and said, "You most certainly do not!"

"Are you telling me how I feel?" On the other end, Pink's words dropped calm and dead even. "Do you want me to say I don't feel anything?"

"Yes, I do," I answered. "I do absolutely, you can bet your life and that's all there is to it. Period," I said.

There followed another silence in which I fanned my hand before my face, as I felt the distinct need to be revived. It was at that moment Jen appeared in the room, stepped toward me, and nodded toward the telephone. "Is it Dad?"

I blinked up at her, then said into the phone, "Excuse me, please." I yanked the receiver from my ear and slammed my palm over the mouthpiece. "Have you ever once," I said to Jen, "one time in your life heard me raise my voice to your father as I have just now done?"

Jen stared at me, shrugged. "Well, no . . ."

I wagged the receiver under her nose, my hand still stifling the sound. "Then does it make a shred of sense that I would be standing here wasting valuable money and your father's big chance for a comeback by shouting at him international long distance all the way to Grenoble, France?"

"Calm down," Jen said, her gaze widening on me. "You don't need to have a spaz."

I closed my eyes, let my breath out slow. "I am talking to Mr. Lindstrom."

And with that, Jen plucked the receiver from my hand and said, "Pink? Wow, am I glad you called."

I dropped back and sank into a chair, which gave me time to regain my composure. After a moment I felt myself relaxing. I sighed with relief, almost grateful that Pink Lindstrom had spoken out. At least the subject was now on the floor, as we say in my committee, and open for discussion. While Jen lamented to Pink about her tentative crosscourt pass, the dragging of her pivot foot, I heard myself telling him—explaining gently—how it sometimes happens that a person becomes fixated, which is not love, but something else altogether. How it might be a phenomenon similar, perhaps, to the attachment of a captive to his or her captor. But above all, I would assure Pink that while his feelings were unfounded, if not entirely perverse, he should not suffer a moment's guilt, worry, or embarrassment about blurting indiscriminately over the phone. Because he is of an age and has had little or no experience in the world. And this, too, I would tell him, will pass.

So I waited as Jen rambled on. I sat, feeling wholly self-satisfied and in control, my hands folded in my lap, the words poised calm and mature at the tip of my tongue. I listened to Jen making arrangements with Pink pertaining to the pivot-foot problem. "Cool," she said finally. Then she said, "It's a date." And before I could get even a syllable in edgewise, she smiled, dropped the receiver into its cradle, and bounded away.

I don't mind admitting that in the large silence that followed, I did move to the phone, just in case Pink Lindstrom might've remained on the line. But I heard only a dial tone.

So, as will sometimes happen, all these words I might've said remain unspoken and are still on my mind as Midge and I wave car after car across this border and over the frigid summit of the Sierra.

In the turnout beyond my lane, our supervisor Marshall hauls himself into a cattle truck bound for the central valley stockyards. After a minute Marshall emerges, stamping manure from his pack boots. He sends the cattle truck onto the interstate, then steps to me, his face grim and gray with the cold.

"I just wish to hell this drought would end," he says, frowning after the truck.

I let Marshall's profanity pass—not out of deference to his position as supervisor, but because he possesses such a worrisome soft heart. It's Marshall's tender nature that's got Midge and me crossing our fingers, hoping his Air Force reserve unit won't be activated for Operation Desert Storm. Standing here in his official O.D. greens—O.D. signifying olive drab—this man may look turned-out and ready for combat. But I'm afraid he'll never make it back from his first bombing mission, or "sortie," as the TV briefing officers call it. Marshall has some idea that "direct hit" means people are killed. And that "heavy casualties" translates to a large loss of human life.

He'll also tell you that these bawling, runny-eyed cattle he's just waved through the station are bound for slaughter, that there are more and more truckloads, because the alfalfa crops have been so poor, what with this drought and no feed, no water—each beast must go for the quick bullet, one deep dull blow to the massive head. There is general panic, Marshall claims. As he sees it, these cattle are milling tight in their vans, clambering over one another for air, for light. They are bawling their eyes out, tears running down their faces. Marshall believes this. He says these animals have some dim understanding.

He slaps his insulated gloves across his broad palm and nods at me. "They know."

I glance to the peaks above town—those bare, dry flanks where every ski lift is closed, or about to be. "I think we'll be getting some precipitation soon," I tell him. "Or snow," I add, summoning the precise word, because I feel such need these days for exactly what is meant.

"It's too cold to snow," Marshall grumbles as I motion a Buick Le Sabre through my lane. The Buick's vanity plate reads DEL ME IN—another weekend gambler making the trip home from Reno.

Right behind the Buick comes a dented Volkswagen van. I bend to the driver's window, which apparently can't be rolled down because the young man at the wheel is shaking his curly head. I step back, bumping into Marshall as the young man kicks open the van's sprung door. The man is moving from Utah, this much is clear. At the thought of that state, my mind leaps to migrating Mormon crickets threatening our farms and rural communities. But regardless, I smile at this man and say:

"Good morning and welcome to California. Are you carrying with you any fruit, vegetables, or animals?"

The young man cocks his unshaven chin. "Just plants."

I glance into the van's chock-full rear, past a fringed lampshade, the neck of an electric guitar rising above a microwave oven. Between cardboard cartons, I spot one wandering Jew and a suspicious leafy plant of such size as to appear treelike, its uppermost shoots crowding the van's roof.

I turn to the man. "Are you aware that you're transporting *Cannabis sativa* across this border?"

"Marijuana?" the young man says, with a casual wave of his hand. "Sure."

I see now that this person is dressed entirely in black, with the exception of a silver chain dangling a peace medal over the words DEAD HEAD emblazoned on his T-shirt. (It's the nature of my work to observe vehicular contents first, individuals second.)

"And your plant, I assume, is in potting soil?"

As I speak, I'm aware of Marshall standing directly behind me, his presence a reminder of our work slogan: "Bugs Not Drugs." This isn't to say we overlook the true trafficker, having at our disposal a twenty-four-hour hot line to the California Highway Patrol. No serious offender gets far. But this young man with his sandals, pierced ear, and the random house plant . . .

I give him a copy of *Golden State*, a magazine free of charge to all newcomers traveling through our station.

"Well, thanks," the man says. Then, as if in return, he reaches into his glove box, tears one square from a fat roll of toilet tissue, and hands me this:

I'm still clutching the flimsy square as the young man drives away, his fingers flashing a V that might stand for peace or for victory. I can't say which.

"Was that guy a hippie, or what?" Marshall nudges beside me and removes his O.D. cap—O.D. as in olive drab. And V is for peace or victory. But I am thinking B-52 and POW, because I've seen the bruised, swollen faces of our downed pilots televised from Baghdad. While on our allied side, it's said that as of Saturday, twelve Iraqi men spent their first day in captivity. These men sat cross-legged in desert sand, bewildered by peanut butter and dehydrated bananas, the Ready to Eat rations of Marines. That number is twelve; my father cannot count higher. *A dozen eggs equals* ______. And I'm thinking I myself can't move past this. Only so far, I think. And Marshall must go AWOL.

"I'm not sure," I mumble. I fold the tissue into my coverall pocket, then give Marshall a shrug. "I think that kid was mixed up." Because I am bewildered—is this war for oil or freedom, victory or peace? I cannot read minds, read lips. I glance off looking for Midge, as if she might provide the answers, but she's left her lane for the warmth of our station's office and a half-hour lunch. And Marshall has stepped away to inspect a truck loaded with bees that have traveled miles to pollinate whatever may have survived our drought.

But nothing flowers before my eyes except dust and diesel exhaust. Until they appear, my father in the passenger seat and Pink Lindstrom behind the wheel of his battered gray pickup. And they are laughing—giggling, really—as Pink eases to a stop in my lane.

"Good morning," I say in my most official but cordial voice. I lean at Pink's open window, keeping my eyes clear of him. I nod to my father. "How was breakfast?"

My father stops laughing and gazes across at me, as if taking everything in—the collar of my coveralls turned up against the cold, hair straggling from a rubber band, my regulation cap pulled low. Maybe it's this winter uniform, padded thick as a child's snowsuit, or the chunky rounded toes of my pack boots—because I feel large and obtuse standing here, and I wish all over again that I'd stuck with college and made more of myself as my parents and my scores in mathematics once suggested. But today—after all this time—my father appears to be seeing me with new eyes.

"It was brunch," Pink says.

And the flicker of pride on my father's face slides into a grin, and they are off again, as if this is some private joke on me—the two of them howling and falling apart in the rusted, peeling interior of Pink's truck.

"Well, honestly," I say. "If you could see yourselves." I step back from the window, tempted to kick one of Pink's bald front tires. "You're both so— Just rude is what you are."

Hearing this disgust, my father subsides. He gives Pink a look. Then he fishes into his shirt pocket and pulls out a folded paper napkin. He gives the napkin to Pink, who hands it out the window to me.

The green napkin says Pastime Cafe printed small in the corner. Not breakfast but brunch after prayer. I open the soft paper and see blue ballpoint, my father's hand shaky with letters he is learning all over again. And I read earnestly, as if these are real words—my father's message to me—because he's trying hard and needs every encouragement. I read:

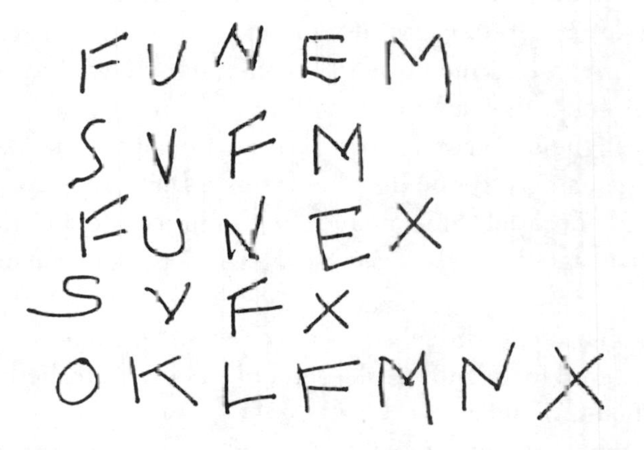

After a minute, I glance from the napkin. My father is smiling, looking at me with his eyebrows up. Waiting.

I nod and refold the napkin. "This is very good. Wonderful," I tell him. "And your handwriting—well, your printing—is excellent. The best ever."

My father beams and thumps Pink on the knee.

Pink lets out a chuckle, then says to me, "I helped."

This strikes me as an odd, if not childish remark, but I give Pink credit. "Well, it's a fine effort."

Behind me, I hear a car pulling into the lane, nosing toward Pink's truck, a radio blaring. Pink mumbles about needing to get back to the newspaper office. And my father is digging all of a sudden into his trouser pocket.

"This," he says, thrusting yet another paper toward the window. I see how he wants me to have it, a crumpled scrap that might add to his napkin success.

I bend to the window again, reaching carefully across Pink. His face and chest are a mere hair's breadth from my hand, my arm. Fortunately, I am gloved and thermally padded.

"Thanks," I say, taking the paper from my father. Finally I glance to Pink. He seems to have entirely forgotten last night's outburst over the phone, for which I'm grateful. I give him a little smile. "Thanks."

"Thanks all around," Pink says. He puts his loose-clutched pickup into gear, pitching his voice above the engine. "That napkin—" He's nearly shouting as the truck rolls forward. "It means something."

I nod. "Absolutely, of course." And I wave them through.

It's only later, after several dozen cars, twenty-seven trucks, eight recreational vehicles, and close to quitting time, that I begin to ponder what, if anything, this napkin of my father's could possibly mean.

As soon as the swing shift crew arrives, I head for the station office where Midge can always be found enjoying a Diet Coke and stuffing all manner of confiscated fruits and vegetables into our industrial strength garbage disposal. Five horsepower, and before you can blink: pure pulp.

For this operation, Midge wears a welder's mask she bought to prevent a splattered face, and she does not like being disturbed, plus there is a fair amount of noise. So, I wait.

I step to our lunch table and pull the scraps of paper from my coverall pocket. As I place these on the table, I feel fresh and important with the cold outdoors on my face, a courier bearing word from the border. Here before me is the likeness of President Saddam Hussein on toilet paper with instructions: WIPE HERE. Followed by my father's cryptic napkin message. And then the wrinkled page I'm about to spread open, just as the disposal's loud grinding stops. I glance from the table, watching Midge yank off her welder's mask and drain the last of her Coke.

After a minute she turns from the sink and sighs. "It's days like these when I wish I was a small blonde dental hygienist."

I nod, reaching for my father's napkin. "I know what you mean." But I cannot, for the life of me, fathom what is written on this napkin. Only FUNEM and FUNEX look as if they could conceivably qualify as words.

Midge steps beside me and points to a far corner of the office. "Don't look now, but we've got a ferret rejection—about an hour ago, family from Tennessee came through. Southern white people, what do they know, riding clear across this country with an animal they believe is a cat."

"They didn't . . ."

"I read them Title 14."

"Well, I should hope so."

In our great state, the putorius furo, commonly called ferret, is contraband, outlawed, and barred entry to our borders since 1935. Furthermore, Midge and I do not like these creatures. It is fair to say that we hate and despise them. So be forewarned, you in these other United States who are the foolish keepers of such animals. Do not come to us with your cute little winsome ferret stories. You will get nowhere with us.

"Except I haven't told Marshall," Midge says. She gives me a knowing look, and I understand her concern, what with the war looming over Marshall. Never mind that as supervisor, Marshall Painter is responsible for disposing of these confiscated outlaws. Marshall has never—war or no—found it in his heart to eliminate a ferret. For this job, as with all nasty business, we rely on Midge, plus a plastic bag and a pressurized cannister of carbon dioxide.

I tear my eyes away from the far corner and that small silver cage, a furry white strip scratching its ear in a manner very much like a cat and still very much alive.

"Midge," I say, drawing her attention to the paper napkin in my hand, "I would like you to read this. My father wrote it at breakfast—or brunch."

Midge sets her welder's mask on the table, then frowns at the napkin I hold before her eyes.

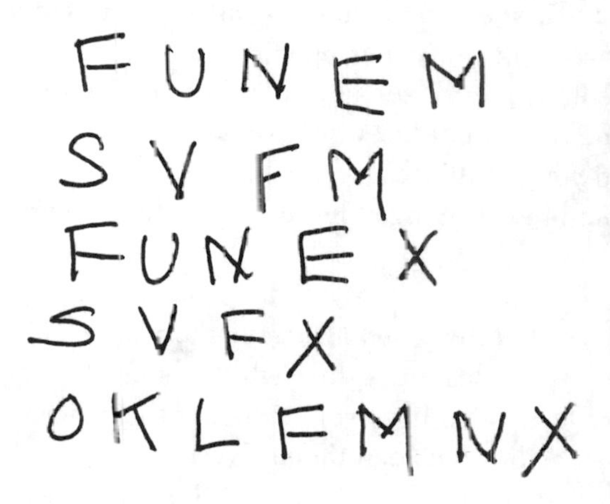

I point out the two possible words. "I think it's supposed to mean something."

"The first sentence needs a question mark," Midge says.

Now, we both know there isn't any sentence, but Midge is reading regardless, explaining as she breezes along.

" 'F-U-N-E-M?' " Midge slides her pudgy index finger under that first line. "The trick is to make these letters into words, so it says: F—have, U—you, N-E—any, M—ham. The question goes, 'Have you any ham?' " Midge glances up to make sure I'm following this. Then she proceeds to the next line. " 'Yes, we have ham.' " She taps those letters. "Here, your dad needs a period. He wants another question mark for sentence three, then two more periods." She directs my eyes down the napkin. " 'Have you any eggs?' " Midge wags her head. " 'Yes, we have eggs.' " Then she shrugs. " 'Okay, I'll have ham and eggs.' "

She turns from me, steps to the table. "Except for the trouble with punctuation, your dad did a good job on that. If you ask me, he's making a lot of progress."

"Yes," I say. I'm still holding the napkin, puzzling and frowning over the lines. "Also," I add in a weak voice, "Pink helped."

Midge nods over. "Well, that would make a difference. The whole thing begs to be read with a Scandinavian accent."

I glance away, feeling somewhat irritated by Midge's know-it-all grin in reference to Pink. After a moment she bottoms into a folding chair at the table. She shakes her head at the square of Saddam Hussein toilet tissue. Then she reaches for my father's wadded white paper. I watch her smoothing the paper open, reading. For the longest while she doesn't look up, and I sense something turning quiet in her. Now she is speaking to me, but her words seem to be standing still.

"Where did you get this?"

I move behind her, leaning at her chair to see the Xeroxed, typewritten passage.

> Wherefore God also gave them up
> to uncleanness, through the lusts of
> their own hearts, to dishonor their own
> bodies between themselves.
>
> Romans 1:24

"Tell me where it came from," Midge says.

I frown down at Midge's face, the sternness in her voice. "My father

—I think Prayer Circle." He often brings home these papers: church announcements, the name of a hospitalized parishioner for whom we might pray—notes sometimes pinned to his shirt by Dorothy Bascombe or Corrine Simonet, as if he were a kindergartner returning from school. Except this Bible passage is different. And I feel a stillness in me as well—this pause which is not silence, but a deep quickening.

I fold my father's napkin, the flimsy tissue square, then the wrinkled page. I understand these Xeroxed lines. I know the Bible. Yet I can't fully comprehend. I stuff everything into my coveralls and glance at Midge.

"I need to know what it means."

"I think the dreaded L word is out," Midge mutters. She pushes from her chair. "There's been some speculation . . ."

I catch Midge's padded elbow. "About what—tell me exactly—what?"

"That Grace Michaels prefers women."

I shove my hands into my pockets, as if to halt those words. Because suddenly I don't want to know. But Midge keeps talking—she won't be stopped. I hear her continuing calmly, sensibly, as if she's still sitting in the gym, defining lesbian, spelling out everything . . .

"*Everything*," she says, "could be on the line."

I shake my head and lean away. But Midge moves with me, her finger tapping, jabbing at my shoulder.

"For once in your life—"

Slowly I swing around. "Careful . . ." I give Midge this word like a warning, because I sense a new drift in the conversation, feel the subject shifting to include not only Grace Michaels and her job, not just the team—but me and not simply me or what Midge believes to be the travesty of my marriage—it seems she's hauling my whole existence into question here. "Don't you dare," I stammer.

Midge shoots me a long narrow look. "Just once," she says, "even *you* might need to take a stand."

I slam my hand down on the table, drilling Midge with my eyes. She starts to speak again, but all of a sudden I'm shouting over her, drowning out her cool tone.

"Hold it, just stop right there." I catch the pitch of my voice, a heat rising to my face. "Are you saying I'm a coward? Is that . . ."

I glance across the room, seeing Marshall standing at the wide open office door, letting in all the cold. Marshall takes off his cap, blinks from Midge to me, grows red in the face, says, "Excuse me," and ducks outside.

"Oh no you don't!" I march after him, unable to stop myself, this anger spilling larger than the moment, this room. "Marshall," I yell out the doorway, "Marshall, you come right back. We've got a ferret in here that needs to be put to death, and this time you're going to do it!"

From the near lane, one of the swing shift turns to stare. I glimpse Marshall darting around our flagpoles and into the trucker's hut. "Marshall, you chicken . . ."

I swing to Midge. "And you—"

"Hedy," she says, in that disgusting, superior tone of hers, "Hedy, you are behaving like the ignorant fool you've always been ever since I've known you."

I ram my hands to my hips. "Is that so? Well, let me tell you . . ." I flick my gaze past her, hunting for something more to say, to do. "You don't know the first thing about me—not even one iota." And with that, I cross the office and bend to a cupboard beneath the sink.

Midge's voice falls above me. "Listen here, Hedy Castle—right from the start you were nothing but a skinny little redneck girl who liked to go riding around in the dark. And right up to this minute, you haven't changed a bit."

"Like hell," I mutter under my breath—this cursing proof, in and of itself, that I am not the same person, because I do not use profanity.

I pull an extra-large plastic garbage bag from a bottom shelf. Then I bang the cupboard door closed and tramp to the far corner of the room.

Midge unsnaps the collar of her coveralls, as if she needs air. "Just what," she says, "do you think you're doing?"

"I'm disposing of this—" I place the ferret, cage and all, into the black plastic bag. Then I move for the pressurized metal cannister, its twelve-inch rubber hose. And though I've watched Midge going through this procedure many times, I have never actually realized how very simple it is: the tip of the hose slips into the plastic bag, then the bag is sealed with a wire twist-tie. And now the cannister valve is turned . . .

"No good," Midge says, nodding to the cannister. "We're out of CO_2 —nothing's in there."

I glance up from the cement floor where I'm kneeling, my hand trembling and still gripping the yellow valve, the ferret rejection rattling its little cage, black plastic rustling. And I've gone to these great lengths, plummeted through every degradation of my God-fearing nature to perform this one thing I have never in my life done—all for the sake of my pitiful pride.

"It can wait until tomorrow," Midge says.

But tomorrow will be too late. Already, I feel my resolve failing. My legs are weak as I stand, the cage suddenly heavy in this plastic. The hose slides away. I tighten my grip on the bag and move for the door. I hear Midge talking to me, telling me there's food in the cage and water, this can wait, asking me, "Where are you going?" And I say, "Leave me."

My Blazer is parked on the concrete island behind our office. For a minute I hesitate at the car, feeling only a deep weariness. Even so, I understand how to proceed. I bend to the rear exhaust pipe. Then I gather the mouth of black plastic around the rusted pipe. But the twist-tie won't work, isn't long enough, and for a moment I can't seem to push my mind past this. I glance west to the summit, peaks dimming in the late afternoon sun—these short winter days.

In our office—only a few steps from where I'm crouched on my haunches trying to think what to do—there's a manila file and inside it, a report issued to us by the California Department of Health Services. This report states:

> Since the year 63 B.C., ferrets have been used as hunters. These quick, sharp-nosed mammals are particularly prized because of the fierce and relentless nature of their attacks. They are known to prey on ground-nesting birds of which California boasts the largest population in the country. The food transit time for a ferret is three hours. They must eat often, and in this respect, they appear to be always hungry. This characteristic also pertains to those varieties kept as pets. Ferret play frequently assumes the form of mock attacks, which may result in bites to humans. Infants often seem to be perceived by ferrets as prey and may suffer severe injury . . .

I pull the rubber band from my hair and stretch it around the exhaust pipe. Then I work the rubber band over the gathered plastic. And everything holds. Throughout all this, the ferret has not made a movement or sound. The animal has food, water, and a folded newspaper on the floor of its cage. This ferret will want for nothing and will end peacefully, drifting off to its death on a dream.

But I am not sure how long to run the Blazer's engine. Midge allows three minutes for CO_2 to work its way, the time required to cook a soft-boiled egg. However, this is simple carbon monoxide, which I calculate might take a little longer.

I climb behind the wheel and start the motor, then crank the car's heater up full force. I'm sitting safe in plush comfort and will be warm for the duration. But after a minute I crack my driver's window as a precaution. I myself am not yet ready for the drifting dream. I turn on the radio, hoping for some soothing distraction. There's only war news and our local country-and-western station and a man singing of his love for his dog: "If I die before I wake," the deep voice croons, "feed Jake." Switching back to news, I learn that the Pentagon is flying 50,000 body bags to the Persian Gulf. I touch my forehead to the steering wheel and rev the engine.

A typical ferret measures seventeen to twenty-two inches in length and weighs between two and six pounds. This particular rejection appeared to be smallish, young, and pure albino with pink pinpoint eyes. I would like to say I glimpsed a rhinestone collar around its neck, but I did not. Title 14, section 671 of the Fish and Game Code pertains to the importation, transportation, and possession of wild animals. Aside from ferrets, our most common rejections at this border include the monk parakeet and gerbils. Field mice are barred from entering, but as I've mentioned, we will admit all domestic races of the order Rodentia—these being rats and mice that are white, trained, dancing, spinning, or laboratory-reared. Circus animals must carry permits. Gliding lemurs are prohibited, but I would still like to see one.

Now and again, some interesting thing will happen. One evening a man driving a new Lincoln Continental barreled through our center lane, not about to stop and the CHP laid two black strips down the interstate in a race to catch him. This man in the Continental turned out to be President Nixon's brother-in-law and the woman beside him was not his lawful wife. So it stands to reason he wouldn't care to brake under our bright lights and submit to certain questions. This occurred before my time. Doug Rankin, now retired, told me that story. Also, it was Doug who saw Elvis reclined on a red velvet sofa in the back of the entertainer's customized bus. Doug said Mr. Presley looked to be an individual of abject loneliness, but I believe we all know this.

For myself, the loneliest man I ever beheld pulled in here after dark at the wheel of a thirty-foot Winnebago with Ohio plates. I said to him, "Sir, I will need to take a look inside." (This was during a period of serious infestation by fire ants.) "Of course," the man said, completely cooperative and polite to the letter of the law. He hopped out of the RV's cab, flung open the side door, swept off his broad-brimmed Stetson, and murmured, "Please, ma'am—after you." Once inside, the man struck a match, lighting a wall-mounted propane lamp. In the dimness I saw that except for a small kitchenette and curtains at each window, the whole interior of the motor home had been stripped bare. Just past the kitchenette with its tiny sink and stove, a thick hemp rope was strung chest-high across the width of the vehicle, from one fake birch wall to the other. Behind this rope, I observed three bales of hay, a large roasting pan full of water, and two sorrel horses with white socks and blazes. The two horses stood big as Clydesdales, side by side on the orange linoleum, resting their drowsy heads on one another as these animals will do. I did not ask for the veterinary certificates we generally require, because this man was plainly not transporting horses, but living with them. Here, in the gutted metal shell of a home, a man hung his hat, his clothes—a row of shirts, pearl-snapped and top stitched, sharp pressed Levi's—hung gingham curtains. Shared his roof. And so I turned to him and said, when at last I could speak, "I imagine they're very good company." And in a voice fraught with all the quiet disappointments humanity might ever suffer, this man replied, "They are the best I know."

Then I hear Midge knocking at the Blazer. I roll down my window and she says, "It's dead." She holds the plastic bag up for me to see, and I force my eyes.

I watch her stride across the concrete and hurl the bag into our gas incinerator. And I cannot say how we should, any of us, live. I have spent my years riding around in the dark. I can't read hearts and minds, lips. I only know I placed a boy's first kiss on my own daughter's mouth and felt such sweet sadness impossible to describe. I put one ferret to death. I met a man who dwelled with horses. Beyond this, I can't say. And I welcome the dusk, already falling.

"Listen to me," Midge says, returning to my window.

I shake my head. "No more—please. I need to get home."

"About Grace Michaels . . . There could be some trouble." Midge steps aside as I drop the Blazer into gear. "I mean, with your church and all."

"It isn't my church," I holler back to her. Then I release the brake and pull from the parking pad, not about to hear another word.

I drive the short distance home, thinking of Coach Michaels. I see her sturdy good looks, the youthful luster of her face, the silver whistle flashing at her chest. Every day, Coach Michaels waves my daughter onto the court. She gives Jen driving instructions. Plus she's teaching this child of mine the facts of life, such as they are, in a class limited by our committee and yet to be revised (no L word is ever uttered)—a course so minor it's combined with Driver's Training under the general title: State Requirements. If it were not mandated by law, I doubt this class would ever be offered.

You, who reside elsewhere—you are off the mark if you believe that all of California clings to the westernmost left liberal edge of this country. Although it's true that my friend and fellow committee person, Corrine Simonet, rates San Francisco among the devil's top three favorite cities, falling after Rio de Janeiro and New Orleans. Of this, Corrine is convinced. Me—I have no opinion. I ride in the dark.

By the time I arrive home, Jen's rushing to get ready for practice. I've heard it said that most family activity takes place in the kitchen. But judging by our household, the central location is my bedroom. No sooner had Ward left than it seemed everybody else moved in. Across the room, Jen's stuffing her blue and gold duffel bag on my keyhole desk. My father watches the war from my bed, his gaze never leaving the little TV. At his right side is Bark, to his left, the large Dustin. Scrunched together on my Heritage spread, the three of them appear to be all of a set. And I'm just too tired to shoo Dustin away.

Jen catches her thick bouncy hair in a plastic tortoise-shell clip. "How was work?"

"Terrible, awful, close to the worst in my life—" (I never quite realized till now how much I hated this day)—"and totally gross." This last is Jen's phrase, but regardless she doesn't respond, which is something of a relief. There are moments when a child's complete lack of interest leaves a parent free to say anything.

I reach in my pocket and toss my car keys and the three scraps of paper onto the nightstand beside my bed. Then I shuck off my coveralls, peel down to my plaid shirt and blue jeans. Shed of my olive drab, I am ready to consider the outside world. But for a minute I simply stand, unable to take my eyes from that crumpled Xeroxed page.

Apart from Grace Michaels' presence at school, I know almost nothing about her. I rarely see this young woman except in passing, the way you might meet anyone in a town our size. Not long ago, I bumped into her—as well as everybody else—at the grand opening of our new Safeway supermarket. The high spot was the produce department, where every twenty minutes certain vegetables are misted lightly and automatically from sprinklers mounted above gleaming bins. What's more, the section's overhead lighting is not fluorescent but soft and subdued, shedding a healthy luster down the rows. Each fruit and vegetable receives such special treatment in that moist, glowing end of the store that you might be put in mind—as I was—of stepping into a hushed hospital nursery reserved for preemies only. This was my thought as my father and I browsed the display of little yellow crookneck squash—when we came upon Coach Michaels wheeling her shiny new shopping cart directly toward us. Coach was dressed for a casual winter weekend—heavy fleece-lined boots, baggy corduroy jeans, and a green flannel shirt of such size as to fit the legendary Paul Bunyan. In one hand she held a grand opening balloon, in the other, a fistful of discount coupons.

Coach nodded down at the coupons. "My mother sends me these." She sounded apologetic, as if clipping coupons were some social gaffe.

I smiled, paying almost no attention. My gaze had fallen immediately to her shopping cart, which is only natural—inspection being a first instinct with me.

After a moment I heard Coach saying to my father, "Do you like peanut brittle?"

I looked up and saw that she'd given him a fifty-cent coupon for that candy.

"How about condensed milk?" she said, shuffling through her coupons.

"Milk," my father answered. He took the coupon from her fingers, then pulled out his smooth leather wallet. He slid the coupons inside, as if the little slips of paper were cash. Otherwise his billfold was empty. Since his illness, my father has difficulty keeping track of money. Every so often I give him a few dollars, which he almost always loses.

Now I caught Coach Michaels glancing into my father's thin, bare wallet, and I felt suddenly ashamed that my father had no money, that the socks he'd chosen to wear that morning didn't match. And no driver's license in his wallet, either. He'd surrendered it to the Department of Motor Vehicles and given up driving, given up nearly everything.

"Have this," Coach said. She folded more coupons into his wallet. "That's twenty-five cents off St. Joseph's aspirin, plus a dollar for Purina dry dog food—any ten-pound bag or more."

"Okay," my father said, sounding very satisfied. He closed his billfold. Then he turned to the produce bin beside him and selected a gnarled stub of gingerroot. He placed the gingerroot in Coach's shopping cart, which I should've anticipated would happen. My father does this whenever we buy groceries—just pulls some random article off a shelf and adds it to the cart.

Flustered, I dug to retrieve the gingerroot from Coach Michaels' basket. "I'm sure Coach doesn't need this, Dad."

"Well, I bet I probably do maybe," Coach said. She nodded down at her shopping cart, the grand opening balloon bobbing above her head, her honey brown hair shining in the low light of produce. "I'm pretty sure I must have a coupon for that." But of course I knew she didn't. Besides which, I doubted Coach possessed even an inkling of an idea as to what it was my father had given her, or how that knobby root might be used.

Judging from the slim pickings in her grocery cart, Grace Michaels hadn't made much progress beyond dormitory cooking: microwave popcorn, instant macaroni and cheese, frozen raspberry yogurt, and creamed corn. Her remaining selections fell into the nonfood category. And such ordinary items they seemed at the time: Band-Aids, rubbing alcohol, a jar of Vaseline.

But tonight, standing in this bright bedroom, in my dark ignorance, these innocent articles, plus Grace's boxy weekend clothes, suddenly take on such sexual mystery as to cause my head to throb.

I cross the room to Jen. "Come into the kitchen with me."

"I hope you don't want to talk," Jen says, hauling her athletic bag off the desk. "I've got to get going."

"Just something I need to ask you." From the center of the bed, my father glances up and nods, as if I'm speaking to him. Then he returns to the war.

I grab the car keys, but Jen shakes her head no. "I have a ride."

She follows me down the hallway, snaps on the kitchen light. It is almost dark.

I step across the linoleum tile and fill the kettle, then switch on the stove.

Jen plops at the kitchen table.

"I need you to tell me if anything's happened at school," I say, not looking over.

"I think my ride's here," Jen says. I hear her closing her bag, the zipper hesitant and halting. Her voice is careful. "Anything . . . like what?"

"About basketball. Coach Michaels, maybe." I pause, listening to the kettle's hiss, heat steaming into my face. Finally I turn to her. "You know—people talking. Rumors."

And as I speak, her eyes spring wide and tight, and I have never from the day Jen was born seen this expression cross her face. She looks stricken.

I move to her. "Oh honey, sweetheart . . ." But I scarcely know I'm speaking, only bent over her, whispering this into her hair and waiting for the word to come out of her mouth: Lesbian.

Finally I feel her deep breath shuddering beneath my chin. Then her voice escapes in a rush. "Tara says she's pregnant; she said she went all the way, she did it."

"Tara—" I snap straight, blink down at her.

A car's horn sounds, streaming and traveling as if for miles, light years from this room. The kettle whistles. I race to the stove; stop this sound.

"My ride," Jen says.

I step after her, through the hall. "Not Coach . . ." I cannot absorb this. My mind is stuck, still waiting for that L word.

Jen shakes her head, slides her letterman's jacket from the closet. She fumbles into the jacket—slow and heartbreaking—like a very old man laboring with an overcoat. Then she opens the front door. She brushes a kiss across my cheek, her lips suddenly cold, aged. Tara Simonet is parked at the curb, watching us. The girl gazes out from the fading light, pink and blonde inside her mother's white Subaru. She hits the horn again.

I catch Jen's arm, suddenly feeling all the danger beyond this room —wanting only to spare her. "Don't go."

"Tara . . ." Jen says. She moves onto the front steps, her shoulders set stiff and straight ahead. "My ride."

I reach for her again, then let my hand drop. I stand at the door, seeing the two of them drive off, my dim eyes following them up the block and through every street, around each corner of this small town, the time it takes to get to Coarsegold High, for a girl to go all the way —however long—I stand here.

Finally I switch on the front porch light, then stumble back to the kitchen. I make a cup of Swiss mocha and wish it was caffeinated. Espresso. Right now I need strength, a sharp pick-me-up.

I sit at the table, and outside I hear a wind, the rattle of this drought. At our border station—just a few miles up the road—you'll find a file, a photo of a child attacked, bitten one hundred and fourteen times by a ferret—raw puncture wounds on a small round face, a neck. Find, too, a Mason jar on the office window sill and one Mormon cricket preserved in formaldehyde, a cricket nearly the size of my shoe. Hear the wind sifting at my house like a storm coursing off some barren desert. Listen. I believe there must be a plague across this land.

I glance up, seeing my father step into the room. He comes to me with two scraps of paper, sits next to me. He places the papers before me. And I bow my head over them, as if to ask a silent blessing on our food, solace from this dark day. I think to myself: *The Lord is my shepherd. I shall not want.*

Then my father takes up his green restaurant napkin. Slowly he says, "F-U-N-E-M?"

"Yes," I whisper, "we have ham."

My father smiles. Then he turns to the crumpled paper, Romans 1:24. He slides the Bible passage beneath my eyes. He points to one word: God. And I realize this is all he knows. He would ask me to read —there's a question in his face. He needs to hear. And I could say anything. Tell him: the L word stands for licorice. L is for left. Lonely. For lifesaver. I could go so far as to say the L word is love.

I clear my throat. My memory is long. I run my finger under the Xeroxed lines, although my father can't follow. I'm reciting by heart. The book is Romans, but I move beyond chapter 1, past verse 24, skipping ahead. My father never notices, his numbers stop at twelve. But I am able to go all the way.

> Let love be without dissimulation . . .
> Bless them which persecute you:
> bless and curse not.
> Rejoice with them that do rejoice,
> and weep with them that weep . . .
> Be kindly affectioned one to another
> Be not overcome of evil, but overcome
> evil with good.

"Thankyou," my father says in that soft rush of his. Then he opens his scribbled napkin. Carefully he spreads it in my lap.

And for a moment we are comforted. We walk beside still waters; we lie down in green pastures. There is a table prepared for us. For just this moment, we live on words alone.

Nine

During the years when my father stood at the high oak pulpit, a Bible open before him, his dark ministerial robes bathed in morning sun—during that time when he preached for civil rights and disarmament, for forgiveness and redemption—the church on the corner of High Street and Kaiser called itself First United Methodist. But not long after my father's retirement, the congregation voted a return to basics. "A Christian backslide," was how my father put it. No sooner had parishioners banned guitars and blue jeans from Sunday services than they took up sacred dancing and became Calvary Bible Church, where members stand alone on the word of God and still stand to this day: Sunday, January 27, 1991.

The title of this morning's sermon is "How Hot Is Hell?" But my father isn't listening. Beside me in the pew, this man who once lamented the occasional snore underscoring his words from the pulpit—this white-haired retired clergyman dozes, his head lolling at my shoulder.

And a good thing, my father's slumber, because Pastor Sitwell appears to be pointing a preacherly finger in our direction when he says, "We have had among us members of the clergy who bear a strong resemblance to permissive parents afraid to spank their children because that would not be loving. But understand this, my friends . . ." Paul Sitwell pauses, his smile beatific, theologically trained. His delivery has come a long way since our debate team days at Coarsegold High. "The Bible does not confuse love with sentimentality. God's love is balanced by justice and an abiding hatred of sin."

Across the aisle, I see Dorothy Bascombe nod in agreement. Corrine Simonet smiles from the choir, her burnished harp silent at her side. Corrine's clear blue gaze wanders the congregation, comes to rest on Tara. Her daughter. My own child has accompanied Tara today, through no doing of mine. I've never forced Jen's church attendance—

perhaps because I myself was not allowed to miss a single service except in the case of true illness, my skinny filial presence a shining Christian example. But this morning I'm here solely for the sake of my father. I lean into him, keeping my shoulder square beneath his drowsy head, the rise and fall of his breath.

" 'Because judgment against a bad work has not been executed speedily,' " Pastor Sitwell quotes from Ecclesiastes, " 'that is why the heart of the sons of men has become fully set in them to do bad.' "

Jen and Tara sit two rows over, not so much crammed in their pew, but clinging to one another as if to sink together into those hot flames. Because it is an inferno, Pastor Sitwell says. Hell, here on earth. And I believe it must be so. This week President Saddam Hussein torched oil wells in the Wafra fields, lofting fiery geysers and billowing smoke that turned day to night. In Iran, black greasy rain drizzled from an oil slick sky. Saddam Hussein spoke to his countrymen, his words reaching Nicosia, that city where Saint Paul once addressed the gentiles. "In the name of God, the merciful, the compassionate," the Iraqi president began. While President Bush bowed his head at Camp David and worshipped. War ships assembled. Marines practiced amphibious landings. Allied forces flew more than 15,000 sorties, detonating bombs of such force as to part all the seas. Iraqi defectors scrambled across lines, fleeing black rain, the rain of terror, smart bombs falling.

How hot is hell?—there's no telling. The Pentagon's exercising Euphoria Control. Defense Secretary Cheney cautioned that "a military operation of this intensity and complexity cannot be scored every evening like a college track meet or a basketball tournament."

But we're trying to keep score regardless. This afternoon in Tampa, Florida, the New York Giants square off against the Buffalo Bills for Super Bowl XXV. I don't follow football as a rule, but this year my attention's been caught by the controversy over whether this event should be called off, what with the Gulf War raging.

It's Midge's opinion that our best move would be to cancel both the war and the Super Bowl. But then, Midge has been carrying a grudge against the New York Giants ever since our last committee meeting, when Corrine Simonet turned up with her personal copy of a videotape titled, *Champions for Life*. Corrine has made a motion to include this video in our tenth grade sex education unit. To this end, our committee previewed the film, which features scenes from the New York Giants' last Super Bowl victory.

All eight of us watched Mark Bavaro catch a pass, followed by his close-up speculation: ". . . with the abortion death squads allowed to run rampant through our country, I wonder how many future champions will be killed before they see the light of day?" After that we saw George Martin sack John Elroy in the end zone. Then George reappeared wearing a snappy blue business suit and said, "I'm glad I was able to help turn the tide in the Super Bowl with that safety. I hope and pray that the Supreme Court has begun to turn the tide against the legalized destruction of babies."

And sitting here, it is clear to me that Corrine Simonet has no inkling that her own daughter believes she is pregnant. Actually, Tara more than believes. She is convinced. According to Jen, Tara has given herself four home pregnancy tests, and on each occasion the little vial of clear solution has turned positive pink. But regardless, it appears that Tara Simonet will never tell her mother. Jen claims Tara would rather die first.

Pastor Sitwell grips the oak pulpit and leans to the congregation. "And so we see today how diabolical evil has been allowed to flourish. Make no mistake—the Devil is real and continues, even at this moment, to reap the tragic harvest of a sinful society."

But it isn't sin, only fear that keeps me in church this morning. I'm afraid for my father, afraid for my daughter and Tara Simonet—those two seated across the rows of polished pews. They are holding hands as girls sometimes do. Tara's gaze aims dead ahead. Below her miniskirt, her right knee is bruised from the game. Basketball.

I fear for Coach Michaels, too. And now, for Pink Lindstrom, as well.

I bow my head, though we are a long way from Pastor Sitwell's closing benediction. I shut my eyes, but I've lost my faith. Fear is the only prayer I know.

Two nights ago, Pink drove through my lane at the border station. It was close to 11:00 P.M., the last Friday of this month—just as Midge has described his crossings.

I actually felt overjoyed to see him. Earlier in the evening, our Lady Miners had played Iola High School, a contest noted on my schedule as a Killer, Iola being the defending league champs. I was having no luck learning the score and had begun kicking myself for ever agreeing to work swing shift on nights when the team played an away game. By ten o'clock I'd resorted to our station's hot line, thinking maybe Norman Spoon at the dispatcher's office might've heard something. But of course, Norm could tell me only that the varsity boys had lost their match.

So the moment Pink's truck rattled under our lights, I dashed into the lane, certain he'd made the hour's drive to cover the team.

I beamed my Everready road lantern directly into the open driver's window and said, "Tell me."

And Pink answered straight off, "We won."

"Oh my Lord, Lord," I said, leaning into the window with such relief and throwing my thermal padded arms around Pink's neck as if it were Midge and me in the stands, hauled to our feet by this remarkable victory. Then I remembered who I was hugging and regained myself, pushing instantly straight.

But behind the wheel, Pink appeared somewhat shaken. He sat blinking up at me.

"Don't say a word," I warned.

Pink nodded and pulled himself a little higher in the seat. Then he dropped his forehead to the steering wheel in a gesture so profoundly forlorn, I cannot rid myself of the sight—not even today, here in the house of God, with my eyes shut and the weight of a crimson cloth-bound hymnal open on my lap.

I gave a small cough. Pink raised his head and gazed at me. "Hedy," he said in such a quiet voice it took all my strength just to hear—"Hedy, I am a red-blooded and lonely man. That's the truth. You are a married woman without a husband, and this whole predicament of ours keeps me up all night every night and that's also the truth. But if it will make you happy, I won't say one word."

I ignored Pink's reference to "our predicament," feeling that I couldn't allow the conversation to proceed any further along those lines. And so I simply said, "Thank you for your understanding."

"Don't mention it," Pink replied, and again he fell silent.

After a moment I saw his hand fumbling in his down jacket. He pulled out a pocket-sized spiral notebook and flipped through its pages. "Give me your light," he said.

Pink aimed the road lantern down his sports column notes—names and numbers slurred in a hurry, in the heat of a killer contest. His breath smoked the icy night. "You should have been there."

"I should've," I said, motherly guilt seizing this first opportunity.

"Jen went into the game at the bottom of the opening quarter and she never came out. She picked off eleven rebounds and scored seventeen points."

"She didn't—" I reached through the window, bumping my gloved hand across Pink's arm to those numbers on the page.

Pink shook his head. "Don't touch me," he said, his voice falling. "Touch me and I guarantee it's all over—I'm good as gone."

I leaned away from the truck's window. "Sorry," I mumbled. "Don't pay any attention to me, I'm sorry. Please just continue." I tugged my cap lower on my forehead so as to avoid his eyes. "What else?"

Pink cleared his throat. "Well, nothing except the team ran a strong man-to-man defense. Mano-a-mano," he added with a soft chuckle. "Plus, Tara Simonet gave the performance of her high school career. She couldn't miss—the ball had her name written all over it. I wish you'd seen." Pink closed the little notebook, slid it back into his jacket. "She played like there was no tomorrow."

"I know," I said, because just then—for an instant—I was there, an hour's drive away, seated on the Visitors side of Iola High. And I could see Tara diving for the loose ball, shoving herself reckless to the rim, playing as if there were no tomorrow. I didn't need to be told, she would rather die.

Pink handed me the light. "It was an upset victory—our kids played over their heads. But if they can hang on to this momentum, they might just go all the way to state finals."

"Yes," I said, hearing my voice a whisper. "All the way."

Then Pink reached to crank his window closed.

"Wait . . ." I turned gazing west to the cold dark summit—no traffic visible this late and lonesome hour.

At this border I'm empowered to detain any vehicle with good cause. And I take the job seriously with good reason. One winter afternoon, not long after I'd first been hired, an older couple drove through my lane and inquired about the weather over the mountains. Above us, the sky had closed like a clam and snow was steadily falling. Visibility will be poor, I told these people. Once you reach the ridge, you'll need to chain your tires. The driver poked his head out the window of his blue Ford Escort. Snowflakes pelted his graying hair, the fur collar of his parka. That bad, he said. I pointed up the slick white interstate, a motel just off the next exit. The man looked to his wife, then back at me. He gave a shrug. There's a new granddaughter in Oakland, he said. The wife can't wait. So I waved them on, hollered, Drive carefully. Not more than fifteen minutes passed before I heard sirens. Then Norman Spoon's voice crackled on the office scanner, reporting a pileup just ahead—a blue '83 Escort traveling at an unsafe speed for the weather, both occupants of the vehicle killed on impact. Since that day, I'm ever aware that my face could be the last a person sees.

I glanced to Pink. "Where are you going?" Here on the job it is my duty to know. "Are you carrying with you any fruit or vegetables? Animals?" Pink grinned out the window, as if we were playing some teasing game. "Tell me," I demanded, "do you have anything to declare?"

"I can't say." Pink cocked his chin like the peculiar, insufferable flirt that he is. "You won't allow a word."

"Never mind," I said.

Flashing the strong beam of my lantern across the truck's frayed seat, I spotted a plastic garment bag draped so as to appear almost human against the passenger door. I played the light down the bag's zipper, aware that my interest had proceeded far beyond the lines of official business. "I'll need to take a look inside."

"I've got to get going," Pink said, revving the pickup's engine.

I pulled off my insulated gloves and reached past him for the lumpy plastic bag. Beyond my lane I heard Marshall hailing an eighteen wheeler, the hiss of air brakes.

"Hedy, cut it out." Pink swatted my hand away, then let out a long breath. He shook his head. "I just wish you'd tell me how to be around you without making you nuts."

"You don't make me nuts," I said, hearing my voice rising a little too shrill.

"Well, nervous then—or scared."

"Scared, my eye," I said.

"I mean, I could try to be more like a friend, if that's what you want. Like with your dad and Jen—"

"Oh, sure . . ." I leaned nearer the truck's window and clicked my tongue. "All the time carrying on with my family . . . I really can't for the life of me—"

"Wait a minute," Pink said, his words suddenly rushing. "I *like* your family—does that seem strange to you? Does it seem strange that Jen and your dad have been just plain nice to me, even when they didn't know the first thing about me? I'm talking about that picnic you asked me to—"

"I never asked you."

He thumped the steering wheel, paying no attention. "You know the day I'm talking about, when you almost . . . the day I . . . we . . . Well, you remember what happened," he said.

And just then, I could've told him: Yes, I know. I could've said: Thank you. And I would be his friend, even as my father and Jen had befriended him. But at that moment, in the dark, I couldn't bring myself to speak, except for the sake of my official duty—for safety's sake.

I aimed my lantern across the seat and down the garment bag once more. "Be that as it may," I said, referring to everything and nothing, "you'll still need to show me what's inside."

Pink let his hands drop to his lap. "Fine," he said, in a sudden even voice that somehow stunned me. "So, we can talk about this another time." He leaned over and yanked the bag open, then sank back behind the wheel. "So, okay."

"You understand I'm required to do this," I said, nodding into his stony face. Then I glanced past him to the bag.

In the light I caught a glimpse of dull brown, a shirt sleeve bearing two stripes above a small gold pin—crossed rifles—an olive green tie strung around the neck of the coat hanger. For a moment my mind raced to extremes, thinking of covert actions, secret meetings, brown shirts. "Who is this?" I whispered.

"It's me until Sunday night," Pink said. He sounded resigned, thrusting his wrist into the light. He tapped his watch. "At 0700 hours, I'm due in Hayward with my reserve unit."

"The *reserves*," I said, swaying back on my heels. I glanced to the truck lane and caught sight of First Sergeant Marshall Painter, Air

Force Reserves. I wanted to tell Pink: Not you, but Marshall. Instead, I flapped my hand at Pink's window, striving for casual. "Well, it could be worse—I mean, you're only going to Hayward, the east bay. Just California."

"I can make it in under four hours," Pink said. He dropped the truck into gear. "I would've left earlier, except I didn't want to miss Jen's game."

"No, of course you didn't." I heard my unfamiliar voice, issuing vague, yet full of convincing brightness, as if some other person had observed my sudden distress and stepped kindly into this conversation, speaking for me. I nodded across to the stiff khaki shirt, green tie. "You must look very nice when you put it all on."

Pink shrugged. "I try my best."

"Well, what are you?" I forced a smile, forcing this idle chitchat just to keep Pink idling safe in my lane.

"Only a corporal."

"I mean, what branch. You know—of the armed services."

"Marine corps."

I glanced away, picturing Marines wading the murky Persian Gulf, practicing their landings, storming the oil-oozing beach. "You wouldn't happen by any chance—" I kept my gaze clear of him, "happen to be amphibious . . ."

He shook his head. "Not me. I'm with the Fourth LAAMB."

"Oh, that," I said with the remarkable calm of sheer ignorance. "Just the Fourth Lamb."

"Right," Pink said. "Light Anti-Aircraft Missile Battalion."

And then I felt the words—a mouthful of weapons—and my blood slammed against my heart. My very bones snapped to, answering a full-out alarm. "Don't move," I ordered, prepared to detain him absolutely, with good cause. And I ran to fetch Marshall.

"Jesus," Marshall groaned as I dragged him out the office door.

"Listen, you're in the reserves yourself, you've got a right. Just ask him if he's been activated—that's all you have to say."

"You ask him," Marshall grumbled. "You're the one who wants to know."

"But you're a man," I said, falling back on any excuse.

Certainly, the vehicle idling in my lane belonged to Pink Lindstrom. But just then, the individual seated in that pickup appeared to be someone else altogether. It was as if a long-awaited traveler had finally arrived safely in my lane, only to be jettisoned away—rocketed with the speed of a missile, faster than sound. Unsafe. And Pink was wrong. In the presence of this sudden imperiled male of red blood, it seemed there'd never be another time to talk.

"Ask him man-to-man," I whispered to Marshall as we stepped alongside the pickup.

Marshall snapped the collar of his coveralls against the cold, then planted his heavy boot on the truck's battered running board. "Man-to-man," he said into the window, "do you figure to see any action?"

For an instant, I saw a slight expression flicker across that solemn face behind the wheel. Then I heard the slow release of the clutch and his truck eased forward, his voice streaming out the window. "I'm not at liberty to say."

We stood—Marshall and I—watching him drive off, the truck's engine coughing as he started up the grade, taillights sputtering off and on in the dark, faltering.

"Bad wiring," Marshall said. "He's got a short. Short-timer. I just wish it were me instead of him."

"Don't wish that on yourself." I tore my eyes away, turned to Marshall. "You hear me? Don't ever." But I wished it, too, and felt ashamed of the thought.

And I believe Marshall must've sensed this. Marshall claims even dumb animals know—each beast must go for the quick bullet. He took me in his arms, hid my face against his chest. "Be strong," he said, "be brave. Ask me man-to-man."

I shook my dazed head.

"Ask me and I'll tell you," Marshall whispered into my cold aching ear. "That guy's as good as gone."

From the pulpit, Pastor Sitwell's voice grows louder, and I lift my eyes. Paul Sitwell calls us to fight the battle at home, rise up in holy horror at a world laid low by pornography, promiscuity, and pollution—those "three P's," he reminds us, "of a humanistic society floundering in hell." Then he closes with a prayer and bids us turn to hymn number 186.

We stand, joining in the recessional . . . " 'Thy saints in all this glorious war . . .' " And the choir marches out, maroon robes rustling. " 'Am I a soldier of the cross, A follower of the lamb . . .' "

My father is full of sleep and unsteady at my side. I brace my arm at his back. "You okay?"

He nods, his voice a quavering hum, trailing the congregation. " 'And shall I fear to own His cause, Or blush to speak His name . . . ' " Until the very end—this word my father knows, sings loud and clear, "A-men."

Then he is hurrying to the church door, beaming as Dorothy Bascombe greets him with a powdery hug.

Once when he was in the stroke rehab unit, I led him up a corridor and down an elevator to the hospital chapel. We sat in the quiet dim light, only the two of us, side by side on a cool nondenominational pew. Then, after a minute my father stepped to the communion rail at the front. He swung one leg over the low rail, then the other. Because he was always looking to escape from the hospital in those first confused weeks, the rehab staff had fixed a small plastic monitor to the cuff of his trousers. He couldn't wander beyond the ward without setting off this monitor—a beeping sound alerting the floor nurse that he was gone again. Sitting in the hospital chapel, I smiled at the idea of that monitor sounding even then, two floors up. I imagined my father as some valuable article shoplifted from a department store—a house detective hustling at the giveaway beep. My father, an endangered species, tagged and released into wild waters—scientists tracking the fading sound. I watched him move behind the small chapel lectern. He gazed out at me, his sole congregation. And in my mind, I heard the monitor sound sky-high, way beyond two floors, so far into the universe I feared God had picked up the signal, and I tipped my head to the hushed ceiling and said out loud, Don't take him now.

Dorothy Bascombe winks at me, then turns to my father. "We're looking as handsome as ever," she says, dabbing her pink lipstick off his cheek. He leans at the church door and grins, always the fool for a kiss.

Jen steps beside us. "Catch you at home. We're hitting the books." She means herself and Tara, the SATs—they missed their Saturday study session due to a baby-sitting job. Or child care, as Jen calls it.

"So here are the famous basketball stars," Dorothy murmurs, leaning to Jen and Tara. They flash goofy smiles and are out the door and down the steps.

Then Dorothy swings to me, speaks close to my ear. "I hope they aren't getting too attached to Grace Michaels."

"Well, she's a very good coach," I answer.

I could tell Dorothy that they're already attached—every girl on the team. At practice, I've seen how each of them looks to Grace, watching for her approval. How they copy her loose, athletic walk, the way she shrugs one shoulder.

"Plus she's a nice woman," I add vaguely.

I glance beyond Dorothy, all my attention drawn to those two zooming down the street in Corrine Simonet's white Subaru.

This baffles me—how Tara is still cramming for the SAT, still putting her mind to it and keeping her fingers crossed for Harvard, Berkeley, Brown, or Oral Roberts U. Still giving her all, on and off the court, as if everything remains possible, and there is no tomorrow.

I nudge my father past Herb Renfrow's handshake, then Pastor Sitwell.

"Good to see you, Hedy," Paul Sitwell calls over his wife's permed head.

I nod, wanting to explain that I'm only here for my father. I'd remind Paul Sitwell of our Junior Prom in the far distant spring of 1970. With Ward away at college, Paul had pinned a corsage of yellow baby roses on my white dotted Swiss and taken me out after the dance for steak and prawns, then driven me straight home, but not before he folded his whole wet tongue into my ear. And I'd mention this to Pastor Sitwell now, except that would not be Christian of me.

"I don't suppose you remember about Paul," I say to my father as we cross the street to our Blazer. He shakes his head no, holds the car door open. "Because I probably never told you . . ."

For a minute he lingers on the street, squinting down the pavement.

Dorothy Bascombe waves from the corner, as if returning his attentions. "You mind those three P's," she hollers with a coy sashay up the sidewalk.

"Would you look at her," I mutter. "Has the woman no pride?"

"P," my father says, sliding into the passenger seat.

"Three P's," I tell him. I start the car and the radio is instantly on.

A voice speaks loud via satellite from Baghdad—our one American reporter allowed to remain behind enemy lines. "Peter Arnett." I nod at my father. Then I snap off the sound, so as not to be reminded of that reserve corporal as good as gone, but not gone yet—only the east bay, our native land.

"Anyway, this boy Paul always had his eye on me—always from the beginning."

My father glances over. "Peter."

"Not Peter, but Paul."

We enter traffic, cruise by the new Safeway market, then past Longs Drugs with its motto, "Take the Longs way home." But we go directly, pulling into our driveway behind the white Subaru and its bumper message: *My Boss Is A Jewish Carpenter.*

"Three P's," my father says, and for a minute we sit quiet in the drive, just pondering the thought.

After a while I open my hand, counting for him on my fingers, "Peter, Paul, and pot roast."

My father smiles. "Sunday."

"You are one hundred percent correct—pot roast, peas, and potatoes. Three P's for a good man."

"Potroastpeas," my father mumbles, climbing out of the car. We move up the front step. "Potatoes."

I push open the door, and without warning my eyes well at the simmering aroma of roast and the whole house warm from a slow oven, the thought of a good man. I will ask Tara to stay for Sunday dinner. And it suddenly occurs to me that if he were here, I'd invite him, too. My unexpected company—that one who is not my lawful missing husband, but a man not yet gone, only four hours away. That P whose name I cannot say. That man—not Peter, not Paul. Not mine.

Ten

It's possible we're the only family in America who didn't watch today's Super Bowl. Even now, at nearly 8:00 P.M. Pacific Time, we remain in the dark, ignorant of the final score.

Tara Simonet is still here, having stayed for Sunday dinner. At the moment, she and Jen are upstairs building their vocabularies. My father is across the living room, seated in the green easy chair we moved from his house. He's struggling with his own lexicon, relearning words in his *Reading for Survival* workbook. And I'm struggling with yet another letter to my husband—this latest attempt motivated partly by guilt and a pain in my heart.

However, tonight I've got help. I have before me the notes from a class I once took from our Coarsegold Park and Recreation Department. This class was called "The Art of Communication." Our communication leader agreed with Emily Post that "Letters written under strong emotion should be held for twenty-four hours and reread before being mailed, or torn into small pieces and not sent at all." Our class was also urged to cultivate a passing acquaintance with Latin and French, so as not to appear out of our depths when conversing with cultured individuals. We were given a list of commonly used phrases, which I'm relying on here, French being the native tongue spoken in Grenoble.

With these communication tips in mind, I've managed to write:

January 27, 1991

Dearest Ward, mon cher,

I'm home tonight en famille and thinking of you and the perfect snow in France.

I do not mention our local weather, because my fears about this drought would fall under The Art of Communication's taboo category: "Chronic Inappropriate Calamity Letters." So I move on, striving for the bright side.

Knowing you, I'm sure your daily training is going even better than you expected. And I feel more positive with each passing day that you'll break 140 miles per hour. There's such great sports news in the San Francisco Chronicle*—all of it totally au courant and apropos. Even as I write, Mark Spitz, who we watched win seven gold medals during the 1971 Olympics—Mark, age 41, is preparing for his comeback in the 50-meter butterfly. Plus, over-forty pitcher Jim Palmer says he'll definitely be at spring training camp. And Bjorn Borg has announced he'll enter Wimbledon this June, after eight straight years away from tennis. Talk about encouraging—all I can add is, veni, vidi, vici! Carpe diem! And ecce homo!*

I pause to read what I've written, then let the page slide to the carpet. I feel so infinitely depressed I can't continue. I'd like to ask somebody why it is that people keep going back to find themselves. Why this endless shift into reverse—as if all our pasts are glorious, and each present moment only some vindication of who we used to be. Who are we? Somebody please tell me. Because I could weep for these sad men of old broken records, for the cautious optimism of aging heroes, this controlled American euphoria—this war our biggest comeback try of all.

I move to my father's chair and lean a moment at his shoulder. Somewhere I read that fear is regressive. And in that regard I have nothing to fear—no former self to retrieve. What I'm afraid of is this: I worry that one of these days I'll be driving along and there'll be a woman standing in the road ahead. She waits, waving both arms in the air as I approach. And I drive right past myself, never knowing this woman was me.

My father glances up from his workbook. He's making progress, reading for survival. His workbook lessons are written as little stories, designed to make learning more interesting. Tonight's vocabulary words are followed by a pronunciation key: kisses (kissez), happy (hapee), laughing (lafing), marry (maree). The story goes:

> Ann *kisses* Jack.
> Jack is a *happy* man.
> He is *laughing.*
> Ann will *marry* Jack.
> Jack will *marry* Ann.

I touch the gold band on my father's finger, this wedding ring he still wears, and I wonder: are these words the key to our survival? My father used to read to me from his Bible . . . *The word is nigh unto thee.* I look into his soft eyes. I want to ask if he remembers, to tap his shoulder—Do you remember the word? Your first kiss? Ann kisses Jack . . .

I remember. That Homecoming night, Ward's face shown even brighter in the porch light. I felt the roughness of his mouth, his lips chafed and flaking from the scouring snow. The kiss seemed no more than an instant, then Ward stood straight again. He gazed down. A dry fleck from his peeling lips still clung to my mouth. "What are you trying to do to me?" he said. I blushed at his smile, the little edge in his voice. He flicked the fine shred of his skin off my lip. He said, "Are you trying to eat me alive?"

Now I stand over my father, shaking my head no, I wouldn't . . . Not ever. I tap the notebook in my father's lap.

"Two syllables," I tell him. "Mar-ee."

"Love," my father says.

"Mush," Jen mutters, rambling into the room.

I turn and catch Tara charging after her down the stairs. Tara takes a flying leap into the hallway, her shoulder banging against the front door. I start to say something, wanting to warn her to be careful of herself, go easy. But then, I'm not supposed to know she's pregnant.

I glance at Jen. "Come into my room."

They trail me to the bedroom. Lately I'm feeling that I have two girls instead of one. It seems Tara's always here. And always, two dogs on my bed.

"Give Dustin a pillow," I tell Jen, and Tara laughs. At least this girl appreciates my sense of humor.

She plops onto the bed and Bark bounces. "I scored 1100 on my last practice test," she says. "Except I missed 'egregious' in the vocabulary."

I open the closet. "Well, practice helps." But I don't really believe this, because what I truly think is that Tara Simonet is practicing denial. I turn to Jen. "In a little while, I want you to go upstairs and lay out your grandfather's pajamas—the blue flannel. His electric blanket should be set at three."

But before my father sleeps, I want him to remember. I want his mind returned to him. Right now. He must close his notebook and read to me with all his words restored. Let him read . . . *I have set before you life and death, blessing and cursing: therefore choose life* . . . I need him to do this for me tonight.

Jen nods from the doorway, watching me zip up my Department of Agriculture coveralls. "You working graveyard?"

"No, I'm just going to the supermarket."

"You're wearing *that* to the store?"

"Well, I think she looks cool," Tara says, sitting up on one elbow. "I read where cat suits are making a fashion comeback. They call it the retro look."

"That's hardly a cat suit."

"It's warm," I mumble. "Added protection."

"Protection," Jen says. "What are you expecting out there—chemical warfare?"

"You've got terrific bones," Tara says.

"Thank you," I say, though almost none of my bones are visible. I glance to the closet's full-length mirror and straighten my olive drab collar, then lift the hair from my neck. "I don't know—should I pull it up like this, or leave it down?"

"Down, definitely," Tara says. "And I think gold earrings would be good with that green—a pair of simple hoops maybe."

"She's only going to the store," Jen mutters, sinking onto the bed.

Tara reaches over, plucks a piece of lint off Jen's baggy gray sweatshirt. "But you never know who you might run into—that's what my mother always says."

I shove into my pack boots, then grab my thermal gloves, purse, and car keys from the dresser. In the living room, I move to my father, plant a kiss on top of his head. I let my hand linger on his thin shoulder, but he doesn't look up from his workbook. "Get some rest," I say finally.

"Ohyes," he says.

Then I am at the door with Jen and Tara right behind.

Jen wraps her wide hand around the doorknob. For a moment I believe she might turn the lock. "Isn't it a little late? I mean, you never go to the store this time of night."

"The new Safeway stays open twenty-four hours," I tell Jen, as if that is reason, in and of itself, for going.

"Try this," Tara says, removing a bracelet from her wrist. She is still trying to complete my outfit. This bracelet looks more like a string —colored threads braided into a bright strand. Tara ties it around my left wrist. "A friendship bracelet—Nekuda Adowa makes them. They're supposed to be left on at all times."

"Twenty-four hours," Jen grumbles.

"In the shower, when you sleep—it's a symbol."

"Well, thanks," I say.

I gaze into Tara's blue eyes, so like her mother's, her blonde hair hitched back, a number-two pencil tucked behind her ear—that heavy lead required for filling in those endless blank bubbles of multiple choice. The SAT is coming up soon; Tara needs to raise her score a hundred points. And so they are studying hard—before and after school—these two girls. They're taking practice tests, practicing basketball. In between, they baby-sit. I hear them on the phone, arranging jobs. Jen says they're pooling their earnings—for what, I don't know. But I can guess. I think they are too young, too slight to carry this weight of the world. And I don't know how long this can go on, how far along . . .

Jen pushes open the front door, snaps on the porch light. "We need a half gallon of milk and orange juice—since you're going . . ." She pauses frowning off a moment. Then she touches my sleeve. "Be careful, Mom," she says.

I nod, aware of the countless times I've spoken those same words: Be careful . . . Then I move for the Blazer. I leave Jen and Tara standing at the door, in that precise spot where I've stood—remaining behind and waving good-bye, time and again, to every person I have ever loved.

But Midge is right. I like to drive in the dark. No matter where you go, the ride is always more important at night. And hazardous—it could be that, too. Except I'm only going to the supermaket. Safeway.

The store is huge, nearly empty of shoppers, and wild with light. I wheel a brand-new silver cart over the shiny black and white industrial floor. Doing the aisles, my mother used to call this. But I'm just here for orange juice and low-fat milk.

At the register, I write a check for $10.00 over the amount, for no reason except in case of emergency. An individual should always carry a little cash.

I leave the store and head for the border station. Fortunately, Midge isn't working tonight—it's just Marshall and the tail end of a swing shift crew.

"I see you came dressed for work." Marshall chuckles, following me into the office. "Can't stay away, day off or not."

I ignore this and move to the desk where none of us ever has a moment to sit. In the bottom drawer, I find our Coarsegold phone book and flip through. I commit the street address to memory.

Then, for the sake of passing a little time, I sit—off duty as I am—and prop my boots on the desk. Across the room, Marshall is pouring bleach into the fruit-stained sink. "Slow night," I say to his back.

"Everybody stayed put to watch the Super Bowl," Marshall says over his shoulder. "The Giants won, I guess you know. But I still lost on the point spread."

"I'm sorry to hear that." I look to the clock over the office door, noting that it's almost ten "This light traffic must make the drive home easier. I mean, if you were returning from the Bay area after one of your weekends in the reserves. Wouldn't you be just about here?"

"I guess," Marshall says with a shrug.

"Well, what time does a person . . ." I glance away, hunting the correct word, "does a person—you know—fall out?"

Marshall turns to squint at me, and in this little quiet, I can hear his mind ticking with the clock, his stubbly chin bobbing along, putting two and two together. Finally he says, "Hedy Gallagher Castle . . ." His voice drops at each of my names and his face colors up, as if I'm strangling this information out of him. "If you've got to know," he says finally. "The guy's probably back. Or almost."

I swing my boots from the desk. "Marshall, I don't believe you are aware that this individual we're discussing did save my life—twice. And he is as good as gone according to your own words. So I certainly think it behooves me to pay the man the courtesy of my respects, last or otherwise."

"Well, if you put it like that . . ."

"I do."

On my way out the door, I stop at the sink where I've spotted Midge's welder's mask resting on the counter. I grab the mask and tuck it under my arm.

"Look," Marshall says, walking me to the Blazer, "you don't need to explain anything to me. We're in a war—strange stuff happens."

" 'Shit happens,' " I say, quoting Midge's bumper sticker. I toss the welder's mask across the Blazer's front seat and climb in. "People get *killed*, for God's sake." I slam the car door shut and Marshall steps back. It's then I notice his grim Air Force Reserve face and remember exactly who I'm talking to. I crank down my window. "Marshall, forgive me . . ."

"Never mind," Marshall says. For a minute he lingers beside the window. "Listen, I'm off at eleven. Hang on and I'll drive you. You look pretty upset."

"Oh I'm fine, fine." I sound like my father, the words streaming.

"Then just be careful," Marshall calls as I ease away.

That's twice in the space of forty-five minutes I've been advised to take care, so to be on the safe side, I drop the Blazer into four-wheel drive. Dry pavement can prove deceiving, particularly at night. Black ice.

I leave the window open, feeling unusually warm in my padded thermal uniform. But then, I have every right to this nervous perspiration. In an effort to calm myself, I make a second stop at Safeway where I return like a criminal to the dairy case, scene of my earlier purchases. At the checkout, I hand over good money for a pint of half-and-half, a high-fat product nobody in our household ever uses.

Then I drive to Pink's house. It's a small place set back from the street, with a yellow lawn, thanks to our drought. The house is old brick—square and steep-roofed—and reminds me of the Three Little Pigs, Seven Dwarves. Of course, Pink himself is not a large person. A light glows behind a front window, smoke curls from the chimney. He is home.

I lean across the seat for Midge's welder's mask and place it snug on my head, dropping the clear visor over my face. This might seem extreme, but a little added protection never hurts. I may owe the man my life, but not—as Marshall's suspicions might infer—my body.

And so I proceed up the stone walk, protected from tip to toe and looking entirely official. The only exception to this drab regulation is Tara's bright string bracelet, which could be construed, I suppose, as friendly.

The front door is low and rounded on top like a portal. My thick-gloved knock is muffled, but I hear movement—the stirring from a sofa, perhaps, a door quietly closing as if to hide an unmade bed, damp towels strewn on the bathroom floor. And in this moment while I wait, a sensation suddenly overcomes me—not a sinking thought, but a full-blown certainty. One common French phrase bandied about by cultured people leaps off the long list and swarms my mind: Cherchez la femme—look for the woman. Because I am sure there's a woman standing behind this door, and I should've known she'd be here. Pink Lindstrom is young and available and not overly unattractive. Red-blooded, as he himself has said. Plus as good as gone to war, which—harsh reality aside—can tend toward romantic interest.

A light blazes on above the mailbox—too late to dash back to my car. But never mind. When she appears, I'll be gracious, neighborly, Jen's mother . . .

The light glances off my plastic visor, blinding me so I can't see as the door swings open.

"Hedy," he says.

And I answer, "Oh, it's you." I feel oddly disappointed.

"Come in, come." He holds the door wide and I fumble over the threshold, tottering and enormous in these clothes, my eyes groping behind my welder's mask.

He closes the door after me, smiles as I enter the tiny front room. "You look like the riot police."

"Thank you," I say, unaware that I'm speaking. I note only that there's a breath remaining, clouding the plastic visor, condensation forming.

"I guess you just got off work."

"Yes, thank you—a slow night. Light traffic. I drove directly." This is the truth—I was verifiably at the station not more than a half hour ago. "I did stop at Safeway." There's a slight silence, and I realize I've dropped a nonsequitur. "It's awfully nice—Safeway. New."

Pink nods. "I shop there."

"Well, I'm very happy for you. Sad, I mean—sad." I dash my hand into the air, as if to be gone. "I just stopped by, only for a minute—I can't stay—to offer my condolences, or sympathy—support—in the event you are truly activated."

"Coming from you, I appreciate that," Pink says. He moves to an extremely small sofa and gathers up newspapers, magazines. "Here, sit." He scolds the magazines straight on a coffee table no bigger than a TV tray, then turns to me. "Can I take your hat?"

"My hat? Oh, this . . ." I'm reluctant to give it up, but visibility is becoming something of a problem. Behind my fogged visor, the sofa blurs, forcing me to remain standing.

Pink leans at my side. "Allow me," he says and he lifts the visor, then the whole apparatus straight up and off with both hands, like you would a crown.

And I see all around us, colors—everything brilliant and clicking into place with the precision of a kaleidoscope. Carefully I lower myself to the sofa, my voluminous coveralls pocketed with the cold outdoors, whooshing like balloons deflating, heavy breathing everywhere.

"You have a lovely home." I cross my legs, hearing thermal fabric sizzle, the hot strike of a match.

"Thanks, I'm renting for now." Pink sets the welder's mask on the cushion beside me, then steps around the coffee table to a blue rocking chair—this furniture arranged in a space that appears the size of my bedroom closet. Pink nods across. "Sometimes it feels a little claustrophobic—you know, cramped."

"Oh, I don't think so, not at all. I mean, for just one person like yourself . . ."

His hands are linked loose in his lap. He sits with his right leg crossed wide, foot resting on his left knee, which to the fully conversant, must convey some message in body language. He's wearing rust-colored moccasins, no socks—ankles painfully white and larger-boned than I would've thought. The narrow leather belt is wrong with the Levi's, but this is Pink and to be expected. His shirt is fine—blue denim the color of his eyes and double top-stitched. Relatively speaking, he looks quite nice, although I'd counted on his Marine khakis—the two of us dressed strictly for the job, our official attire keeping us at a safe distance, maintaining some perfect impersonal order. I was relying on my belief, despite popular opinion, that men and women are not in any way attracted to uniforms.

We suffer another spell of quiet, then I lurch to common ground. "My father enjoys Safeway. He puts the strangest things in our shopping cart, you wouldn't believe—"

"Can I make you a cup of coffee," Pink says, "tea, maybe a glass of wine? How about decaf?"

I nod and Pink ducks around a corner. I hear a cupboard creak open.

"What kind of things," he calls, "in the shopping cart?"

"Well, once a package of hair nets."

I scoot to the edge of the sofa, thinking of the store's grand opening and Grace Michaels—how Midge said: Even you might need to take a stand. But I feel such trepidation. Like now, for instance—even now, I'm using all my courage just to keep myself sitting here. Just to come this close.

"I don't know where my father found them," I add loudly. "The hair nets, that is. He picks things up, drops them into our basket." I ease back into the cushions. It seems easier carrying on this conversation without Pink physically in the room. "We go through the checkout, and there's always some surprise. Like tequila with a worm and he doesn't even drink. Dad just gets a little confused sometimes."

"Or maybe the trouble is we don't know what he's thinking."

"Maybe . . ." I glance around, a radio almost mute in the corner. Pink must've turned it down when I knocked. No fireplace, but a smoking chimney. Oil heat. A painted duck decoy beside the blue rocker. Green carpet like healthy grass. Walls painted adobe. A plaid blanket folded over the arm of the sofa. Purple pillows. All the colors of Tara's bracelet are in this room. And on the side table nearest me, a photograph of a woman. I stare, thinking I've found her, she's here.

"What else in the cart?"

But I can't take my eyes from her. Her hair is sandy, blunt cut in the style of Coach Michaels. She appears nearly as young as my girls—I mean, Jen—one girl. Her features are small and pert. "Petite" is the word that comes to mind—she fits this room.

"Tell me one more thing."

I frown down at my clumsy gloved hands. My lackluster hair should be up, held tight in a rubber band. This bracelet is not official. "Well—" I clear my throat. "One time a Japanese pear." I pull off my gloves, but my bare hands look no better. "These pears are round like apples and pale yellow." I twist the rings on my finger—two gold bands, my own and my mother's. "Each pear sits in a little white casing that looks crocheted."

"Like baby bonnets." Pink comes around the corner and sets our cups on the coffee table. "I've seen them in the produce department."

I reach for my coffee, thinking *bonnet*—my word exactly.

"Of course, they're very expensive," I put in. "I mean the pears . . ." I edge my eyes toward the photograph. "Expensive for fruit, that is."

"I hope you don't take cream."

"No thank you." I wave vaguely across the room. "I have dairy products in the car."

"That's good," Pink says, and I believe he means this, given his Minnesota farm upbringing. He eases into the rocker and sips at his coffee, a steaming brown mug. After a moment he looks up, smiling over the cup's rim. "What do they taste like, those pears?"

"Well, we only had the one . . ." I hear myself and detest my earnest voice, but fruit is part of my business. So I plunge on. "We kept saving this little pear for the right time—you know, special. But then finally we just couldn't bring ourselves to eat it at all."

"Because it cost too much to eat?"

"Because we liked it too much."

"I like you too much."

I raise the coffee cup to my lips—calmly, as if I didn't hear this.

Then he smiles and says straight out, "If I'd known you were coming, I'd have baked a cake."

This common phrase is one with which I have more than a passing acquaintance and the words unsettle me, cause me to glance to my hands, my mother's ring. Years ago, this was their song. I gesture toward the door. "If you care for half-and-half, I can get mine. It's out in the—"

"Would you like to dance?" Pink says. He fairly leaps from the rocker and slips the coffee mug from my hands.

"I don't actually dance."

"Your father says you do."

"He said that?"

Pink turns, takes four steps—all that's required to cross this room—and turns up the volume on his radio. "Like a dream, is what he told me."

Then Pink's back at my side. His right hand slides to my waist, his touch negligible through my coveralls. The other hand he folds firm around mine. It's a short reach to his shoulder; he is short. I am elephantine.

We turn in place and just that quick, we are around the dance floor. On the radio, it's late night listening. Elton John sings "I Guess That's Why They Call It the Blues," and it seems right—the voice of such a diminutive entertainer filling this little space.

Pink drifts light as a cloud against my bulk, says: "Just like a dream."

On the second pass around, I look for the woman. I nod to her photograph and speak in my most matronly voice—Jen's mother.

"Your girlfriend?" I glance off, searching for a more appropriate common phrase—woman friend, significant other . . .

"My wife," Pink says.

I snatch my hand off his blue denim shoulder. "Your *wife?*"

"I mean, my ex-wife—Julie," he says. "My first wife."

I step back, bumping the coffee table, thinking: this is what comes of a married woman such as myself cavorting with the likes of Pink Lindstrom. I've arrived at this place under my own false pretenses, only to be upstaged and undone by the devil himself—a man who refuses to remain in uniform, stick to safe common ground. Ask a simple question and what do I get?—a reminder of my own sneaking dishonesty hurled smack in my face.

"Your *first* wife?" I turn to Pink, aware of my voice rising full of self-righteousness—that barking sanctimony born entirely from self-disgust. "Tell me this, Pink Lindstrom, how many wives, exactly, have you had?"

Pink shrugs. "Only one." Then he adds, "But I'm going to do it again. I want to be married, I like being married—me for her, her for me. Like that." He reaches past me, turns the photograph over. "Anyway, I don't see what you're getting so worked up about. People get divorced—you were married once yourself."

"I *am* married, you crazy person, you—"

"Then tell me what it is you're doing here." He grabs my hand, as if to resume dancing. "Just try telling me there's nothing between us—go on, say it."

I stumble against him, stumbling for words. "You shrimp," I yell hot in his ear, my lips brushing with such scorching indignance I feel utterly faint. "You whacked-out son of a dairy farmer . . ."

"He's a psychiatrist."

"Stop pumping my arm." He clings to me, but I cling even harder to this absurd anger. I hang on for dear life, as if wrath is my only salvation, my last chance to safety from this sinful close call.

"We got married young."

"I'll just bet you did. Pink Lindstrom—child groom."

"We were in college."

"Try kindergarten." And with that, I'm moving to the door, when he blocks my path like the soccer goalie he most likely was and reels me down to the sofa—which I realize now is an illicit love seat—where he wrestles me with supernatural strength and says,

"Listen. This is the honest to God truth of what happened."

"Don't you dare drag God into this!"

"Try and listen." He grips my shoulder, his breath hard along my cheek. "We'd been together—Julie and I—since spring semester of our freshman year. And we were always talking about getting married—young people do that when they believe they're in love."

"Then I'd like to hear how old you think you are now," I sputter into his face. "Because you're young this very minute—younger than young. Christopher Columbus could've sailed the Nina, the Pinta, *plus* the Santa Maria behind your ears."

Even as I speak, his ears flare red. "I'm thirty-three."

"You are an egregious liar."

"Just hear me. At the beginning of our senior year, Julie got pregnant and it was a hard time, because we both wanted a baby—we did. I still do. But we couldn't figure it out, see our way clear. We kept going back and forth, back and forth, worrying until it was impossible to think straight. We both had these college loans we'd piled up, no money. It got to where we didn't know what anything really meant—not anything."

Pink sits back, slumping into the sofa cushion. His mouth flickers, as if his words are wind across a flame. "So," he says, his voice dropping low, "we had the abortion—Julie did. By the end of that last year, I think we both knew marriage wasn't ever going to work for us—we *knew*, can you understand? We were already seeing ourselves in the past. We should've been just old college sweethearts, with nothing more between us. But we went ahead anyway, because there *was* something—between us." Pink frowns off. The collar of his shirt is open; his neck looks raw, too exposed. He glances down at his hands, closes them. "Somehow it seemed like we had to get married because of the abortion. But we only made it worse—we just couldn't do one thing right." He stops, his face wholly flushed, the color of his name.

For a minute I don't speak. I push straight on the sofa, feeling the welder's mask hard at my back. Then I shift to look at him and my heart slides like freight. People should never be young, because it means too far to travel. And whatever leads us to adulthood will surely kill us in the end—these old aches, this ancient suffering. Pink Lindstrom has told me an honest and true story from his life, a life I can't deny, though I have tried and tried.

"I don't know," he says, and his voice is hoarse—ragged from too many words. "Does this make any sense to you?"

I nod. It makes no sense and all the sense in this troubled world. "Tara's pregnant," I whisper before I even realize what I'm saying. I duck my head and press my hand to my mouth to stop the hard-kept secret I've already told.

Pink leans to me. For a moment there's no air in this close room—no space to breathe except his sore breath falling over me. Then he draws my hand away and his mouth is here, as if his lips never left mine since that hot August day. It seems I'm burning from the sun, drowning all over again. Yet I sink gladly into this scalding sea. His breath sears through me. How hot is hell?—do not ask me. If there are any bridges left behind me—burn them. He breathes my name. "Hedy . . ." I burn. At the back of my eyes, my daughter's face melts. The words are: kissez, hapee, lafing, maree—it is their song. The melody grows faint; the words escape me. Across the water, my husband wades the snows of France. He looks for the woman, cherchez la femme. But my life jacket surfaces empty on the waves. Then his image fades. And suddenly I want to cry, Come back. I'm here, look here—I'm dying. Tell me, how shall I be saved? I blink dizzy past Pink's shoulder, his mouth. And in the distance, a voice thunders from the high Sunday pulpit. Except it's not my father—where is my father? —only a thunder rolling over the pews, calling, Rise up . . .

"Hedy—" Pink reaches to hold me.

But I struggle from the sofa, as if to answer that call.

Pink presses beside me. I stagger dazed against him, whispering "No" into his blue shirt, whispering "Please." I whisper, "Are you the devil?"

He stares. For an instant there's no sound, only his mouth forming the word in disbelief.

I turn my eyes from his gaze. I could be the child I once was, asking in the dark. Or the woman standing up ahead. But he takes my hand and leads me to the door. And I pass her by.

"You need to go home," he says. "We mustn't do this, you mustn't." He looks away, shaking his head. "Devil," he mumbles.

And I'm rendered speechless by the sudden shame I feel.

The walk is stony under my feet. Mist rises from the freezing, parched grass. The glow of the front window dims behind me. He waits while I climb into the car, until I start the engine. Then he closes the front door. Beside me on the seat there is half-and-half, orange juice, milk. I bought all this years ago, when living was safe. I carried protection.

For a minute I sit gazing down in the darkness. Then I feel my way across the seat, my fingers searching. I reach into the glove box for a flashlight. But Midge's welder's mask isn't here. And I believe she'll never forgive me; he never will.

Midge wears it on the job. She paid for that mask, provided it for herself. Her friendship means the world to me. Life goes on—she told me this. But I could not go on without Midge.

I turn off the ignition and trudge back up the walk. The light is still shining above the mailbox. He opens the door before I can knock.

"My mask—"

Then his arms enclose me. His words rush to me. "I'm mortal," he says. "Mortal."

Eleven

Our committee is charged with the following from Appendix C of the California State *Family Life/Sex Education Guidelines:*

> The local Family Life Education Advisory Committee will make recommendations to its school district regarding how controversial issues such as homosexuality, abortion, and contraception will, or will not, be addressed.

And so we gather month after month in the school district's conference room—as we are tonight—and we struggle all over again with Appendix C. With us, everything is Old Business.

Across our conference table, committee member Mae Arnold shoves from her chair. Mae reads from a twelve-step quiz she's designed for evaluating tenth graders' attitudes. "True or false," Mae says, rattling her handwritten sheet. "Marriage is the only proper context for sexual intercourse."

"I believe Corrine has the floor," Midge says, acting in her capacity as committee chair. For a moment Midge sits back, kneading her temples as if with a very bad headache. Then she sighs and pours herself another cup of coffee.

Tonight I've brought a thermos of my usual decaf, plus Corrine Simonet has provided her famous almond brickle cookies—these homemade refreshments being the one issue upon which our committee unanimously agrees.

Of course, Midge claims there's a reason for our committee's terminal stalemate. She says it's the hidden axe, tool of what she calls the suppressive Christian movement. But there's nothing furtive about our members—we're all openly present, with the exception of a few frustrated middle-of-the-roaders who've stopped attending our stalled meetings altogether. Three of us seated at this walnut veneer conference table are Lady Miner basketball mothers: Corrine Simonet, myself, and Margarita Avent, whose daughter is our quick little point guard.

At the moment, our girls are at team practice. As I left the house, Tara pulled up to give Jen and my father a lift to the gym. My father doesn't normally attend practices, but the further basketball season progresses, the more our Lady Miners seem to want him around. Or "need" him, as Coach Michaels puts it.

Beside me, Corrine smiles and waves a pale hand. "I'm always more than happy to yield the floor to Mae."

"True or false," Mae continues, "My ideal future would include being married to one person for a lifetime." She pauses, tapping her pencil along the paper. "In other words, no divorce."

While Mae proceeds down her list, I glance over at our school nurse. Jane McCullom attends these meetings faithfully. We're all women here, which isn't surprising, females being traditionally more active in home, school, and church functions. I imagine that's why our half of the human race is so often deemed to be preservers and transmitters of the culture.

Angela Tucker speaks from the far end of the table. "Madame Chairman . . ."

"*Ms.* Chair*person*," Midge corrects her.

"I move that we accept Mae's twelve-point attitude evaluation."

"I second that," Penny Bower says.

And so it goes. The floor is open to debate. Nurse McCullom moves to amend the motion to include some mention of spermicides and condoms. Midge concurs. There's a stunned quiet around the table. Then jangled discussion.

Nurse McCullom gives us those numbers we've heard time and again: Over 25 percent of all fifteen-year-olds have already had sex, one million teenage girls find themselves pregnant each year, every three minutes somebody in the world dies from an illegal abortion.

"Abortion is not a method of birth control," Angela Tucker says.

Jane McCullom nods patiently and continues. "Adolescent mothers deliver fourteen percent of this country's infants . . ." Nurse McCullom pauses, turning at the sound of a phone ringing in another part of the building.

For a moment every face around the table is tipped toward that muffled noise issuing from behind a locked, after-hours, office door.

We've learned from experience the phone can't be answered, but it's still mildly distressing. We're eight mothers here. And we're all aware that every second of every minute, twenty-four hours of every day and night—always—someone, somewhere is trying to reach a mother. So naturally, when the phone rings there's a little leap inside each of us to answer.

Nine rings, and then silence. Jane McCullom moves along. "The number of teenagers contracting AIDS continues to double each year."

"You can attribute that to homosexuality and IV drug use," Penny Bower puts in.

This remark sends Corrine Simonet to her college-lined notebook. "In 1986," Corrine reads, "the U.S. Supreme Court stated: 'To hold that the act of homosexual sodomy is somehow protected as a fundamental right would be to cast aside millennia of moral teaching.' "

"Which brings us to Grace Michaels," Angela Tucker says.

I look up, sitting straighter at the mention of Grace's name. But instantly Midge is tapping a spoon against her coffee mug for order.

"We're not here to discuss a rumor about sexual preference," Midge says.

"There you go again!" Penny Bower flaps her hand at Midge. "We're talking about sexual *perversion* and you keep calling it *preference,* as if sodomy's just fine. And if I say it isn't, you tell me I'm *homophobic* which is a made-up word—a word that's supposed to make me feel like I'm the one who's wrong." Penny turns to Margarita Avent for no reason I can guess, except that English is Margarita's second language. "*Homophobia,*" Penny says, her voice rising, "isn't even in the dictionary."

I watch Margarita's high dark cheeks flush deeper. Margarita is Latino, Roman Catholic. For the good of our schools and the good of Family Life Education, we are as diversely represented on this committee as our small community's population allows.

"All words," Midge says brusquely, "are made up. Where do you think language comes from—the stork, a cabbage patch?" Then Midge falls silent, as if checking herself, striving for chairperson diplomacy.

Jane McCullom clears her throat. "There are five seventh graders pregnant in our middle school."

" 'In the beginning was the Word,' " Corrine Simonet murmurs. " '. . . And the whole earth was of one language, and of one speech.' "

Midge raps her coffee cup again. "This meeting is entirely out of order."

I gaze past the table, to the dark, thermal-paned office window. Somewhere far from this small paneled room in our Coarsegold Unified School District office, gavels are sounding in state legislatures. Executives gather, filling top-floor suites of corporate headquarters. The U.S. Congress is in session, the Supreme Court—law of this land—these hallowed halls of power. Men file in. We are eight women talking at odds and out of order, seated at a fake walnut table—only here to recommend. And all the while, men speak and men decide. So I wonder—how is it that we are the transmitters of culture? And what culture? What one language? What speech?

I give a little cough and raise my hand, though this procedure isn't required by *Robert's Rules of Order*. "In a recent national poll taken by the Mattel Toy Company . . ." I pause, nodding around the table. "According to this poll, 54 percent of Americans believe that Barbie should stay true to Ken."

"Hedy," Midge says in that slow, indulgent voice of hers, "Ken and Barbie are dolls."

"And we're people," I mumble. "We're only human."

For just this minute, I am speaking out of order on my own behalf—I understand this. In the past ten days, ever since that Sunday night of January 27 in Pink Lindstrom's little brick house, I have had sexual intercourse twelve times—all of it outside the ideal and proper context of marriage. I carry on my person, even now, in my simulated leather handbag, a box of lambskin condoms—the very kind that Jane McCullom is at this moment describing as inferior when compared to condoms made of latex. I glance down, frowning at my purse propped beside the chair.

When I look up again, I see Nurse McCullom removing a banana from her briefcase. She peels a latex condom treated with nonoxynol 9—the most effective spermicide, she says—over the banana's yellow skin. Watching her, I'm transfixed. I will never lose my great interest in agricultural products. Around the table, my cocommittee members appear equally overwhelmed. Penny Bower shields her eyes, as if from a bright light.

"There's no absolute safe sex," Jane explains. "Abstinence needs to be emphasized first and foreskin—I mean, first and foremost . . ." Her face colors up, then she clears her throat and continues. "Understanding the correct application of a condom with spermicide could save a child's life."

Angela Tucker squares her cashmere shoulders. "My child has already been saved, thank the Lord. And if you plan to introduce bananas as teaching aids . . ."

Quietly as possible, I unscrew the cap on my thermos and pour a little more decaf. Not too long ago, on a slow night at the border station, Marshall told me a true story about a laboratory rabbit. This story he found in a book titled *Russian Experiments in Parapsychology*. It seems that one week after giving birth, this rabbit was separated from her litter of six. The adult rabbit was placed in a cage and taken miles out to sea on a submarine. The Russian submarine descended 1,500 feet below the surface of the water. Researchers attached wire electrodes to monitor the animal's heartbeat and brain waves. Then, at a fixed time on shore, the six infant rabbits were systematically chloroformed and killed. At each death, the mother rabbit's heartbeat accelerated. Brain activity became erratic. Deep under water and far removed, the rabbit flailed in its cage. According to Marshall, this is the documented truth of what happened.

"School isn't the place." Penny Bower drops her hands flat on the table. "All that needs to be said is that if you have sex you might get AIDS and die."

"You might get pregnant," Corrine adds.

I set down my coffee cup and think of Tara. I look over, trying to read Corrine's face, but she's flipping through her notebook, her head turned away.

Nurse McCullom glances to Midge. "Our young people need tools for survival."

And what Midge needs is a hundred-pound gavel. If there's a hidden axe here, it's disguised in the form of total confusion. The one bright spot of this meeting is that Grace Michaels isn't obligated to attend. And for that, I'm grateful. I worry that if our committee should ever proceed to New Business, Grace Michaels' rumored sexual preference will be the only subject on the agenda.

Now Angela Tucker takes the floor. She opens a book titled *The Joy of No Sex*, which she recommends as a valuable teaching tool for survival. Angela reads, " 'One technique to allay sexual agitation is to reflect on the true nature of the material body. The body is a bag of blood, pus, urine, bile, and stool.' "

Mae Arnold winces, then recovers herself. She gestures toward Jane McCullom's sheathed banana. "The body is *not* just some piece of fruit."

Midge stares at me from the end of the table, gives me a look that orders, Speak up.

Except I don't dare. My handbag is full of condoms and fruit is on the tip of my tongue. Never mind Angela Tucker's material body. My heart brims with the Song of Solomon . . . *As the apple among the tree of the wood, so is my beloved among the sons. I sat down under his shadow with great delight, and his fruit was sweet to my taste . . .*

But Midge is still frowning in my direction. I scoot closer to the table. "If the chair pleases . . ."

"Hold it!" Angela Tucker rushes in, anticipating that I'm about to move to adjourn, which according to the rules of order is a privileged motion taking precedence over all others and undebatable.

It's generally understood among our committee that I am wont to so move when the hour draws near 9:00 P.M., our prearranged time for adjourning. But there's another arrangement known only to Midge and me: when the discussion grows too heated and the battle mounts with the outcome muddy and doubtful, I am sworn to sound retreat. Any unfinished business (which in our case amounts to everything) and all deciding votes are thus tabled until our next meeting. It's no idle boast when I say that tabling is my major contribution to our efforts for Family Life Education.

But Angela Tucker has successfully intervened. "Please take one and pass the rest," she says, brandishing Xeroxed sheets. "I'd like your reactions and some input when we meet next time."

I help myself to another of Corrine's cookies, then scan Angela's Xeroxed page, which is a detailed analysis of lyrics to a hard rock album *As Nasty As They Wanna Be*, performed by the band 2 Live Crew. Given that I'm eating and not about to risk possible nausea, I fold the paper into my pocket, saving these details for later.

Then Corrine leans closer on my left and slices a small white card under my eyes. "Just a little something else to take home and think about," she says in a voice angelic as her harp. But she deals these cards like a seasoned deadeye, sailing them around the table. I hold mine gambler-style, close to the vest. This card could be a winner—Queen of Hearts, the Ace of Spades. But this is no game. I drop the card to the table, turning it face up.

My Personal Pledge

I, Tara Simonet,
am a (virgin, secondary virgin). I vow to maintain abstenance until death do me part
I will be answerable to Jennifer Castle
for my decision.

Signed Tara M. Simonet
Dated Feb. 6, 1991

"It's the right size for a wallet," Corrine explains. "This card will always be there as a tangible reminder—black and white and perfectly clear."

But I understand nothing. I stare at Corrine. "Tara . . ."

Corrine nods. "I used her as an example, so you'd have an idea of how it's done." Corrine holds up a card, her daughter's name in the palm of her hand. Tara has signed this, committed herself eight times over so everyone at the table will see how it's done—her name detained in this room like a child kept after school, writing: I will not . . . will not . . . a hundred times across a chalkboard.

I catch Corrine's sweater sleeve, point to the name of my own daughter. "Answerable?"

"Well, more like support," Corrine says. "A friend, sibling, parent—somebody to confide in, help keep our girls strong."

Corrine moves on, describing secondary virginity—another chance for a girl who's gone all the way. " 'No' is a love word," Corrine tells us. "Usually you'll see 'until marriage' written in the space referring to length of abstention. But Tara is such an original little cutup."

"God love her," Angela Tucker pipes in.

"I love her," I whisper.

"These wallet-sized commitments could be available to every girl at Coarsegold High."

"Plus our middle school," Angela says.

From the head of the table, Midge gives me her nod, trying one more time. But it's no good. I feel like Old Business stalled in committee, my heart stopping still at the line "Until death do me part."

Then Midge strikes her spoon on her pink ceramic cup. "Does the chair hear a motion to adjourn?"

On cue, seven faces turn my direction, eyes expectant, anticipating what I am wont to say when the hour is at hand.

I look away, my eyes sore from staring at the bright white card, those names. Finally I mumble, "I so move."

But for a moment not one of us stirs. Down the carpeted hall beyond this room, the telephone is ringing again. The sound comes faint and insistent—urgent to our ears.

I glance around the table, my friends and neighbors, preservers and transmitters of the culture—all of us, such creatures of habit, so desirous of everything in its place. Fear, I've read, is regressive. And I wish I could offer these women some assurance—recite that old church doxology . . . *As it was in the beginning, is now and ever shall be* . . . If it were in my power I'd make a privileged motion, undebatable. Say to them: World without end—no phone rings for us. Our children are safe in the garden of childhood delights. They will abstain, never taste that forbidden fruit. Not know.

At last the telephone stops and we push to our feet in a scrape of chairs. We smile as we gather up our papers, standing adjourned and sheepish with relief.

Except there's no reprieve here, no going back. Maybe it's just this dark starless night we step into, a limp yellow ribbon hanging above the school district door, reminder of 500,000 troops, bombs falling. Or it could be the barren spine of peaks rising behind us, black streambeds dry as my throat. But this present life—right now—feels like a real fight, as if there is something at large and truly wild in the world.

I hear the slam of car doors in the parking lot, then Midge's voice as she tails me to the Blazer. "A letter fell into my hands today," she says, sounding so stiff and unlike herself, I want to plug my ears.

"Tell me about it tomorrow."

Midge shakes her head. "You going straight home?"

"Where else?" I lean beside the Blazer, just daring Midge to mention what she can't possibly know—that as of late, my car is apt to make an abrupt turn onto Evergreen Street, where I'll find Pink Lindstrom home, the full shelter of his arms raising a roof over my head, his sturdy legs, the notch of his shoulder, all tongue and groove, his chest the only place to close my weary eyes, to sleep in my own bed, to house me.

"I'll meet you there," Midge says.

I look up, blinking at her.

"Home," she says. "Your place."

The driveway is jammed. Cars line the curb out front, forcing me to park down the block, like some late arrival at a party.

Midge pulls in behind me, scoots out of her Honda. "Jesus," she says. "Looks like they're holding practice at your house."

I nod, staring up the sidewalk. We move past Coach Michaels' red Volkswagen, past a Dodge Colt driven by our weak side forward, then Rita Avent's Toyota. They're all here, from the starting lineup to the bench. Tara's Subaru is in the drive. They're halfway through the season, these girls, with a record of three wins, two losses. They're fighting for a playoff berth. And I would like to believe it's only basketball that's gathered them at our house on a Wednesday night getting late—a scrimmage inside, my living room lamps blazing behind closed drapes like those lofty lights of the gym.

So I choose not to notice Pink's truck parked beside the Subaru. And Foster here, as well—Midge halting now at her son's Camaro.

I walk on, climbing the steps to the front door. But for a minute I linger outside, in need of this fresh air. The cold on my face is a relief and the house will be stuffy, what with all these people.

Maybe this isn't true, but I read somewhere that the time in a woman's life called menopause isn't as clear-cut as we've generally thought. Experts are saying that changes can begin as early as our mid-thirties. And I tend to agree, because a few years ago, while sitting at the foot of my mother's bed, I experienced my first hot flash. One minute I felt fine, moving as cool as you please down the hall to her room—my mother so sick from chemotherapy it seemed she might die of the cure before the disease ever took her—and the next minute, settling onto her bed, without warning, gazing into her tired eyes, I was suddenly drenched in sweat, my cheeks full of heat, the crease between my breasts streaming. She gave me a smile, my mother. She waved a shaky hand. "Open a window," she said. "Your father thinks if he keeps this house like an oven, I just might live."

But tonight—right now—I believe it could be only basketball—a hot contest burning at my temples, flushing my face and instantly flooding me.

I turn as Midge trudges up the porch steps. She glances over, then squints past me. "Your dad home?"

"At practice." I blot my mouth, heat beading my upper lip. Take care of him, my mother told me that last afternoon. "I mean, here. He's . . ." I nod to the front door, my voice slow and falling. "Dad."

"It could be a team meeting," Midge says.

"It could . . ."

"So okay," Midge says, and she reaches around me, turns the knob, and pushes open the door.

For a minute nobody notices we're inside, except Dustin. He pads into the hallway, his big square head bumping our legs. I move to take Midge's coat, but she grabs my arm, nudges me into the living room.

The team is bunched at the sofa, except this is no time-out huddle, no game. And the room is too quiet.

"Dad," I whisper, crossing the carpet. Then I'm shoving through the pack of them—girls falling back on either side, the smell of gym shorts, sweats, rubber. Girls make little sounds in my ear, mew like pups, newborns. But I am soaked with the change of life and you won't catch me crying.

"Dad?" He's stretched on the sofa, eyes closed, his head in Coach Michaels' lap. His face looks lopsided—I have seen this before—mouth sagging at the left corner. His nose is running. I reach into his shirt pocket for a handkerchief, feeling his pacemaker, the web of his breath up and down. "Daddy?"

"Mom," Jen says, pushing behind me, her voice high and scraping. "We tried to phone you—Grampa fell."

Coach Michaels glances up, her fingers smooth in my father's white hair. "At practice—I think he blacked out."

"We tried to call."

I nod, because it seems now that I knew this. After the fact, I'm sure that ringing in the school district office was for me. It's a backward memory—this certainty. And I believe it must be the curse of our existence—why the news so seldom surprises, why we feel such a world of guilt. Because in the midst of all our ignorance we know things.

"The paramedics came," Grace Michaels says. "They told us that he had a TIA." She looks off, squinting as if to recall exactly. "I'm not sure," she mumbles. "Is that what they said—TIA?"

"Yes," I answer, so full of knowledge my head hurts. I can quote almost word for word from that library book, that chronicle of strokes from victim to victor.

Grace bows her head over him, her golden brown hair trailing. "They told us that he's supposed to rest. Take it easy is what they said."

I slide my fingers down his arm. "Dad . . ." His hand is clean and dry and light in mine, his face crooked and still. "Dad, listen—you've had a Transient Ischemic Attack." I speak directly to him, give him these words like medicine. He deserves to hear; he has a brain. I need to hear this—a balm cool as a breeze to break my fever, such drenching heat. "This isn't like the last time, not a real stroke. But you might feel weak for a little while . . ."

"He fell and couldn't get up," Jen says softly.

"You could have some numbness on one side . . ."

"We called Mrs. Stiverson—Midge," Jen says. "She was still at the meeting, so Foster came over with Nekuda. Then we phoned Pink and he left a message with Dr. Vernon's answering service. And now Pink's in the kitchen talking to Uncle Dex. And Foster decided to make tomato soup, because Tara got sick at practice and she's in the bathroom."

"So that's everybody," a voice chimes from the rear.

"The whole team," Jen says.

And at my back, these girls cram close, like a full-court press, a thicket of bare legs. They lean with me, blinking down at my father. He's suffered a floor burn, a raw smudge on his cheek. But I take no notice of this, scarcely hear the girls' whispers, their hard hands braced along my shoulders.

"You might have a little trouble speaking. There could be some problem with your vision . . ."

And I'm thinking of a time in the hospital. A time when he woke in the middle of the night, full of energy, as if it were a brand-new day and not enough hours for a busy man. I watched him rushing, struggling into his bathrobe. Then he fairly flew from his room. He marched down the sleep-hushed corridor of Rehab and headed directly to the showers. I ducked into the tiled room right behind him, coaxing him, saying, "Dad, it's still dark outside—not time for a shower yet. Let's go back, come back to bed." But it seemed my father no sooner stepped inside that bright, shiny cubicle, when the whole notion of bathing escaped him. Instead, he leaned back against the slippery blue wall and allowed himself to slide slowly down on his haunches. Then he glanced up and crooked a finger for me to join him. So there we sat—not saying anything, but just hunkered together on cool tile in a shower stall slick with light. We stayed like that, smiling over at each other, for a minute or so. And then suddenly my father let out a gasp—a suck of air, gruesome and moaning in that small echoing space. My father sprang back, slamming me with him against the wall. His eyes glittered wild, his face so twisted with terror, I shook just to look at him. Then he pointed quick, to the floor. His mouth gaped speechless, his finger jabbing for me to see. And though there was only blue tile, a large metal drain, I cowered with him. Because it was unspeakable, whatever lay on that cold floor, whatever hovered just beneath the dark metal drain. Unspeakable, what he beheld in his sickness—what I could not see.

"Whatever it is," I whisper now. I cup his slack chin. "Whatever you're feeling, it won't last." I nod over at Grace Michaels, but she doesn't take her eyes from him.

"We were winding up practice," she says in a voice so quiet I need to bend closer. "He had all the basketballs in his bag except one. And I was teasing him with it—I mean the ball. We do that—play this little game of keep-away. So when he turned, I let go and bounced the ball off his butt. And he laughed, you know. And then he . . ." She falters, glancing to her lap. "He just sort of fell."

"Don't worry, Coach," somebody says over my shoulder.

"Listen—" I jiggle Grace's hand, her fingers in his fine hair. "It could be a few minutes, maybe an hour, or overnight. But a TIA is always temporary. Always," I add, hanging on for dear life to everything I know. "This isn't—" And just then he reaches up and touches my face. "There, you see?" I gaze down at him, overjoyed and fickle with relief—forgetting in an instant all the words ever written about Transient Ischemic Attacks—thinking only that here is a miracle. I grin at Coach Michaels. "See?"

"You," my father mumbles.

All of a sudden our living room is full of girls' chatter. Grace Michaels sinks back against the sofa cushions, looking exhausted. I'm exhausted.

Julie Dwyer, who starts at forward, squeezes beside me. "Mrs. Castle, you are so brave." She turns to Jen. "God, your mother—I can't get over her—doesn't she just remind you of Desdemona on 'All My Days'? I mean, she's exactly like her." Julie nods into my face, clamps both hands on my shoulders. "And that's a compliment, Mrs. Castle. Honest to God, no lie—believe me." (This is the most earnest child on whom I have ever laid eyes.) "You could be twins."

I glance over, catching my father struggling up on his elbows. "Excuse me, Julie—"

"Jewels," she says as I bend to my father. "That's what everybody calls me."

"Dad, stay put a minute." I ease him down on the sofa and turn to Coach Michaels. "He needs to be in bed, except I don't think he should try the stairs right now."

"No, not the stairs," Grace says.

"Maybe my bed."

I feel a tap on my back. "The Royal Jewels is what they call me."

Grace nods. "I think your bed."

"The royal jewels." A girl laughs behind me. "That's what my brother says he's got between his legs."

I ignore this, because we are a team here, after all, and I recognize locker room talk when I hear it. Plus, the aftermath of a scare will sometimes bring out the random vulgarity, just for the sole purpose of taking a jab at death—score one off-color remark for the living.

"Be right back," I say, touching my father's knee. I speed up the hall stairs and pull the electric blanket off his bed. He'll want this. And his slippers, flannel pajamas. I bundle everything in my arms and move swiftly downstairs—a woman with purpose, a brave woman, perhaps like Desdemona on "All My Days." Some afternoon, I will tune in and see precisely who she is.

I dart through the dining room and discover Foster and Nekuda Adowa sitting down to saltines and tomato soup.

"Your father . . ." Nekuda says. "Your father is like the saint." Nekuda is leaned so far over his bowl, one dreadlock is swimming. "For him, I eat the very bad soup, which is begging for one tiny pinch of dill, bay leaf, slice of lemon. He should be spared, this saint."

Foster gives me a look. "It's from the can—even Tara ate some."

"And she threw it up, every bit." Nekuda turns, his dark arms moving like tidal waves. "The soup goes in, comes out, except so big I'm thinking, Whoa—this must be the guts, the hair of the dog, the skin of the cat . . ."

I back from the table, bumping into Midge.

"She's just got the flu," Foster says.

I steer Midge into the kitchen. "Listen, will you fix some coffee, hot chocolate—I need to make this bed and call Dr. Vernon and—"

"The doctor phoned." Midge glances to the clock on the stove. "About five minutes ago. Pink talked to him."

I listen as Midge repeats that telephone conversation as if she was a third party on the line. I'd like to ask why I never heard the phone, ask where in this house is Pink Lindstrom when I need him—him of all people.

"Anyway," Midge says, "Dr. Vernon wants you to bring your dad into the office tomorrow if he feels up to it."

I nod, sidling into the hallway. As I pass the closed bathroom door, I hear the flush of the toilet, water running in the sink.

"Tara?" I knock, and the door opens a crack.

"How is he?" she sniffles.

"I think he's okay. It wasn't a real stroke, you know."

"Well, I was praying for him. In here . . ." She opens the door a little wider and I smell sickness, see wet towels sopping the floor, toilet seat up.

For a moment I lean against the door jamb. "Tara—honey, listen . . ."

"I'm going to clean it up," she says in a rush. Then she moves to close the door. "Don't worry."

"Right," I mumble, turning for my bedroom.

I strip covers from the bed and smooth my father's electric blanket over the top sheet. "Don't worry," I whisper, and as I speak the words, it occurs to me why people are always leaving to strike new ground, set new records. Why they strive to be first in the world. The reason, I believe, is that daily life extracts too much—takes it all. And true adventurers understand this. Whole governments know. You can rise or fall a hero on a distant shore. There are some odds in such singular struggles: records and enemies, these can be broken. But the home front—here—will break your heart every time.

Since his stroke, my father tends to feel the cold, so I add another cover, then my Heritage spread. I'm on my knees, plugging in his electric blanket, when I hear a rustling across the room. I glance to the open closet. It's a walk-in, crammed full, but deep, with a ceiling light. And Pink is standing just inside. For some reason I don't find this surprising. But he's holding the little dog Bark in one arm and that, right there, undoes me.

"Come here," he says, and without a word, I stand straight up and walk directly into the closet.

Pink slides the door closed behind us. Then he snaps off the light and I'm glad for this, because two entire wardrobes are hung here—Ward's and mine. Plus, the sight of my father's dog has brought me to utter tears, when through everything prior I'd been holding up so well.

"I found Bark hiding out," Pink says. "Probably all the noise." He props the dog higher, nods past me. "Then I got to looking at your clothes. And I was just thinking how I'd like to see you wearing every one of these."

"Well, there are too many," I sniff. "I have this trouble—"

"I talked to Dr. Vernon."

I nod against his Minnesota Vikings reindeer sweater. "Trouble parting with things." And though I've often felt this, I don't think I quite realized the truth of it till this moment.

"Listen, Hedy, you mustn't cry now—please. Your dad's strong, I don't need to tell you."

I feel my way along the crowded hangers behind me, until I come to a wool jacket which I'm certain belongs to Ward. Inside the roomy pocket there's a wad of Kleenex and I pull it out, blow my nose. "Could you—" I whisper. "Could you put Bark somewhere?"

Pink opens the door a little. "Bark's just upset is all." He nudges the dog outside. Then he slides us into darkness again. "Anyway, I want you to know that I think your husband is a very snappy dresser—I'd be the first to admit."

"Well, so are you—just a wonderful dresser." This is an out-and-out lie, but sometimes we must spare the ones we love. "Really," I say, "you are."

Then Pink reaches down for my hand, raises my fingers to his lips. It amounts to no more than this—a touch—mouth brushing across fingertips. And I am tinder struck and moist in all new places. Not more than twenty minutes ago, I flashed mid-life menopausal, only to find myself in this dark closet, instantly ablaze with the three-alarm hormones of an adolescent.

"There's a dance after Friday night's games," he says into my palm.

"Here," I whisper and draw my hand away. I raise my lips to his, clinging to him in the presence of dresses, suits, sweaters, slacks—the empty garments of some other couple I once believed I knew better than my own self.

For a minute Pink cups my face in his hands. Then he says, "Your dad should be in bed."

"My bed," I whisper. I open the closet, hearing the front door, girls calling good-bye. And from the kitchen, a clatter of dishes in the sink.

As we move into the hallway, Pink says, "About the dance . . . I'd like to take Grace Michaels. I think you know why."

"Yes," I answer quietly, "I do."

We pass the closed bathroom door. "Tara needs to call her mother—it looks as if she'll spend the night."

Pink nods. "I'll sleep on the sofa. For your father," he says, then grins.

I flick his sweater sleeve and step away as we enter the living room.

Pink moves to help my father to his feet, but Coach Michaels is already there.

"Reverend . . ." Grace whispers. She eases him up, her arm firm around his shoulders. "Galen," she says, and he is alert at the sound of his name. He gives her a little smile, which seems a good sign, weak as he is—still charmed.

I follow them down the hallway. Grace Michaels is a full head taller than my father, her long legs in charcoal sweats, a white T-shirt reading Coe College, 1988 Women's Softball Champs. Her shoulders are broader than his, her gait strong and steady. But even propped against this young woman, my father appears to be escorting her.

At the bathroom, I drop back. I hesitate a moment, then knock. The door opens and Jen steps out. She shoots me a serious, tight-eyed look. "Tara's staying over."

"Phone her mom," I say. Then I move through the doorway, stooping for a wet towel.

"Don't tell her I'm sick," Tara calls after Jen. She glances to me. "I wouldn't want my mom worrying."

I shut the door, then turn to the sink where Tara stands. I look into the mirror above, Tara's face reflected pale, eyes red from vomiting. "I'm worried," I say, keeping my gaze straight ahead in the mirror.

"Your dad'll be okay, Mrs. Castle—really." Tara nods at my reflection. "He's got God watching over him, I can feel it."

I shake my head. "I mean you, Tara—I'm worried about you."

"Just a little flu bug. . ."

"Tell me this—" I lean, taking her by the shoulders, as if to shake some sense into her. But my words are calm. "Tell me, who's looking out for you?"

Her breath comes quick and loud. "Nobody," she says. She pulls away, her chest heaving under her Lady Miners sweatshirt, and I believe she'll be sick again. She goes down, kneeling over the toilet bowl, her head averted, bowed. "Sometimes . . ." she whispers, her voice a rasp. "Sometimes I really believe I'll slash my wrists and go to hell and live with Satan."

"Oh Tara, no." I bend beside her, my legs weak from her words. "Honey, please."

"And do you know why?" She rushes on, as if I hadn't spoken. "Because I'm trash." She swings her head, looks directly at me, and I have never seen eyes so cold blue and hard. "Trash," she whispers, like spit in my face. She raises a fist and I jerk to catch the blow. But she strikes her own chest. "Trash," she says, her voice rising.

I glance around, as if for help—for somebody here to lend aid, help this girl, help me. She slams her chest again, then again. I grab her wrist, bracing my free hand on the rim of the toilet, because she is so strong—strong everywhere, this power forward, playing like there's no tomorrow. She means to hurt herself.

But there isn't any help, nobody watching over her—her mother looking only to heaven, a gold harp in her right hand, white card in her left: *I, Tara Simonet, have made a choice to remain abstinent until death do me part . . .*

Only my hand here, slipping on the porcelain rim as Tara yanks away—my fingers plunging into the clear cold bowl. I am no match for this girl, only my hand like a cup in this water and my father's words drifting a thousand times over as he stood at the holy font . . . "What name shall be given to this child?"

And she cries again. "I'm trash!"

"You're pregnant," I say. I reach for her, my arm sweeping up from the bowl, my hand dripping water like rain in her hair, down her face, the tip of her chin.

She puts a hand to her streaming cheek. "Pregnant," she says slowly, as if she's never before heard that word, never felt the water or her own tears.

I push to my feet. For a moment Tara leans back, blinking in the small quiet. Then Jen is calling from the hallway. "We'll be right there," I answer.

Tara fumbles up beside me. I wring a washcloth in the sink and wipe her wet face. I lift her hair, trailing the cloth at the back of her neck. Maybe it was only the sound of my own child's voice at the door. Or the weight of Tara's blonde curls on my fingertips, the scent of her full skin. But my thoughts are suddenly gravid, delivering a vague flicker of morning sickness that would place me in this room at dawn, my breasts aching and tender. And I marvel at the work of the body—how the flesh both restores and anticipates the passages of our lives, as if every cell holds a memory of the journey already completed, even as we are traveling through.

I glance to the mirror and Tara turns. I gaze at her bleak, anxious face in the glass, her eyes so blue they look bruised. "There's something—" I hitch my fingers in the elastic of her shorts, holding her beside me. "Maybe if you could just remember . . ."

"I'm pregnant," she whispers.

"Maybe if you could remember—I mean, no matter what anybody tells you—and say to yourself."

She grabs her sweatband off the Formica counter, suddenly antsy, moving from the sink.

"Maybe if you could just say . . ." My words trail after her. "Say: I am fearfully and wonderfully made."

She pulls up her white socks, opens the bathroom door. I watch her hesitate, as if preparing herself to step out. She sighs, her back to me, straight shoulders falling. Then I hear her take a deep breath—and after a moment her small, weepy voice. "I am fearfully and wonderfully made."

Twelve

My father has insisted on being here tonight, game six of Lady Miners league play. And Tara, too—on the court taking warm-ups with the team, having recovered, it seems, from her bout with the flu.

Tara's parents sit a few bleachers behind me. To the casual observer, such as Midge at my left and Nekuda Adowa on the right, it might appear that Corrine Simonet and I are engaging in idle chitchat, what with Corrine remarking on how good it is to see my father up and about, considering the scare he gave us two nights ago. "Thank God it was only an ATI" she says.

"TIA," Midge mutters off.

"I just hope Reverend's had his flu shot." Corrine leans down, speaking louder to be heard above taped warm-up music blaring from the gym's public address system. "Such a stubborn virus this year—I was beginning to think Tara'd never shake it."

I turn and nod solemnly up. "They say this flu's the kind that keeps coming back on you."

"Oh please, don't tell me," Corrine groans. "That's the last thing I need to hear."

But I must tell her, because I worry that any moment during the next forty-eight minutes of play, we may glance to the team's bench and see Tara sidelined and heaving into one of those white Athletic Department towels my father is even now dutifully folding

Greg Simonet ruffles his wife's blonde curls, then squeezes her close. For a moment it appears the two of them have been sitting cozy in these bleachers ever since their own high school days—a going steady good-looking All-American couple. There have been times when the sight of this loving duo has set off a low buzzing in my brain which I've taken to be sheer envy. But now I feel nothing but irritation at their nuzzling. Tonight I'm inclined to agree with my daughter, who scorns public displays of affection—or PDAs, as she terms them.

"What do you hear from Ward?" Greg Simonet calls down. It seems Greg seldom addresses me without using my husband's name. But then, people are forever asking after Ward, the entire town inquiring about their local boy made good. And as always, it's a question that fills me with sheer loneliness—not for Ward, but for myself.

"He's in Grenoble," I answer. "I phoned him yesterday." This is true. Afraid for my father and needing just then to hear my husband's winning, upbeat voice, I dialed that string of international numbers—codes connecting me to a continent, a country, a city. But not to Ward. Regardless of what those long distance ads would have you believe, you cannot reach out and touch someone if that person isn't there.

"Well, let's just pray that hubby of yours stays put right where he is," Corrine says, giving me a look. "You don't want him anywhere near an airport, not with all these terrorist threats."

I nod as the warm-up music reaches a deafening pitch. At the bench, my father sits with his empty canvas bag. He's spread the bag over his legs like a lap robe, and I steer my eyes away, not wanting to see how like an invalid he appears. He's here tonight over Jen's protests. Since his TIA, Jen seems painfully aware of her grandfather—how easily he becomes confused, how quickly he forgets which toothbrush is his, how to tie his shoes. "He's only had a little setback," I explained to Jen after yesterday's practice. And I was irritated—I admit—because it seemed Jen wasn't so much concerned for her grandfather as she was suddenly embarrassed by his presence among her teammates and friends—embarrassed by his lost ground.

But for the moment Jen appears focused only on the contest about to get underway. It's a Killer game tonight, and as Pink mentioned in his sports column, there can be no neutral blood on our court.

And so the warm-up tape is Shriekback—heavy metal pumping our Lady Miners and vibrating the bleachers. No neutral blood anywhere, with yellow ribbons draping the gym's double doors and butcher paper banners blazing across concrete walls: GO MINERS, HIT PAY DIRT . . . WE'LL SCARE THE SAND OUT OF SADDAM.

Then Shriekback fades to the national anthem. We rise. Our Home side is filled with more fans than I have ever seen for a girls' game. Below us, Lady Miners turn in the direction of the flag hung from a rafter. The team stands straight and still, girls covering their hearts and a patriotic patch sewn just above. Yesterday a team vote was taken and miniature Stars and Stripes handed round. Just yesterday I sewed that flag to Jen's uniform. I phoned my husband to no avail. Phoned my brother, then Dr. Vernon on my father's behalf. For Tara, I dialed the Eastside Women's Medical Group, telephone lines humming over the mountains a hundred miles away, humming like that jump rope song I used to know . . . "Called up the doctor, and the doctor said . . ." But that doctor didn't answer, "Give that baby some shortening bread." Tara made an appointment. Just yesterday. I heard Saddam Hussein say, "In order to decide who will lose and who will win, it is based on who has the Devil on his side and who has God on his side." Our President said, "Of this we are sure, our cause is just. Our cause is moral. Our cause is right."

"Lord . . ." A voice booms into the crackling silence following the anthem. "Lord, we know you do not hate the Iraqi people . . ."

I turn, blinking at Midge, dumbfounded as to why . . . Why before the center court jump is the voice of Pastor Paul Sitwell suddenly echoing in our gym.

". . . We know you take no joy in killing. And so we come before you tonight . . ."

On my right, Nekuda Adowa has sunk back onto the bleacher, shaking his dreadlocks. He will not be party to this—not any of it. Nekuda alone is striving for neutral blood, his loyalty divided between our Lady Miners and the Warriorettes from Seven Persons High. Those opposing players stand antsy at the Visitors bench, all nine of them with one exception, people of color, as Nekuda would say—Native American.

". . . We ask your blessing on our troops in that distant land, and most especially those courageous men and women we call Coarsegold's own."

On the gym's far wall, their names are listed in thick red felt pen—eighteen alumni of this high school now serving in the Persian Gulf. And if I believed in prayer, I would add Pink Lindstrom as well, because just yesterday he received his activation papers. "I'm scared," I told my father, as if he could fully comprehend. And my father, in his sickness and confusion, nodded and dropped a paper plate into the electric toaster, thinking that stiff white paper was bread. Just yesterday this happened.

". . . Finally, Lord, we pray that you topple the evil despot and lead us to victory in our righteous cause. This we ask in the name of your son Jesus Christ whose blood was shed for us . . ."

Suddenly the bleachers erupt—"Amen!"—with cheers, a buzzer sounds. Down the row, Sylvestro Avent, our point guard's father and head maintenance engineer of Coarsegold High—this slight dark man presses a string of rosary beads to his lips and crosses himself. Then the referees wave the teams onto the floor. Beside me, Midge sinks onto her Booster Club cushion, shaking her head.

At center court, the tap goes to Seven Persons High. "Defense," is the foot-stomping cry from our Home bleachers. As usual, our pepless cheerleaders sit lock-kneed and virginal, saving themselves for the boys' game to follow.

But judging from this turnout, Pink's newspaper write-ups are beginning to take hold. Pink devoted the better part of his column to tonight's contest against the Warriorettes, a team that one week ago defeated us in double overtime by a basket scored just as the final buzzer sounded. To quote Pink, those winning points were made with "a prayer shot launched by the Warriorettes' offensive omniscience, Sonia Louise, who soared for the hoop with her holy medal flying up from beneath her jersey and her long legs stretching from hell to breakfast."

Fortunately, our team's last-second loss took place in the town of Seven Persons, so I was spared the sight of Lady Miners slouching hangdog for the Visitors locker room and a long, silent bus ride home. If it weren't for my responsibility as team statistician, I'd consider foregoing tonight's rematch.

Earlier, in the throes of what Jen calls pregame butterflies, I telephoned Midge's son Foster with the hope that he might consider attending this mere girls' contest. I have not forgotten my daughter's first varsity performance and Foster beside me—his large calming presence when I couldn't bear to look, the sound of his soothing play-by-play in my ear.

Instead, Nekuda Adowa sits grimly at my right, his eyes closed and head in his hands. Below us, the Warriorettes have already jumped to a 12-point lead—that team, legendary beyond the Paiute reservation from which they hail. In a dusty town littered with broken bottles and losing bingo cards, Seven Persons High has built a basketball dynasty that year after year manages to power its way to state competition.

I mark another unanswered Warriorette basket on my stat sheet, then turn to Midge. "Did Foster say anything about coming tonight?"

Midge shrugs. "He can't leave the house until he makes his bed." This is one of Midge's wry little jokes. Foster's bed is the least of it. But he did promise over the phone to be here. He assured me in that gruff, amiable way of his, "Just try and chill out, Mrs. Castle. Remember, I support our troops."

Three turnovers in a row, and Coach Michaels calls time. Jen scoots down the bench to make room for our winded starters. My father reaches for plastic water bottles, then blots a towel to Tara's glistening face. Coach rests her clipboard on her knee and dashes X's and O's with her felt pen. I hear her saying, "pick up," "switch." Grace is dressed for the dance following these games. Her usual loose, pleated slacks have been replaced by a suede miniskirt—navy blue with soft camel-colored tights and sweater. Statuesque is the word that comes to mind. No matter that tonight she'll be on Pink's arm—in three-inch heels, she appears proud of her height. Besides which, Pink—as I understand the politically correct term—is not one for feeling "vertically challenged." Although lately I myself have been wondering if perhaps Pink might fail to meet some physical standard of our Desert Storm forces—to fall short, as it were, which for me would be utter relief.

Below us, a Warriorette guard takes the throw-in, dribbles directly to the basket and scores. I watch Jen duck from our bench, reporting to the scorer's table.

"About time," Midge says as Jen enters the game. "Our girls are playing scared."

I mark the substitution, wondering how my own skittish daughter could be expected to make a difference. Beside me, Nekuda creeps his hand and squeezes my arm. Still, he keeps his eyes averted. And I take little comfort from his touch, or the bright braided bracelet that circles his wrist, matching mine. For the duration of this game, it's clear Nekuda is not one of us.

In the opening minute of second quarter play, the Warriorettes rack up an uncontested set shot from left of the lane, then a quick spinning one-hander. But there's nothing flashy about that team. The Warriorettes score quiet points. On defense, time and again, they run our Lady Miners into those dead ends where chaos happens—a drive abruptly halted, the ball popped loose.

With the clock reading just under five minutes to halftime, the score stands Warriorettes: 27, Lady Miners: 11. Then, as if to heap further hot humiliation upon us, Sonia Louise—that offensive omniscience—is tapped from the Warriorette bench. Midge groans as Sonia sheds her maroon warm-up jacket and ambles onto the court. Otherwise, our dejected Home fans sit leaden.

Given this substitution, Coach Michaels calls her second time-out. In the lull, Greg Simonet suddenly finds his voice and hollers from the bleachers, "Use that glass, Tara! It won't break." And Tara glances up, her moist face sagging and bleary.

Midge nods down at her. "She's moving like a sloth. I've seen two good drinkers take more shots than she has all night."

"She'll be okay," I answer, thinking if only she can hang on till next Thursday. Her appointment is set for 10:30 A.M. She is—as close as she can figure—nine weeks along. Other than this present sorry contest, there are no immediate games looming. The upcoming holiday noted on our Lady Miners schedule is "Ski & Skate Week." To my knowledge, we are the only town in all of California to cancel school for five full days of such frivolities. Forget this drought—the total absence of ice and snow—we are bent upon Ski and Skate. Still hopeful.

And still hopeful, the sound of Grace Michaels' young, level voice. "Hands in," she says, and our huddling girls move closer. They stack palm upon palm. Then my father leans in, resting his light fingers over theirs. It's a reflex of his lifetime faith—this laying on of hands. Only yesterday, Dr. Vernon assured me: "His long-term memory will be the last to go." As if I could find even a shred of consolation in those words.

"Team!" girls shout in one voice, one handshake. Then they're up and onto the court.

I glance to the far basket and Pink standing near the exit, his sports column notebook wedged under his arm. I'm aware before I even look that his eyes are on me. He smiles, then points furtively toward the open double doors. I nod. Halftime. The parking lot. I'll be there. Yes. All this goes without saying.

It's no accident that Sonia Louise has entered the game with four minutes remaining in the second quarter. This towering girl is the lone Warriorette of full Caucasian blood. She's also asthmatic. She rides the bench with a small white inhaler in her hand and a cannister of oxygen at her Reeboked feet. Four minutes of play is the maximum her straining lungs will allow.

"Nekuda," I whisper, leaning to the boy's bowed head. "Look—there's a white girl in the game for Seven Persons." I tap his shoulder. "Take a look—it isn't just them against us."

"Lowly people," Nekuda mumbles into his lap.

"No, no—she's a giant," I tell him. "And besides, they're winning. Open your eyes." But Nekuda doesn't budge.

On the court below, Jen checks Sonia Louise close to the hoop, conceding a height advantage of five inches. But it looks more like infinity. This wheezing white girl leaps over my daughter—indeed, our entire team—in a single bound. Her arms bolt straight up for the pass. She takes a little turnaround jumper, misses, snatches her own rebound off the boards, and puts up another shot. All this without ever once touching down.

I lean to Midge. "Listen—maybe we should go phone Foster."

Already, Home fans are lumbering down the bleachers, as if this game's all over before the first half even ends. And I think now's the time to meet Pink in the parking lot. But Pink's still at the far end—just leaning there grinning. He appears to be transfixed by a solitary figure standing at the double doors. As I gaze over, this gymnasium apparition—because that's what it seems—suddenly bursts through the doors and tears along the opposite sideline, circling the gym with both arms raised high. The creature is dressed in baggy fatigues and combat boots. A deflated regulation basketball covers its head like a helmet, a gold satin cape sails from broad shoulders. The face is halved straight down the nose and chin with Lady Miner colors—one side painted yellow as a moon, the other a royal blue sky.

There's a roar from the crowd. Then, all around us, arms shoot up from the stands, arcing in the direction of the streaking caped figure. "It's the wave," I say to Midge.

"It's Foster," Midge says.

"Not," I answer, sounding like my own child.

Midge shakes her head. "A mother knows."

"Nekuda, open your eyes." I poke at his Haile Selassie sweater, scrambling for anything to make him look. "Down there—a person of color."

At last Nekuda raises his head. He squints along the sidelines and nods. "My brother."

The Warriorette coach has called time-out. Sonia Louise folds her six feet, four inches onto the Visitors bench and presses her white inhaler like a beak to her face. At our bench, my father stands smiling up at the waving bleachers. After a moment he raises his fumbling arms over his head, mimicking the crowd. I watch Jen frown in his direction. Then she turns for the huddle and Coach Michaels' quick instructions.

"They're going to a 1–3–1 offense," Midge says, gazing down. "It's the only way to draw that giant out from under the basket."

Fans quiet for the throw-in; we have possession of the ball. The caped figure has disappeared as quickly as it arrived—one turn around the gym, then off into the night. But the air still holds a lingering pull that feels strong and tidal. It seems possible this single wave may have shifted the game our way.

Below us, Lady Miners run the offense. Jen skims the key, up and back. She plays the rover. She lures Sonia Louise outside the paint, leaving the hoop undefended. And Tara's shot drops through. Then Rita Avent drives for a lay-up. One minute, thirty seconds. The rattled Warriorettes launch a long crosscourt pass and Julie Dwyer zooms to intercept. The ball is ours, and ours again. Back door here. Give and go there. Pick and roll. I note them all, until the halftime buzzer sounds. And we've closed the gap: 29–21. Instantly the silent bleachers burst with whistles and applause. It seems this is always the way—whenever a losing team rallies, there's a redemptive chord struck in even the most downtrodden fan.

As the cheering subsides, I glance across and see Pink ducking out the exit. Our official game manual states that the duration of halftime intermission is ten minutes. And so I hurry, thrusting the stat sheet into Coach's hands as I zip past the bench.

In the quiet rear lot, I find Pink waiting at his truck. He flings the pickup's door open and immediately we are parked in every sense of the word and demonstratively engaged in any and all behavior such an activity might entail.

I didn't plan this. My handbag, stuffed with those inferior lambskin condoms, is inside the gym, three Home bleachers up and understandably well beyond my reach, given the position I'm in, which is slightly more upright than missionary. But this is the cab of a truck, after all, and a steering wheel to contend with, plus armrests. Nevertheless, I feel infinitely blessed and boundless as Pink murmurs, "I'm wearing double-reinforced ribbed latex treated with vitamin E and nonoxynol 9."

"I love you," I respond. "You—Pink," I blurt. And for a moment it seems I'm reliving a youth I never had—this dark high school parking lot, asphalt silver with frost, the quick chill of slick worn Naugahyde up my spine, scent of oranges in a forgotten lunchbox, my hair ponytailed, socks rolled exactly so, twined around his vernal legs, myself unfolding with this kiss, the fall of his stunning breath, just the sound of his voice—then the sudden *slap* of a windshield wiper on the glass, and we two are sprung apart.

Pink shoves me down, out of sight. "Sshhhh. Hedy," he whispers, his voice quick and falling.

I hold myself still beneath the dash, my eyes shut tight as if this alone will keep me from being seen. In the silence, I strain to listen. I hear the clock on the dash, faint and meticulous, then a pebbly sound —coat buttons—someone brushing up against the driver's door. I am a married woman, thirty-eight years old. I have a child nearly full-grown and a father who needs me. I'm crouched on the gritty rubber floor mat of Pink Lindstrom's truck, my good wool slacks hobbling my ankles, sweater bunched high and binding, bra straps dangling slovenly down my arms. I know who I am. But I tell you now—I would rather die here on my knees than lose this love to cheap discovery.

Pink is pitch black above, covering me as if from a bomb blast. I blink against his weight. It seems I can feel his heart beating in my hair. Then after a minute I hear a woman's voice calling across the parking lot—another answering. I press the flat of my hand across my face to stop the sound of my breathing. And then there's only the night, quiet. "They've gone," Pink whispers.

Carefully he eases straight, then pulls me up. Somehow I've surfaced behind the steering wheel. And it seems a foreign place, this driver's seat. My fingers grope with instinct, tugging to fasten the safety belt.

Pink draws my hand away. "Hedy, no," he tells me. He speaks gently, as if I've wandered into my father's jumbled mind. "We can't leave now. Anyway . . ." He nods to the windshield. "They never saw us."

And I believe this could be true. The windshield is completely fogged over, like an old steamy joke.

"Look here," Pink says. He leans to the blurred glass and streaks my name clean across. Then he trails his cool, wet finger down my cheek. "See?"

"Yes," I answer. I see a white square folded under the windshield wiper. For a moment I believe it could be a wedge of snow clinging there—a reward for all our dry-eyed prayers. But now my voice is dry too, my tongue parched with words.

"They left a note," I whisper.

Pink fastens his blue jeans and runs a hand through his hair. He opens the passenger door. "Probably some school announcement," he says, his breath pale in the air. "A car wash coming up, or maybe something about the dance."

And I think, yes, maybe it's only that. I smooth my sweater, fumbling to put myself back together. Then I grab my coat and slip outside.

"Don't—" Pink reaches over the hood for the folded paper, but my hand gets there first. "Don't read it."

"I won't," I tell him, I lie.

We turn from the truck and start across the lot. I feel vaguely sodden, a slight pressure with each step. Along a row of cars, I stop, glimpsing white papers dotting windshields. On my own Blazer I see a folded page.

Pink slides his arm around my shoulder and steers me on. "Leave it," he says.

We move through the double doors, the heat of the gym rushing my face. The third quarter is already under way. In the Home bleachers, I spot Midge with one hand on the empty space beside her, saving my seat.

The score is tied at 35 all, the sound of the drumming ball urgent. Jen's in the game, and the sight of her pure hard effort and my father leaning from the bench, as if his sole striving vigilance could bring the win safely home—this keen devotion holds me like all the Earth's gravity brought to bear.

And so I make no move for the girls' restroom down the corridor—a stop that only moments ago seemed absolutely necessary. Instead, I hurry to my place, leaving Pink at the door, leaving the note still folded in my hand and his double-reinforced condom inside me. It feels like a tampon inserted there, feels like almost nothing at all. I tell myself these things sometimes happen in the act of love. And maybe I should know better. But I take my seat.

Midge squints up at the big gym clock, as if calculating the length of my absence. Finally she tips her chin my way. "Well?"

Hot as it is, I pull my coat tighter, slipping the white paper into my pocket. "I went to call Foster."

Midge levels her gaze on me, as if deliberating whether to accept this. "Come on, Hedy," she says. She nods, dropping her voice low. "Tell me what's going on with you—not that I don't have my own ideas."

"There's nothing going on, not one thing whatsoever," I answer.

I look Midge straight in the eye, trying not to let the thought of Pink enter my mind for fear she'll see. I admit there have been moments lately when I've felt so flooded with joy, I can scarcely keep myself from blurting everything. And maybe I would, if Midge didn't dislike Ward so much. Call this some kind of perverse fidelity or misplaced guilt—but I can't bear to give Midge such satisfaction at Ward's expense.

Midge drops the stat notebook into my lap. "All right, don't confide in me," she grumbles. "I'm only your best friend since Horace Mann Elementary, since I gave you the two steelies and my one green cat eye. But just forget it—don't mind *me*."

"Midge, please . . ." I shake my head over the stats, hearing the close, blistering game below. It seems I've lost all track and will never be able to concentrate. I shift in the bleacher, crossing my legs, aware of Pink's condom.

Finally I slide the notebook back to Midge. "If you could just keep the stats for the rest of the half . . . I mean, you've already started."

Midge heaves a sigh. "And considering you're a total wreck." She leans past me and taps Nekuda's knee. "Will you kindly tell her it's only a game."

"It is the beginning of the end," Nekuda says.

I let my gaze wander to the far wall, those eighteen alumni glorified on butcher paper, and Pink Lindstrom not listed among them. But I could write my own name there. I'd don Pink's desert camouflage, even as I'm wearing his condom, and take his place in war. I believe I could.

"Tara's three-point shot's finally connecting," Midge says. "Any second the Warriorettes will be bringing that mouth-breathing scoring machine into the game again."

I nod, imagining aerial bombardment and light antiaircraft missiles. "Midge," I say after a moment, "have you ever wondered if you could actually kill?"

"Ferrets, yes," she says, in a most cheerful voice. She marks a Lady Miners free throw. "That's Seven Persons' fourth foul—from now on, we're in the bonus."

"Well, of course ferrets . . ." I mumble.

Nekuda gazes down to the court, then slumps back. "We are doomed," he says.

"Doomed to win," Midge chuckles.

And so we are, despite the last-ditch substitution of Sonia Louise. The Warriorettes' quiet offense has been corrupted. Shots miss their mark. The ball strikes the rim, bouncing high and deep, or shudders against the glass, then lobs off slow and straight down. And always, that ball falls into a frenzy of Lady Miner hands.

I glance to Midge, then reach into my pocket for the folded white paper.

"Air ball!" a voice heckles from the bleachers.

I look to the floor, seeing Jen edge downcourt, anticipating the fast break.

The Warriorette coach yells, "Get back, Sonia." But it's too late.

"Way to be!" Greg Simonet calls as Jen takes the ball on the break and drives all the way for a lay-up. "Hey, Hedy," Greg hollers, "did you catch that?"

I nod, gazing down to the paper in my lap. On Wednesday, a letter fell into Midge's hands. Tonight, this same letter fell like snow. It struck Pink's windshield, struck the fear of God. Now it falls upon me to read.

Beloved Friends,

Greetings in the wonderful name of Jesus! The spiritual revolution sweeping across this land has begun at last. As parents, we can no longer abdicate our leadership to teachers, coaches, physicians, or any others who would demonize our children. Heed these prophetic words from 2 Timothy . . .

> *For the time will come when they will not endure sound doctrine; but after their own lusts shall they heap to themselves teachers, having itching ears. And they shall turn away their ears from the truth, and they shall be turned into fables.*

Dear friends, that perilous time has already come. Our public schools are in a moral free-fall and our children are in mortal danger. Join God's glorious army NOW! Together we'll return our great American heritage and bring Christ into every classroom. How? By COMMUNITY IMPACT EVANGELISM!

Your local chapter of Parents for Excellence in Education invites you to attend our next . . .

I sit frowning at the page, then turn to Midge. But she's on her feet with thirty seconds remaining and the win assured and the Home crowd yelling across to the somber Warriorette bench, "Go start the bus—Go start the—" I glance at the score and with sheer relief, I crumple the paper in my hand, forgetting all those words.

Then the buzzer sounds and our bleachers erupt. One game closer to State Tournament, and our Lady Miners have finally caught on. But standing here, watching these fans drain out the door, I wish for the recent past when it was only Midge and me, plus Nekuda and a few straggling others bunched small and close. Maybe this sounds disloyal, but that's how I feel. Until I glance below. At the bench, Lady Miners bask in a circle of upperclass admiration, those cheerleaders suddenly all white dazzling smiles. And beside Jen—bobbing cool on his toes—a young man I believe to be the student body president himself. This satisfying sight is enough to make even a veteran spectator such as myself light-headed and smug with victory.

I wave Midge off, unable to take my eyes from the court. Then Greg and Corrine Simonet clatter down the bleachers.

"What a game," Greg says, his voice fairly bursting.

I give him a little smile, this Lady Miner triumph disposing me to charitable acts. Tonight, I could almost grow to like Greg Simonet, although I still concur with Midge's estimation of the man as a "weenie."

"Now, tell me the truth," Corrine says, resting her hand along my arm. "Are you sure you're feeling all right about next week—Tara won't be too much trouble?"

I blink at Corrine, her words shoving me past this stadium glow. Tomorrow the Simonets are packing their skates and skis and heading for a week in Sun Valley, Idaho, with their two sons, James and Nicholas. On Thursday, their only daughter, Tara, is having an abortion and a few days after that, this same girl will sit down for one last try at the SAT with the hope of improving her score a hundred points, which might—just might—gain her admission to the college of her choice. Eleventh-hour cramming, plus mandatory team practices are the pretexts under which the Simonets are leaving Tara behind in my care. And I am not—in any way, shape, or form—feeling all right about this. Furthermore, I do not believe Corrine Simonet possesses a bone in her beautiful second runner-up body, or a single brain cell in either lobe or any hemisphere, that truly knows what trouble is.

Nevertheless, I smile at Corrine and say, "No trouble at all." Then I sink onto the bleacher, as if to catch my breath. Deceit can be thoroughly exhausting. But then, I've developed no stamina. Throughout the years, I've made a point of avoiding the invention or transmission of a lie, large or small—all this time striving to keep my slate clean by my own statistical reckoning, only to come to this: chalking up falsehoods right and left. Yet somehow I have never felt so painfully honest as I do now. And this confounds me. Maybe it's that rub people talk about, or the location between a rock and a hard place. But I believe something extreme is happening to me—something acutely taxing.

Greg Simonet unfolds Corrine's wool coat from his arm and holds it open for her. "I can't tell you how much we appreciate your offering to let Tara stay at your place," he says. "For a while, we thought we'd need to scrap the whole trip, considering everything Tara's got herself into."

"That's what senior year is all about," Corrine says, slipping into her coat. She winks at me. "You'd better prepare yourself. Jen'll be there before you know it."

I wrench myself from this thought and watch Corrine buttoning up. She starts at the top. My eyes follow, fastening with her. The crumpled white letter is still in my hand. I lean forward slightly, toward my feet—that narrow crack between the bleachers. There are four large, jet black buttons on Corrine's coat. I'm counting. And as I nudge the wadded paper through the crack in the bleachers, I hear those buttons click against the pickup's door. I see the letter fall soft as snow.

"Anyway," Corrine says, "I'll call you before we leave. And thanks again, Hedy." She turns, letting Greg lead her down the stands. When they reach the floor, she glances back at me and smiles. "You're a real lifesaver—I hope you know that."

And just then, I want to tell her—regardless of all consequences and any fear—to say to her: Don't go. Your child . . . Listen, Corrine, your child . . . Instead I give a little shake of my head, as if to be modest. I am no lifesaver.

After a minute, I slink off the bleachers to where my father waits. He sits alone on the Home bench, our team long gone for the locker room and showers. "Wait just a minute more," I tell him. Then I hurry to the girls' restroom. In a white painted stall scratched to the metal with initials, a heart, cupid's arrow, and the words "suck dick," I remove Pink's condom, I flush the toilet, and I don't look.

When I return to the gym, I find Pink and Grace Michaels flanking my father on the bench.

Pink nods up. "Your dad's feeling a little weak."

Grace gives me an anxious look, then glances to my father. "Galen . . ." She scoots from the bench and crouches before him. In that nervous time-out habit which has become so familiar, Coach tucks her hair behind her ears. Then she holds up a finger. She moves it left to right, and my father's head turns. Then Grace says, "Touch your nose." And he does. "Now your eyes." He creeps his halting hand, then stops and leans toward her. "Your eyes," Grace says. But he reaches to touch hers. I watch his mouth working to form a word. He looks so drawn—these games are too much, I think. The days too long for him, everything just too hard.

"Honey," he mumbles.

Grace smiles. "Can you stand up?"

He nods, his face almost sheepish, as if there's some reason for shame here. But he owes no apology—this man who has given his all, this one now riding the bench. He places his hands flat on the wood to either side and rocks himself, preparing to stand.

Across the way, varsity boys crowd their locker room doorway, basketballs under their arms. Behind us the bleachers are starting to fill once again.

Pink reaches for my father's elbow as he struggles up. I place my hand at his back, the deep blue of this sweater he wears for our team.

Then Grace presses close. "Let me," she says, taking his arm.

I fall back, trailing them as they move onto the hardwood. Pink stays alongside a moment, then he steps away too. Somehow they seem to require privacy, my father and Grace.

Her high heels clip the shiny court. She raises her coach's hand to the boys craning at the door, impatient for warm-ups. She walks my father to center court, and I think how easily he is led these days. I remind myself that I must watch him even more carefully now—stay on the lookout.

It's possible that just a minute ago my father suffered another TIA. Yesterday, Dr. Vernon warned me about these episodes, and I've read it for myself: *Transient ischemic attacks are often the precursor to a major stroke. However, because the symptoms of TIAs last only a brief time, patients and families alike tend to forget them . . .* But I haven't forgotten. As a precaution, we've increased his daily dose of Coumadin, hoping to prevent any more blood clots from forming. And on Dr. Vernon's advice, I've reread my father's Living Will . . . *If I have an incurable or terminal condition or illness and no reasonable hope of long-term recovery or survival, I desire that life-sustaining or prolonging treatments not be used. In accordance with these wishes, I, Galen S. Gallagher, do hereby designate and appoint Hedy G. Castle as my attorney-in-fact and by this document grant the above named durable power of attorney in the event . . .*

And so I'm trying to prepare myself. But tonight, my father's will is to live.

Grace moves him on, down the court. Along the sidelines, the scorer's table sits empty. Fans are still straying through the big double doors for the boys' contest. At the other end, a few youngsters shoot hoops—a between-games opportunity for those artless newcomers who haven't yet learned to worry about appearances or how the world tends to watch and choose up sides and then leave everybody else behind on a judgment call.

I step beside Pink as Grace leads my father under the basket.

"They thought all they needed to do to win was show their sneakers," she says, and my father smiles. She points past the free-throw lane. "Right there, Tara took the set shot that tied it up." She turns to him. "Remember?"

"Sure," my father says, the word tumbling from his slack mouth.

"And over here, Rita sunk one off a fake and put us in the lead."

"Hey, Coach!" a man's voice echoes down from the bleachers. "You ever hear a song called 'When Grace Met Sin'?"

Slowly my father turns and looks up. He nods, as if that hollering has been directed at him. It's a piece of sacred music he remembers well, my father—an old hymn speaking of salvation. Except now the words take on a meaning that causes me to wince.

I take my eyes from the bleachers and glance to Grace. But her face registers nothing. She clears her throat, keeps her eyes on my father.

"And Jen," she says, her voice rising slightly, "the way she made that drive from center court for the lay-up . . ."

"Coach—you listening? I'm talking to you!"

At the top of the key, I feel Pink stiffen beside me. He squints into the stands. Then he moves to the basket and touches Grace's sleeve. His words fall quiet and calm. "I think we should be getting the Reverend home."

Grace turns. And now the color rushes to her cheeks. Her eyes flick up toward the crowd. "Well, of course," she stammers. "Yes, you're right—he needs to rest. But anyway . . ." Grace sways toward my father, looking suddenly as if she's never worn high heels. "It was a wonderful game." Her voice trails off. She grips my father's hand. "Anyway, it really was . . ."

For a moment I stand dazed in the key. I watch Pink steering my father and Grace toward the double doors. At the other end of the court, two referees stride to the scorer's table. The table is full now, official record books open, a timekeeper setting the clock for warm-ups.

Then, from the tight silence, somebody yells, "Let's get this show on the road!"

Instantly loudspeakers crackle as if with relief, and hard rock grates the gym. Then a rumbling starts up in the bleachers—a stamping of feet like legions on the march and fans chanting, "Miners—Miners . . ." But it sounds like God's own army falling on my ears. *Beloved Friends*, the letter began. *Greetings in the wonderful name of Jesus!*

I walk along the sidelines, hesitating, staring up into the stands. I want to ask somebody, Do you know this song, "When Grace Met Sin"? Are you the one who hollered those words like a curse? I scan faces—my daughter's classmates, mothers, fathers—my neighbors. I need an answer from these people. I want to hear from them how the song goes. But I lack all strength to keep this steady gaze.

At last I turn away. I'm the attorney-in-fact—of this I'm sure. But here, under the harsh lights of the gym, I do not feel any durable power. It seems only my father possesses the will. He alone knows the true words. And I believe he'll sing me the song.

I move toward the double doors, bumping past the boys taking the floor, the relentless slam of basketballs. I'll ask my father how it is possible to live so long in this woeful world. Before we leave here and step across that white littered parking lot I will understand from him the way to be.

"Dad," I call to him. I step beneath the butcher paper banners, the outsized yellow ribbons. "Dad?"

At the sound of his name, he turns. He appears slight in the expanse of the doorway, but still alive under the blazing lights, alive to this chanting crowd. He hears the music. His chin bobs, as if the school dance is now and he stands prepared, with Grace at his side. He smiles. Then he lifts his arms. And in a perfect curve, so far removed from judgment calls and all earthly salvation—having no need for answers—he creates a wave.

Thirteen

This morning I regret our Blazer's bucket seats confining me solitary as a chauffeur, while Jen and Tara huddle together in back. At the edge of town, I pull into the border station, aware that this seating arrangement will not be lost on Midge.

She steps into the auto lane, bends at my open window and nods. "I see you've finally achieved pariah status."

"They're studying for the SAT," I tell her, looking to the rearview mirror.

But Midge just shrugs, reaffirmed in her belief that no living adolescent would choose the immediate proximity of a parent. I suppose in Midge's motherly experience this may be true. Midge describes whole weeks passing with virtually no sight of Foster while she waits under the same roof, reading from her dog-eared paperback edition of *What To Do Until The Adult Arrives*.

In the backseat, Jen riffles her SAT practice manual, as if offering proof of diligent study.

Midge pays no attention, glancing to the empty seat beside me. "Where's your dad?"

"Prayer Circle—they're having one of their picnics at Sutter's Fort." It seems our entire household is heading off to Sacramento on this unseasonably springlike Ski and Skate day. Soon, my father will be enjoying a corned beef sandwich and potato salad on the rich valley floor of California history, even as Tara terminates her pregnancy across town.

"Well, I hope you know what you're doing," Midge says. Then, catching my startled look, she adds, "I mean, letting your dad go off for the whole day with that bunch."

I rev the engine, anxious to get past this border check and Midge leaning through my window. I gaze into my best friend's face, wishing I could just tell her the truth. Maybe if I hadn't already given Tara's secret away—blurted it out to Pink—I could've confided in Midge. I would've welcomed another mother's voice, the help of somebody like Midge. But it seemed I couldn't betray these girls' trust a second time.

I nod out the window. "I'm sure Dad'll be fine."

"Right," Midge snips, "especially when you consider Dorothy Bascombe has the unadulterated hots for him." Midge flashes me one of her sarcastic smiles. Then she thumps the Blazer's door and steps back.

"Anyway," she calls as I ease the car through, "just try and stay out of Nordstrom's!"

I tap the horn and speed away, my deception complete. Midge believes I've taken the day off to give these girls a shopping trip. And it seems conceivable, what with no school in session and this mild weather, the first week of Lent already upon us.

We climb the interstate, weaving up the steep eastern flank of the Sierra. WEATHER CHANGEABLE AHEAD, a highway sign reads. CARRY CHAINS. But the pavement stretches bare and smooth as a strap. All around us, granite mountains rise like mausoleums, sealed from the elements. Pines stand brittle with thirst, dying from their tips down. In the distance, Blue Canyon Reservoir is a shallow beggar's bowl, is not blue. And last week Marshall claims he stepped out his back door to a coyote picking delicately at the dog's meal of hard, dry kibble.

" 'A family insures eighty percent of their property,' " Jen says from the backseat. She reads from a practice test, quizzing Tara who hasn't uttered a word since we set out. " 'This family pays a two and a half percent premium amounting to $348. What is the total value of their property?' "

We start down the western slope, and I lean to the wheel, thinking of my father. "He'll be just fine," I whisper under my breath. I picture him riding in Calvary Bible's white van, his paper bag lunch clutched on his lap. He deserves this outing, needs the company of friends. And I need his friends as well. No matter that these Christian companions sit so fearfully close in their righteous judgment, forever watchful. I'm depending on them regardless. Today my father's absence is required —not just for Tara's sake, but for my own peace of mind.

Twice this week I've woken in the night, aware of my father roaming our quiet, sleeping house. Both times I've raced up the dark hall, flipping on lights and remembering his first words from last summer, the hospital: *How do we get out of here . . .* And I worry that a night will come when I won't hear him—won't wake to lead him back to bed, my hand holding him secure while his eyes wander bewildered as if his mind has already left, traveling miles away. Some night I'm afraid he'll walk right out the door as I sleep on, not knowing. And so today while we're out of the house, Pink is installing dead bolts. New locks with keys, to keep my father safe inside.

"Okay, listen close," Jen commands, and I hear Tara give a sigh. " 'Two dozen shuttlecocks and four badminton rackets are to be purchased for a playground . . .' "

After a while I reach to turn on the radio. Jen's voice rises. She reads one question after another, flipping pages. This thick book is called *Test Buster: Expert Help for Higher Scores.*

As we approach Sacramento, the interstate widens and I move into the safe middle lane. Last Tuesday afternoon while Jen was vacuuming, my father poured an entire box of detergent into the washer. I came home from work and waded across our laundry room, suds climbing and billowing at my knees. After supper, I found him rummaging through the bathroom cabinet. I pointed to the top shelf, that crowded row of medicine. "All yours," I told him, "to make you well." And my father nodded, "Sure." Later, helping him undress for bed, I emptied eighteen aspirin from his trouser pocket—a handful of little white pills.

Jen clears her throat, then says loudly, " 'Six runners—Jim, Lou, Dave, Brad, Mike, and Paul—compete in a series of races. Paul never finishes first or last. Dave never finishes immediately behind Jim or Lou, but always runs just ahead of Brad. Based on this information . . .' " Jen reads down a list of multiple choice, then says, "Think."

But I'm trying not to, just striving to let the highway take me—the road dropping down, down into the valley, the radio playing soft and this day turning so warm with sea level, I believe the weather report must be for us. . . . *Look for that high pressure to continue building off the Gulf as easterly winds diminish. Today's high should reach right around 66 degrees in the capital city. We're calling for sunshine throughout the region and another beautiful day for bombing.*

I snap off the radio. Sunshine yes, but no clear skies over Baghdad. Not on this Day 30 with more than 70,000 missions flown—that jammed air space a high-flying nightmare for traffic control. And nightmare below. This past week, four bridges crumbled into the Tigris River.

Two blinding fireballs big as city blocks rolled billowing through the vicinity of Haifa Street. "We're starting to see miles of blackened earth and bomb craters," an Air Force pilot reported. And I've heard that the lights have gone out, there's no water running, and food is scarce. It's said whole families stand wailing on street corners.

We enter the city limits and I glance to the rearview, seeing Tara's eyes go wide. But I don't dare speak, because Jen is still reading from the test, still hoping to steer Tara's thoughts past that appointment, only a few miles now, and a half hour away.

" 'Which of the following,' " Jen asks in a tight voice, " 'is an acceptable finishing sequence of the runners . . .' "

Here at home, I've read that we're adjusting to the conflict. There's speculation about when we'll start the ground war. Saturday, the President met privately with advisors, then stepped into the Rose Garden to say he felt "pleased, very satisfied with the progress so far." He had no further comment, except to object to the "myths and falsehoods" spread by the Iraqi government regarding civilian casualties.

" 'If, in an acceptable finishing sequence, Jim and Lou run first and fifth respectively, which of the following must be true . . .' "

I take the business route, watching for exits. I'm looking for Florin Road. Word has it that the sand of northern Arabia is as fine as talcum powder. Frontline Marines will sleep on the desert floor. Not long ago, an item appeared in the *San Francisco Chronicle,* asking for donations of athletic socks suitable for marching.

" 'Where would Mike finish?' "

Then, in yesterday's paper, a triage officer at a medical station explained how he'll use a grease pencil to sort the ground war wounded. He said the letter *I* will stand for Immediate, indicating surgical priority for those with a good chance of living.

" 'If Dave comes in second, does it follow that Mike must finish sixth?' "

The lightly injured—those able to wait for treatment—will be identified as *D* for Delay. I slow, turning onto Florin Road. All of these wounded will be marked on their foreheads, designated with grease pencil in plain view.

"Are we almost there?" I hear Tara's voice small from the backseat—these words the first she's spoken.

I nod, glancing to the clock on the dash. The gravely injured—the ones most likely to die—will be set aside. I ease into the right lane, then swing into the clinic's parking lot. These fatally wounded will be marked with the letter *E* for Expectant.

In the backseat, Jen closes the test manual with a soft thud. "Mike finishes sixth," she says, like an afterthought.

For a minute I leave the motor running, as if we aren't really parked here. Then Tara gives a cough, and I glance around. I see her scared young face, and I think of mortal pain, of choices slung hard as the awful truth. And I wonder: How is it that we are what we never in this world thought we'd be? How does it happen that we do what we believed we never would?

She is wearing loose, comfortable clothing as the receptionist advised over the phone—blue Lady Miner sweatpants and an extra-large T-shirt from summer basketball camp. Last night I packed her athletic bag with extras, just in case she needed a change. I added sanitary pads and more athletic socks. Lately I've been buying these socks in economy packs—down the Soft Goods aisle in Safeway—eight pairs at a time.

Jen shifts on the seat, staring out. "There are people here," she whispers. She speaks as if caught by surprise, when in fact we anticipated this. We've traveled to the state capital after all, a city where laws are made and decisions handed down. During the past few days, we've discussed every possibility, trying hard to visualize. But it seems nothing has really prepared us for the sight of these protesters.

I turn to Tara. "We can just leave, you know."

"It's okay," she says. "Really . . ."

Finally I cut the engine. I swing my door open, wishing there were a few more cars in the lot. Considering how long Tara stayed on the phone trying to secure an appointment, it sounded as if today might be full.

Tara climbs outside, then reaches back for her canvas bag. She glances to Jen. "Should I take my jacket?"

"No, honey," I answer, aware of the warm morning sun.

"Well, I'm bringing it," Jen says firmly, hauling herself off the seat. And I can read my daughter's mind, see those TV news clips of chanting crowds and women being hustled through, their coats hooding them, faces concealed.

"Tara, you walk between us—we're going to hold hands."

"Jeezus." Jen lets out a groan, as if it's her duty. But she takes her place, easing the athletic bag from Tara's grip.

I flank Tara's right. Beyond the parking lot, traffic zips past on busy Florin Road, and it astounds me how constantly—all the time—life just goes on as if everything everywhere is perfectly normal. I could be a mother, young again, walking little children to school, the store, instructing them as we go . . . Stick together. Stay in the crosswalk. Don't speak to strangers.

"Hold your heads up high," I tell them. And I realize how I've always wanted to say this—a phrase it once seemed nobody but my own mother could use without appearing the fool. I repeat these words now, exactly as she would. And they mean something.

Three wide cement steps lead to the clinic's door, where there are maybe a dozen people carrying hand-printed signs. Along the front of the cinder block building, a ramp for the handicapped slopes to meet the door. This sight heartens me. Regardless of what's said about trendy California, we do try very hard to provide for everything.

As if in deference to any possible women in wheelchairs terminating pregnancies—of which there are none this morning—I note that the protesters stand well away from the ramp.

"Hurry," I whisper. "This way." I yank Tara toward the ramp, and Jen comes sweeping from behind like crack the whip.

Tara's bag bumps along the wrought iron railing as we rush up the asphalt. Beyond the railing, blazing red signs suddenly shift in our direction. "Don't look—don't," I order. Then fast, I whisk the clinic door open and shove both girls inside. For a moment, I feel such relief. Then my breath catches as I see my mistake, how I'm still out here, standing rigid with my back to the door. I duck my head, unable to move, aware of these people clumped just below. I hear a deep voice calling me off the ramp, calling me to pray. I blink down at my feet, the dark asphalt.

Then a woman shouts up, "God loves the child growing in you. Don't kill God's love!"

Slowly I lift my eyes. I squint out, tongue-tied and dim-witted. I want to ask this woman, What child? Who?

A man starts up the ramp, holding a little boy against his chest, a sign above his head: MURDERERS WILL PAY. In a rush, more people climb closer. I push my gaze past faded denim jackets, somebody lugging a leather briefcase, a flash of gold bracelet. Signs flap at my face. FIFTY PERCENT OF THIS DOCTOR'S PATIENTS DIE . . . COUPLES THAT KILL TOGETHER, BURN TOGETHER . . . Then a big red heart—and filling that heart—the curve of a fetus, the words, HAPPY VALENTINE'S DAY, DEAR MOMMY. PLEASE BE MINE, I DON'T WANT TO DIE . . .

I sway against the door, leaning weak, as if the blood has drained from my own heart. These signs cram tight around me, grim faces press. I smell aftershave. A young woman with a smear of lipstick red as a valentine hollers, "The wages of sin!" I turn away, clapping my hand to my mouth, because I believe I will be sick. Then I feel the door giving and Jen's hand is at my shoulder. She pulls me inside.

"Mom," she says, "Mom, are you okay?"

Across the small waiting room, Tara scoots from a plastic chair. "Come sit here," she says, steering me with a shaky hand.

We take seats along the far wall. The room is almost empty. Aside from the three of us, there's just one couple who look to be somewhere in their thirties, plus a young black man pacing.

Everything here seems two-tone—turquoise and white—these chairs where we sit with me in the middle, blue linoleum buckling the floor, white textured walls decked with glossy nature posters. The piped music is soft rock and instrumental. A hand-printed note beside the door reads, PLEASE HAVE YOUR RIDE PICK YOU UP AT (BY) 4:30 P.M. I sit back, telling myself to relax, stay calm, we have plenty of time.

At my right, Tara balances a clipboard on her knee. She leans over an official-looking form, filling in blanks, checking off boxes here and there. I watch her flicking a wisp of blonde hair from her eyes. She taps the ballpoint, then counts on her fingers, calculating. For a moment it seems she's finally taking the SAT.

Jen leaves her chair and saunters to the nearest table for a magazine. She's attempting to appear casual. There are five coffee tables arranged in this room, which strikes me as excessive, given the number of seats. But then I see how each narrow surface holds three full boxes of pastel Kleenex.

After a moment Jen returns, slumps down on my left, and opens a well-thumbed magazine called *Rider*.

"What time is it?" I whisper, nodding to her watch.

She rolls her wrist my way, as if too engrossed in these many pages of full-color motorcycles to answer.

I give her a nudge. "It's ten minutes past our appointment—they told us ten-thirty."

"Don't worry," Jen says.

"I'm supposed to pee," Tara says, clicking the ballpoint. "They need to check my urine to be sure."

I pat Jen's knee. "I'll go with you."

Jen waves my hand away, giving me an exasperated look. "Not me," she says.

I follow Tara across the waiting room to the receptionist's window. A young woman slides open the glass and takes Tara's clipboard. Then the woman steps to an adjoining door and motions us through. We trail her to a tiled bathroom, where she hands Tara a small, clear plastic cup.

"Try and catch it midstream," she says in a voice so pleasantly kind, I myself would like to oblige.

There are two stalls in this restroom and the music drifting here as well. On a Formica counter, I count four more boxes of Kleenex. Women must be crying their eyes out, I think. Everywhere, women bawling, wailing. But the room is cool and quiet, only Tara and me on this Valentine's Day—a sweethearts' holiday—hardly the time for such an appointment, except for Tara asking softly on the phone for the first available date. And me, keeping my calendar by the war, forgetting the 14th, aware only of Day 30.

"Did you catch it?" I ask, my voice echoing nervous and louder than I intended from this overly large stall. I see now that I'm occupying the raised padded seat provided for the handicapped. After a minute, I reach over and grasp the shiny handrail. I pull myself up, feeling truly infirm.

Tara waits at the sink, her little plastic cup gold with urine, gold as her hair. "You all right?" she asks, nodding to my fingers gripping the faucet, a slight tremble. "God," she says, the urine suddenly sloshing in her own shaking hand. "I'm so sorry I'm putting you through this, Mrs. Castle. Just so sorry . . ."

"Tara, no." My voice falls, scraping over the water splashing hot and hard in the sink.

As we move out the door, Tara glances down to the cup. "I hope it's enough. Do you think—"

And I see how she's trying even now to do everything right, striving to please. "It's fine," I tell her.

"Perfect," the receptionist says, stepping beside us. She takes the cup from Tara's hand, then leads us down a hall. At the third door on the left, she pauses. "Would you like your mother to be in the room with you?"

I shake my head. "I'm not—"

"Yes," Tara says, glancing to me. "And Jen," she adds.

The receptionist nods, opening the door. Jen is already inside, seated in a white plastic chair. Tara's athletic bag rests at her feet. She looks up from her magazine. "They told me to wait here."

"Be right back," the receptionist says. Then she closes the door behind us.

After a minute, a nurse breezes in. The nurse looks from Jen, to Tara, to me. "Tara Simonet?" She mispronounces the last name, but this seems no time to correct her. She's a small woman, Japanese, with silver streaking her glossy black hair.

Tara leans forward. "That's me."

"Sit here, please." The nurse pats a long, cushioned examining table. Then she rolls a stool closer to the table. She glances over at me. "We'll bring another chair for you."

"Thank you," I mumble. I look away, trying not to listen as the nurse turns to Tara. In the corner, Jen has buried her head in the magazine again. Last week, I heard these two girls talking at the kitchen table, Jen saying: "We're both in this, just like at practice—like when I set a pick for you, and you roll straight off my screen and go."

Still, it never occurred to me that my daughter would be sitting in the actual room. I didn't think I'd be here either. Somehow I imagined we'd wait anxious and concerned from a safe remove.

I step over to Jen. "Sweetheart," I say, careful to keep my voice low, "you don't have to stay for—"

"I do," she whispers. "I told Tara I would and I need to do it." Her words sound certain, but I catch a waver in her eyes.

"Jen, I don't want you here." I say this as her mother.

She shakes her head. "I've got to stay. I need . . ."

I reach for her hand.

"Let me," she says.

I look closely into her tight face, knowing she won't budge. Finally, at the sound of the door I step back.

The receptionist returns with a blue chair and sets it beside me. I hear her speaking to the nurse—words I can't make out. But I assume it's about Tara's urine sample, which is positive because the nurse nods, and we already knew this, although I suppose they need to be sure. I need to sit down.

The nurse moves closer to the table where Tara sits, her legs dangling over the vinyl cushions. "Just a few questions," the nurse says, and she clears her throat. "Are you still certain of the decision that's brought you here today?"

"Yes," Tara says.

"Have you told your partner about this decision?"

Tara glances up. The sanitary paper strip running the length of the examining table crackles as she shifts, fidgeting. She whispers, "Partner?"

"The biological father," the nurse says.

Tara shakes her head. "He doesn't know—not anything." She clears her throat, then looks past the nurse. "We broke up a month ago." She nods at me, as if explaining what's never been discussed. "He got upset—I mean, he went ballistic on me. I couldn't tell him."

"Of course you couldn't." I want to cross the room to her, hold her. But my legs are weak. I should take this seat.

The nurse pricks Tara's finger and smears a drop of blood onto a small glass strip. She presses a square of gauze to the finger and says, "Please hold." Then she pumps a blood pressure cuff around Tara's upper arm. "You're a little elevated—130 over 82. Nerves," she says. "Try and relax."

And I'm trying, nodding as the nurse pops a thermometer into Tara's mouth, then opens a little booklet, her pleasant voice briefly touching on diaphragms, the Pill, a sponge, and of course, latex condoms with nonoxynol 9. From the corner, Jen looks up and cocks her chin, listening. I watch my daughter absorbing this information, and I think how I've yet to give Jen that manual she asked for. I think of our Family Life Committee—of the facts stalled in Old Business, everything tabled. And I could weep that these girls have traveled such a distance over the mountains, come to this place—this extreme, Tara going all the way—to be given a lesson in sex education.

I glance around, relieved to spot Kleenex. It seems here, of all places, we are going to need it. But the room appears unmedically cheerful. A poster of wildflowers hangs on the white wall. Above the examining table, a plastic mobile turns slowly—bright little sailboats drifting this way and that.

"Sexy nightwear at no additional charge," the nurse quips, unfolding a blue hospital gown beside Tara. "We need all your clothes off—the gown ties in back."

Before the nurse has even walked out the door, Tara's shucked her sweatpants, as if this is nothing more than the locker room and we're all teammates here—sisters-in-arms.

Jen moves to the table, collecting everything—sweats, T-shirt, panties, bra. Then she slips back into her chair and opens the magazine over Tara's wadded clothes.

Tara turns to me. "Can I keep my socks?"

"Yes," I tell her, not caring if this is right or wrong. I step beside her and gather up the blue gown, holding it open for her. "Right hand through this sleeve . . . Now the left." I could be dressing a small child, lifting her yellow hair from her neck. "Ties go in the back like so."

The nurse returns and rolls a boxy machine alongside the examining table. She positions the cart opposite. "Please lie flat," she says to Tara. She explores with her fingers, looking for a vein in the tender spot inside Tara's elbow. Then she says, "Make a fist," and she takes a hypodermic from the cart. "This will help you to relax."

After a minute the doctor appears. She wears a snappy white medical coat that looks more fashionable than professional on her slim, high-heeled frame. "You must be Tara's mother," she says, giving me a smile. She glances to where Jen sits.

"I'm a friend," Jen says in a nervous rush.

"And Tara," the doctor says, resting her hand on the girl's arm. "I'm Connie Sayle—your doctor today. How are you feeling?"

"Fine," Tara murmurs.

"Sleepy?" The doctor slips her fingers behind Tara's head and pulls the gown's cloth ties. She eases the blue fabric down, listening to Tara's heart. She examines the girl's breasts, then smooths the gown back in place. "What sport do you play?"

"Basketball," Tara mumbles.

Dr. Sayle nods. "You have an athlete's heart—strong, slow pulse. A large heart."

"Oh yes, she does," I put in. "She's our starting forward and such a wonderful . . ." I glance over, catching Jen giving me a look that orders, Enough.

But I can't say enough, can't sit myself down.

"I hope you're remembering to check your breasts every month," the doctor says. Then she moves to the end of the table. "Scoot my way, Tara. That's it—slide down a little more, bend those long legs." She adjusts the table's stirrups, devices I recall from checkups—the feel of frigid metal on my feet. But these stirrups are wrapped with soft fleece like mittens. And Tara is wearing her socks.

"This isn't real sheepskin." Dr. Sayle smiles, fitting Tara's feet into the stirrups. "We're a bunch of animal lovers here." She settles onto the stool at Tara's feet, then glances to the nurse. "Right?"

The nurse nods, rolling the metal cart closer. I watch the nurse drape a sheet over the girl's bent knees, so the white cotton falls like a tent, hiding all of Tara from the waist down.

Jen closes her magazine. I step for the counter and grip the box of Kleenex, just to quiet my jittery hands—something to hold.

The doctor snaps on tight rubber gloves, these gloves the filmy color of cream. "I'm going to give you a pelvic exam and make a Pap smear for the lab. Take a long, deep breath, Tara. Okay, let it out slow." Dr. Sayle pauses a moment. I hear the sound of instruments taken up, then replaced on the cart. But I'm not looking, just keeping my eyes on that mobile spinning slow overhead.

"You're doing fine, Tara. You'll feel a little pull at the mouth of your cervix, some pressure here—we're giving you a local anaesthetic now—a couple of quick stings. Let everything go, breathe in again . . . then out. Good," Dr. Sayle says.

Jen slips out of her chair, creeps beside Tara. "You hear that?" she says, her voice climbing high and halting. She smooths Tara's hair from her eyes. "You're doing good."

I pull out a Kleenex and touch it to my forehead, my cheeks. Then I plunge in, aware of the small quiet. "At our house, we're just crazy about animals. We have two dogs—one's my father's and . . ."

"Hold my hand," Tara whispers, blinking up at Jen.

For a minute I'm aware of the machine's muffled sound and Dr.

Sayle's soothing voice. I wrap my fingers tight around the Kleenex box, bracing myself.

Then Dr. Sayle sits straight on the stool. "We're all done," she says.

I stare down the length of the table to Dr. Sayle pulling off her cream-colored gloves. "Done?"

The doctor nods, "That's right." She takes Tara's feet from the stirrups, then switches off a bright lamp beside her. This lamp I haven't even noticed until now—that's how fast all of this has happened.

"Are you sure?"

Jen is still standing there, gripping Tara's hand.

"I mean—finished?"

The nurse smiles. "See you in a minute," she says. She sweeps from the room, carrying a tray of crumpled blue paper towels.

I glance at Jen, speechless.

Dr. Sayle helps Tara slide flat on the table. She rests her hand at the girl's shoulder. "You doing okay?"

"Okay," Tara mumbles.

"We need you to lie still," the doctor says. "Take it easy for ten minutes or so. We're going to run a tissue check in the lab. But everything looks good." Dr. Sayle rocks back on her heels and shoves her hands into the deep pockets of her crisp white coat. "You're altogether lovely, you know—lovely inside."

Tara turns her face away, and for a moment it seems that of all that's transpired in this room—"lovely," just a single word—will cause this girl to cry.

Dr. Sayle moves to the counter, scribbling a ballpoint across a prescription pad. She hands me three slips of paper. "The antibiotic should be taken twice a day, starting tonight. The Methergine is for bleeding." Dr. Sayle turns to Tara. "A little discharge is normal, but if you're soaking through a sanitary pad within an hour or less, you need to take one of these pills. I'm giving you Anaprox for pain—you may feel some cramping similar to menstruation."

Tara nods. I stand studying the prescriptions, trying to commit everything to memory. I think of my father's medications—those pills lining the top shelf—and I don't know how we'll ever keep all of this straight.

Then Dr. Sayle says mercifully, "Your nurse will give you an after-care instruction sheet. And don't hesitate to call if you have any questions." She heads for the door. "Also, no P.E. for three days. No baths, only showers for a week. And that goes for intercourse—seven days, no sex—understand?" And the doctor waves and is gone.

Such a silence falls in this room. Intercourse appears to be a word long lost to our language, so far from the tips of our tongues and this girl lying straight and still under a white sheet. It seems years ago, I glimpsed that little white abstinence card bearing Tara's signature and my own daughter's name there as well: answerable.

"I'm cold," Tara whispers.

I glance around the room looking for a blanket, towels, anything. But I hesitate to open those cupboards along the wall. Finally my gaze settles on Tara's athletic bag, and I haul it to the table.

I unzip the bag, removing a clean sweatshirt. "Just drape this on top of the sheet," I tell Jen. "Spread these corduroys on the bottom."

"Moth-er," Jen says, but she unfolds the clothes.

At the canvas bottom, I find three pairs of athletic socks, and I realize what a state I was in last night, packing this bag—three pairs hardly necessary. Yet I'm aware that now and again, wisdom can randomly occur during hysteria.

"At least your feet will be warm," I assure Tara. I lift the sheet and pull off her old white socks, resisting the temptation to touch my lips to her cool toes. I'm stretching the third sock over Tara's thick-padded right foot when the nurse appears.

"Are you feeling ready to get dressed?" she asks.

Tara nods, lying stiff with that extra change of clothes corresponding exactly to her shape beneath the sheet—everything arranged perfect as a paper doll.

"I'll help her," Jen says.

I turn to the nurse. "Could I speak to you outside?"

As we move into the hall, the nurse hands me Tara's after-care instructions, plus the little booklet. "Before you leave," she says, "we'd like your daughter to be sitting up and resting for at least a half hour."

She leads me to the doorway of a room near the clinic's entrance. Somehow this room reminds me of Midge—or maybe just Midge's idea of house beautiful: sculpted pile carpet, overstuffed sectional sofa, four La-Z-Boy recliners in various shades of green, a console-sized TV equipped with remote control and stereo sound, one popcorn maker and two Mr. Coffee's . . . Eleven boxes of Kleenex.

"Our Recovery Room," the nurse says, nodding in the doorway. She glances to the lone woman seated there. "We're a little slow today."

I unfold the slips of paper from my purse. "About these prescriptions . . . We live in a small town, and I was wondering—I mean, we haven't told anybody . . ."

The nurse touches her small square finger to my sleeve. "There's a pharmacy just up the street—maybe a mile. Turn right out of our parking lot, it'll be on your side of Florin Road." She taps the little squares of paper. "If you have any problems filling these, just ask the pharmacist to give us a call."

"Thanks—thanks so much. Thanks for everything." I gush, but I mean this. Then, from the corner of my eyes, I see Tara moving up the hall. She walks slightly bent, as if with a stomachache. But otherwise she looks all right, considering—her clothes changed, hair combed. Jen trails behind, lugging the athletic bag, Tara's blue Nikes tucked under her arm.

"She wanted to wear all the socks," Jen says, her voice falling low and confidential as they step alongside. "We couldn't get her shoes on—no way." Jen arches an eyebrow at me. "I think that shot they gave her hasn't worn off yet."

Inside the Recovery Room, Tara is already reclined in a La-Z-Boy. Jen stumbles after her, looking thoroughly worn out.

The nurse glances at her watch. "You may get lucky—there's usually a little break during the lunch hour, before the next shift arrives." I look over puzzled. "The protesters," she explains, with a wave of her hand. "It amounts to a changing of the guard out there."

I take a chair and for a while we sit like three old cronies—Jen, Tara, and I—parked quiet in our La-Z-Boys. On the big console TV, it's daytime soaps with commercials for Cross Your Heart bras, toilet bowl cleaners, and roach and ant spray. We've watched fifteen minutes of "All My Days," but so far, no glimpse of the brave Desdemona to whom I'm purported to bear a resemblance. Instead, one steamy scene follows another in which designer wardrobes are unbuttoned and unzipped on designer sheets and an occasional silk strap slips off a sleek polished shoulder and the shoulder is nibbled by a man with chiseled lips and small teeth.

Finally, I can tolerate no more. I turn in my recliner to Jen. "This isn't about real-life love, you know—not the way it actually honestly is."

"I understand about love," Jen says with a cool shrug. "I see how you and Dad work it."

I glance away. "Well, your dad and I . . ." My words snag. "I mean, we're a little different."

"Right," Jen says, her voice suddenly thick and gruff. "He's gone."

I frown down at the papers in my lap, despising myself for raising the subject of love here in the Recovery Room of an abortion clinic, and on Valentine's Day. I am devoid of human sensitivity. And I feel sorely used up and bone-tired.

"Anyway, do you think I care about stupid love?" Jen asks. "Do you?"

Before I can answer, she punches the TV remote control, her anger channel-hopping way past the subject. Finally she pulls up at CNN. On the screen, I glimpse the dwarfen features of Peter Arnett, our lone reporter in Baghdad. And behind him, smoke rising from a concrete building and sirens sounding, the charred bodies of children being carried limp in the arms of wailing mothers and grown men keening with their heads in their hands. The camera shifts to a sign reading SHELTER in Arabic and English, then to rescue workers digging on their hands and knees for survivors. "At least two hundred thirty-five of the dead have been recovered," Peter Arnett says. "But it's believed that some three hundred more civilians were trapped behind these walls when an American Stealth fighter dropped two bombs in a predawn strike early yesterday morning."

I avert my eyes, but I can't stop the sound of those sirens, then a foreign interviewed voice speaking broken, weeping English . . . "I am sleeping and suddenly there is a heat and my blanket burning. I turn to try and to touch my father, but he is nothing there, only a piece of flesh."

And I think there can be no recovery in this room. The pain is still here, carried wailing via satellite through our Recovery Room with four recliners and eleven boxes of Kleenex—that number not nearly enough to dry all the tears, to ever stop the pain or the signs waiting just outside, signs demanding respect for the unborn, while before our eyes the born die in living color. No. From this pain, we will never—not any of us—recover.

"Let's go home," I say, pushing from my recliner. I touch Tara's cheek, aware of the TV's continued coverage, but she appears unmoved, her face still soft with a residue of tranquilizer. "Tell me," I whisper, "are you bleeding?"

Tara nods. "Jen gave me a pad."

I look to Jen. "The two of you stay here. I'll bring the car around to the street and park out front, so Tara won't have far to walk." I step for the door, then turn to where they sit. "I'll come right back for you."

In the Waiting Room, the nurse intercepts me. "Sorry," she says, "the second shift's already out there."

I shake my head, slipping past. "It doesn't matter." At the front door I pause, folding the prescription papers and Tara's instruction sheet into my purse. I rummage for the car keys. Then I move outside.

For a moment I scarcely notice the straggle of protesters standing below. I am numb, and I take the three cement steps, without even glancing toward the handicap ramp. They're singing a hymn, these people. " 'As with a mother's care, For Thee the lambs within her bosom bear . . .' "

I pass between them, not looking right or left. No signs press close—only the familiar words of the song falling over me. And then the sudden clap of a hand on my arm.

"Hedy!" a voice slams in my ear.

I spring back, as if to run.

"Hedy, my dear merciful Jesus—what are you doing here?"

I grip my purse tight to my chest and stare into this woman's shocked round face. "Dorothy," I whisper.

"Here of all places," Dorothy Bascombe says, stunned breathless. "What—what on earth!"

I shake my head, take another step back. "I was only—" I hear my frightened voice, timid as a child, and I loathe myself. "I mean, I'm just . . ."

"Oh Hedy, don't tell me." Dorothy blinks up, gazing overhead. "God, no."

My hand flutters from my chest. "But Sutter's Fort," I stammer. "The picnic . . ."

Dorothy's head bobs, nodding, nodding. "Our lunch on the lawn, but we always try to stop here on our way home. Wherever and whenever the spirit moves us, we stop for Operation Rescue."

"You should've told me," I say, trying to calm myself, aware of Prayer Circle gathered all around. "You had no right bringing my—" I jerk toward Dorothy, my voice suddenly shrill with alarm. "My father, where is he?"

"Hedy, please," Dorothy says. "Your father shouldn't see you in this place. Spare him . . ." She glances down my sweater . . . "He's a sick man, Hedy. A sweet sick man."

But I'm already shoving through the circle, dashing to Calvary Bible's white van, with Dorothy right behind. "He wanted to come," she says, her voice faltering, fingers fretting at her dress collar.

"Where?" I'm shouting now, hollering into her powdery face.

And she steps aside, sweeps her arm toward the clinic's asphalt ramp.

He stands on the grass, just this side of the ramp, standing very still. It seems someone has leaned him there—propped him against the wrought iron railing.

"Dad," I call to him.

He moves as if to raise his hand to wave, beckon me over. Then he glances down, and I follow his gaze, seeing a glint of silver at his wrist, restraining him. There was a time once, he drove his old Dodge sedan to Folsom Prison, a place not far from here. He objected to the death penalty—believed it to be barbaric. And he handcuffed himself in protest to the prison's chain link fence.

"He volunteered," Dorothy says. "He wanted to be the one . . . Besides, he kept wandering off." Her voice fumbles in my ear. "Hedy dear, listen . . . we couldn't keep him still."

But I pay no attention, rushing across the grass. I throw my arms around his neck, and he feels so strong in my grip, his cheek stubbly with afternoon shadow. By the look of him, no one would think him feeble, seeing him planted so firm, his wide wrist circled with a silver cuff, its mate locked around a wrought iron slat. Only his eyes give him away.

"Oh Dad," I whisper, shaking my head against his rough cheek and not caring anymore what I say, knowing he'll never understand. Only asking myself, "Daddy, is this how it's going to be? From now on—is it?"

My father nods. "Babies," he mumbles. "Dying."

I shut my watery eyes and press my forehead to his shoulder. Then I slide my hand into his shirt pocket. I think of home and dead bolts on every door, keys locking him in—keys hidden from him. But he must have this one—I feel it in his pocket, small as a cops and robbers toy.

"Look," I say softly, holding his wrist. I turn the little key and the cuff springs open. "Look at that," I tell him. "You're free."

For a moment he stands smiling down at the empty cuff dangling from the rail. Then we turn away. I walk my father past Dorothy Bascombe, past Prayer Circle. I lead him up the clinic steps.

"Not in there," Dorothy calls, watching me swing the door open. "Don't take him inside. Honor your father!"

"This isn't my father," I whisper. We enter the waiting room, and I nod to the receptionist, as if this halting man's sudden presence is perfectly natural. Then I guide him down the hall and through the open doorway of Recovery where Jen and Tara sit.

Jen glances up, startled. "Grampa . . ."

My father raises his eyebrows, looking amused at her surprise. He leans to pat Tara's shoulder, then sinks into a La-Z-Boy. He appears pleased to be resting in this indulgent recliner, a chair he once took Puritan pains to avoid.

"Not Grampa . . ." Jen lets out a sigh and snaps herself straight. "Can't we go anywhere without him? I mean, not even here?"

I shoot Jen a look to be still. Then I turn to Tara, keeping my voice low. "Mrs. Bascombe and four others from Prayer Circle are outside. They're singing hymns." I pause, as if we might catch a scrap of melody. But there's only the television and Peter Arnett's sober voice. "Anyway," I tell Tara, "I'm going out to talk to them. You mustn't take a step from this room until they leave. Do you understand?"

"Yes," Tara says. The sound of her voice is thin with fear.

I look at Jen. "Understand?"

Jen nods, my father nods. I bend to his chair, releasing the lever so he's fully reclined. "Okay, Dad?"

"Wonderful," he says.

Then I am hurrying through the clinic and out the front door. I walk directly into the middle of Prayer Circle and Dorothy Bascombe, knowing precisely what must be done—what I must say.

"I'm pregnant, Dorothy."

"Oh my dear girl," she breathes.

"I came here, but then I realized . . . I mean, I can't go through with it. I'm going to keep my baby, and that's the truth—I am."

"Well," Dorothy says, her voice swinging low and grasping. "My, oh my, well . . ." For a minute she moves away. She stands kneading her eyes, as if with a headache. Then finally she steps beside me again. She wraps her arms around my waist and hugs me close. "You've made the right decision, Hedy—the only decision a Christian could. And we're a hundred percent with you, every one of us."

Around the circle, I hear relieved sounds of agreement. Herb Renfrow murmurs, "Amen."

"You mustn't worry," Dorothy says softly. "When your time comes, we'll be right there to hold your hand. Especially with Ward so far—" Dorothy steps back, blinking at me.

I shake my head. "Not Ward's."

"Not Ward's," Dorothy whispers.

I look off, beyond the parking lot. "I've fallen so low, Dorothy. Just so low . . ." And this, I realize, is the first truth I've told.

"Oh, how deep we sink in carnal sin," Dorothy says, swaying against Herb Renfrow. "The very weakness of our mortal flesh . . ." She appears to be in something of a state of ecstasy.

"The thing is . . ." I reach for Dorothy's hand, my fingers trembling from so many lies. "Right now I just need to be alone with my father. Please Dorothy, if you could leave me—if everybody could just go now. I need to be with my father."

Dorothy stands straight, staring at me closely. Then at last she lets out a sigh. "Well, of course you need your father, you poor pitiful child. There isn't anybody knows better than me the comfort of a father's shoulder to cry on."

"Thank you, Dorothy," I mumble.

She gives my hand a squeeze. "We'll be in touch. You can rest assured, we won't let you down. Meantime, trust in the Lord, and when things weigh heavy—as they surely will, given the condition you're in—just buck up and tell yourself: 'I am an upstream Christian in a downhill world.' "

"Yes, I'll do that—I will," I assure her.

Herb Renfrow and Alfred Welch nod. They gaze at me, making awkward noises of sympathy. Beside them, Ellen Short and Cybil Edwards sigh.

I bow my head. "Thank you all."

Then the five of them swing away, heading for the curb. I watch them pile into Calvary Bible's white van. As Herb Renfrow eases onto Florin Road, Dorothy blows me a kiss, and I wave.

I wait until the van disappears in a stream of cars, then I turn for the clinic. I climb the steps thinking, I am an upstream Christian in a downhill world. And I am in terrible, terrible trouble.

In the Recovery Room, I adjust my father's recliner to a sitting position. "We're going home," I tell him.

Across the room, I spot Jen and Tara already moving for the door. "The parking lot," I call after them.

"Come on, Dad," I say, bending to help him up. And then I notice how his eyes are welling.

"Hedy," he says. He gazes past my shoulder, nodding to the big console TV, the sound of women wailing over the commentary of Peter Arnett, wailing over small bodies lined on a sidewalk. "See," my father whispers. "Babies."

I take him by the arm and we leave those sounds and the picture, leave it all behind.

As we cross the parking lot, I make him a promise. "When we get home, the first thing we're going to do is buy you a La-Z-Boy and we'll have a cake, because it's Valentine's Day. This cake will be shaped like a heart . . ."

And I'm remembering an evening when he took it into his head to make my mother a cake, and this was going to be a surprise because she'd gone down to church for choir practice. My brother and I were in grammar school, at an age when everything seemed a wonderment—just how our father rolled up his shirtsleeves and sifted the flour, measuring everything exactly so. He cradled the plastic bowl in the crook of his arm and stirred that chocolate batter to beat the band, stirred so hard the bowl spun right out of his grip and splashed milky Dutch chocolate all over our kitchen floor.

I open the Blazer's door, and my father climbs into the front. In the back, Tara is sprawled across the plush red seat with her head in Jen's lap.

So, on this cake disaster night, my father proceeded to step around the spilled batter to our kitchen's screen door. He whistled for our black dog Gus. Then he walked calm as you please to the drawer where she kept the best silverware—our mother—and he counted out three big sterling spoons. He said to my brother and me, "Shut your eyes for a moment of prayer." Then, all in one breath, he thundered: "God is great God is good let us thank Him for this food A-men." And as the dog lapped, we slid down on the white tile floor—my father, Dex, and me—and we spooned cake batter. Remembering our manners, cloth napkins tucked under our chins, our proper left hands in our laps, we ate Dutch chocolate cake straight off the floor.

I turn out of the parking lot, staying in the crowded inside lane, not wanting to miss the pharmacy.

After a few blocks, my father reaches over and taps my arm. Then he points into the backseat and the girls—Tara's athletic bag wedged against the door. "We won," he says, soft.

"Uh-huh." I keep my eyes on the road. Though it's only a little past two by the clock on the dash, this feels like rush hour.

"Angels," my father says, nodding at them—the girls.

And I think he must believe we're driving those two home from a game. He sees them soaring for the hoop. "They fought the good fight," I tell him, aware of how he loves these old familiar phrases.

I slow, flipping my turn signal, because I've finally spotted the drugstore. "They went the distance," I add. "They flew like God's own angels." In the next block, I find a parking space along the street and glide in.

Jen leans from the backseat. "What?"

"Tara's prescriptions—we need to fill them before we start home." I turn off the ignition and move to open my door.

"Honey . . ." I look over at the sound of my father's voice. He gazes past me, out my window. "See," he says, with a smile. He stretches toward the glass, wagging a finger as if to show me. "Trees."

I squint across the lanes of streaking cars, beyond the street and storefronts, above rooftops—I glimpse the tips of eucalyptus, shaggy with leaves, even in this withering drought, the dead of winter—those biblical trees from ancient times, their anointing oil, fragrant in the house of the Lord, the Holy Land.

"Beautiful," I say to him. I brush a kiss across his knuckles, his hand resting on the steering wheel. I turn to Jen, and Tara dozing. "Stay here—I'll be right back." Then I grab my purse and slide out my door.

Five stores up, I reach the pharmacy and hurry inside. I notice with relief that nobody waits at the prescription counter. I hand the pharmacist the three slips for Tara's medication. One antibiotic starting tonight, I remind myself. The pharmacist studies the little papers, then sets to work, stepping behind a glass partition. He asks no questions, and I think this might be due to the address printed on those slips. Methergine is for bleeding . . . I nod, pulling my checkbook from my purse. Anaprox for pain . . .

As I open my checkbook, it occurs to me that I never saw Tara pay for her abortion. Last night, she tucked the money into a side pocket of her canvas bag. Tara, Jen, and I had gathered the $264 well in advance. Seventy-five of it came from Jen and Tara's baby-sitting—or child care—efforts. I added a hundred and my father contributed the remaining eighty-nine dollars from his pension check. Well, not exactly contributed, but it's safe to say that had he been aware, he certainly would've offered. I know my father.

"Mom—" It's Jen tapping me on the shoulder.

"Go back to the car," I tell her, not looking over. The pharmacist slides three plastic vials onto the counter. I reach for the pen beside the cash register.

"Mom, I need to know what you said to Mrs. Bascombe at the clinic. Before Tara wakes up . . ." I feel Jen's breath fall along my cheek as she leans around. "I'm worried."

The pharmacist rings up the total and places the sales receipt beside my hand. Finally I glance over. "The truth is, I lied." And I could do it again for Jen, make up some story as false as my whole life now seems—forever naming my husband as my true spouse, locking my father's illness away, refusing his living will, believing the end of this Desert Storm is surely in sight and the peace won, the world made safe for democracy at last, and the drought over, snow imminent any moment, snow falling everywhere. But standing here, I feel so weary, my shoulders sagging with the weight of falsehoods. I can't continue.

"Tell me," Jen says.

I make out the check and sign my feeble name across the bottom. "I said I'd come down here for an abortion, but then at the last minute, I had a sort of revelation and I decided against it."

"Oh Mom, you didn't."

The pharmacist nods. "That's what they call a foxhole conversion. We got a lot of those in the war—Korea, that is." He takes my check, then stands a moment, staring. "Are you sure you really need these drugs? Could be, you don't."

"We do," I tell him. I turn as Jen swings away. "Listen, about the money for the abortion . . ."

"I can't believe you said such a thing to Mrs. Bascombe," she hollers, dashing off. "This is just the worst!"

"Jen," I call after her.

But she races on, down the pharmacy aisle. At the door she halts and yanks round. "Don't worry," she yells. "We paid!"

I sway against the cash register, then blink across to the pharmacist. "Do you have some water," I ask. "Just a little water in a paper cup."

He tosses Tara's medicine into a bag. "These drugs are contraindicated for pregnant women."

I nod. I will give them each a pill—Tara, Jen, my father. And if I weren't driving, I'd take one myself. Anaprox to kill the pain.

The pharmicist gives a shrug, then moves behind his glass partition. After a moment, he returns. He brings me water in a clear plastic cup.

"Thank you," I say, my words tired and slack as my father's.

I take up my purse, cramming to make room inside for Tara's pills. My fingers brush across my checkbook, then sink into lambskin condoms, and I say to myself, We paid.

The plastic cup is almost full to the rim, so I walk carefully. I see that Jen has stomped off leaving the pharmacy door wide open, and this will make it easier for me to go without spilling. But then, Jen's still in the doorway—or maybe rushing back to me. That must be it, because she's tearing up the aisle, her eyes enormous, and the sound of my name—a sharp intake of breath, a gasp,

"Mom—"

Water splashes down my sweater as we collide. The cup falls, rolling into the aisle.

"Grampa, he—"

And I'm out the door, my legs churning the sidewalk and Jen racing to catch up, my athlete daughter—swift and agile, running the opposition ragged. But I am faster, slammed quick with dread . . . The Blazer's doors hang open—backseat and passenger. Open.

On the street, four lanes of cars, buses, trucks are stalled. Nothing running. Only me, brash with frantic speed, the air tearing me apart, my chest exploding, raining red like valentines dropped down the sky, this beautiful day for bombing. Blood stains the back of Tara's pale corduroys. Roused from sleep, she goes without shoes, stands in the middle of this dangerous road, her feet swathed in white cotton. She cries, "Reverend," and I believe in my aching hopeful heart the word she speaks is "reverent." The sounds so close. A voice so close in my ear . . . Honor your father. "I do," I answer, the words falling, shuddering. "This is my father," I yell to a man sitting still in his halted Buick. He holds a car phone, his face ashen. "Call a doctor!"

"This is my father—Dad!" I will not let these gawking drivers forget how they've left him lying helpless in this road. I grope to feel his pulse, his sturdy wrist chafed red from that handcuff. "Daddy . . ."

"You mustn't move him," somebody says, dropping a hand to my shoulder.

"I know CPR, how to save him," I say to this person, to anyone who'll listen. "My job requires me."

"Mom," Jen falters. And I believe she is no girl, but a colt, stamping the pavement and walleyed.

"There were too many cars," Tara cries. "They tried to stop, everybody tried . . ."

"He never looked where he was going."

I hear this, but I won't let my gaze leave his still face. "He always knew where he was going," I tell whoever. "Always."

Then I whisper, "Jen, help me lift his head."

"Mama," she says.

"Help me."

She cradles him. He needs to be elevated, his head should be high.

I press my mouth to his. *Do you remember your first kiss?* He called me Helen that night, my mother's name. The doctor said, Take a long, deep breath. Now let it out slow. Those most gravely hurt, the triage officer explained, will be marked on their foreheads with the letter *E*.

"Not him," I say, because I see no wound. But next to me, a man is speaking broken English, saying . . . I turn to try and to touch my father, but he is nothing there, only a piece of flesh . . .

"Daddy, open your eyes." I whisper fierce—"Don't!"—because I believe he is going ballistic on me. "Don't go."

A woman kneels beside me. The sound of sirens fills the air, coming closer. This is the scene of a tragedy. We will never know how many are trapped inside. His first words after the accident in his brain were, How do we get out of here?

This woman nudges a small box across the pavement. She moves gingerly. I'm on my hands and knees, searching the rubble for survivors. The letter *I* will signify Immediate, meaning those with the best chance of living. But we will, none of us, recover.

The woman offers me Kleenex. She gives me the box, and I think women must be crying their eyes out. Everywhere, women wailing.

I wail. I could fill a cup, catch my tears midstream and ask him to swallow this pill to deaden the pain.

"He never felt a thing," a voice says above me.

I look up, stammering, telling a stranger, "He felt everything."

My father's face is dark with afternoon shadow. But there isn't a cloud in the sky. The sun falls low, striking rooftops, filling the shaggy eucalyptus with gold. Sunlight cascades through this corridor of cars. These people ring us like a circle of prayer.

Jen cradles him; I hold his feet in my lap.

The woman dabs Kleenex, soft on my streaming face. She whispers, "Tonight—I promise you—I'll pray for his departed soul."

I nod to this woman, nod to them all—the ones standing with gaping, anxious mouths, brimming eyes, shy men holding their arms stiff at their sides, useless hands red as bricks.

I'm telling them now, he knew exactly where he was going.

But my words are lost in the sound of an ambulance, its siren winding down, like a last breath falling slow over us. I loosen the laces of his good black shoes. His socks are not suitable for marching. But I believe he went the distance. Tonight, I will kiss my father's weary feet, the ground he walked on.

I turn to the medics bending near. "He looked," I tell them. "He saw the trees."

Tonight, I will anoint his head with oil.

Fourteen

On Monday, my father was buried.

My husband rushed home.

My brother flew in from Chicago.

Tara took the SAT in tears.

On Tuesday, the Lady Miners pinned black ribbons to their uniforms and defeated Meadow High.

And today, Friday February 22, a sorrowful Pink Lindstrom is leaving for active duty with the Fourth Light Anti-Aircraft Missile Battalion, U.S. Marine Corps Reserves.

My father was memorialized, eulogized, and laid to rest beside my mother. He wore his dark ministerial suit and his black Bostonian dress shoes. He held his soft leather-bound Bible with his name stamped in gold. I placed a white rosebud in his lapel. The Lady Miners—except for Jen, who stood beside me—acted as pallbearers. In addition to Prayer Circle and Pastor Paul Sitwell, Pink and Coach Michaels paid tributes.

We sang this hymn . . . "Lead kindly Light, amid the encircling gloom . . . And with the morn those angel faces smile; Which I have loved long since, and lost awhile . . ." And then we read aloud and in unison from Revelations:

> The dwelling of God is with men.
> He will live with them, and they
> shall be his people, and God himself
> will be with them; he will wipe away
> every tear from their eyes, and death
> shall be no more; neither shall there
> be mourning nor crying nor pain any more . . .

And I believed all along that the pain of these days was a test to be passed, like Tara's SAT. It seemed if I made the required arrangements, paid attention to details and did everything right—if I saw to the death certificate and answered all the questions correctly, and if Dr. Vernon signed it, and if I climbed the stairs to the second floor of the Illardi Brothers Funeral Home and a showroom of coffins and chose the exact one in deep mahogany and opened his closet and picked out his suit and tie and wound his old wristwatch and telephoned those who should know and wept but stayed strong throughout and opened my home and spoke to each one who stepped inside to pay respects and hugged them all and fastened the rose in his lapel and sang the hymn, said the words, sat at graveside on green AstroTurf hiding withered grass and took a handful of earth, dry as sand, and scattered it over and allowed the dog Bark to sleep on my bed for seven days and nights—if I did all this without fail and proved it, then I believed everything would be over and done. And my father, who I have loved long since, could come back—lost only a little while. We would go home, bolt the door behind us, and say: Well, we got through that—we passed with flying colors. We'd breathe a sigh of relief and take up our lives again. Somehow, I believed every hard hour was leading us to reunion.

But this afternoon, standing out here at the border station—back on the job—I realize my error. I see how, in the frantic blur of arrangements, it's possible to mistake all the details for death.

From the far lane, Midge waves. "Need a break?"

I shake my head and lift my collar against the cold. I've scarcely been at work ten minutes. But then, Midge maintains I should've stayed home in the first place. She says I've accumulated a string of sick days—time off for illness—that I could use. But I need to be here. Because just now, at the end of arrangements—right now, deep down, the loss of my father sets in. I feel it cramping my legs, tightening my chest. Perhaps grief can be described as an emotion, but this loss is wholly physical. Loss scalds my face, turns every bone brittle. It dams my eyes, so tears can't fall.

Yesterday Ward told me, "Go ahead and cry—let it all out." He's trying hard to be a comfort right now. And on these nights when I cling to the edge of the bed, shying from him, he tells me not to worry. He says this is only grief, and it just takes a while.

He's been home a little more than a week. The minute his plane landed in San Francisco, he rented a car and drove over the mountains. When his car pulled into the driveway, Jen was upstairs. My father had been gone three days, his memorial service set for the next afternoon. I'd just begun a load of laundry and didn't hear the car over the washer's noise. I was rushing to make the house presentable, knowing that after the memorial service, a host of people would stop by. Also, in the sudden chaos of my father's absence, I felt the need to create some kind of order. I'd straightened every room, including his. Jen and I changed the sheets on his bed. Half the dirty clothes I'd just emptied from the hamper belonged to him—his gray sweatshirt, twill trousers . . . I wandered into the kitchen, thinking, Everything's practically done. We're almost ready . . .

When suddenly Jen bolted down the stairs, hollering, "He's here!"

I raced to the window and stared out. In the drive, I saw a brand new white Lincoln, big as a cloud and only one person inside, the one door swinging open. Standing there, I felt my whole body leap. But I didn't move.

From the hallway, Jen yelled again. "Mom, he's here—Dad."

And I saw that it was Ward climbing out from behind the wheel. He zipped his World Cup windbreaker, then reached back into the car for his flight bag. The noise of the washer subsided, clicking into its soak cycle. Then the car door slammed and I jumped, startled at the sound.

He strode up the front walk—with Jen waiting in the doorway—and came right inside, as if he did this every day. Every day, in and out. But I kept thinking to myself: These are my father's clothes inside the washer, my father's favorite cup in the cupboard, his bed all made. And for a moment, I honestly couldn't think what Ward was doing here.

"Honey," he said. He crossed the kitchen to me, his blue eyes blinking tears. "Oh, honey . . ."

As he pulled me to him, I caught Jen watching from the table. She leaned back in his chair, the one where my father used to sit—Ward's chair.

"Ward," I whispered against his stunning, cool cheek.

"It's all right," he murmured. He stroked my hair. "I'm home now, sweetheart. I'm here."

I nodded, though it seemed nothing would ever be all right again. And I cannot, even now, let everything out. I can scarcely admit to myself how it could happen that just when we two are finally reunited I should feel so woefully estranged.

At the approach of a blue Honda, I move into my lane. "Good afternoon," I say to the driver. I squint to see the clock on the car's dash. Not long, and the Lady Miners will be driving through on their way to Foothill High School. It's a game night, Friday night. Tonight, Pink is leaving.

"Are you carrying any fruit or vegetables?" I ask. "Animals?" I hear my voice, a dry rattle. I wave this traveler up the road, my gesture hollow, my eyes tight and stinging. The man drives west, in the direction of an ocean. But I believe I'm headed for a long, dry spell.

Maybe what Ward says is true. It's a manifestation of grief, this barrenness I feel—my father's death, or the thought of Pink leaving for war—some rock-bottom understanding of how quickly life can be lost. Whatever the reason, all week I've been wishing I truly was going to have a baby. But then, it really isn't so preposterous when you consider those inferior condoms. Plus the night I wore Pink's double-reinforced latex throughout the entire second half of Lady Miners play.

Not that I could actually be pregnant, although there was something about telling Dorothy Bascombe, and not just saying it, but standing so resolute outside the clinic in front of all those people I know, as if I was making a real announcement. And something, too, about the way they took me at my word, every one of them. How on Monday they edged near at graveside, their hands supporting me as if I might not bear up under the weight of the loss, my condition. And how I felt the gaze of others as well. The eyes of the church. How news travels. As we stepped across the yellow grass, leaving the cemetery, Dorothy drew me aside. She blotted her mournful face, then spoke close. "I know what a difficult time this is," she whispered. "Such a strain, so much to attend to. Ward says you haven't had a minute's sleep. But if you want to keep your baby, you've got to try . . ." Dorothy gripped my shoulder. "Try hard not to overdo." And I nodded, nodded, wanting to explain that I was trying—I really was—and overdoing, doing everything required of me in the futile hope that my father would come back. Just trying to keep my father.

Across the asphalt, our team bus pulls into the truck lane. Heavy metal pounds loud as Jen opens a window. "Mom," she calls, waving me over.

Girls glance my way, still shy with sympathy. Our Lady Miners sit near the front, according to the athletic rules of the road. In the rear, Varsity men—those boys—occupy premium seats, sprawled at a cool distance from coaches and driver.

I gaze up, thinking how small Jen looks, lost in the royal blue bulk of her letterman's jacket, her face so pale. It seems the color hasn't returned to her cheeks since that moment she raced down the pharmacy aisle, gasping her grandfather's name. Even now, she can't say the word—Grampa—without sliding her eyes away. And I know she's thinking how, during those last days, she wished to be free of his befuddled presence, how ashamed she felt of him.

She blinks out the bus window. "I forgot my homework."

Tara leans across the seat, shaking her head. "Do you believe it?" she says, because Jen without homework is a first. This is so unlike my daughter. But we are no longer like ourselves—not Jen, not Tara, not me.

"The red binder and my math book," Jen says.

She thrusts a paper my way. I reach for it, seeing numbers, the combination that will enable me to open her school locker.

She gives me a pitiful smile. "It's locker 33. Could you . . . before they close the school?"

"Yes, absolutely," I answer. I stand on tiptoe under the window, straining toward Jen's anxious face. I long to ease her mind, to tell her: I know how much you loved him—he knows, too. But this subject seems off limits. All week, Jen's avoided my attempts to talk.

So instead I slip the locker combination into my coverall pocket and say, "Don't worry."

At the front of the bus, Coach Michaels gazes out, then gives me a little wave. I'd like to tell her as well—Don't worry. Throughout these past days, I've hardly had a moment to think about Coach, or the letter folded on Pink's windshield, or that heckling call from the bleachers. By now I'm sure the whole team is aware of the rumors. But when I mentioned there could be some trouble, Jen simply shook her head in disgust. Somehow this made me feel better. It seems our Lady Miners are nothing if not loyal.

Then the driver drops the bus into gear.

I swing around, hearing Marshall hollering out the station door. "Give 'em hell!" He glances to me with a shrug. "Or heck."

"Bring home a win," Midge calls.

For a minute I stand, watching the bus rumble off. And I remember our first game of the season—that nervous night we came away empty-handed against Foothill High. *Play ball*, my father said . . . I give our Lady Miners one last wave. "Fight the good fight," I whisper under my breath. Then I head for the office.

We're allowed a half hour for lunch—or supper, considering this is swing shift—and I figure Marshall will cover for me while I make my run to the school.

"Sure thing," he says. He gives me a long look, his voice softening. "Fact is, you didn't even need to come to work today—you really didn't."

I grab my purse and car keys, scarcely listening.

Marshall trails me outside. As we reach my Blazer, he heaves a sigh. "Listen," he says, "I need to ask. Are you here because of him? I heard he's due out tonight."

"Who?" I ask. But I know full well.

"Oh Jesus," Marshall mumbles. Then he gives a little cough. "Hedy, I've got to say this, regardless of the state you're in, and I know it's bad for you right now . . ."

I climb inside my car and start the engine, but Marshall has hold of the door. "Marshall, please."

"I think you should hear this," he says. "Last week four guys showed up at my reserve meeting, and like overnight, they'd tied the knot. Gold bands, the works. That's what happens—what guys do when they're scared any day they'll be called up and won't come back."

I shake my head, because this makes no sense—no sense at all that a person would get married if they believed they might not ever have a marriage.

"It's how guys think," Marshall says, as if he's read my mind. "Call it aid and comfort, maybe security . . . But we all need to feel we've got somebody—somebody back home."

I gaze off, aware of Ward's attempts to comfort me, his words: *Remember, I'm here for you . . .*

"I'm married," I whisper.

"That's my point," Marshall says quietly. "You've got somebody. But Pink Lindstrom . . . Well, the way I see it, he doesn't have anyone waiting for him—not really. And I'm asking you to consider if that's fair." Marshall lifts the cuff of his coverall and taps his watch. "Think about it—if Saddam doesn't haul his ass out of Kuwait by 0900 hours, we've got a ground war happening. And Pink Lindstrom's walking smack into it." For a moment Marshall rests his hand on my shoulder. "Just try to put yourself in the poor guy's shoes," he says. Then he shuts the car door.

I ease off the parking pad and turn for town. It's not quite 3:30 and there's plenty of time before the school closes. I feel better driving, placing some distance between what Marshall just said and the truth of the matter, which is that I care about Pink to an utter distraction. And it fills me with such dread that by tomorrow morning the Mother of All Battles may have begun, with a million troops moving through blowing sand and the black smoke of burning oil wells, a dusty plume of tanks stretching for miles—all these soldiers moving toward each other. Tomorrow, this could happen. Just tomorrow. And Pink will already be gone.

In my bedroom closet, I collected socks for him. On Valentine's Day, Pink bought me roses—red and long-stemmed. Roses wilted on the seat of his pickup truck while he waited all hours for us to return from Sacramento. But my father was struck down. My husband flew home. Socks and red roses, these gifts we never gave. We never exchanged lovers' kisses. I took no solace from grief in his arms. We haven't spent a moment alone. The last time I touched him, my father was alive.

But as I pass the Safeway, it occurs to me that I can still give him socks. When he pulls into my lane tonight, I can send him off with a little something. I check the clock on the dash. Then I make a sharp turn into the supermarket lot.

I rush inside, down the Soft Goods aisle, and grab three economy packs. That's twenty-four pairs—athletic-type, white, with cushioned sole, reinforced heel and toe. It seems that number might see him through. Some analysts are predicting the fighting could be over in a matter of days. They say even the weather's cooperating. I've read that "moonlight is limited and the tides are in our favor." But I'm not entirely convinced. A war on the ground could last much longer. And a guy needs to have somebody waiting back home.

For a minute I linger in Soft Goods, just trying to keep my mind from wandering two aisles over. Then finally I give up. I speed my cart to Feminine Products, past deodorants and disposable douches, until I reach the location of that 99-percent-accurate pregnancy test called Answer.

I pull up before the row of blue and white boxes. I tell myself to be sensible—forget this. But then, there might still be some slight chance. And in the face of uncertainty, as my father used to say, there is nothing at all wrong with hope. I toss the blue and white box into my cart. Then I'm through the check-stand and out the automatic door.

Fortunately, the high school is only another mile down the road. By the time Jen returns from the game, I'll have her homework waiting on the kitchen table. I'll fix her a sandwich, and make myself something as well. I've scarcely had a bite all day, and now more than ever, I should be eating to keep my strength up, maybe even eating for two. Plus getting plenty of rest, because Ward is right, I've hardly had a minute's sleep and that kind of deprivation eventually starts to tell on a person, like now, with my shaky fingers gripping the steering wheel too tight. And here—where just the ordinary sight of the school parking lot is enough to put a tightness in my throat.

I climb from the Blazer, relieved to see a few cars remaining in the lot. But I hurry anyway, because suddenly there doesn't seem a moment to spare. I race through the front entrance with Jen's locker combination in my pocket and the blue and white box in my hand.

Lights blaze down the central corridor. Janet Martell, our school secretary, still sits at her desk.

"Jen's homework," I blurt, scooting past her open office. "I'll just be a minute."

"Take your time," she calls.

But this pregnancy test takes only one minute, and I can vouch for the time because I've bought three kits since Tuesday and have received three separate negative answers. Nevertheless, I duck into the empty girls' restroom, thinking: You never know.

I add the solution from the little stopper to my urine sample. Then I begin counting the seconds under my breath, "One–one thousand, two–one thousand . . ." Anything's possible, I tell myself. Just anything's . . .

I check my sample. Then carefully I count again from the beginning, giving the test another minute, allowing myself this one last chance. Then finally I slide the kit back inside the box. I place the small carton in the trash bin and cover it with paper towels. This is a high school restroom, after all. Despite everything, they're only girls.

Outside, metal lockers line the corridor walls. But even with these overhead lights, I can barely make out the numbers. At last I locate 33 along the bottom row. I kneel on the stained indoor-outdoor carpeting and unfold the scrap of paper Jen gave me. Up the hall, Sylvestro Avent, our point guard's father, patiently vacuums.

Try as as I might, I can't read Jen's combination. I squint to focus on the sequence she's written, but my eyes blur, playing tricks. I see a green paper napkin, Pink behind the wheel, my father smiling across as I strain to make sense of the letters printed in his wandering hand: F U N E M . . . S V F M . . .

And I want the lie I told on the day of his death to be true. I think Marshall must be right—a man feels the need to get married, so he can have somebody back home. Maybe this wish runs deep, echoes from long ago and those games we played, jingles we used to sing. Until here it is years later, a man grows up and finds he's still that old farmer in the dell. A man stands inside the circle and takes a wife every time. But the woman always takes a child.

I blink to clear my flooded eyes, and I wonder where in the world is the justice. In the space of one week, my father is gone and Pink Lindstrom's been called to war. So somebody tell me why I shouldn't have this baby.

I glance up as the sound of the vacuum cleaner drones close, then falls silent.

"Trouble?" Mr. Avent says. He crouches beside me, smelling of pine disinfectant. He studies the combination, his eyes clear and bright as his daughter's. Then he cocks his head my way. "Those girls are playing a very tough one tonight."

"A squeaker," I whisper. I duck my face from his gaze, because suddenly it seems I can't stop these tears.

"Of course, we are going to see a little miracle because of how they keep playing above their heads." Sylvestro turns the locker dial this way and that. "They have wings, those girls."

I nod, trying to hold my voice straight. "Angels."

Mr. Avent opens the locker door a crack. He taps the silver dial. "Sometimes they act up on you—these things." Then he glances away, as if to respect Jen's privacy.

"Thank you," I murmur. My words are watery, my eyes still swamped—every test negative. My nose is running.

After a moment Mr. Avent stands straight, fidgeting at his shirt pocket. He removes a folded white handkerchief and hands it to me. "I'm sorry about your father," he says quietly. "He was a very good man. I lit a candle for him."

I dab at my nose. "Thank you," I whisper again.

As Sylvestro returns to his vacuuming, I gaze after him. Maybe it was only his reticence just now, but I find myself kneeling here, hesitant to look through Jen's locker. Still, she did ask me . . . I wipe my eyes, reminding myself: math book, red binder.

Then I open the metal door. And suddenly it sounds like an avalanche crashing. Textbooks, old test papers, gum wrappers, a wad of Silly Putty, and a black banana tumble into my lap. A musty T-shirt falls from a shelf, floats down, and settles on my head. I grope for Jen's binder, fumbling over the broken spine of a paperback romance that claims to be historically sensual. I pull out the binder, its red cover soggy from a leaky water pistol.

For a minute I sink onto my haunches. I check the name written in the binder's front cover, because I can't believe this inconceivable mess could possibly belong to my fastidious daughter. Nothing in the fifteen years of this girl's overly organized and controlled existence has prepared me for the calamity of her locker.

Except for her book and binder, I pile everything back inside. And I wonder, What is the meaning of this? Who is she? It seems I've unlocked the door to a closet adolescent—Jen's secret life.

Finally, I move to shut the locker. But on the inside of the narrow door, I catch a glimpse of Tara's smiling face—her senior cap and gown photo taped to the metal. Next to Tara, I see Foster posed in his football uniform and dropped to one knee, the ball tucked under his arm. And below these two, at the center, a grainy picture from the *Coarsegold Register* and a headline reading: SPEED IS HIS GAME, CASTLE'S HIS NAME.

The newsprint is already yellowing, though the article isn't that old. It begins, "Ward Castle, two-time World Record Holder and former member of the U.S. Speed Skiing Team, heads for the French Alps this week looking to nail qualifying times that will vault him onto the World Cup circuit and a comeback aimed at shattering the present record of 139.7 mph. Relaxing at home recently, the well-known Coarsegold resident smiled when asked about the decade difference in age between himself and the current champion, 32-year-old Michael Prufer of France. 'That man specializes in arterial medicine,' Castle said. 'For him, skiing's not much more than a hobby. But this sport is my life. Velocity is my one and only specialty . . . ' "

I push the door closed and spin the combination dial. This afternoon, Ward is making the drive to watch Jen play the Foothill Cougarettes. But for months he's stood locked inside this narrow metal darkness. In the photograph, his skis are positioned for a vertical drop of nearly 2,000 feet. His face is concealed beneath a streamlined helmet. He's gloved and suited in a second skin of swift synthetic. His leg fairings are aerodynamic. But he's never moved from this spot in her locker—this place of honor to which she pays homage, kneeling every day, opening the door to him—every day finding him home. Here, she keeps her secret, her homework. Every day she's got somebody waiting. She turns the combination and comes as close as she can get to a father.

"Jen," I whisper, gathering up her math book and binder. I say her name down the corridor and into the cold gray air, breathe her name over the Blazer's wheel, stream it out the window and all the way to the station. I pull onto the parking pad and sit for a while in the falling dusk. I picture Jen's tired young face, and I think I would do anything —give the world—to lift her guilt, spare her all loneliness and pain.

When I finally step back on duty, it's nearly dark. "Sorry I'm late," I holler over to Midge. I fold the locker combination into my pocket. "Jen needed her homework."

Midge nods. "You missed Ward. He just came through on his way to the game."

But it wasn't long ago, I caught sight of him there in her locker.

And something else," Midge shouts across. "A phone call—but it can wait."

I look away, thinking it could've been Pink calling. Since Monday, he's phoned only twice, and one of those times was to arrange to meet Jen after practice. "He wants to say good-bye," Jen said at dinner that night. Ward turned in his chair, curious. This was Wednesday; we were still eating leftovers from the neighborly spread of casseroles, cold cuts, and desserts following my father's memorial service. Jen hadn't touched a bite. "Pink's a friend," she told Ward. She ducked her head over her plate. "He took Grampa places . . . Mom knows him." At this, I felt my face flush. "He's a sportswriter for the paper," I put in quickly. "He's new." "Pink," Ward said, frowning at the name. He lifted his fork, then set it down. "Well, I hope he doesn't want a story from me. These guys are always hunting for an angle, no matter when." Jen folded her napkin, not glancing up. "They used to go on dates," she said softly. "Grampa and Pink." I saw her look to Ward, as if hoping for his smile. Then she mumbled, "At least that's what Mom said." Ward shook his head. "Listen—if he wants an interview, just tell him this isn't the time."

Across our lanes, the wind picks up, cold deepens. I lean to car after car, feeling forever on the verge of tears. In my mind, I keep kneeling at Jen's locker. I swing the metal door open, hearing Ward saying, Let it all out. And everything comes tumbling, like loosed floodgates. In that narrow space, I find a world of grief Jen has kept hidden from me.

It's hours before traffic finally slows a little. But then, this is Friday night and the beginning of a weekend. I wait for the next lull, then step from my lane.

"What time have you got?" I call to Midge. On this eve of Pink's departure—with every minute moving us closer to Day 38 and that deadline in Kuwait—I've neglected to wear my watch. Only Tara's bright string bracelet circles my wrist.

"Almost nine," Midge says, stepping over. She rests her hand on my sleeve. "I wasn't going to mention this until we got off work. But it was Corrine who phoned a while ago."

I look toward town, not paying any attention. "Do you realize that the deadline for the ground war is only twelve hours away?" I think of Pink packing, zipping his uniform into the garment bag. "They've got to get out of Kuwait."

"Corrine Simonet," Midge says gently. "She believes you should resign from our committee."

I shake my head. "Why don't they just leave, so it can be over and everybody . . ." I blink down at the pavement. "Resign?"

"It's only a suggestion. Corrine said considering the strain you're under since your dad—" Midge glances off, shuts her eyes a moment. "Oh, hell—nobody needs to tell you how you feel. Corrine just thought it might help if you eased up a little. And as much as I hate agreeing with her, I think she could be right. I can't see that you're doing yourself . . ."

"Ease up?" I whisper. I snatch my arm from Midge's grasp, my whole voice rising. "Well, let me tell you—"

"Hold it," Midge says.

I stamp the asphalt. "I know exactly what Corrine thinks."

Midge reaches for me. "Calm down."

"She thinks I'm pregnant," I yell, not caring who hears. My father is dead and all tests have failed. There is no world without end. In a matter of hours, the ground may shake and the burning desert sky will open.

"What," Midge chokes, "are you trying to tell me?"

"I'm saying they believe I'm pregnant—not just Corrine, but everybody."

"Pregnant," Midge mumbles. Throughout all the years, I have never before seen Midge flummoxed. "Why . . . " she asks. "Why didn't I know this?"

"Because you're not a Christian and you don't go to church," I reply hotly. "What's more, they think I'm an adulterer, which just happens to be true."

"Well, that part I figured," Midge says. She draws herself up to her full stubby stature. "Give me *some* credit at least."

"And furthermore—"

All of a sudden Midge grabs my shoulder and nods past me. "It's him."

I swing around, seeing Pink's gray truck rolling under the station's lights.

He slows to a stop beside us and rolls down his window. "We won," he says.

And all my anger, my fear, falls away, because I believe he's saying they've finally pulled out and the war is over. He won't have to go, and the worst—everything—is over.

But Pink's rattling off a final score, rebounds, and free-throw conversions—the stats. "I phoned Foothill," he says, then smiles. "That leaves two games to go—we'll breeze by Rich Lake, no problem, but Iola will be another story. I only wish . . ." He pauses, catching me staring across the pickup's seat—a khaki sea bag propped there.

Then he says, "Hedy, I need you to . . . I mean, could you just climb inside here for a minute?"

Pink jumps out and tosses his sea bag into the truck's bed. He turns to Midge, as if she's boss. "How about it—for a minute?"

Midge nods to me. "How about it?"

I gaze toward the station, Marshall standing at the door. "I'm only going as far as the first exit and back," I holler to him. I feel Marshall's eyes and hear my voice straining too loud, "I'm coming right back . . ." But I doubt he cares if I ever return.

I step across the lanes to my Blazer and fetch the grocery bag full of socks. Then I slide into the pickup beside Pink. We roll away from the station, out from under the arcing lights.

"Sit closer," Pink says. He reaches for my hand as I scoot over. Then, after a minute he says, "Let me feel your grip."

I tighten my fingers around his.

"Harder," he says.

I glance to him, aware of my ring digging. "I don't want to hurt you."

"Sshhhh," he says.

The exit is five miles ahead. We ride the first mile scarcely speaking, just pressed like this, with our shoulders firm together, hands locked in the dark. Pink stays to the slow inside lane. The road rises gradually, holds us in rippling stillness.

We are not large people, neither Pink nor myself, which I find a comfort just now. We made love in the space of this worn Naugahyde. My father sat here. Several times, Jen caught a lift home from practice. Suddenly it seems such a short season—basketball.

Pink nods out the windshield, his leg tensing along mine. "I guess you know your husband phoned me."

I stare over. "Ward?" My mind leaps to Prayer Circle and Dorothy Bascombe. I think of how word travels.

"He called yesterday. The Olympic Committee's voted to make

speed skiing a demonstration sport. He said it was late-breaking news —he wanted me to have the scoop. They'll be holding time trials, putting a team together for Albertville next winter."

"He phoned you?" For a moment I gaze off, seeing Ward poised for the vertical drop, hear him saying, *Velocity is my one and only. . .*

Pink eases his hand away and shifts down, taking the exit. "He believes he can make the team. His goal—and he said I could quote him—is to represent America in the Olympic spirit of international peace and goodwill." Pink hits the brakes, his voice dropping rough. "He didn't come home to you, Hedy. He just came back for the funeral —he flew in, like your brother."

"But today . . ." I tap my throat, as if to dislodge the words. I want to tell Pink how I opened Jen's locker and there was this picture, how all week she's tried so hard with Ward. "But Jen—" I need to make Pink understand how this love isn't just between us. This love can cause collateral damage, people can get hurt. And I won't do anything more to harm Jen. I don't think she can take it—I can't take it. But sitting here, I'm unable to speak. I feel my father's illness—an implosion of words in my chest. Truly, there is such a thing as wounded silence. "Jen," I stammer.

"We're not talking about Jen," Pink says. "And not you." He crosses the freeway overpass and eases up to a stop sign. "Don't you get it—the story he gave me is only about him. Just him."

Pink sits back from the wheel and for a minute we idle at the sign. We haven't ridden far into the mountains, but the darkness is impenetrable. I feel the close granite flanks rising black and steep around us, the cold sinking solid through the pickup.

"Look . . ." Pink says. His hand gropes, falling along my arm. "All I want is for us to live our lives—you and me."

"I already have a life," I whisper. I sit very still in the dark, holding still under his blind touch, trying hard not to give myself away. "And besides . . . " I clear my aching throat. "It isn't fair to you."

He straightens in his seat and clamps both hands to the wheel. "Christ," I hear him mutter, soft under his breath. Somehow the irritation in his voice is a relief. I need to feel his anger this minute—now, before he leaves. There seems no other way to send someone off to war except just angry.

He eases the pickup onto the interstate, turning back in the direction we've come. Below us, I see the lights of town. Any time, Jen will be back from the game, and Ward too. Not long and I'll be coming home to them. Tonight, I'm making my big comeback try. Ward told me, Sometimes it just takes a while. And I intend to do my best. But just now it's requiring all the strength I've got.

"I'd like to know what life it is you're talking about," Pink says. He lifts his arm, smears his sweater sleeve across his face. "And don't give me that married business. Because you may already be taken, but you're not spoken for."

"Well, I am so," I sniff. I cup my hand at the steering wheel as a precaution. Along this last stretch before the border station, Pink is suddenly wandering us all over the road and I don't think he's seeing too straight, even though we are going extremely slow. I nod over at him. "I am so spoken for."

"That's not what your father told me."

I shake my head.

"Stop crying," Pink says.

"You stop."

Pink wheels into the station, picking up a little speed here at the last minute. He lurches alongside my Blazer and applies the brakes. The truck jerks forward, then settles. "Plus he loved your bathing suit—that one you wore Labor Day with those dolphins all over it."

I glance to my car, wishing I could see the clock. I think it must be getting very late. The sun's probably already rising over Baghdad. Across the border, allied forces will be gathering. They've drawn a line in the sand.

I hear my voice faltering toward Pink. "You put words in my father's mouth. You're always—"

"I love you, Hedy." Pink shuts off the engine, then sinks back. "For myself, that's all I can say."

"Please," I whisper.

"I love you."

I duck from his embrace, trying to steady my breath, escape the heat of his touch. Until this moment, I never knew how pure desire could be so filled with dread.

I rummage at my feet for the grocery bag, those socks. I feel my way, my hands trembling—my whole body shaken. I've heard it said that in battle, a person sometimes lives on for a few seconds after death. There was a story from another war, a soldier shot through the heart—a man fatally wounded, reporting into his field radio with all politeness, saying: "Please allow me to break this connection . . . I have been killed."

Pink reaches up beside me and snaps on the truck's ceiling light. He smooths open a blue-lined paper and holds it under my eyes. "I hope you can read this," he says. "The number's 1–800–523–2694. It's the Marine hot line. Somebody will always answer, twenty-four hours a day. But you need to be family, so tell them you're my wife."

But I am not his wife.

He folds the paper into my coverall pocket, then hands me a silver key. "This will let you into my house, in case you want to water the plants."

But he has no plants.

"They haven't told us exactly where we'll be. I heard they're moving troops up the Tapline Road along the border, so maybe . . . I mean, if I ever see a phone . . ."

I shake my head. "No," I tell him. "You mustn't call. Promise you won't." Because I don't believe I can survive the days waiting by the telephone, leaping every time it rings—every time afraid and hoping. Even now, just hearing his voice—even with Pink right beside me and still safe—the sound of his voice is breaking my heart.

I turn, emptying the grocery bag into his lap. "Have these," I say to him. I give him twenty-four pairs of socks as an offering. If he will let me go—allow me, please, to break this connection.

I toss the bag to the pickup floor, then fumble to open my door.

He catches my shoulder. "Hedy, wait," he says. "Something for you."

He reaches across, opening the glove box. The wristwatch he wears says 10:45. Not long and he'll be on the coast and activated. By morning, he could be nowhere in this country.

"I'm not going to let anything happen to me," he says. But his lips on mine are mortal. Just mortal—he told me so himself.

Finally I turn from his arms. I stumble out of the truck. Along the far lane, Marshall inspects a load of alfalfa for bindweed. Inside the station, Midge will be pulverizing oranges, grapefruit, and Idaho potatoes.

Pink leaves me with a Japanese pear. I cradle it in my hands as he pulls away. This pear is round and the palest shade of yellow. It rests in a soft white casing that looks crocheted. Like a baby bonnet, Pink told me. That night we lay down in his bed. It was safe sex. But this departure is taking my life.

I walk to the edge of the lanes, rocking myself, rocking this little pear. When his pickup lifts with the grade and rounds a curve—when his flickering taillights disappear—it's then I wave him through. And in these few moments, I'm aware of my heart beating, blood coursing, how the lungs fill and bones do hold. I feel myself living on.

Fifteen

I'm using my sick days. The last shift I worked was Saturday. By 7:00 A.M., I was in my lane on duty, when Marshall passed the news that Iraq had made one last halfhearted stab at negotiations before the deadline. Inside the station, Marshall kept his little battery-operated TV tuned to Cable Network News. The deadline passed. Shortly after nine, our President emerged from the White House. He rejected Saddam Hussein in the Rose Garden. That night, he faced the cameras and announced, "The liberation of Kuwait has now entered its final phase." Then the President asked that all of us stop whatever we were doing and say a prayer for those men and women in uniform who were risking their lives. He said, "May God bless and protect each and every one of them and may God bless the United States of America."

And while I didn't fall to my knees in prayer and have not spoken to God during the three days since, I did stop what I was doing. I climbed between cold white sheets—took to my bed—and have remained here, more or less, up to this late afternoon, Tuesday, February 26, and the five o'clock news.

The television sits on my dresser. It's the set my father used to watch while reclined on my pillows. Although he never could manage the remote control. And Bark is curled at my elbow now, not his.

But some things haven't stopped, haven't changed. The Lady Miners are still playing their home game tonight against Rich Lake High. Jen's across the room, packing her athletic bag on my desk as she's done time and again. She places immaculate Nike Air Rebounds at the bottom. These dazzling shoes are brand new and need breaking in. But she'll wear them tonight regardless. Ward bought the shoes for her. He analyzed her arches, the stability of her ankles. He researched durable outsoles, adjustable lacing systems, and reinforcements along the big toe for what he termed "overpronators."

I couldn't bring myself to ask the possible astronomical price a person might pay for such features. For Ward, money isn't a consideration, even with everybody else tightening their belts. Ward knows what a difference the best equipment makes. It can mean a split second, a championship. On the slopes, he's a streaking endorsement. The boots that bear his seal of approval are sleek Solomons. His skis are custom Dynamics with the name printed clear. He wears a racing bib emblazoned with Subaru and his helmet says Kodak. He speeds across the finish as advertised. His sport may be expensive, but his body costs even more—especially in these high-profile comeback times.

It seems just about everybody and everything is poised for some big recovery. Commentators talk about redeeming our national pride. Our President said from the beginning, "This will not be another Vietnam." Instead, ex-military brass resurrected as network consultants bring us Gulf War analysis alongside reruns of parachute divisions dropping into Normandy and troops wading Omaha Beach. And now we hear that if the ground war ends quickly and casualties are low, we should see a drop in oil prices and a full economic comeback.

But my father won't be coming back—he's passed on. And I fear Pink Lindstrom will never return. When he left, Pink promised not to phone me. But in the early hours of Sunday morning, he called the station and left a message with graveyard shift. This message was for Midge and said only that he was boarding a bus and not to worry, everything was okay and he'd be in touch.

Midge found nothing surprising about Pink leaving word for her. "After all," she said, "I *am* the first friend he made in Coarsegold." Midge had stopped by the house to give me this news. "Anyway," she added, "if he's on a bus, we know he's safe." I looked up from my bed, baffled by her logic. "Number one," I told her, "we have no idea where this bus is—I mean, upon whose soil? And two, traveling anywhere right now—war zone or not—is dangerous and everybody knows it."

Just last week when Ward flew home from France, there were three separate reports of terrorism in international airports. Plus, Ward told me that trains carrying skiers to weekend holidays in the Alps were subject to delays while military personnel with attack-trained dogs searched the aisles. But despite this, it seems my husband is prepared to book a flight for those speed-skiing time trials. He hasn't actually said as much, and so far no Winter Olympics scoop has appeared in the *Coarsegold Register*. Still, I'm waiting . . .

Ward pokes his head around the bedroom door. He smiles, then steps in. "Try and drink this," he says. He sets an iced glass of Gatorade on the nightstand. Then he tears the foil from an instant energy bar and places it beside the drink.

When I was pregnant with Jen, Ward gave me thirty-two ounces of Gatorade and six energy bars a day. He used these supplements himself, claiming they provided extra stamina on the slopes. And, in retrospect—in utero—I think they might've helped Jen, too. Just to look at her as she hauls her bag off my desk—her sturdy, arresting legs, the steadiness of her gaze.

She nods over. "They're leading cheers for us tonight—the pep squad."

"Oh, sure," I tell her. I flap my hand over the blankets. "Now that you're winning, they'll climb on board. Those cheerleaders don't deserve you."

At my desk, Jen hesitates, giving a little shrug. "Have pity on them," she says. Then she turns to Ward. "Ready?"

"Ready, Hedy," he says, with a wink for me.

Gazing at Ward, I almost believe I could be that girl on his arm—that one who walked with him years ago, out the door and into the high school gym.

He hasn't aged. I doubt his blue eyes will ever fade. Nothing can keep his blond cowlick down.

"Get some rest," he says, leaning to me. "We'll be back right after the game." I want to ask, What game? Because he already looks Olympian, his body lean, with a racer's finesse—on his way to the Winter Games of '92. He is death-defying.

I nod up from the pillows. "Tell me again . . ." I slide my eyes from his gaze. "Tell me what you heard about foreign travel."

He holds my chin in his hand. "If you travel overseas," he says, "your chances are 1 in 650,000 of ever being killed by a terrorist."

Jen leans around. "I won't be straight home tonight." She speaks tentatively, as if she doesn't quite believe this herself. "There's a dance—but don't worry." She clears her throat. "Foster said he'd give me a ride."

I blink up from the pillows. I think of her locker, that shrine taped to the inside of the door. "Foster?"

"It's just a ride." Jen pulls her father away, her voice high and prissy. "Foster has a driver's license. He's got V.V.—and that's all, period."

I squint off, racking my brain for the meaning of those initials. But all I can summon up is our Family Life Committee and discussions about S.T.D.s. Finally I mumble, "V.V.?"

Jen nods as she and Ward step from the room. She calls back, "Vehicular Value."

I hear the front door close and then the sound of our Blazer pulling out of the drive. For a few minutes I lie taking in the stillness of this house—the only sound the muted running commentary of the war. Presently, Dustin wanders in and fumbles up onto the bed. A pile of newspapers crackle as the big dog stretches across my blanketed feet. At my request, Ward has been bringing home the *San Francisco Chronicle*, *Los Angeles Times*, and *Sacramento Bee*. I've spent part of every day in bed, reading from first page to last. I sleep with the television's continuous coverage. It seems I myself will never make a comeback from the weight of all this. I won't ever move on. Just struggling to stay abreast has laid me low.

When the ground war began, allied trackers still hadn't found any chemical weapon units on the battlefield. But some Pentagon officials believe these weapons are there. And so our troops have been readied. *A first indication of the presence of nerve agents may be an odor very much like that of broccoli or cabbage . . .* Warnings to civilians have been posted along the streets of desert towns: *If you are inside your car and see birds dropping . . .*

Yesterday evening, a Scud missile struck one of our Army barracks in Dhahran. At that same moment, a U.S. helicopter-borne maneuver —the largest in history—was droning fifty miles into Iraq. As one of our briefing officers announced on TV, "The pregame show is over, folks. Stay tuned for the Soldier Super Bowl!"

But judging by tonight's news, it's beginning to look more like a mop-up operation. I prop myself higher in bed and reach for the TV's remote control. On the screen, Iraqi soldiers scramble from a sandy bunker. They fall to their knees, waving tattered white flags over their heads.

Then the camera cuts to a young American pilot, just returned from a mission. "I honest to God thought we'd shot into the doggone farm," he says with a grin. "We had them dropping and running every which way. It looked like somebody opened the sheep pen down there."

At the station break, I sink back into the pillows. I hold myself perfectly still, as if my empty quiet will allow some revelation to enter. I want to understand these killing fields.

It appears there is no first line of resistance. Bridges have crumbled into the Tigris River and armored columns are crossing the Euphrates near the ancient town of Ur. The cradle of civilization is not civilized. Blood spills like the Red Sea. I shut my eyes and pull the blankets over my head, but there's no relief. The phone is ringing.

I stumble to my desk. It's Midge calling from halftime. She tells me we're kicking butt. I nod. She gives me the stats, which she's keeping. "Read 'em and weep," she says triumphantly. And I could truly weep, because I can find no revelation from this war, no foxhole conversion. Somehow it seems the harder this country fights to make the world safe for democracy, the more unsafe I feel.

On the other end, Midge keeps rambling. Her voice drops as she mentions a rumor that surfaced during the first quarter. "It's about some club Grace belonged to in college," she says. "Gay Life. But I don't think anybody will dare go after Grace so close to the end of this season—not as long as our girls keep winning. Besides, they can't just force her out because she might be gay."

Midge's words are climbing, working up. She gives me one of her committee chairman facts—90 percent of all sexual abuse is perpetrated by heterosexual males against minor females. She rattles this off in a smug voice, although it's a number I already knew, given my penchant for statistics.

"So," Midge says. "Would you fire all of our male teachers on the basis of that percentage—does that make sense? Then does it follow that you'd fire Grace Michaels?"

I gaze off, thinking Midge made a wrong career choice with pest exclusion. Trial law seems her true niche. "Of course not," I tell her. Even so, I recall the vague flicker of fear that rose in me the first time she mentioned the L word . . . and then the large anger I felt at myself.

"I'd never do anything to hurt Coach," I answer.

"I don't mean you literally," Midge says. "Not you per se."

Midge lets out a long, irritated breath. Then she moves on. I hear her supplying complete details of Ward's popular presence in the bleachers.

"I'd just like to know how you could allow this," she says, her voice loud in my ear. "I mean, letting him breeze right back here—smack into your life all over again. I just hope you're not still calling this mess a real marriage."

"It's not a mess . . ."

"Because you know what's happening to you," she says, paying no attention, rattling on, "I'll tell you what's happening. You've been doing this for so long, you're starting to turn into an old bachelor. You think I haven't seen it coming—think again. A dried-up old bachelor, that's you."

I listen, feeling her words score a direct hit.

"Your only sign of life is that half the town believes you're pregnant. And that happens to be a lie," Midge snaps.

I frown down at myself, my thin flannel nightgown. In my hand, the remote control lies small and black as a dead bird. "My true life . . ." I whisper.

"Which makes Pink Lindstrom your last chance," she says.

I shake my head, because there is no chance. The human heart can take only so much, and I surrendered days ago in Dorothy Bascombe's arms, at graveside, at the open door of Jen's locker. Call me a coward, but I cannot do one more hard thing, such as end this marriage of mine —I just can't.

"Midge, listen—" I cough to clear my throat. "About Pink and me . . . We're . . . Well, we're all over."

"*Over?*" Midge yells. "Let me tell you something, Hedy Castle—you're the one who's all over. You got that—just you!" And she bangs down the phone.

For a minute I stand clutching the receiver, hearing only the dial tone. Then I move for the bedroom closet. I rummage through my work coveralls until I find the paper Pink gave me on the night he left. The Marine's hot line number is written there. Below it, his rank and serial number. Following this, the address and telephone of his parents. I stare at their names, marveling at the solid fact of them—both of them still living.

Finally I dial the 800 number. Somebody will always answer, twenty-four hours a day, and I need to leave a message—a message, which no matter how afraid for his safety I might sound, no matter how painful to deliver—the listening party will surely interpret as Dear John. But I hear only a beeping signal.

I try again, remembering Midge's words . . . "Which makes Pink Lindstrom your last chance . . ." although, if you know anything about Midge, you understand she's an unreconstructed feminist who would never hold that a woman's salvation depends on any man. I dial another time and then once more. I'm certain Midge was referring to love rather than gender. And in this, she'll get no argument from me.

The telephone keeps beeping in my ear. It seems every Marine is busy—liberating Kuwait with incoming, outgoing fire, taking prisoners, mopping up . . .

I redial one last time. Pink's mother's name is Martha. I study the address, how she lives in Alden, Minnesota. Then a voice answers and says, "Pentagon family hot line, how may I help you?" I hear a woman speaking.

"Mom," I whisper and put down the phone.

In the bathroom, I open the medicine cabinet, wondering how it should happen that at my father's death, I have never felt so bereft of my mother.

The plastic vials holding my father's pills are still lined in a neat row. And on the middle shelf, the ones Tara left behind. Methergine for bleeding, Anaprox to stop the pain . . . Tara scarcely used them, young and strong as she is. One night's sleep, and she appeared good as new. But I am not good and will never be new.

I tap two Anaprox into my palm and move to the bedroom for Ward's Gatorade. The nightstand beside the bed is strewn with the clutter from his pockets—breath mints and French chewing gum. A tube of lip balm reads *soin de lèvres*. For a moment I let my eyes linger on the little Japanese pear sitting in the midst, still cradled in its white casing. Then I wash the two pain pills down with Gatorade and grab the instant energy bar. Before I leave the room, I turn the TV up.

I run the bath water hot and hard. It's been three days since I've washed my face or any other part of myself. And cleanliness is next to godliness, is what my mother said. I climb in and soak a minute before eating the energy bar. Most drug labels warn that pills shouldn't be taken on an empty stomach and I am one for following instructions.

Beside which, I wouldn't want to O.D. in this steamy water. Not that two pills alone would ever amount to enough. But I'm already feeling no pain, just sitting here, nodding along to the sound of the war wafting from my bedroom.

I hear Field Commander Schwarzkopf's calm, genial voice. It's a repeat of his earlier press briefing from Riyadh. The general is fielding a few questions. I ease down in the tub, listening for those lines I've already heard. "Has the resistance been light because the Iraqis are retreated," one reporter asks, "or are they simply not engaging you, are they surrendering? I mean, what exactly are they doing?" I tip my chin and wait for the chuckles I know are coming. Then, with expert timing, the general answers, "All of the above." And the room erupts —tinny as a canned-laugh track.

Then the noise fades, and I hear my own laughter clattering off the bathroom tile. But these are tears streaming down my cheeks. I look off, trying to compose myself, trying to focus on a plastic bottle of shampoo beside the bath soap. The shampoo's label says, *la ligne de bain pour l'homme.* But if this is a common French phrase, I don't recognize it; I can't understand.

I sink lower, my hands combing the bottom of the tub as if to find some familiar healing language. My father's last word to me was "trees." He officiated at our wedding—Ward's and mine. We stood before him with half the town packed inside the church. My father said, Marriage is honorable in all. And into this holy estate these two come now to be joined . . .

I fumble for a washcloth and drizzle warm water down my chest. My breasts appear much smaller than I seem to remember. I blink to clear my vision, deciding it could be just these slobbery, weepy pills I've taken, although I notice the soap is still true to size and floating, which I doubt could be a hallucination.

But to be on the safe side, I drop my bony knees beneath the warm surface, anchoring myself. I have this odd feeling that my body might ramble directly after my wandering mind. My mother should be here. I'm sure if she were right here, rocking me on this drowsy water the way she used to do when I was little—if I could feel her beside me now, I believe I'd find the strength to escape the rapid fire issuing from my bedroom, all those bullets ricocheting around me. I'd rise above my sold-out, shriveled self—this dried-up old bachelor I've become.

Instead, I'm falling. I drape the warm washcloth over my eyes and drift under, from top to bottom, dropping down, with all the questions circling faint . . . Round and round . . . Is she retreated . . . failed to engage . . . surrendered . . . I swallow my tears, my watery pride . . . I mumble, "All of the above."

Then, from the bathroom door I hear Ward holler, "Hedy!"

And quick, he's across the blue tile. He plunges to his elbows and lifts me sopping against his windbreaker, dripping over the bath mat.

He lugs me up the hall, into the bedroom, and lowers me between the dogs. "You fell asleep in the tub," he says. He shakes his blurred blond head. "Just a good thing I got home when I did."

"Don't mention it," I mumble in all modesty. It seems I've endured so many attempts to save my life that the entire process has completely self-effaced me.

Ward places his hand on my forehead, as if checking for fever. "God, I can't believe how much weight you've lost." He sounds truly awed. He dashes around the corner then returns, unfurling his words in a white towel. "Just lie still," he says. "We need to get you dry before you freeze to death."

I close my eyes and sink into the pillow. Please let it be known that at the chaste age of nineteen I married for eternal love. Throughout my childhood years—a period referred to as formative—I favored any and all stories involving the feats of heroic animals. My mother, on the other hand, was partial to novels featuring male characters exhibiting wild and adventuresome spirits. Not to excuse myself, but it's possible these reading habits have some bearing on the way I turned out.

Weakly, I hold my fingers up to Ward. "I think I O.D.'d," I rasp. "Two pain pills."

"You've got no resistance," Ward says, blotting the towel at my neck. "Corrine Simonet is absolutely right. Your dad's funeral—"

"His death." My voice gains a little with this distinction.

"It's done you in," Ward continues. "You need to take yourself off that committee and tomorrow won't be too soon. You're in no condition."

"Corrine said that?"

"You bet she did."

I blink up at the ceiling, remembering Midge's words: Your only sign of life . . .

After a moment, Ward moves from the bed and snaps off the war.

"Please . . ." I lift my groggy head. "Leave it."

Heavy artillery fire resumes as Ward dries one limp arm, then the other.

I nod over, my mouth slow and dry. "Did she tell you I was pregnant . . . I mean, Corrine—she thinks . . ."

Ward laughs, settling beside me on the bed. "Hedy, you are out of your gourd on those pills." He dips the towel into the hollow of my collarbone. Then he lets out a sigh. "Anyway, the girls lost to that half-assed team. The offense went all to hell in the fourth quarter. Tara Simonet fouled out and that little guard . . ."

"Rita," I say softly.

"She sprained her wrist. But Jen played like gangbusters—she's the genuine article, a real athlete."

"Such a credit to you . . ." I gaze up, attempting to bring some order to Ward's face. He appears to have two straight noses and one blue eye. "Ward, I've been wondering—I mean, have you ever considered . . ." For a moment I look away, then I plunge on. "Because sometimes the thought does sort of cross my mind every now and then about . . . well, having another baby . . ."

Ward sits straight and his features fall suddenly into place. "Hedy, come on," he says, tapping my chin. "We're way past that—you and I. Jen's almost grown up. Besides, you remember how lousy I was with babies, even my own kid." He lifts Bark from between us and drops her at the foot of the bed. I hear Dustin groan in his sleep. Then Ward runs the towel down my chest. "You know me—I never did get the hang of taking care of Jen when she was little. But tonight—I mean, just watching her play—now, that's another story."

I turn my face away, wondering how it could be lost on him—how the secret to the care of a child is in caring for the child—something that simple. He could go the rest of his life never understanding.

He cups my breasts, drying the pale skin beneath. "And you, too," he says, his voice softening. "Another story."

Across the room, the television flickers under my painless gaze. "This just in," a voice announces. "We've confirmed reports that early this morning, Arab allies entered Kuwait City. South of the capital, two divisions of U.S. Marines carried the day in a strategic battle at Kuwait's international airport . . ."

Ward bends over me, dabs the towel lightly between my legs. For a moment his hand lingers in the dark nest of my hair. "It's been so long," he says. "I'd almost forgotten how beautiful . . ."

But I'm scarcely listening. I raise up a little, squinting to see past him. The screen shifts to idling tanks and grinning Americans wearing Kevlar helmets and armored vests, rifles slung over their shoulders. Jubilant women cloaked in black lift a flag of green, white, and red. Bearded men kiss the Stars and Stripes and each other, kiss a camouflaged Marine.

Pink kisses me. But no—this is Ward leaning into my vision, his touch. "I've never seen a woman so strong . . ."

"The war's almost over," I whisper.

"And all the time you've been here," Ward says. He wraps me in terry cloth. "I never deserved you, Hedy. Not even at the beginning—even then, you were too good for me."

I sigh, nodding up from this soft white banner of surrender. "Everybody needs someone waiting back home," I mumble.

"Well, I count myself lucky," Ward says. "Just touching you . . ." He runs a finger down my cheek, then draws me close. "Next winter, God willing, I'll bring back a gold medal and give it to you, just for you."

But I'm waiting at home now—this minute—waiting for a girl who's wandered off with a boy of vehicular value. Beyond this safe place, it's dark and they are out there, riding around. There is no Jen forever coming home, climbing the stairs to her room—only me here, forever waiting.

"That's a promise," Ward says. I feel his breath, warm in my ear, then his mouth along my shoulder, at my breast. "Dear Hedy," he whispers. After a minute he shifts, gazing into my eyes. "Sweetheart . . . Honey, listen, I need to ask—are you still taking the Pill?"

I shake my tearful swamped head. "Only for pain."

"Well, you don't need to hurt anymore," he says softly. He takes my hand and kisses my fingers. "Just wait one second."

The bed creaks as he slips away. Across the room, I hear him rummaging through his brown flight bag—his carry-on, or *valise*, as the cultured might say. This is a word I know, but otherwise . . . Ward steps quietly over the carpet, opening a little foil packet. And I wonder vaguely, What is the French word for condom?

I reach for the blankets, thinking tomorrow I will telephone Dorothy Bascombe. I'll tell her that I've lost my child. I'll say this loss has drained me, but the ache is subsiding. She'll advise me to rest, sleep as much as possible. Yes, sleep, I tell myself. Sleep. And I close my weary eyes.

Somewhere far away, a light switches off. But the glow of the screen remains. People throng the streets.

"Hedy?" Ward says, but I can barely make out my name among the crowd. In Kuwait City, they're performing the wave, waving hello, good-bye. I feel only the slight touch of his hand at my shoulder. Flags are waving. "Honey?"

I drift off, pulling the blankets higher. But after a moment, a nagging question steals through my slumber. I toss in the pillows, casting about. It seems something's missing, a last word needs to be spoken here. Except I have no voice.

Or maybe I'm dreaming this hours later. Because the streets are finally empty. I'm dialing the hot line number. On the other end, my mother picks up the receiver. She whispers, *Semper fidelis*. Then she passes the phone to Midge. This is your final chance, Midge says. Answer correctly, and you'll improve your score by one hundred points. But you must keep your reply simple and direct.

And from the pulpit, my father speaks. He answers clearly . . . Those whom God has joined together, let not man put asunder. Then he adds without hesitation: The common French phrase for condom is *Après ski*.

Sixteen

Our Home bleachers are packed. At the gym's entrance, members of the Junior Achievement Club sit at card tables, hawking miniature Stars and Stripes for seventy-five cents apiece or two for a dollar. Business is booming—the noisy stands flutter with red, white, and blue. Before the opening tip-off—before a shot's ever taken—we're celebrating a win.

On Wednesday, our President declared victory over Saddam Hussein's army and ordered a midnight cease-fire. In a televised address, he reminded us that "winning is not the time to gloat." But we do, anyway. This cold Friday night, March 1, feels for all the world like 4th of July.

On the glossy court, Lady Miners take pregame warm-ups to the amplified beat of the ten-decibel band, Slaughter. Our team is still sporting patriotic patches on royal jerseys—and over each heart, a somber black ribbon. My eyes well at this glimpse of dark grosgrain. I blink down, past the open stat sheet on my knees. In the midst of this jubilant racket, it seems Grace Michaels and I share a hard silence. Coach sits gravely below, as if at a mourner's bench. Beside her, there's an empty space that no mere ball person could ever fill.

I look up, feeling Ward's arm slide around my shoulders. "They've got some bruisers," he says, referring to our opposition.

He squeezes me close in what I take to be a public display of affection. Tonight, we appear extremely married, and the very sight has left Midge disgusted—so much so that she's shoved to her feet as if to move to some other spot in this crowded gym.

I tug at her stadium cushion. "Midge, don't—"

But my voice is lost in the roar of fans as Slaughter fades and our feckless, fair-weather cheerleaders take to the floor. They strut clapping along the sidelines and the stands thunder:

We have style,
We have class,
We're going to kick
Iola's . . .

Down the row, Nekuda Adowa nods at the insinuated silence. As Midge sinks back beside me, Nekuda leans around. "Tonight," he says, "a must-win."

"Don't remind us," Midge mutters.

But we're ever aware, Midge and I. A must-win for our Lady Miners, and for those Iola Highlanders as well. Tonight, as they say in the big leagues, an entire season comes down to a final game. After the next forty-eight minutes of play, one of these teams will be bound for State Tournament. And so, with the boys' squads beyond any hope of the play-offs, all of Coarsegold appears suddenly riveted on this girls' contest.

Two rows back, Greg Simonet hollers down. "I told Tara if she fouls out tonight, I want her to walk off that court like a Christian."

He's speaking to Ward. Corrine Simonet hasn't directed a word my way since we climbed into the stands. Considering that Dorothy Bascombe is sitting right beside her, I'm certain Corrine's heard how I've miscarried the baby I never actually conceived. Even so, I sense Corrine staring down, still waiting for me to resign from our committee.

The bleachers quiet for our national anthem and Ward rises beside me. He stands respectfully still, facing the gym's far end, with his hand over his heart. It seems he's already climbed to the winner's podium, the flag unfurled in Albertville and snow falling from Olympian heights.

"When are you going?" I whisper as we reach the home of the brave, because I know it won't be long. Yesterday, the pre-Olympics scoop finally appeared in the *Coarsegold Register*, minus a byline.

"Later," Ward says, not looking over, "we'll talk."

Then, from the loudspeakers Paul Sitwell's voice crackles, "Let us pray." Pastor Sitwell gives thanks for our swift triumph over evil, the enemy slain in countless numbers and our own courageous ranks scarcely touched by the battlefield's scouring winds. He prays for our returning troops, for the safe return to families and solid American values. It seems our conflict in the Gulf truly was a holy war. Paul Sitwell's voice rises loud, calling us to a moral victory at home.

At the closing "A-men," our Home side roars, "We're number one! We're number one!" and the bleachers rock with the game's opening tip. My father no longer sits on the bench, but he told me once that the New Testament amounted to a covenant with God founded on love and mercy. Yet sitting here I feel only an almighty righteousness filling these stands—the vengeance of an Old Testament born again. Our national comeback.

From the first exchange of baskets, the game is quick and physical. Tara's counterpart—Iola's top-scoring forward—appears to possess far more than the little bit of meanness purported to be found in everybody. Plus, I expect this girl is looking to redeem herself, along with the rest of Iola's defending-league champs. The last time the Highlanders met our Lady Miners, they suffered a 12-point loss on their own court. Pink supplied me with the details of that contest. This happened only five weeks ago, but it seems light years—ages since I saw Pink's face, heard his voice—forever since he was here.

We've received no further word from him, neither Midge nor I. But I read in yesterday's newspaper that certain reserve units will be the last to leave the Gulf. It's possible that Pink is stalled on that clogged highway of death north of Kuwait City—caught with the smoldering remains of Iraq's Republican Guard and all the phone lines down. Or maybe he is giving me time to think, or just giving up as I have—surrendering to this New Old World Order. I'm prepared to entertain any speculation about Pink's silence, except the possibility that he could've come to harm.

Midge nudges me in the ribs. "Those officials better keep a tight rein, or this game will get away from them."

I nod, forcing my attention to the struggle at hand. I mark a Lady Miner turnover on my stat sheet, then glance down seeing Iola's big forward crashing over Tara's back for the offensive rebound. There's no whistle on the play, only Pink's replacement from the *Register* catching the foul in the lens of his camera.

"Hey ref," Ward hollers. "You got that whistle stuck in your throat?"

Behind us, Greg Simonet calls to the official, "Whose uniform you wearing tonight—huh, fella?"

Rita Avent takes the inbounds pass after Iola's basket and brings the ball upcourt. Rita is taped and wearing a wrist guard, but her fast, elusive dribble seems unhampered by Tuesday night's sprain. She fakes left, then right, and guns up a 20 footer that bounces high off the boards. Iola's weak side forward lashes for the loose ball, throwing an elbow that buckles Julie Dwyer to the hardwood.

Grace Michaels signals a quick time-out as the crowd groans with another uncalled foul. At the opposing bench, Iola's coach drapes his arm around his panting center, his free hand stabbing the air as if diagramming a play.

Ward nods to our bench and Coach Michaels in the huddle. "She's letting Iola walk all over us—what's the point of her being a dyke if she can't hang tough?"

I turn and stare at him, but he just shrugs.

"You know what I mean—we've got this woman on the ski team and she doesn't back off for a minute. It takes balls."

"You mean courage," I tell him, looking to the court again.

Iola has possession for a quick 3-point basket and a foul in the act of shooting. It's Tara's second penalty and too early in the game for collecting fouls. Tara shakes her head, glancing up the stands toward her parents. Then she moves to her place along the free-throw lane.

"Michaels ought to use her bench," Ward says loudly, as if he wants Coach to hear. "We need some horses on the court." He means Jen, still sitting in her warm-up jacket—one horse.

Greg Simonet takes up the call. "How about it, Coach," he hollers. "Can Jen come out to play?"

Tonight, Greg is more vocal than usual—partly due to this must-win game. But mostly, I think Greg is rising to the occasion of Ward's celebrity presence. Otherwise, I doubt you'd hear any support for my daughter. It seems she's been tainted—Jen has—by rumors of my adultery and near abortion, these rumors I myself spawned on a week called Ski and Skate, with Prayer Circle stationed on the grounds of that clinic and my father shackled to the handicapped rail. I freed my father. I spared Tara. But we still paid. And now Jen has lost her best friend. By order of Corrine Simonet, Tara is no longer allowed to enter our house. Tara cannot spend the night, can't drive Jen from practice and stay for supper, can't phone. I'm a bad influence and Tara cannot come out to play.

Since my father's funeral, she's dropped by our house only one afternoon. "Just to pick up a few things," she told me, when I answered the doorbell. She slid her eyes from my gaze. "My mom—" she mumbled, then stopped herself. Jen trailed her through the house, dogging her up and down stairs, lingering at the bathroom door, offering little scraps of strained conversation as Tara rummaged through the medicine cabinet. Tara left, taking every trace of herself—SAT study guides, two sweaters and a skirt she'd loaned Jen, red sweatpants, fingernail polish, prescriptions bearing her name. At the front door Jen said, "Catch you later." But Tara never glanced around. "See you," I called as she stepped down the driveway. It was then that I glimpsed her mother sitting behind the wheel of the idling white Subaru. "Later," Jen whispered, watching the car pull out. For a minute we stood in the quiet hallway. Then finally I moved to close the door. Jen nodded. "She's bailed on me." "Not on you," I said. I reached, catching her arm. "Oh honey, not you. It's because of me—because of what I told Mrs. Bascombe." Jen blinked toward the door, her face pinched as if with tears. But her eyes looked like this barren land of ours—dry and scalded.

Now Dorothy Bascombe is here in this gym—even here. Except I don't believe it's basketball that's suddenly drawn her. Tonight may be a must-win for our tournament chances, but for Grace Michaels there's much more on the line.

Midge still believes it's possible we won't see any serious trouble. "There's no law against joining some college club," she sputtered to me over the phone. "Plus, I figure if Grace is a lesbian, she's in the closet—at least in this town she'd better be—and we've got to hope to God she stays there."

From the left corner, Tara launches a shot that rattles the rim, then drops off into a bolt of arms. Chris Nye comes up with the rebound and lays the ball through the hoop. I note all this in my stat sheet as the home fans break their silence with whistles and a loud "Hoo-ah!" This is a yell I recognize from my many hours of television viewing, as our Gulf War expression of direct hit approval. But we've still got a distance to go before closing this lopsided score. As the buzzer sounds, ending the first quarter, the big red numerals overhead read, Home: 8, Visitors: 17.

"They're not letting us penetrate," Ward mutters beside me. "We've got to break that sagging defense."

I nod, leaning to Midge. "Listen, did Foster mention anything about coming?" I glance to the gym's double doors as if to see him standing there. It remains a mystery—whether that caped and camouflaged person known as The Wave is, or is not, Foster. But it doesn't matter. I feel the need of Foster's undisguised calm presence.

"He's with Walt," Midge says. "They're grooming Duchess for half-time."

"Oh, right," I mumble. Duchess is Walt's two-year-old Doberman pinscher and member of the Coarsegold Doberman Drill Team. At their first competition, this drill team won top Kennel Club honors in the Light Entertainment category. They're on the program tonight, volunteered by Midge's husband as a special added attraction for this last game of regular league play. And something of a closing tribute to our team and the entire season as well—this storied season, as Pink might say in his sports column, if we should make it all the way to State. If Pink should ever come home.

I take up my pen, seeing the Lady Miners hustling back on court for the second quarter—and Jen in the game with them. On my left, Ward has fallen suddenly quiet, as if his racer's concentration will keep Jen's eyes on the ball, set her feet firm in anticipation of the opposition's drive, send her arms high to block the shot.

And then the ball's in play, and her hands shoot out for an easy interception. Jen looks to speed the pass, but our guards can't shake the pressure defense. At the other end, Julie Dwyer's trapped in the corner. Then Tara pops free. She starts up the key as if to meet the ball. But just as quickly, she hesitates and drops back.

I stare down. Now that Jen's on the court, it seems Tara has stopped playing. All of a sudden she's abstaining. It used to look so easy—Jen and Tara on the give and go. Drive, dish, and deliver. Their 3-D offense, Jen termed it, grinning with confidence. But now I sense the tension, these two girls racing to avoid each other. I hear the tight, halting dribble, Jen calling, "Help," calling to anyone but Tara.

Jen crosses mid-court and pulls up, double-teamed and harried—at a loss. Frantic, she swings around, drags her pivot foot, and it's Iola's ball.

Ward slumps back with a sigh.

"What's going on," Midge says. "I mean, where's Tara?"

I glance behind me, up the bleachers to Corrine and Dorothy Bascombe. What's going on?—I'd like them to answer. Let them tell Midge how Tara isn't allowed—how girls must pay.

With six minutes remaining until the half, I mark another Lady Miner turnover. And I wonder: if I were to resign from our Family Life Committee, let it be known this minute—would Corrine Simonet lift her hand like a majority vote and send her moral victory signal down the bleachers. If I withdraw, will she lift the losing sanction and allow these girls to give and go?

"Midge, I'm tendering my resignation." I turn, nodding into her nonplussed face. "Effective as of now."

Then Ward groans, "Oh, God."

I look to the court, seeing Tara ram Iola's rugged forward out of bounds. The referee's whistle blows shrill at the flagrant foul.

"That's three on Tara," Ward says.

"Take her out of there!" This is Midge yelling—Midge, who has never once in her son's entire football career tried to tell a coach what to do.

"Listen, Midge—did you hear me? I'm quitting." But I don't look over, my gaze clinging to Tara as the scorer's horn sounds for the substitution.

Tara stumbles off the court. She appears almost dazed, sinking to the bench, blonde hair falling loose from her high ponytail. She presses a towel to her dripping face, and I wish my father were sitting beside her in his loyal Lady Miners sweater. I wish his comforting arm would slide around her. Instead, it's Coach Michaels who shores her, placing a strong hand at her back. And just then—with that touch—I see Tara turn, gazing up, up to her mother. And in Tara's eyes, I catch a look of dark surrender.

Three weeks from now, more or less, Tara will learn the outcome of her last, best effort at the SAT. This spring, she'll receive notification from the colleges of her choice—those sacred offices of admission. On June 15, she'll march to the strains of "Pomp and Circumstance" and graduate with honors. And this season—this game of basketball and hard striving, of painful, pairless abortion, of a white card signed and answerable friendship abstained, and an afternoon blood-stained, when she stood in her thick-stockinged feet and saw an upright man struck down . . . Three weeks from now, or this spring, or possibly June 15—this storied season may fade. But just now it is sore in her eyes, and I believe something far more threatening than foul trouble is bowing Tara's head.

"Anyway," Midge says after a moment, "your resignation is absolutely not accepted."

I ignore this, turning to my stat sheet. But I cannot bring myself to enter Tara's flagrant foul.

As play continues, Tara's replacement hits a driving lay-in from right baseline, then an off-balance jumper at the top of the key. Both shots leave this second-string Lady Miner thrilled with her unexpected success. The girl gives a little jump for joy, which is not cool. But her mile-wide grin seems to relax our nervous team. While down the row, Nekuda Adowa appears to have fallen instantly in love.

"Yes!" Nekuda calls to the giddy scoring forward. He leans out, smiling at Ward. Tonight, as if in honor of my husband's winter sports fame, Nekuda is decked out in a forest green Tyrolean hat and what must be the longest wool scarf in captivity.

Midge pulls herself straight and glances at Ward. "Allow me to introduce our exchange student," she says grudgingly—the first words she's spoken to Ward all evening. "Jean Pierre, otherwise known as Nekuda Adowa. Plus," Midge adds, "the spiritual son of Haile Selassie, Martin Luther King, and Mahatma Gandhi."

"Good to meet you," Ward says, shooting me an amused look. He smiles, despite these closing moments to halftime and a Lady Miner deficit of 15 points.

Midge turns to Nekuda. "This is Jen's father—a two-time and possibly two-timing record holder who, to the best of anyone's knowledge, has never been separated from his luggage."

"Ahh, Midge," Ward moans. He leans past me, winking at Nekuda. "Midge and I go way back."

"Too far," Midge says.

"So I see you went all the way," Nekuda beams.

Sometimes I do seriously question this boy's grasp of our language. But Nekuda has obviously read yesterday's newspaper, because all of a sudden he's thumping his wool tweed knees and singing in his clipped reggae rapper's voice:

> we be hobbin' and bobbin',
> strainin' and gainin' . . .

And with this fight song of the Jamaican Olympic bobsled team, with the buzzer sounding and flags flying, players heading for their locker rooms and one small boy rushing to hurl a quick shot, referees leaning at the scorer's table, and sixteen Doberman pinschers straining at the double doors to strut their stuff, the first half ends.

The Dobermans prance four by four onto the shiny court. Their nails are clipped and a silver choke-chain gleams at each arching neck. These dogs drill a capella. They know how good they are—trained to such crack precision, not one pair of quick yellow eyes looks over at the signal to about-face. They wheel as one, and without breaking stride, they thread the needle. The crowd applauds, but no proud Doberman acknowledges—every sleek head held aloof, ears pitched in perfect black triangles.

"I just wish Marshall was here," I whisper, poking Midge.

This is a sight Marshall would truly appreciate, given his penchant for the animal kingdom. Just yesterday—having climbed from my war vigil bed and once again on the job—Marshall handed me a newspaper clipping pertaining to the unspeakable fate of 440 creatures in the Kuwait City Zoo. According to this article, occupying Iraqi soldiers killed and ate all the gazelles, llamas, and African porcupines, in addition to every hitherto happy clan on display in the petting zoo. Among the two dozen known survivors, the Kuwaiti director of collections listed only seven monkeys, an elephant, two hippos, five lions, one wolf, and three Syrian bears. However, as Marshall was relieved to point out, our southern city of San Diego has offered immediate aid in rebuilding, including the gift of a rare Arabian oryx. So maybe there's hope—this generous gesture from San Diego could bode well for each and every famished, displaced person wandering the bombed-out streets of that liberated country. You never know.

"I believe Duchess has put on a few pounds," Midge says, nodding to the court.

I gaze down, unable to distinguish Duchess among the trim Dobermans streaming into their legendary double pinwheel. "Well, if she's gained a little, it certainly doesn't show."

On cue, the dogs spin from their pinwheel and halt at attention, facing our Home side. Then, as our applause straggles, the handsome Dobermans snap into their exit maneuver. They strut down the free-throw lane, two abreast, a flash of silver collars under the gym's bright lights. When they reach baseline and the basketball standard, the Dobermans peel off in singles—the blue metal pole separating them like that old game of bread and butter.

"They're just wonderful," I say, looking up as Foster squeezes into our row.

Foster nods, stuffing a dog biscuit into his enormous letterman's jacket. For a moment he squints to the overhead scoreboard. Then he settles his hefty frame on the bleacher and tosses a crumpled paper into Midge's lap. "This shit's gotta stop," he grumbles.

I glance at that familiar wad of white paper in Midge's hand, then I force my eyes below. On the court, the last Doberman to round the pole seems to have suddenly lost composure. The dog hesitates, sniffs at the metal standard, and lifts a lean hind leg.

Midge glances over. "That wasn't Duchess."

"Of course not," I answer. But my words are lost in the crowd's snicker, then the quick drumming of basketballs as the teams burst into halftime warm-ups.

Beside me, Midge is spreading the white Xeroxed paper smooth on her knee. This could be one more bake sale announcement, or another car wash—it's just possible. But even so, I want to tell Midge, Don't read this now. We've got a must-win on our hands, we're only halfway through. *Not now*, Pink said that night, leading me across the white-littered parking lot. I dropped the wadded paper down the dark underside of the bleachers. We need this win.

Regardless, Midge shoves the paper under my eyes. In vain I look away. Suddenly, all around me, fans are rising. I glimpse the crumpled paper rising, blazing white and born-again from the bleachers, blood rising. Flags are rising. The ball soars. We're number one.

A posterboard sign wafts high in the stands: IMMIGRANTS AND FAGGOTS, THEY MAKE NO SENSE TO ME. The words belong to heavy metal, Guns N'

Roses. Down the row, I see Nekuda cringe at the sight. In vain, I take the Lord's name. God give us strength. This country. Another sign thrusts up. GRACE, YOU'RE UNDER PRESSURE. The white paper says:

> TO ALL CONCERNED PARENTS AND LEGAL GUARDIANS:
>
> Your local chapter of Parents for Excellence in Education has learned of LEWD MISCONDUCT on the part of a staff member employed by the Coarsegold Unified School District. On Friday, March 1, A SIGNED COMPLAINT was filed with Superintendent of Schools, Jeffrey Siglar. In this complaint, A FEMALE HIGH SCHOOL STUDENT CHARGES TEACHER AND ATHLETIC COACH GRACE RENEE MICHAELS WITH IMPROPER PHYSICAL ADVANCES AND ACTIVE HOMOSEXUAL RECRUITMENT.
>
> As these grave charges come under review, we urge you to contact Superintendent Siglar at the district office (telephone 694–2811), plus our school board trustees (names and home numbers listed below).
>
> Our battle against the GAY RIGHTS AGENDA OF SEXPLOITATION must begin today. In the words of one committed Christian, "Homosexuals have hijacked the freedom train to Selma . . . That train never stopped in Sodom."
>
> DEMAND THE IMMEDIATE RESIGNATION OF GRACE RENEE MICHAELS. Send the message loud and clear—THIS EVIL WILL NOT STAND!
>
> Act before it's too late. YOUR CHILD COULD BE NEXT!

Midge jabs her finger into the paper, noting the date typed there. "That's today," she says. "This was written just today."

"Yes," I answer, because the timing's clear. Grace has had no opportunity to respond. Watching her at the bench, her arms strung around Tara and Rita Avent, holding them in the huddle, I doubt Grace even knows about these charges.

"Jesus." Ward shakes his head as he scans the letter. "What are they trying to do—sabotage the whole game?"

I open my stat sheet and turn to Ward. "This is about more than a game," I tell him loudly.

"Team!" girls shout from the huddle, palms stacked together in a handshake. Then our starters take position for the second half.

At the throw-in, I glance back, seeing the two empty seats beside Greg Simonet. I picture Corrine and Dorothy Bascombe moving methodically in the darkness outside our blazing, noisy gym. Tonight the icy parking lot is full, all the cars and trucks of Coarsegold frosted with this weather. Windshield wipers snap tight as traps over white papers containing Grace Michaels' name, a female student unnamed.

I rap my pen on Ward's knee. "It's about more than time trials or medals or playoff chances."

On the floor, Tara hollers "Switch!" But I hear only the sharp click of coat buttons against car doors.

"Hold on," Ward says, glancing over. He points to the letter in Midge's lap. "Don't take this out on me."

Tara's voice rises rough from below. "Get back! Get back!"

But I'm taking it all out on Ward, unable to shift my gaze to the court. I catch his hand, my fingers digging. "Listen to me, Ward Castle!"

"Hedy," he says quietly, as if to lower my sudden shouting voice.

But it's too late. I feel Midge's stare, Greg Simonet's gaze drilling my back. From the bench Coach Michaels swings around. She glances swift up the bleachers, eyes widening at posterboard launched again, this time for her full benefit. IMMIGRANTS AND FAGGOTS . . . I see her open face dim. Then slowly she straightens her shoulders and turns back to the game.

"Honey, please," Ward says, startled by my grip on his hand. "Don't make a scene here—honey, don't."

Finally I tear my gaze from him. The Iola Highlanders thunder downcourt on a drive. Dorothy Bascombe and Corrine stand at the gym's entrance, their parking lot Christian duty done. They linger, as if waiting for a break in the action before resuming their seats.

But there's no letup. Iola's power forward takes Tara into the corner, then spins away for a curt jump shot.

"Defense!" Corrine calls like a cheerleader from the door.

Tara's head snaps round, as if stunned by her mother's bright voice. Then she stumbles after the ball.

"There's more to this than you'll ever know," I whisper, releasing Ward's hand.

I enter Iola's basket, my head pounding with the words of that wadded letter. Improper physical advances, active homosexual recruitment—signed charges made by an unnamed student. Except I can name her. She's here on the court and among my statistics. These columns of numbers reveal a personal running account . . . Steals and Recoveries: 1, Assists: 0, Turnovers: 4, Field Goals Attempted and Made . . . Free throws . . . At the next column, my eyes stop. My hesitant fingers pull up, finally clicking the ballpoint. Here and now, I charge Tara Simonet with the flagrant foul.

"Somebody better call a time-out," Midge says, still frowning at the letter. "This game's just drifting away."

I glance up. The Visitors score flashes forward, as if those red-beaded numbers are on a roll of their own.

Our Lady Miners inbound. Rita Avent stutters the ball across the center line, her fingers crossed, signaling a back-door play. But Julie Dwyer's muscled on the crossover. She falls aside, tossing up a futile shot. Then Iola's beefy forward hammers Tara for the rebound.

"Hey!" a voice booms from the Home stands. "Is there a ref in the house?"

"Referee, hell," somebody shouts down. "We could use a coach."

On the bench, Grace Michaels doesn't look around. She sits motionless, facing the court as if transfixed. With five minutes remaining in this third quarter, Grace already seems resigned to a merciless rout —resigned to the charges, her resignation tendered.

Only Jen glances up, her eyes careful, as if avoiding the thrust of posterboard. She looks to the still-empty seats beside Greg Simonet, then to Ward and me. Finally her gaze slips down the row, coming to rest on Foster.

"How about it," a loud Home fan persists, "we got a coach in the house?"

"Uh, excuse me," Foster mumbles, prying himself off the bleacher.

For a moment I think Foster may be answering that call to coaching duty. He lumbers down the stands, pausing a moment behind the bench. Then he moves on. I watch him slipping past Corrine and Dorothy Bascombe at the door. Corrine gives Foster a little smile, then touches a pale distressed hand to her mouth as Tara's defensive assignment sinks a 3-point shot.

It seems Tara's playing it safe this quarter, wary of collecting another foul. Up and down the court, she backs away from the opposing forward's challenge. Or maybe Tara feels restrained by the constant sight of her mother standing just beyond Iola's baseline. Or it could be that Jen's painful gaze from the bench has finally caught her, or Coach Michaels calling encouragement, the clap of Grace's earnest hands. Grace, under serious pressure—a letter which she knows nothing about.

Only Tara knows. With a toss of her head, she shrugs off another Highlander basket, as if it doesn't matter. But her eyes flash at the opposing forward's cocky smile. The big power forward lopes ahead as our Lady Miners bring the ball upcourt.

Midge shakes her head at the maddening Highlander defense. "Wherever you look, they're in your face."

But Iola's number 7 allows Tara plenty of room. The girl waits, positioned under our basket, her taunting hands giving Tara the come-on.

"Tara's wide open," Ward calls, as if our offense can't see with their own eyes.

Just outside the key, Julie Dwyer sends Tara the ball on a skimming bounce pass.

Behind us, Greg Simonet hollers, "Put it up!"

Tara glances to the basket, hesitates.

"Shoot!" Greg yells.

But Tara drives.

Cheerleaders leap from the sidelines, kicking their sassy legs. "Sink that ball—all the way—all the way!"

The clock says a minute remaining in the third quarter.

Tara blisters the hardwood.

Under the basket, Iola's power forward cocks her chin and rocks back—come on.

Fifty-five seconds. But the drive seems to take forever, and Tara isn't stopping, only streaking head-on like a game of chicken. She plows the big forward to her knees, then wafts a shot off a little finger roll. Swish. The whistle squeals and Tara's cited with the charging foul. She nods, knowing full well. Iola's forward rises to her powerful height and grins over. "No basket."

Even I hear this, six rows up. I see the girl's wide orange hip checking Tara hard as Iola takes the ball on the penalty. Then Tara's blatant hand shoves the girl away. But the opposing forward lunges back.

"Hoo-ah!" a Home fan yells as Tara's elbow knifes into the girl's ribs.

Instantly, both referees are on the call, jammed between Tara and the Iola forward—that livid girl shouting at the top of her lungs, "Fuck you!"

The lead official jerks his thumb. "You're outta here."

He means both of them—two blunt ejections from this game.

In the bleachers, fans turn quiet, transformed to simple onlookers. Under our basket, Lady Miners cluster around Tara, shaking their heads and panting for breath.

Coach Michaels folds Tara's warm-up jacket over her arm and steps along the sideline. At the opposition's bench, Iola's coach sends his fuming power forward to the locker room with a pat on the rear. For a moment I let my gaze linger on that time-honored bench familiarity—the balding coach planting his nonchalant hand just there.

"Good riddance," Greg Simonet hollers down as number 7 strides away.

At the double doors, Corrine is leaned against Dorothy Bascombe. The two of them blink to the far end where Coach Michaels stands holding the royal blue jacket open for Tara.

And I do not know exactly what's expected of a girl admonished to walk off the court like a Christian. But the jacket hangs heavy. Tara raises her dull eyes, squinting at the score, as if to commit those numbers to memory. She glances to the bench, to her mother swaying at the distant end. But she does not look again to that spot where Grace Michaels stands. After a moment she turns away, moving up the baseline for the Home locker room. The bright clip that held her high ponytail is gone, her hair loose and falling. Her head is bent. I watch until she disappears, down that corridor to a room of cement showers, sprung metal lockers, wooden benches—a room where the game is told in echoes to a banished girl straining alone to hear.

The clock has stopped with forty seconds remaining, and I think when this third quarter ends, I'll head for the locker room and keep

Tara company. I'll tell her, Listen—this is more than a game. Grace Michaels is wrongly charged . . . we've got to stop the lies. I'll help you.

These are the thoughts streaming through my mind as the crowd sets to roaring around me. With Iola's top scorer out of the action and our springy reserve forward playing what tomorrow's *Coarsegold Register* will surely term "the greatest game of her young life," we appear to be putting a dent in the Highlanders' long lead. When abruptly the buzzer sounds, ending the quarter, 28–41.

"There goes all our momentum," Midge says. She runs a finger down my stat sheet. But I've stopped keeping track since the double ejection.

I hand Midge the stats and my pen. "Quick—help me out."

Midge speeds the ballpoint across the columns. "I don't think we'll take them in one quarter," she says after a moment. "But at least this loss is looking a little more respectable."

"*Loss?*" Ward says, flapping his swift hand at Midge. "We've got all the time in the world to catch up."

I study the red numbers overhead. Judging from the score, I tend to agree with Midge. It would take a non-stop fourth quarter rally to bring this game home. Or maybe the appearance of The Wave—just now, with these teams in their sober huddles. Foster did make that not-so-subtle exit, after all. But I see no sign of a caped figure—only Dorothy and Corrine stepping our way to resume their seats.

"So we don't make it to the playoffs," Midge says. "These girls have still chalked up their best season ever."

Ward grins. "Next Wednesday night—you've got my word—we'll be on that bus to State."

"Oh you." I laugh, struck by the sheer simplicity of this man's confidence, this easy optimism I've taken on faith—in the absence of faith—through all my married years.

"Such a dreamer," Midge mutters as she tallies a column.

I gaze off across the court. Eighteen years—in the absence of faith, in the absence of a marriage, I've called myself married.

"Go!" Lady Miners shout from the huddle. Then they break their handshake and step onto the hardwood for the final quarter.

In the absence of faith, it isn't so hard to live by conventions. I understand this—it seems the world requires almost nothing. In the absence of faith, it's possible to ride forever in the dark, to stand silent in a closet and never come out.

"Look . . ." I give Ward a little nudge, my thoughts distracted by the sight of Jen kicking into the air for a rebound. "Jen's in the game. She's playing the high post—and you know how much she hates that."

Ward nods. But he has no idea, sitting in these bleachers, so reassuringly self-assured.

With Jen on the court, I settle back into my seat. Any minute, The Wave may make his swing around the gym. Then I'll find Tara. I'll lead her from the locker room. And we'll come out with the truth—come out of the closet, Tara and I.

A cheer goes up as Julie Dwyer scores and the Lady Miners narrow Iola's lead, 32–43.

I reach for the stat sheet in Midge's lap. "How can it be," I mumble vaguely. Midge looks up but I'm not really speaking to her, only wondering out loud . . . "I mean, how is it that the very quality that draws you to a person is the exact same thing that leads you to leave him . . ."

Midge snaps straight. She stares from me to Ward. "You're *leaving* him?"

"Hold it," Ward says, glancing over.

There's a whistle on the inbounds pass, and I mark Iola's foul. I squint down the columns of numbers, trying to think, trying to believe my own ears. Did I say leaving?

Below us, Jen steps to the line and converts the free throw, her first of the night.

"Anyway," Ward says, leaning back on the bleachers, looking casual. "I'm the one who's leaving, remember?"

"Well, you are, yes." I cross my fingers as Jen dribbles the ball three times, then sets herself to take the bonus shot.

Ward touches my sleeve. "Although if we ever got some snow, I could—you know—stay home . . ."

Jen flicks the ball and it circles the rim—once, twice—then drops through. Somehow all this anxiety—Jen on the court, Tara in the locker room, Grace hunched at our bench—this worrying on three counts has spread the strain so thin, I feel oddly well balanced, speaking to Ward with the coolest equanimity.

"No, staying home won't work," I tell him. "What we need to do . . ." I lower my voice, glancing at Midge.

But Midge is paying no attention, concentrating only on the game. She groans as the whistle sounds. "Half our team's on the verge of fouling out, for God's sake."

"Don't worry, Iola's in the same boat," I tell her. I gaze up at the scoreboard—just under four minutes left, and we're down by 8. Finally I turn back to Ward. I lay my hand on his knee. I see now that my fingers are trembling beyond my control, but I try to ignore this. I give a weak shrug. "I think what we need to do is get a divorce."

For a moment Ward looks off, shaking his head. "Jesus," he says. Then he leans close. "Listen—I hope this isn't one of those extramarital deals. I mean, Greg did mention a rumor." Ward slips his arm around my shoulder. "Because if there's somebody else . . ."

"There's me," I answer, soft under my breath. Just me, I say to myself—and I'm coming out.

"Or . . ." Ward forces a chuckle. "Maybe it's only that time of month making you squirrelly."

"Could be," I answer, hearing my voice rising loud above the game.

Midge pulls herself straighter on the stadium cushion, fidgeting, glancing around. "Where *is* Foster, anyway?"

Below, the Lady Miners are suddenly on a tear, their shots falling all bottoms, blue jerseys soaring. Their hustle rocks the Home bleachers.

I slide out from under Ward's arm. "Or maybe I'm just whacked-out menopausal."

"Hedy, come on," Ward says, catching the sarcasm in my voice.

But I won't come on, because I'm coming out.

As the crowd cheers, Midge reaches over and grabs my hand. "Feel here," she says, touching my fingers to her forehead. "Honest to God sweat."

I squint overhead and see the game clock stopped for a Lady Miner time-out. There are thirty seconds left and the score reads Home: 54, Visitors: 56.

"I mean, think of what we've been through." Ward speaks close to my ear to be heard above the boisterous fans. "We've kept everything together for so long."

I nod, because it feels like forever *I've* been hanging on, holding us together. "Later . . ." I holler to Ward, as if I'm all the way across the gym . . . "we'll talk."

Behind us, Greg Simonet whoops at this down-to-the-wire comeback. Corrine sits tight beside him. Dorothy Bascombe holds a hand to her chest—I assume to quiet her racing heart.

"Sometimes you just need a couple of kids mixing it up," Greg yells down, "to set a fire under the rest."

Midge gives a snort, glaring straight ahead.

I flash Greg Simonet a peace sign. "It takes more than a fight to get a win," I shout up the bleachers. "And don't you forget it!"

"Calm down," Midge says.

And then I realize we're on our feet, gripping each other—Midge and I.

The teams set themselves for these last thirty seconds of the game. Grace Michaels stands beside the bench, her hair tucked behind her ears, one hand at the open neck of her green silk blouse. Ward is at my other side, braced against my shoulder. And Nekuda is standing, too—everybody standing.

We have possession of the ball at our end of the court. Iola's coach has primed his team, sending his quickest players toe-dancing along the sideline to pressure the inbound pass. Behind the line, Julie Dwyer casts about through a thicket of arms, then ducks the ball to Rita Avent. As Rita dribbles for the key, a harassing guard forces her outside. But no matter. Lady Miners swarm into position for their final play.

The crowd falls quiet, waiting. Iola presses even closer, but careful not to foul. I tighten my fingers around Midge's arm, thinking our Lady Miners will go to Julie for the shot. A veteran, she's strong in the clutch. Fifteen seconds. Sure enough, she's got the pass. But then all of a sudden it looks like Rita's play. Rita starts up from the corner to the ball. Julie fakes, as if to shoot, then hands off to the little point guard. Rita works the ball to the top of the key. Nine seconds. Under the basket, Jen and Chris Nye muscle through a blur of orange for position. The ball arcs, spinning with Rita's release, rattles the rim and bounces low off the boards. Then suddenly a sharp whistle sounds away from the ball.

The official signals the foul, his voice rising in the tight stillness. "Orange 19."

I lean to Midge, hearing such an audible sigh of relief from the bleachers, it sounds like wind in my ears.

Then my breath catches as Jen moves to the free-throw line.

"That's my girl," Ward murmurs beside me.

"She's shooting with the bonus." Midge speaks so quietly it seems she's afraid to even voice the words. "She could tie it."

I glance to the clock, seeing the game as good as over with one second left and the score unchanged, 54–56. Only these two free-throws standing between Iola and a win. Only Jen standing there.

Granted, I consider myself a fairly strong person. I've endured much over the past weeks. And throughout this entire heart-stopping season, I've attempted to remain calm—even here tonight . . . Tonight, when for all intents and purposes, I ended my marriage. I've tried hard to keep my composure. But I cannot watch my daughter alone on the line, awarded one free-throw, plus a penalty shot, with virtually no time remaining and our team down by two.

I ease away from Midge's grip and hand her the stats.

Ward reaches after me. "Stay . . ."

"I am praying for her," Nekuda says as I squeeze past.

"Thank you," I answer. I sidle down the bleachers, through the hushed Home fans. "Excuse me," I say quietly. "Pardon me . . ." Until I reach the floor.

I walk the long way around, keeping to the sidelines, not looking back. Jen will be wiping her nervous hands on her shorts. She'll blow a loose strand of hair from her forehead. I move through the far door. She bounces the ball three times. I hear this now—these separate sounds ricocheting from hardwood and booming thick down the dim barrel of this corridor, catching me halfway. She takes a deep breath; she concentrates on a spot just above the rim. Even here in the dark hallway, I see her. The trick lies in the angle of the arm, tension in the wrist, the touch of her fingers giving the ball its soft backspin.

And then the roar comes swift, rushing at my back like a flash flood. I cling to the door of the locker room until it subsides. 55–56. She is handed the ball again. In the taut silence, I hear a shower running, sizzling on cement. Then an ocean surges. She's tied the game. It's overtime.

"Jen," I whisper, my legs shaky with relief. "You did it."

I step into the locker room and across the cement, toward the drumming water. Tara's uniform lies folded on a bench. For these next three minutes and the one time-out allowed each team, I'll sit with Tara. I won't mention Coach Michaels—the charges. Only after the game is over . . . Together, Tara and I will come out.

No ringed, plastic curtains divide these showers. There are only girls here, and one cavernous communal stall. But as I peer inside, it's Foster glancing up startled—Foster, drenched and disguised.

"It's cold," he says, his voice bubbling under the rattling spray. His flooded eyes are dazed and blinking. He holds his palm under the spray, as if to show me. "The water. She was in here—I called 911. I thought the water should be cold."

"Tara—" I clamp my hand to my mouth.

"We need to keep her awake." Foster lifts his soaking gold cape from her curled form.

I drop to the cement, water streaming around my knees, gurgling down the big metal drain. Tara's head rests in Foster's desert-camouflaged lap. Except for thick red wrist bands, she's utterly white and naked. I scramble to feel for her pulse. But beneath my fingers, her wrist is torn and loose with red.

Above me, I hear Foster's chattering teeth, the scrape of his voice. "I used my socks for tourniquets, but she wasn't bleeding too much. And I think she took some pills, because there was this . . ."

Foster opens his right hand and a plastic vial rolls from his fingers. I stare at that white label, scrubbed and mealy from the wet.

"Please no," I whisper. I tap my palm against Tara's cheek. "Tara, open your eyes—wake up." The shower stings icy as hail, catching in her yellow hair. I bring both fists down hard on her chest. "Breathe!"

Foster fumbles for his cape, raising the slick satin like a tent over us. "I told them not to turn on the siren and to use the other door. The crowd," he says, his words falling low. "They should be coming. And I tried not to look at her, Mrs. Castle. Except for her wrists. And to see if she was breathing. And I only came in here because I thought she might be upset about getting kicked out like that—but only crying, you know. I mean, it was just a game. And now—" Foster's voice breaks, and I look up at his painted face running blue and gold, school colors bleeding down his boy's neck. "Now, I don't know if she's going to make it."

"She is," I tell him. I strike her still cheeks, once, twice, shake her pale, smooth shoulders. The shower beats heavy. I tilt her face, forcing all my breath inside her. Beyond the din, I hear the muffled cry of the crowd. They pray for the tide to turn, for their cups to run over. Everywhere but here, the dry land is waiting and people are thirsting, crying out for one perfect wave to carry them safe to shore. She cries —I feel a shiver stir her.

"Coach . . ."

My hands drop from her chest and I stare into her blinking eyes.

"Coach . . ." Her voice fades, riding low on her shallow breath. "Sorry."

"Tara, it's me—Jen's mother." I reach to cradle her higher. "It's Hedy. And Foster. We're in the locker room—the shower."

For a moment she squints off, as if struggling to focus. And I believe she sees the game. She hears the Home fans cheering.

"You hurt yourself," Foster says, his hand creeping cautious in her hair. "Any minute, they're coming."

Tara strains up at me, struggling to sit. Water runs from her nose.

"Breathe through your mouth," I tell her. "Keep breathing."

Her hand flickers toward me, her whispery voice gaining a little. "Am I . . . will I die?"

I shake my sopping head. And then the paramedics are here, entering through the rear door, unfolding a gurney. A quick hand reaches in, shuts off the shower. Two men, one woman, step inside. It seems before I can speak, they're pumping a blood pressure cuff around Tara's arm, finding a pulse at her neck.

Foster watches a moment, then turns to me. He tips his streaked chin. "I think the game might be over," he says in the slow dripping quiet. "But maybe I could hold the team."

"Yes, go." I grab his soaked cape from the concrete. "Go fast."

Foster draws the gold cape around his shoulders and squishes into his combat boots. For a moment he hesitates beside Tara. Then he steps out of the big gray shower and is gone.

The paramedics buckle Tara onto the gurney, her arm already threaded with an IV. As they wheel her off, I hurry alongside. I keep hold of her hand until we reach the rear door.

"Ma'am?" A paramedic gestures for me to step back.

Then I see Tara striving to speak. I bend close as the door swings open. The night air rushes over us. Wind gusts across the parking lot, sailing white papers. I hear a sound swelling. From the gym, it seems the lofty lights blaze brighter. The sound rolls louder. Foster is circling the court, once around, his dripping arms raised high. His face streams blue and gold, setting the moon and stars. He turns the tide and holds them all—the winners, the losers, Home fans and Visitors.

"Listen . . ." I nod down, squeezing Tara's weak hand. "Do you hear?"

She labors to lift her head, her lips groping. "Please," she mumbles.

I smooth her damp hair. "You mustn't worry—everything's going to be all right."

She turns her face away.

"We'll be there as fast as we can—Jen and I . . ."

Then I feel her fingers flutter in my grip. I lean closer.

"Please," she whispers, faint along my cheek. "Don't tell my mother."

Seventeen

I dreamed about a pure white ferret. I held this ferret in my hand, my fingers cuffed loosely around its neck. Then Midge called to me across the station office. And as I looked up at the sound of her voice, this ferret sunk its long sharp teeth into my index finger. I felt almost nothing, though the animal's razor teeth pierced all the way through the bone—pale incisors glistening with blood. I kept my hand—my whole self—very still, waiting for the creature to release me. I believed that if the ferret could withdraw its teeth swift and straight up, the pain might not be so great. But if the animal moved its sleek head, or wrangled against my hand in any way, then the ripping hurt would be unbearable. And I was trying to remain calm, explaining this to Midge and waiting, when I suddenly woke up.

This happened on Saturday night. At my blanketed feet, Bark twitched as if with her own bad dream, and across the bed, Ward slept slack-mouthed, snoring into his pillow. My finger seemed to throb with the memory of that nightmare, and I couldn't get back to sleep. I tossed, thinking of Tara still in the hospital—for observation, Dr. Vernon said. I pictured her lying in the same Sunday morning twilight, lying in white sheets and another blue gown, her wrists taped and finely stitched, her stomach pumped clean. I thought of how soon Paul Sitwell would step behind the pulpit to deliver his sermon titled, "Turn Your Scars Into Stars." This homily had come to him the day before as he sat beside Tara's hospital bed, gripping her hand in prayer. Reluctant to intrude, I'd lingered at the door to her room. I watched as the pastor interrupted his own bedside prayer. He let Tara's hand fall to the sheets, then he reached into his pocket for a small notebook. He jotted his sermon inspiration across a red-lined page headed: Preachables.

So it was a dream, plus these thoughts, that caused me to make my first migration through our dark chilly house, upstairs to Jen's room—from my bed to hers. "I had a nightmare," is what I told her.

The next night—close to twelve—Jen lifted her groggy head as I climbed under her covers again. "Another bad dream?" she mumbled. I nodded, although I couldn't recall anything specific that might've roused me. Jen thumped her pillow and rolled to her edge of the mattress. After a minute I heard her say softly, "She wasn't at school today—Coach wasn't." "I know," I answered, because all weekend Midge and I had been stopping by Grace's empty duplex and leaving messages on her answering machine. "Anyway," Jen added, "Rita's dad ran practice for us." I was aware of this, too. And I would've mentioned it at supper, except for Ward. Ever since Friday night's game—since I first brought up the subject of our marriage—these meals with Ward still seated at the head of the table are silent and strained. I also knew that Tara had been released from the hospital. She'd left that room without Jen so much as setting a foot inside. Where Tara was concerned, it seemed Jen wasn't about to relent. So at this late hour, I kept to my side of Jen's bed, hesitant to speak. Then, hearing her sigh, I crept my hand a little closer and said, "Don't worry, sweetheart. Coach will be back." Jen gave a yawn—too loud in the dark quiet. "Better get some sleep," she said.

On Monday night, I made my third trip upstairs—this time without any excuse. I found Jen awake and waiting. The sheets were turned down. She whispered, "Is your side too cold?" "Not bad," I said. I remembered how only three weeks ago we'd kept the furnace higher, when my father lay sleeping across the dark hall. "I miss him so much," I said. "Your grandfather . . . " I let my voice trail, aware of the guilt Jen still carried, how the mention of his name pained her. I felt the bed creak with her shiver. After a minute she whispered, "I miss them all." And then she said, "I'm freezing." I slipped my hand to her flannel waist, but she eased away. These days, she does not like to be touched. "Listen," I told her. "They're coming back." For a moment I closed my eyes, thinking of Pink. "Not Grampa," Jen said, barely audible. I turned to her. "But Coach Michaels and Tara—" "Not Dad," she whispered.

For a moment I sat up on one elbow, trying to see her face. I wondered just what Ward might've told her. That morning after Jen left for school, Ward had brewed another pot of coffee and poured me a cup. He sat down across the kitchen table and reached for my hand.

"Hedy," he said. "Darling . . ." He leaned to me, his eyes so earnest they seemed a darker blue. His hair looked darker too, deprived of the bleaching California sun—all those months he'd been gone. "You know I don't want to go away again. You do realize that, don't you?"

I glanced down to the table, our hands meeting in the middle, his thumb tracing my knuckles. "You mean not leave for good," I whispered.

"Listen, there's never been a time I didn't want to come back—not once," Ward said.

"But that's just it . . ."

Ward shook his head. "Try and see it my way. If I wanted things to be over—us to be over—would I be sitting at this table?" He straightened in his chair, his hand slipping from mine. "We've put in a lot of years, Hedy. You just can't walk away from that."

For a minute I stared into Ward's troubled face, wishing I could tell him that we'd been walking in different directions from the moment we stepped down the church aisle—all that time trying to maintain our marriage at some safe remove from our separate lives. But I believe now that every effort I ever made to keep our marriage out of harm's way also kept us from love. And I see that it's just not possible to hedge all bets, to cut our losses. Here I am—finally arrived at my middle age—and it seems the sum total of what I've learned is that there is a difference between loss and letting go.

Across the table, Ward sighed. "It's my life we're talking about here—I don't need to tell you." He cocked his head toward the window. "Everything's out there for me. Now I get the feeling that after all these years, you think I need to make some kind of choice. Is that what you want—are you asking me to choose?"

I set down my coffee cup and laid my hand on his arm. "Yes," I told him. Then I said to my husband of nineteen years, after all these years: "Choose life."

And so that night, lying in Jen's bed, I waited and wondered. Finally I heard Jen clear her throat. "There's one thing," she whispered, her voice thick with drowsiness, "Dad says if he makes the time trials, I can go to the Olympics." I shifted toward her, struggling to honor that little distance of white sheet she seemed to require. "Well, that would be nice . . ." For a moment I felt Jen's eyes. "I mean, really wonderful," I added. Jen nodded, her words falling quick and low. "Joint custody."

I'm not sure of the exact statistics, but I read somewhere that death comes in the middle of the night more often than at any other time. Maybe deep down, this is what keeps the drowsy toddler calling from a crib for one more bedtime story, another drink of water. It could be why the phone sits by the bed and the late, late talk shows stay up for us. But Jen and I have known grief at all hours, and these whisperings in the dark seem only the ministrations of death. Across the sheet's pale demarcation, we give soft halting voice to what goes unsaid in the full light of day.

Yet on this Tuesday night, I remain downstairs. I lie awake in my own bed and wait for dawn to lift. I tell myself Jen needs her rest. Tomorrow these girls leave for State Tournament and their first round of competition on Thursday. The Lady Miners will be sent off with a five-star pep rally. No ordinary school bus will carry them over the mountains. These girls—as Jen might put it—will be living large. Julie Dwyer's parents have provided their thirty-foot Winnebago. After school, this motor home will be idling in the rear parking lot, with digital sound blasting and a refrigerator stocked like a minimart. At 6:30 P.M., the Lady Miners will take their allotted practice time on the lustrous hardwood floor of Sacramento's Capital Events Center. They'll sleep two to a room in the River View Ramada Inn. Reservations have been made and all the meal money collected. In the continued absence of Coach Michaels, with Tara still sidelined and under further observation at home, and the whole town buzzing to know what on Earth . . . there are some few of us just trying to hang on for our Lady Miners and doing our utmost to attend to details and make the very best of things.

As the hall clock strikes midnight, I slide deeper beneath the blankets. Ward slumbers close beside me, his fingers curling, shuffling with the vague insistence of a sleepwalker through my hair. I suppose there are those who would tell a person like myself that the end of this marriage shouldn't be so hard. They could be telling me now, saying: Think of it this way—you can't let go of what you never had. But they'd be a hundred percent wrong. Out there—beyond this house—the world is groaning with the collected despair of people relinquishing their best, waking dreams. Every second of every minute, a multitude weeps. Everywhere—men, women, and children drop their empty hands—letting go of what they never had.

I glance up from my pillow—a soft rustle at the bedroom door. After a moment I hear Jen creeping across the dark room. "Mom?" she whispers. She gropes at my side.

I catch her hand. "Sshhhh. Your dad . . ."

"Mom, listen—I can't find my uniform."

I gaze off, my dull mind hunting. "I think it's in the dryer," I answer, soft as possible.

"Oh God." She drops her face very near, fine hair brushing my forehead. "You mean I didn't iron it?"

"In the morning," I whisper.

"Well, what if I forget?"

I ease the blankets away, careful not to wake Ward. Then I swing my weary legs to the carpet and lead Jen from the bed.

"Sometimes I get the feeling I'm turning into sort of an air head," she says as I move her up the hallway. Her voice is scratchy from the chill of this silent house, this wee hour. Her pink gown hangs crumpled around her legs—that flannel favorite, faded and finally too small.

At the foot of the stairs, she hesitates. "Anyway . . ." she gives a little cough . . . "when are you coming up?"

I snap on the light to catch her face.

But she sees me first. "Mom," she says, blinking in the brightness. "Have you been crying?"

I shake my head, habituated to lying as I am. "It's just my age." I dab at my weepy swollen eyes. Finally I mumble, "I guess I could come now . . ."

"Well, okay," she sighs. Her voice fills with such utter resignation you'd think this was all my idea.

I switch us into darkness again. "When you get to be a woman of my years . . ." I climb the stairs, feeling my way after Jen. "You fall asleep and everything just puffs up on you. Really," I say to her flannel back, "that's what happens."

I sense her quick shrug. "Maybe you should try cucumbers on your eyelids. Tara said—" She stops, as if to catch herself. Then we move into her room.

"Dustin's in here," she says. She latches her hand at the big dog's collar and drags him off her bed and out to the hallway. Then she steps back inside. "I couldn't even think about sleeping because of how he's always licking his lips."

"Dustin?" I squint to read her alarm clock—it must be after one, and I can't imagine how she'll get through six periods of classes, a five-star pep rally, and a thirty-foot Winnebago ride over a hundred miles of highway with eight crazed, keyed-up, and absolutely terrified girls. Like herself.

"Dustin—who else," she says, snapping the blankets straight, plumping the pillows. "You wouldn't believe how loud . . ."

I crawl under the covers. She sags to her side, and for a minute the night seems to settle darker over us. I keep my voice even, striving to match this somber quiet. "Your bed is very cold."

"Like ice," she says. Then she whispers, "Tomorrow . . ."

I nod. "You mean today—it's already Wednesday."

Her voice fades even softer. "Today . . ."

I turn to her, shifting onto my side. "Today—before I go to work—I'll iron your uniform."

Then suddenly her face wedges tight at my shoulder. My arms fall around her. I feel her breath shuddering through me. "Grampa," she whispers. Yet it seems she cries for everyone, for everything. And I can find no reply, except to hold her. I can't keep her from pain, can't spare her. But still she presses closer, her hands locked at my waist. There's a word for this—a word that means both to cling and to be split asunder.

And so we cleave to each other—Jen and I—cleaving as one, even while a new day steals slowly into the sky and every cell divides, and divides again as if from the womb, cleaving us apart.

A few years back, our California Department of Health conducted a study which resulted in forty-six stapled pages documenting the dangerous nature of domesticated ferrets. The study was sent to us here at the border station and filed under "Ferret Exclusion." This afternoon, while waiting for Midge to relieve me from duty, I've used our office machine to copy a section of historical background from the document. This section includes the account of a London doctor, dated 1834.

Perhaps, as Marshall claims, I truly am in a severe state of anxiety—my mind fixated on ferrets, even with the school pep rally scheduled to get under way in one hour and both Tara and Coach Michaels still absent, plus no sign of the spiral-bound notebook in which I keep the stats—that notebook last seen in Midge's lap. Midge claims she gave the missing stats to Coach after Friday night's game. And there's the problem. Such a complete record of individual performances would certainly be helpful to our interim coach Sylvestro Avent. Besides which, I do absolutely need that notebook for tomorrow night's play-off.

I step into the truck lane and shove the historical account under Marshall's eyes. "Read this," I order.

"For Pete's sake," Marshall says. He waves the report away, just as I figured he would. Marshall claims he has no time for all the mailings that come to us as a government agency. But the fact remains—given his soft heart, Marshall has no stomach for the ugly truth.

So I read out loud and fully determined, trailing him to a linen supply truck . . .

" 'Some few years ago, a poor mother, holding a mangled infant in her arms, rushed screaming with fright into my house. The woman implored me to save the child's life, who, she said, had been nearly killed by a ferret. The infant's face, neck, and arms were dreadfully lacerated, the jugular vein had been opened, as also the temporal artery; the eyes were greatly injured, and indeed the child, who is still living, has lost the entire sight of one of them, and has very imperfect vision in the other . . .' "

I tap Marshall on the shoulder. "Are you listening to this?"

Behind the wheel of the linen truck, the driver mumbles, "I am."

"Good," I tell him. I glance up, seeing Midge pulling in to replace me. Then I return to the page. " '. . . Having stopped the infant's still bleeding vessels, I accompanied the mother to her cottage. Upon entering, the child began to cry piteously. Instantly the ferret was seen rushing from behind some bavins—' " I nudge Marshall. "I believe this means firewood. But whatever . . . 'the ferret was seen rushing from behind some bavins, where it had taken shelter. The animal, of large growth and much distended with the infant's blood, came boldly forward. In the middle of the room, the ferret met the fearful parent still holding the infant in her arms. When I set about kicking at the creature, as the first impulse of protection, the ferret endeavored to seize my leg. Not until the animal's back was broken by repeated blows did the ferret give over its earnest and reiterated attempts to renew its sanguinary feast . . .' "

For a moment there's quiet. Then Marshall turns slowly from the linen truck. "Honest to God," he mutters. "I could've gone my entire life and never once regretted not hearing that."

"Well, there's your whole trouble," I snap back.

At the truck's window, the driver gives a weak nod. "Anyway," he says, "I heard those killer bees are on the march again—all the way across the Texas border."

Midge heaves a shrug as she steps alongside. "If it's not one thing, it's another."

"Please relieve her," Marshall says, jerking his thumb my direction. "Right now, *please*."

But I'm already hurrying away. I check my watch, then climb into the Blazer. It occurs to me that if I forego stopping at home to change clothes, I'll have enough time to give Grace Michaels' duplex another try and still make the pep rally.

"I'll call you later," I yell, honking to Midge. Then I'm off, with the cold air streaming and Jen's ironed uniform seesawing from a hanger at the backseat window.

Of course, I don't actually expect to find Grace home. But regardless I pull up to the curb, feeling some little hope. For a minute I sit gazing out at the empty driveway separating those duplexes, the drapes on every window drawn. Then I trudge up the front walk.

I knock at the flimsy door of 220-A, then try again. I check Grace's mailbox, as if to find the missing stats crammed there. Then I pull off my thermal-padded gloves and rap louder. Standing here, large and reinforced inside my official Department of Agriculture coveralls, I believe I could break through this door single-handed. And it's seriously crossing my mind, when I spot a white envelope wedged at the corner of Grace's rubber doormat.

I glance to the adjoining duplex, in case anyone might be watching. Then I bend, lifting the rubber mat. As I snatch up the envelope, I feel my blood rush—the adrenaline of a criminal. A brass key lies in the square of fine dirt left under the mat.

I'm doing this for the good of our Lady Miners—that's what I tell myself as I curl my fingers around the key. There's a state championship on the line here. At a time like this, Grace would want us to have the stats.

Somehow it's reassuring to be dressed in my official attire while breaking and entering. There's a certain added authority. Plus, I feel a little less culpable, seeing that Grace has left a spare key in such an obvious and naive place.

I slip the white envelope into my pocket, then I turn the key in the lock. At my touch, the door swings open. I step inside, already hunting that notebook. The duplex is small and sparsely decorated. But then, a first-year teacher's salary doesn't allow for much more. In the living room, Grace's gym bag sits empty on a plaid sofa. Her silver whistle gleams beside books scattered over the coffee table. My gaze wanders across John Wooden's *Winning Basketball*, an illustrated copy of *Black Elk Speaks*, and a thick paperback called *The No-Nag, No Guilt, Do It Your Own Way Guide to Quitting Smoking*.

I stare at this last book a moment, then slide it off the table. I notice from the worn cover that the book was formerly titled *The Smoker's Book of Health*. "Grace?" I whisper. I return the paperback to its place, thinking: Grace Michaels, coach and instructor of physical education . . . Grace, 1988 Coe College women's softball champ . . . Grace, a smoker?

But in the kitchenette I catch the stale smell of tobacco. And on the kitchen counter, in Grace's handwriting, I find a list headed, Ten Good Reasons To Quit!

For a minute I lean at the counter. I straighten a pile of clipped coupons and remember that grand opening—my father taking those little slips from Grace's hand, how he folded them like cash into his empty wallet. Then I scan Grace's quit smoking list. Reason number 3 says, "I want to set a good example for my students, especially the team."

As I turn from the counter, I pull the white envelope from my pocket. The envelope is unsealed and addressed simply: "Grace M." Inside, I glimpse a blue pamphlet, the words, "Hope for the Sinful Homosexual." I take out the pamphlet and read an attached stick-um note that states in a careful, flowery hand: "Remember, only our Lord possesses the power to transform the emotions and rearrange the hormones . . ."

I fold the pamphlet back into my pocket. Then I step down a narrow hall to Grace's bedroom. The faint smell of tobacco trails me—an odor I would never in this world have considered heartbreaking. But I can't stop thinking how a young woman, so harassed and persecuted, should take herself to task for setting one poor example. I keep thinking how guilt and shame are heaped.

Gold trophies crowd Grace's bedroom dresser. The stats lie on her nightstand. I grab the notebook and sink with relief onto the edge of her bed. I'm tempted to call Midge immediately and give her the good news. Grace's phone is on the nightstand, just inches from my elbow—and beside the phone, an answering machine blinking urgent red.

For a moment I sit clutching the stats in my lap. I debate just exactly how much is going too far, even for a nervy trespasser such as myself. Then I fumble for the machine's flashing red light. I press Play . . . "Play ball," I say to myself. But this is more than a game. The beep of the machine deletes no obscenity. "Fist-fuck," I hear, and "tongue slut." People call and call, "Resign . . ." "If that girl dies . . ." "Cunt sucker . . ."

And I remember how, at our last Family Life Committee meeting, Angela Tucker handed out that analysis of 2 Live Crew's, *As Nasty As They Wanna Be.* Angela had taken such pains to catch each and every alarming word. I figure she suffered no end for the sake of our children, playing those songs over and over. But the words recorded on this answering machine aren't shouted from the mouths of outrageous performers looking to shock and rake in an easy buck. These are citizens of my town talking—I know some of them by voice alone. And I wish Angela were listening with me. Somebody should be sitting here with a pencil, censoring these censors. Because these people appear to have no limit, they're as nasty as they want to be.

So it's something of a relief when the superintendent of schools abruptly identifies himself and states the time and date of an emergency school board meeting—Grace's presence required. And I welcome the respite of Midge's calm encouragements, followed by my own echoing words. Then—wonder of wonders—someone named Izzy calls from Iowa and says everybody's still on for Yosemite the last week in June. Then a mature voice breaks in, registering a mother's eternal complaint. "Your phone's busy day and night . . ." I nod, because this is obviously no exaggeration . . . "Anyway, about Jill's birthday . . ." But at the next sound of the tone, comes "Bitch!" And then mercifully —the soft, halting voices of girls. I lean to the machine, picturing them on the line—every team member but Tara, passing the phone, speaking one after another, from guard to forward to center. I catch Jen's voice . . . "Coach, everybody— Well, we love you, Coach." Then all together . . . "Come back, Coach," they say from their huddle on the other end. "Take us to State." And I'm unable to listen anymore. I reach to stop the messages, only more obscenities streaming now. And reporters calling, too—news hounds looking for a scandalous scoop, weighing in from as far as San Francisco, Santa Barbara . . . Yuma . . . "I'm still in Yuma," Pink is saying. The notebook slides onto the carpet. I press Rewind, backing up for fear I'll miss a word. ". . . still in Yuma," Pink says, "but I phoned the paper and they told me how hard the team played, and I know how hard for you . . . Grace, hang in, okay? Hold on. God, I wish I was there—all this paperwork just to come home. But don't let them keep you away from State. And tell the team congratulations, tell everybody good luck. And if you could, give Hedy Castle a message from me—please say, O-K-L-F-M-N-X . . . And I guess that's all, except try and stay tough. Stay strong . . ."

I turn up the volume, then rewind to hear his voice again. His words fall over me. He speaks my name and I close my eyes. He is safe.

Then the machine gives its rude beep and I push from the bed. Grace's clock radio says 2:40—still time to make the pep rally. Quickly I bend for the stat sheets. But before I leave, I move to the answering machine and I press Erase.

I step out of the duplex and tear a blank stat sheet from the notebook. I sit on the concrete step, scribbling in a rush: Your mother called—Jill would definitely prefer the green over the mauve for her birthday . . . Izzy says everybody's on . . . I dash my ballpoint down the page. The Lady Miners—your team . . . Pink Lindstrom says . . .

At the end of this list, I jot my own message. I give Grace the team's practice schedule, the name of their motel, their play-off time. Then I fold the message sheet inside her mailbox. After the rally, I'll make a phone call and deliver everything again on that answering machine, just to be sure.

I slip the house key under the mat and start down the walk. Then I stop and turn back for the mailbox. To the long list of messages, I add: P.S. Good luck quitting smoking—I'm keeping my fingers crossed.

The band plays "El Capitan," and Ward's still saving me a seat. At first glance, I can't see that much has changed since my own high school pep rally days. Except no butcher paper banner ever hung above our bleachers, declaring in red, white, and blue: Victory! Peace! Pride! But otherwise, the gym is festooned in all the old familiar crepe paper ways.

Team parents sit directly behind the empty Lady Miners bench. I scan our row, noticing that Greg and Corrine Simonet are clearly not among us. In the bleachers above, rowdy juniors and seniors occupy the privileged Home side, while those underclasspersons are jammed opposite, relegated to Visitors. School principal, Bob Ledbetter, stands at the big double doors, his feet spread wide and arms folded across his chest. As is the case with so many administrators, this bulky, knit-shirted man is an ex-football coach. I seldom see Mr. Ledbetter without imagining what a successful career he might've had in the areas of personal bodyguard or home alarm systems. He appears always to be expecting trouble.

But today, sinking onto this bleacher, I sense something too—not trouble so much as a buzzing tension in the stands. All week, excitement's been building for our trip to State. And all week, the word has been out about Foster finding Tara in the locker room and how Coach Michaels has disappeared. Plus, by now I'm sure the whole town's read that Xeroxed letter. So I don't know if it's support for the Lady Miners, or just all-out curiosity that's filled this gym with so many extra people from our community—not to mention a few journalism-type strangers lurking at the sidelines.

Only our superintendent of schools—that leaver of abrupt messages on answering machines—that man is conspicuously absent. Never mind that it's been four years since we've sent a team—male or female—to state championships. With the pressing demands for Grace's removal, I suppose Superintendent Siglar is feeling the heat of his position. So this afternoon he's steering clear—his politically expedient absence not to be confused with cowardice.

After a slight pause, the band lurches into the theme from *Rocky*. Our cheerleaders bounce across the court, their blue skirts flipping short and gold body suits clinging and riding the curves high or low, depending. Somehow I don't believe we ever truly comprehended in my time the exact meaning of hard bodies.

Ward leans close and familiar, as if nothing at all has transpired between us this week. He speaks loud, to be heard above squeaking clarinets and a final crash of cymbals. "Tara's here," he says.

I blink toward the the door leading to the Home locker room—that far corner from which our team will emerge to a hero's welcome and a warrior's send-off.

"She was in her third period class today—Foster told me."

I nod, because I know what this means. The Miners' handbook states that in order to participate, an athlete must attend at least half of his or her classes on the day of a sports event or team travel. This eligibility rule is part of our school district's efforts to elevate scholarship above athletics—we're trying hard to put learning first.

At center court, our cheerleaders flounce their shaggy pom-poms, coaxing the raucous student body. "Give us an M!"

"Of course, Tara won't be able to play," Ward says.

I know this, too. What I can't understand is why Tara would risk the open stares of this crowd and her teammates to be here today. My only guess is that pride has brought her. But then, pride can sometimes be a form of shame. Or it could be her stubborn persistence—a quality I've watched all season long on the basketball court and in my own house, Tara's head bent for hours over those practice tests. Of course, this was before . . .

"Give us an I!"

The crowd's deafening answer falls from the bleachers, and I gaze off, away from the sound. On Friday night, Tara swallowed—as close as I can count—thirteen pain pills of minimum strength. Then she sat on a locker room bench sipping a 7UP—until she felt her mind begin to drift. This is what I've come to understand must've happened.

"Give us an N!"

Until after a minute or so, the game faded entirely and Tara no longer saw Grace Michaels standing at the sidelines. She also lost the sound of her mother's voice, but I believe she still carried with her some church words that had come to her a few days earlier while taking a shower. And she did not want to ruin her uniform or the number she'd been wearing on her jersey since junior high—this number she considered lucky. She'd never in her life used alcohol, and she hadn't once seen her parents touch a drop. But she'd offered both her breasts to a boy who did. Drink. And on those dark nights he nursed at her nipples—nursed his penis slowly inside her. But then, he came very fast. And it felt like—well, she didn't know. But she still got pregnant.

"Give us an E!"

So she had the abortion, and then—this is my own opinion—she learned everything that should've been put first. This new knowledge was not hard won, only hard. On that same day, she watched my father die. And she lost blood. But she didn't want to ruin her uniform.

"Give us an R!"

So she removed her jersey, her shorts—she took everything off, as if she was going to bed. She folded her clothes on the locker room bench. And she wondered vaguely if she could be dead drunk, though she'd never swallowed alcohol, just pills. But Dr. Vernon said the pills were what kept her alive, because her fingers fumbled weak, and the double-edged razor blade which she'd bought especially never got very far.

"Give us an S!"

So she wasn't bleeding profusely, only stumbling into the locker room shower where she'd first thought of the words. For a minute she got mixed up with the hot and cold. And then, when she felt the water as good as she could get it, when she went to speak the words she'd carried with her—the ones she wanted to say right at the end—she discovered they'd entirely escaped her.

And I feel quite certain this happened, because after her stomach was pumped and her wrists stitched, she mumbled into my ear that she wanted to see God. Outside, her parents were fairly storming the door to enter the Emergency Room. But I'd arrived first, before the curtain was drawn separating her bed, before those urgent procedures had begun. So, for the next twenty minutes the Simonets were forced to wait outside. If I'd been in a position to do so, I would've kept them away forever. But I did finally open the door just a crack to offer an update. "She wants to see God," I told them. And I shut the door.

"What does it spell!"

I was at the Emergency Room door only a moment. When I stepped back across the room, the nurse was opening the curtain, sliding it along the metal track above Tara's bed. Maybe it was this sight, or the sound of the curtain's silver rings that prompted the forgotten last words to return to Tara. Perhaps she still believed death was near. Regardless, both the nurse and I distinctly heard her fully conscious voice. "And after my body has been destroyed," she whispered, "yet in my flesh I will see God."

Our cheerleaders cartwheel off the court to the roar of "Miners!" Then the stands rock with the rhythmic stamp of feet and the call rising "Mi-ners, Mi-ners . . ."

At this point in the rally, it's customary for the team's coach to bring out all of his or her players. I look for Grace, thinking there could be a chance. She was the one, after all, who told Jen about playing to the pain—how sometimes it doesn't hurt quite as much if you go right back onto the court.

For a minute my gaze moves to every door and wanders the stands. Then my eyes catch. In the bleachers, I spot Greg and Corrine Simonet sitting way up on the Visitors side, with their freshman son James wedged between them. From that far remove, they appear to be hunting Grace, too, their heads turned and craning.

But it's Rita Avent's father who steps to mid-court. He speaks into a cordless hand mike, which seems an amazing technological advance for our budget-crunched school, and a little daunting to Sylvestro Avent as well. Mr. Avent sees these students every day as he makes his maintenance rounds. But this afternoon he appears overwhelmed by the murmuring and expectant crowd—his new role as acting coach. He pulls at his unaccustomed necktie. Today, the chain dangling from his trouser pocket isn't a loop of keys to this building, but his rosary and the glint of a crucifix.

Sylvestro clears his throat, and I strain for his voice. But from his low rush of words, I hear only "Miss Michaels . . ." And then a long, uneasy pause . . . a little cough.

Finally, with a flourish of gold cape, The Wave dashes to mid-court, preempting his own scheduled appearance. The student body whoops as Foster lifts the hand mike closer, catching Mr. Avent's words. The sound comes clear but still quiet, hushed as a prayer—each name he speaks a bead on his rosary.

And suddenly they're streaming onto the court—our Lacy Miners racing one by one as their names are called and we are all standing, cheering and whistling and the band is playing our rousing fight song, which sounds exactly like "On Wisconsin" without the words. But it doesn't make a bit of difference. No matter that some might do it better . . . Gulf heroes ticker taped down Park Avenue . . . In Hollywood, all the big stars on hand and perfectly turned out to hail the troops on Rodeo Drive . . . Sleek jets spewing vapor trails of red, white, and blue over Pennsylvania Avenue . . . I am overcome by the sight of these girls lined on the court, all royal blue and gold in their warm-ups. These girls standing straight and still, hands linked behind their backs as if at attention.

The crowd quiets as the final Lady Miner is introduced. Parents settle back onto the bleachers, clutching Instamatics and camcorders in their laps. But Ward is still on his feet. I stare as he hauls up his relic letterman's jacket.

"They asked me to say a few words," he says, shrugging into the jacket. "I found this in the closet and I thought—well, for old time's sake . . ."

Even as Ward speaks, his name is announced, a local hero coming back to inspire his daughter's team—these play-off athletes of his alma mater.

He steps from the bleacher, his jacket trailing the scent of mothballs. But all the pins on the pockets, shoulders, the chest—everything still glitters gold. And the jacket still fits.

Ward takes the mike, and I hear his rallying words echoing, stirring this assembly. He's a natural born speaker and a born winner. He's been on the victory stand and on the public address countless times before. His words and his downhill races are record-breaking short and sweet. He says, "If you fall behind, just stay in the game—hustle. Don't defeat yourselves. Remember, in order to lose, somebody's going to have to beat you." He turns, nodding to our Lady Miners. "And if you keep that number one attitude, *nobody* ever will."

The crowd claps long and loud, and I wait for Ward to return the mike to Sylvestro Avent. But he still has the floor as the applause subsides. "Tonight," he says, raising his hand for complete quiet, "tonight I'll be in San Francisco, boarding a plane to begin a journey that I hope will end this time next year in Albertville, France, and the games of the 16th Winter Olympics. So I won't be here to see you take your winning season to State. But in my heart, I'll be with you every step of the way, from the opening tip-off to the final buzzer. And together—tomorrow and a year from tomorrow—together, we're going to bring home the gold. And Hedy . . ." He pauses as the cheering straggles off . . . "Hedy, we need you to come out here now." Ward waves for me, then grins up to the bleachers. "She wasn't expecting this."

I shake my head, because no I wasn't and no, I haven't the slightest intention of walking onto that floor in the middle of this entire student body. With the exception of my high school graduation, which took place right here during ancient times, I have never set foot anywhere near a live microphone. But then, Margarita Avent is leaning down the bleacher to give me a push, and a few conscientious students are reflexively clapping, just to be nice, because that is their hapless lot in life, trying always to be nice. And then Nekuda Adowa, with his dusty dreadlocks and eternal Haile Selassie sweater, offers me his arm.

Ward chuckles into the mike, crooking a gleeful finger at me And I realize there's nothing in the world I'd rather do than impale this man completely through his lean hard body with one of his own aerodynamic ski poles. But finally, with utter loathsome resignation, I set my teeth, lurch to a standing position, and grip Nekuda's ragged, immutable sleeve.

As we approach mid-court, Ward reaches out, drawing me into the center jump circle. "These girls have a little something," he says, off mike and confidential.

I turn to the team, and up and down the line they're giving me knowing smiles—everybody except Jen, who's playing it self-consciously cool, what with my being her mother. Plus Tara, who won't even look, although I catch the scent of her cologne, a little too strong, and the showy gold ribbon holding her hair, tied a little too big—just every little thing, trying way too hard.

Julie Dwyer and Rita Avent, team co-captains, step forward. They share the mike. And what poise—these girls—so self-possessed. Standing between them in my bulky border station uniform, I wish I'd had the sense to drive straight home and change into presentable clothes.

"On behalf of all of us," Julie says.

"And in appreciation for all he gave us," Rita adds. "For the encouragement he offered, for making sure everything we needed was always there . . ."

The mike both blends and separates their voices. Between these girls—one song, two melodies.

"For the way he smiled and for being our friend and never giving up on us."

"And because we miss him—because Reverend Gallagher can't be here . . ."

"We voted—all of us . . ." Julie glances around to her teammates. "We voted to dedicate this season to him. And we want you to have this." Julie reaches into her warm-up jacket. Then she takes my shaky hand which doesn't seem to want to open, and she places a large block letter C in my palm. "For him."

I blink down at the letter, a little gold basketball pinned to the fleecy royal blue.

As applause fades, Ward nudges me. "Say something."

Rita guides the microphone into my hand.

I gaze up to the bleachers on either side—freshmen, sophomores, juniors, seniors, all of them fidgeting, waiting to get on with things. They desire the large noise, the band's blare, a cheerleader's rocketing back flip. But I would like to give them a calm word. Though the mike slides in my panicked wet grip and my eyes well, I need to say something here. And I wish for my father's voice, because I'm accepting this honor for him. I long to hear his words issuing from the microphone . . . to tell Corrine Simonet seated far above with her arm wrapped around her first-born son . . . You, way up there—*Put on bowels of mercies, kindness, humbleness of mind* . . . To implore these young, restless faces, *Put on learning. Put on forgiveness. Walk in wisdom toward them who are without, and redeem the time.* I'd send these words ringing to the rafters and echoing down the bleachers to settle full on every listening ear . . . *But above all these things put on charity, which is the bond of perfection. For you shall inherit the Earth. And in your flesh you will see God.*

But at the end, my father lost his voice. And all the words—except for a very few—got stuck on his tongue.

Ward pokes me a little harder. I glance again to the team, surprised as Jen gives me a nod. For an instant I catch a trace of pride turning her smile shy, then she looks away. But Tara is gazing straight at me. "Tara," I whisper. And I remember when my father was in the rehab center—how they told me that speech amounts to only 10 percent of all communication. Standing here, I think this could be so. I believe—just now—Tara has caught my entire unspoken but well-meaning speech. I watch her leaning out from the line. She mouths the words and I lift the mike.

"Thank you," I stammer up to all those rows. "Thank you very much."

Then fast, I turn and start off the court. But Ward stops me. He gives me a hug and a kiss. Then he moves to Jen and wraps his arms tight around her. To those watching, this must represent an intimate family moment, like the ones glimpsed so often at various large ceremonies. But it's also the comfortable gesture of a man who leads a public life. Seeing him now, it occurs to me that the whole world is Ward's walk-in closet—that place where he hangs his laureled jacket and pins his high hopes—a place so commodious, I doubt he'll ever come out. Yet here on this court, he gives Jen and me his best effort. This public display of affection is heartfelt. This is good-bye.

And so I sit alone now, as Foster races the gym in a tumultuous wave and Nekuda takes the mike to perform what appears to be his much-anticipated reggae rap.

> Listen to the words
> of the prophet I and I
> as I speak in praise
> of the Coarsegold High . . .

Nekuda bobs to the beat, his dreadlocks snaking wild around his dark head.

> I'm waiting for a fast break
> a run and a gun
> like an ex-o-dus
> straight out of Babylon . . .

I grip my father's bright blue letter in my lap, determined to keep myself here. At home, Ward will be packing—his departure hastily premature. If it weren't for me—this marriage ending—I'm certain Ward would've stayed for Jen's play-off game. I believe he would've given anything . . .

> To see Rita, Julie,
> Jen on the go
> like Shadrack, Meshack
> and Abednago . . .

So I hope Nekuda stops soon, because his reggae rap is tearing me apart. Granted, Nekuda is our Lady Miners' most loyal fan, with us from the beginning—from that very first game, with me. He deserves this moment at center court—this slight boy of color, wearing the hues of mother Africa and weaving bits of thread to circle our wrists like rainbows. Friendship bracelets. I'm still wearing mine. It's supposed to be left on, Tara told me. She said, In the shower, when you sleep . . .

And then, at last, Nekuda's words come to an end. He steps away to loud whistling applause, which is a relief when you consider how hard he must've worked just to memorize that epic.

As the gym quiets, a cheerleader smiles into the mike and announces the rally's wind-up event. Soon this crowd will be gone, and I'll walk Jen to the rear parking lot. I'll stop at the Blazer for her ironed uniform. Jen will smooth the uniform straight, hooking the hanger over her fingers, casual but careful. She'll say, See you tomorrow. And maybe she'll give me a kiss, maybe not. But somehow I believe she will. Then she'll step across the asphalt to the Dwyers' thirty-foot Winnebago. Most likely, there'll be too much luggage—gym bags, garment bags, a legitimate suitcase or two. Chris Nye will definitely be bringing her sleeping bag because, according to Jen, her mother "has this thing about motel mattresses."

There's a stir in the bleachers. Four students have been chosen—or perhaps browbeaten—into representing his or her class in a competition that appears to involve the use of toilet paper.

With the class standard-bearers in tow—one freshman, a sophomore, junior, and a senior—the cheerleaders step across the court to our team lineup. As the cheerleaders approach, Lady Miners break their soldierly ranks for the first time. They duck, giggling behind one another to avoid this pep rally foolishness.

If you happen to be traveling in our golden state this afternoon and decide to stop overnight in Sacramento, it's possible you may see these girls. You might spot them ordering double cheeseburgers and large fries. You could check into the same motel. They're staying at the River View Ramada Inn. If there's an indoor swimming pool, they'll be there. My daughter is the tallest one—the one with light brown hair and brown eyes she got from my side. All these girls will be wearing letterman jackets. And you'll notice how they carry themselves like the excellent athletes they are. After 9:00 P.M., I'm fairly sure they'll be congregating at the closest ice machine. It's my observation that young people—particularly those from towns small as ours—derive no end of pleasure in filling up those cardboard buckets.

From the team lineup, the cheerleaders have tapped our four seniors—Julie Dwyer, Liz Kauffman, Rita Avent, and Tara—girls whose days of high school play are nearly at an end. Not that Tara will be suited up for tomorrow's game, or that Liz Kauffman will see more than her usual minute on the floor. But no matter—these two are listed on the roster. And whatever her motivation, I believe Tara has suffered no small humiliation attending classes and appearing on this court in order to travel to State with the team. No wristbands can completely conceal her white bandages, and no amount of cologne or brassy gold ribbon can spark her dim eyes. Plus, given the distance her parents are keeping from these proceedings, I'd guess that Tara is also here over their fuming protests.

The object of this class competition, as I understand it, is to wrap each of the four Lady Miners in toilet paper. "We want these Miners covered from head to foot," a pert cheerleader says, nodding to the class representatives. "You leave anything showing, you're disqualified."

There's a smattering of guffaws from the bleachers. But the chosen representatives are seriously straight-faced. They're allowed to use as much toilet paper as they need, and they've stockpiled at least six rolls—each of them.

"On your marks," a cheerleader commands. "Get ready . . ." And the whistle bursts shrill. The students grab their rolls and leap to work. From both sides of the gym, the cheering racket is enough to buckle the bleachers level. It seems even the most defiant sophomore, the aloof senior, is suddenly compelled to holler, Go, go, go . . . Oh God, you missed her knee . . . You dork, you dweeb—get another roll . . . Go!

They're winding frantically from the feet up, and the freshman appears to have taken the lead. Julie Dwyer is already wrapped to her chin. Down the row, Tara's also disappearing fast. But with a final surge the freshman boy makes one spectacular spin, and he's over the top. Julie is a pillar of white. Next, Tara's covered. Then Rita. The sophomore finishes last, although I'd give the job on Liz Kauffman very high marks for neatness.

A cheerleader steps to the freshman and raises his arm straight up, like a prize fighter. This boy is so thrilled he vaults his last roll of toilet paper steep and unfurling into the senior section. Instantly, there's a serpentine response from the also-rans on the floor, until the whooping bleachers are striped and crosshatched. I blow a torn, fluttering piece from my face. In the midst of this ruckus, Principal Ledbetter gazes grim from the double doors.

Out on the court, our five remaining Lady Miners gather around their mummified teammates. I watch Jen run her hand along Julie Dwyer's thick, wrapped shoulder. Jen's fingers peck as if to find an opening, a crack in all that white.

Here in the parents' row, Instamatic cameras flash at either side of me. A few smiling parents duck onto the court—camcorders aimed, film rolling. A little bit of family history is being recorded here. We will never witness such a spectacle again. Even the quieting stands seem aware. The principal himself has left his post, wadding toilet paper in his fists, cleaning up. This is a first, and once is enough for him.

But on the bench, Sylvestro Avent doesn't move to lift a finger. For this pure white space of time, Sylvestro is our acting coach, his necktie still in place and maintenance-free. He sits watching, hunched in the dark suit he wears to Sunday mass, his hands laced with his rosary beads. If he ever has grandchildren, I believe he will tell them . . . Once, your mother was spun like a cocoon . . . Once, they wrapped her in white swaddling clothes . . . They shrouded her with winding cloth . . . And then . . . This is true, he'll say. I saw it happen. Then these three girls—your mother suddenly among them—appeared as angels in shining garments. They said, woman, why do you weep . . . Tara, why are you crying?

She comes across the court, trailing those flimsy white strips. In her hair, the big gold bow is smashed flat and hanging. Somehow she looks larger than she is, so padded and tattered in paper and stumbling for the cheerleader with the mike.

She clamps the microphone in her fumbling grip. For a moment its screeching feedback startles her. She blinks at her shaking hand, the awful noise. And just then, I see her mother plunging down the bleachers.

"Tara," I call as if to warn her, or stop her. I don't know which, or even what I'm doing—only moving onto the court because she just keeps crying, her voice drowned in the high shrieking mike—and her mother still coming with such a wrathful face. "Tara—"

But the girl raises her trembling hand quick and flat out like a traffic cop. Corrine hesitates at the sidelines. I step back, feeling Sylvestro Avent tug my sleeve. Suddenly the piercing sound of the mike ceases, leaving a stunned quiet that swells down the bleachers and from all the doors—this silence more deafening than any noise.

Tara rakes the gold bow from her hair, her face loose and twisted with tears. She rips the white streamers off her arms. In the stands, there's an uneasy shifting—whispers, as Tara peels the sweatbands from her wrists. Then she lifts an edge of white bandage, and she yanks.

"No!" her mother cries, lunging onto the court. It seems in these few moments, Corrine has aged far past her years, beyond all memory of second runner-up beauty. Her face looks smeared. She sways into Foster's wide receiver arms, and he holds her clear.

The gauze bandage reels from Tara's left wrist. She glances down, fretting with the mike, her right hand. Then she stumbles toward the cheerleaders and says, hoarse and urgent, "Help me." But those girls have no stomach for this. And besides, she did this to herself—she's saying so, stammering into the mike, both hands finally free.

"I did this . . ."

Tara lifts her left hand. She turns her wrist this way and that. But for a moment it seems she's forgotten the crowd. She stands staring at her wrists. "Coach," she whispers. The name breaks in her voice. My breath catches, seeing her fingers tear at her wrists. But the wounds are thin and the stitches hold—all those stitches lined black as ants.

Then her breath plows loud through the microphone.

"I lied."

And again her mother cries, "No!"

Along the baseline, the team stands absolutely still. A roll of toilet paper hangs caught in the basket's net. Jen's face is pale and so open as to appear utterly blank.

Tara's voice falters up to the bleachers. "Coach . . ."

On either side, a ripple moves along the rows.

"Coach . . ." "Coach . . ."

But I'm whispering, "Tara . . ." I step toward her, holding out my hand, as if she's a child caught in swift current, or my father crossing that dangerous, busy road. But I couldn't save my father. And Tara will not come.

She swings away, pushing the hair from her face. She blinks up. The discarded white gauze curls at her feet. A remnant of toilet paper drifts down her back.

"Coach, if you're here—" She puts a hand to her streaming eyes, her shoulders sagging over the microphone. "Everything," she mumbles. "Everything . . ." She shakes her head—keeps shaking her head. ". . . lies."

Tara's words fade into the gym's steel rafters. For a moment, Sylvestro Avent lingers beside me. Then he moves toward his somber Lady Miners. Cheerleaders drift to the sidelines. Greg Simonet turns his wife away, as if leading her from the scene of some terrible tragedy, a loved one suddenly lost and gone forever.

Only Tara remains. I watch her bending, her hands still shaking as she gathers up the limp gauze. But she isn't lost—she does not seek the living among the dead. In this moment, she redeems the time. She puts on learning. She puts on the bonds of charity.

And she sees God in her flesh.

Eighteen

I am going to State. For the ride, I've brought along a thermos of Swiss mocha decaf, plus a bag of extremely rich double-chocolate-chip cookies studded with chunky pecans. I can use the calories. Rummaging through the bedroom closet this afternoon, I found that most of my vital statistics have decreased a full size since the last time I had the occasion to seriously deliberate what to wear. I also discovered—and this seemed even more startling—that almost every article of crammed clothing I vaguely counted as my own actually belonged to Ward. My cupboard, as the nursery rhyme goes, was bare.

Last night—with the exception of my own tossing self—my bed was empty as well. The whole house creaked dark and vacant. Jen slept a hundred miles away. I couldn't creep upstairs to slide under the covers beside her. And across the hall, my father's bed remained painfully made without even one wrinkle. Finally, around 1:00 A.M., I sat up on my pillows and switched on the lamp. I reached for the stat book, which I'd been studying earlier, and I copied out this passage from the white leather Bible my father had given me. "Whereas ye have always obeyed, not in my presence only, but now much more in my absence, work out your own salvation with fear and trembling." In the absence of my father, my daughter, and Ward, these words struck me as worth noting. And it occurred to me that, while no one finally needs permission to go, sometimes permission must still be given—to a parent, a child, a spouse, or a lover—if only for one's own liberation. This also seemed worth observing. It seemed, at that lonesome hour, both exhilarating and profoundly sad.

Before I turn the Blazer onto the highway, I drive by Grace Michaels' duplex one last time. Just as I expected, the drapes are still drawn and the driveway's empty. And so I speed on.

I pass our high school, where all the yellow ribbons fluttering from car antennas, trees, and doors have been joined by bright bows of royal blue. At Safeway, the advertised specials have vanished from the windows, every sign of private enterprise replaced by team spirit: WE SALUTE OUR LADY MINERS!

And just ahead, the border station's flags appear to be flying higher —those stars and stripes and the banner of our great golden state, flapping into the wild blue yonder for our winning girls.

As I pull into the lane, Marshall steps alongside.

"Welcome to California," he says, then he gives me the goofiest grin. "Where're you headed, ma'am?"

I glance to the dash clock. "Listen, Marshall—" I sit back, mustering my patience, "I'm going to State, as you very well know. And there's sure to be rush-hour traffic holding things up, so I haven't got time for your silliness, which I'm normally only too happy to endure."

Marshall leans oblivious into my window. "Where's Ward?"

"Gone," I answer, shortly.

"So I hear," Marshall says, raising an eyebrow.

"Marshall, please."

"Anyway . . ." He nods closer. "She called here this morning—Mrs. Simonet. She thought you were working. And the woman was pissed, excuse my language. She's got some notion it's all your fault—what happened with her daughter at the assembly yesterday."

I stare into Marshall's ruddy, windblown face, and he shrugs.

"Of course, I did my best to convince her that whole idea didn't seem too likely. I mean, a person in your state of mind helping somebody else come to their senses."

"Well, Corrine could've phoned me at home . . ."

"Nope," Marshall says. "I pretty much discouraged her from doing that." Marshall pauses a moment, squinting into the backseat. "You giving those away?"

I glance to a tangled pile of wire hangers bound from my new sparse closet to our local thrift shop. "Be my guest." For just this minute, I've got time to spare—all of a sudden picturing Tara leaning from the team lineup, mouthing those words . . .

Marshall grabs an armful of hangers, then steps from the lane.

"Wait," I call after him. "What exactly did you say to Corrine?"

"Nothing much. I told her I was the Antichrist, and if she bothered you at home, I'd personally see to it that she burned in hell."

Marshall drops the hangers beside the office door. "Good luck at State," he shouts across the lanes. "And drive carefully." Then he waves me through with a flourish, using both hands as if to lift me over the mountains and set me safe on the other side.

I start up the grade—that straight stretch rising before the wide curving turns to the summit. For a minute I stay in the slow lane, careful not to spill my coffee. Then I take a long swig and tramp the gas.

Along these first miles, the bare interstate feels desolate, our little town disappearing fast from my rearview. We live in what's called a rain shadow. And I'd like to think that here, at the end of this storied season—on this day, the sky will suddenly open and lightning will flash the close high horizon and send thunder rolling—that as I climb, this riddling torrent will sheet and drift into the long soft falling of snow—that white will fill this granite chain and put new flesh on the dark prehistoric spine—that even my windshield wipers will hush and the sharp blades surrender with the pure gathering of altitude and quenching air.

But the sun is in my westward eyes and riding low. Here, the coffee steams from my hand like dry ice. And I can't say that any of us should feel wholly thankful for the victories of this passing season. As our gloating President pointed out, "This is no time to gloat."

Yesterday after that assembly, Tara stumbled from the gym, her tearful face still swamped from all her hard telling. And she asked everyone—just anyone—to share a room at the Ramada Inn. The rear parking lot was already shadowed, the thirty-foot Winnebago waiting. I don't pretend to understand why it is that the major events of these past weeks seem to have taken place in the potholed expanse of our high school parking lot. But standing there watching Tara, the white gauze still curling through her fingers—hearing her ask each teammate . . . Can I? With you? because the reservations made very clear, two to a room—and observing that no girl stepped forward, not even my daughter, who was once a friend, my own eyes faded. And my face fell with Tara's. I saw her parents, her pale younger brother, buckle their seat belts and drive away without so much as a glance or a wave goodbye.

The Lady Miners drifted past Tara toward the motor home. I handed

Jen her ironed uniform. "Honey—" I said. "Sweetheart . . ." But though I might tell Jen the forgiving words to say, it seemed compassion could only be demonstrated. And there wasn't any more time. Mr. Dwyer revved the Winnebago's engine. Heavy metal already bumped loud at a long side window. Then Tara brushed by. I grabbed her arm like one last chance, and she glanced over. Her dull gaze fell to my gripping hand. She said, "Don't worry, Mrs. Castle." I scarcely heard, following her eyes, fumbling with the frayed strings of my bracelet. I tied the bracelet around her scarred wrist. For a moment Tara blinked down. Then she nodded, striving to smile. "Everything will be all right."

But descending from this granite tinderbox, I'm not so sure. I believe our drought will never end. Down the western flank, every creek bed still runs empty and all the machines are out of ice. Continents away on that other desert road, they're still tallying up the casualties, 150,000 dead, still counting, and a sheikdom of cross-eyed trillionaires still ruling Kuwait . . . Pink still in Yuma.

Gradually, the rocky shoulder of the road levels to pale sedge grass. I drop into the dusky valley. As I pass the exit to Sunrise Mall, I think of Midge and reach for a chocolate chip cookie. Midge called this morning after my sleepless night and said, Eat something. According to her, Foster had returned from the pep assembly with a blow-by-blow description of the proceedings and the added detail that I appeared gaunt—a word Foster would never use, but never mind. I *have* lost one size and could've easily avoided driving alone if I'd left earlier with Midge, Foster, and Nekuda, plus escaped my own gloomy company. And eaten a large meal at Macy's third-floor cafeteria, besides. Except I didn't feel up to extreme comparative shopping, an activity Midge pursues to the utter exclusion of actually buying something. During this time of temporary economic downturn, Midge will simply not settle for less—only drastically reduced.

And of course, I anticipated this heavy traffic clotting every urban artery. I told Marshall as much. Even so, I had no idea. It seems nothing on Earth could've prepared me for the three-lane business route and a sign ahead reading Florin Road and the sheer memory of Jen shoving toward me, up the aisle of that drugstore and my feet carrying me frantic into the street, my father lying there, somebody proffering a box of Kleenex at my bended knee, the leaves of the eucalyptus shimmering distant and the sirens wailing close, but too late. This Sacramento revisited.

I can't bear to look. A horn blares beside me, and I hit the brakes. Here, at the end, I seem to be veering all over the road.

"Hey, lady," somebody yells from the bumper-to-bumper on the right. "Get a grip!"

It's nearly six o'clock and the light is almost gone. No one should have to make this trip alone. Here, in the dead of winter, a fog settles into the valley. It rises from the lowlands and the citrus heights, from the fallow rice fields and the American River wallowing to thick muddy bottom. Some people call it tule fog, but I believe this haze tonight could be just exhaust.

All around, I hear the muffled noise of car radios and slow engines. My rearview mirror is blanched in headlights. Ahead, strings of red flare brighter with brakes applied. Sitting here, caught in the murky middle lane at rush hour, I feel a sick panic. Maybe it's this sign I'm now creeping past—the words FLORIN ROAD. Or the large pale dome rising off the next exit, those lights casting a glow into the thick exhaust. There is no air; this tournament is called single elimination. And I want to turn and rush back to higher ground. I want to go home.

But my seat is reserved—Midge phoned ahead. My ticket waits at Will Call and the stats I must keep lie on the dash. And so I gulp the dregs of my coffee, eyeing that next exit and I think to myself: Get a grip.

I hold out until the last possible moment, then I signal for the right lane. But as I ease over, I see dozens of cars flashing with me. All of a sudden it appears everyone's looking to take the exit, as if this is a sold-out pro game with national coverage. But tonight's attraction is high school girls and we're—each of us—bound for State. This heartens me. I turn down the ramp following these others, until gradually my mounting stage mother fright subsides, falling to that acceptable level of nervousness which is only natural and normal. Parental.

The stadium easily holds 12,000. But parking here is cramped, plus hazardous, with cars constantly pulling in and out. Several teams have reached this first round of competition, and ours is the third game scheduled tonight. One ticket will admit a person to all contests, so some spectators are randomly arriving or leaving—some games have already been decided. Only those teams that win this evening will go on to the next round tomorrow.

After a long, cruising hunt, I finally pull into a space. I slide the stats off the dashboard and climb outside. But as I turn from the car, I see a fleet of yellow school buses rolling slowly away. And I think, single elimination—just one chance. I unlock the Blazer and lean back inside for the bag of cookies. Tonight, we're going to need every ounce of our strength, all the energy we can muster.

The trek to the main entrance seems forever. From this distance, the stadium appears temple-domed and the light golden. I hear the crowd, the drifting strains of music. And I hurry, for fear our game is about to get underway.

Inside, the stadium lobby is packed, people surging for hot dogs, soft drinks, souvenir programs, and T-shirts. The line at the Will Call window stands at least fifteen deep, but moving steadily. The racket is deafening, with student booster clubs holding their own competitions in a barrage of school colors and cocky taunts leading here and there to flirtatious games of pickup. But then, love never does abide by the provincial rules of power. Even as I watch, a loyal Mendocino Maverick appears to have fallen entirely under the spell of a Grass Valley Cobra.

"Next," the woman behind the Will Call window says, and I'm nudged forward.

Loudly I give my name, and the harried woman flips through a long tray of envelopes and pulls one out.

But as I reach into my purse for my wallet, the woman shakes her head. "Your seat's already paid," she says, shouting through that little hole in the window. "Your newspaper took care of everything with the press pass."

I blink down as she slides the envelope to me. "Newspaper?"

But the woman is already craning past me, hollering "Next!"

I step away feeling such confusion, my first thought is to find a women's room, which I don't need and will never locate. Not in this mob. So I walk on, opening the little white envelope as I go. My ticket reads Section A, Row 6, Seat 11, and my press pass says *Yuma Star Tribune*.

For a minute I stand glancing from my pass to the milling crowd, allowing myself to be bumped and elbowed. It occurs to me that I might continue around the wide circle of this lobby until I reach the entrance to Section A and find Midge, who can possibly tell me the meaning of this. But asking Midge seems too easy somehow, and from what I can gather, there's still some time before our game begins. These events tend to run a little late, what with four contests scheduled back-to-back. Given my new status as a member of the press, I'm feeling suddenly aware of how all this works. And calm, too. I'm perfectly calm.

Seeing a gentleman wearing a similar pass, I peel the paper backing from my own sticker, then press the badge to my crepe blouse.

"Excuse me," I say, stepping to the man. I hear my voice, cool and composed. "Could you direct me to the press booth?"

The man gives a hearty laugh, which I take to be collegial, as in colleague. Then he squints down. "Yuma?"

I pull at my crepe chest, taking another look at my badge. "*Yuma Star Tribune*," I tell him. "That's Arizona."

"What in hell . . ." my fellow reporter says.

But I pay no attention. "Well, if there's not a booth, how about the locker rooms? I'm covering the Coarsegold High School Lady Miners."

"All the frigging way from Arizona?"

"You're goddamned right," I answer, feeling the full freedom of my position. Cursing aside, I believe I could truly be cut out for this line of work.

The man unfolds a paper from his pocket, then studies what appears to be a detailed map. "Okay," he says after a moment. "Follow me."

We push through the throngs, the reporter speaking loud above my head. "Those girls are up against one of the best inside teams in the state. They sure as hell don't want to let that number 14 come anywhere near the basket. She can shoot the lights out."

"That's nothing," I answer, staying right alongside as we veer away from the noise. I match him all the way down a twisting catacomb of corridors. "The Miners have three horses that can post up the middle and maneuver in a phone booth. They've got arms like windmills and the genius of leap. Plus, a young center with legs that stretch from hell to breakfast."

"Is that so," the man murmurs. He gives me a long, assessing look. "Could be we'll see a real barn burner out there tonight."

"Could be," I say.

The reporter takes a sudden left turn and pulls up to a closed metal door. "This is them," he says. Then he gives a nod and is gone.

For a moment I linger at the door. I tuck my crepe blouse into the very loose waist of my skirt. Then, cautiously, I step inside.

The team stands silent in a room that looks large enough to hold all of Coarsegold High. The lockers are new and limitless down concrete walls. I count three soft drink machines, two snack machines, two ice machines . . .

But these girls are only eight strong, not counting Tara who isn't suited up. And if they are horses, they're running scared right now—running in place and herded small to hear Sylvestro Avent's last quiet words before they take the court.

"Put the season behind you," Sylvestro is saying. "Forget every mistake. This is a brand-new ball game—you're brand new. And I'm proud." He glances to Rita, his voice trailing even more faint. "Very proud."

I tiptoe across the concrete. "They play an inside game." I lean into the team circle, aware of my reporter's voice turning motherly. I would take these jittery girls in my arms, every one. "Keep number 14 away from the basket. Just try and remember—14 can shoot the lights out."

"Mom . . ." Jen whispers.

And then a rap sounds at the metal door. "Eight minutes for warm-ups," a voice calls.

Each head looks up from the circle.

I give a cough, striving for a lighter note as they cram tighter, reluctant to leave this room. "Just go out there and live large," I tell them. But my words fall too soft.

Then Julie Dwyer says, "Hands in."

Their arms meet in the middle like the spokes of a wheel, every wrist girded with brilliant threads—even Tara's. I glance over, watching her fingers hesitate, groping for a place.

Then Sylvestro Avent nods up. "Mrs. Castle?"

I reach in, resting my hand over his. And I feel the strong shake, solid and lifting.

"Team," the girls shout.

"Team," I whisper.

Later, I will remember all this in detail—how a shoelace was pulled and tied again with a double knot, how Chris Nye slipped the birthstone ring off her finger and left it on a bench, how our meager words echoed down the length of that cavernous corridor, the antsy rustle of sleek warm-ups, the click of chewing gum . . . and then the long breaths taken as we near the door to the arena.

"Jen—" I reach for her sleeve in the dim light growing brighter, the music of a pep band swelling. I reach for words before she leaves me here—here at the end—something that will convey it all. There aren't words enough. "Good luck," I say finally.

She nods close. "Thanks." Then she glances curious to my chest—the small badge. But there's so little time left, she won't stop to ask.

Only I will. I keep her a moment more. "Last night," I say, dropping my voice low, "who did you room with?"

Jen snaps the thick elastic at her waist and straightens her shoulders, as if preparing to run with the question. She starts for the door, toward the sound of basketballs already drumming, the crowd's applause. "Tara," she calls, "wait up." I catch her swift gaze returning my way, her carefully cool shrug. "Tara."

I linger in the darkness, smiling to myself and feeling my heart lift. Beyond the door, I hear our Lady Miners take the court. Then I gaze off, trying to remember—how exactly did I get to this spot? I push my thoughts back to the crowded lobby and struggle to retrace my steps. But I was too busy tagging alongside that reporter, too full of my own jabber. And I wish I had that map. In this dim maze of corridors, my previous reliable sense of direction has vanished, and I can't for the life of me think how to find Section A.

My only idea is to follow the team, to step out this door directly in front of me and suffer the embarrassment of finding myself cringing under the glaring lights and on the court, without even a basketball in my hand, just these stat sheets and a bag of cookies.

It seems I have no choice. For a moment I close my eyes, bracing myself for pending humiliation. Outside the door, a band strikes up "California, Here I Come" in honor of these State games—so okay, I tell myself, I am coming out, I'm coming . . . when a firm hand grabs my elbow and I'm suddenly right back where I started from, with my eyes still shut and a voice at my ear. "Mrs. Castle—Hedy . . ."

"Coach," I gasp. I whisper . . . "Coach, is that you?" I grope along a silky arm, afraid to open my eyes, because I think I could be imagining. However, my mother used to say that some things just have to be believed to be seen. And so I'm trying, holding myself absolutely still in the dark—trying hard to believe.

"I would've been here sooner . . . " The words fall out of breath into my hair . . . "But the traffic was awful."

"Tell me about it," I say, remaining casual, although I think I'm starting to reach some sort of blind faith recognition here. I believe this could be Grace. I clear my throat in an effort to contain myself. "Anyway," I whisper, reaching for something more. "Are you having any luck—I mean, quitting smoking?"

She nods against my cheek, and it's then I realize she's got her arm strung around my shoulder, hugging me. "Almost six days," she says, "I've been clean."

And this right here is the clincher, because as everybody knows, it was on the sixth day that God is said to have created man and woman. And God saw that everything was good.

I blink up, staring at her. Outside, the band is launching into another round of "California, Here I Come." But for a moment it seems I'm standing fully in the state of Grace.

Then she takes my hand, and suddenly we're coming out together. As we step from the corridor, I tell her about the inside team and number 14. I say, "I hope you've got your clipboard."

Walking around this arena is as dizzying as circling the globe, which is why I'm striving not to pay any attention to the band, or the ceaseless din of the crowd, basketballs hammering. I keep my eyes steady on the sideline stripe, taking comfort in all the old dimensions that remain the same, no matter how otherwise large this lofty dome might be. I can quote those dependable figures exactly as written in the official rule book . . . The playing court shall be a rectangular surface no greater than . . . Each basket shall consist of a single metal ring, with an inside diameter of 18 inches. The backboard . . .

Grace stops at the scorer's table. She speaks quietly to the officials —the official scorekeepers and the official timekeeper with his quick electronic board that will flash the official numbers high overhead.

I stick tight to Grace, keeping my bag of cookies from the well-groomed official view. "I'm the team statistician," I offer, by way of nervous explanation. "Plus, I'm with the press."

Grace glances over and smiles. "I see you got the pass," she says, just like that—in front of everybody at the table. "Pink told me he was going to pull some strings, since he couldn't be here himself."

"You mean he's *still* in Yuma?" I feel my heart sag because, of course, I've been harboring some little possibility ever since opening that envelope.

Grace nods. "He thinks he'll be deactivated in about two weeks."

I shrug off my disappointment and turn to the official table. "Mr. Lindstrom was called up," I say, for the purpose of clarification. "He's a member of our desert forces in Arizona . . ."

But Grace is already leading me away.

After what seems many miles, we reach our team bench. At the far end of the court, our Lady Miners are still taking warm-ups, and not one of them has yet spotted Coach Michaels. Only Tara seated in her street clothes and Sylvestro Avent wearing his good Sunday suit have noticed. They leap from the bench. And in this instant, I observe a girl transfigured. I glimpse Tara's face shining like the sun, her clothes dazzling. This girl, as you can imagine, possesses an amazing wardrobe. But fortunately, Jen and I have plenty of extra space in our closets, plus many spare hangers lying on the backseat. Ever since the Simonets stormed off yesterday, I've been thinking that Tara might be needing another place to stay after the Ramada Inn.

Then at last I hear Midge calling my name. I look up six rows, over a silver railing, and my empty seat is there, in close proximity to the bench, which I should've known all along, given I'm the one keeping these team stats.

As I turn for my seat, Grace reaches after me. "Thanks for taking all my messages."

"I probably shouldn't have," I mumble.

But Grace shakes her head. "They did me good."

The silver rail is about four feet high and runs the entire circumference of the arena, I assume to discourage overly enthusiastic fans from gaining the floor. Yet, I easily duck under to the spectator side. And these are not bleachers rising before me, but actual metal chairs padded for extra comfort.

I step up the wide aisle, climbing to my row. Midge certainly doesn't need her Coarsegold Booster Club cushion, but she's planted firmly on it regardless. She slides her souvenir program from my reserved seat, and I sink down. At my left, Foster is wearing his blue and gold letterman's jacket, despite this hot crush of people. Another seat over, Nekuda is also warmly layered, the wool profile of Haile Sellasie vaguely visible under a T-shirt emblazoned with a big red basketball circling the great seal of California and the words: I SURVIVED STATE TOURNAMENT, 1991.

"We were beginning to think you'd never make it," Midge grumbles beside me.

"And miss this game?" I open the bag of chocolate chip cookies and pass it down the row. We are going to need every ounce of strength. I give Midge a shrug. "Is the Pope a Catholic?"

"Well, it's just a relief to see Grace here . . ." Midge's voice trails —she stares at my chest. "*Yuma Star Tribune?*"

But the two-minute warning buzzer is sounding, and I can't reply, because our Lady Miners are loping across the court for the bench, smiles spreading as they come.

Grace leans to them, clapping her hands, and I can almost hear her calling, "Hustle round," because this is single elimination about to get underway and no time for reunion, except in the familiar language of hook shot, screen, and give and go—the language of play.

Sylvestro Avent moves to Grace's side, studying his game notes—her right-hand man. At the end of the bench, Tara bends with the big canvas bag, scooping all the loose basketballs inside.

I glance away, unable to watch how she reaches for the balls one after another, tugs at the drawstring . . .

For high school girls, the rule book says: The basketball shall be of an approved orange or natural color, with seams no wider that 1/4 inch. The ball shall measure 28 1/2 inches in diameter and inflation must not exceed . . .

"Mrs. Castle . . ." Nekuda's sweatered arm stretches from the short sleeve of his T-shirt. He reaches past Foster and presses me with chocolate chip cookies. "Don't worry—we'll win. We'll go on to the next round tomorrow. Please," he says, emptying the entire bag of cookies in my lap, "take more than two."

Foster nudges me. "Jen's out of her warm-ups—she's looking good. I think she's starting for Tara."

He points, but my hands are full of cookies and my eyes can't follow. I repeat to myself . . . The playing court shall be a rectangular surface no greater than 94 feet in length . . . Each basket shall consist of a metal ring . . .

Foster nods. "I mean, she's looking kind of right."

Midge opens the stat sheet in my lap.

There is a mercy seat. My father told me. And this seat shall be made of pure gold, and the length thereof, two cubits and a half. And the width thereof, one cubit and a half. And there shall be two angels of gold, rendered from one piece, on the ends of the mercy seat . . .

I feel the game gathering. Here, even the air is athletic—sounds clear and rounded—music traveling as if from the celestial vault itself. I blink across the sheen of the beautiful floor, everyone gathered. No Home Side, no Visitors. Before the bench, these girls huddle close.

And you will see one angel on the end of this side, and another angel on the other end of that side . . .

Drums and angels, my father said. And I hear drums; I glimpse the angels there.

Girls lean in, their hands melding in the middle. "Grace!" is the call.

Then the teams take the floor for the center jump. The colors are blue and gold—these are the ones I'm watching.

According to the rules, the referee shall toss the ball. The toss shall be straight and slightly higher than either player can jump . . .

Jen positions herself inside the circle. She is the tallest member of our team. Her right arm stretches up, already reaching. The girl opposite—that girl in green and white—shakes out her hands, then steps to the center line. She is reaching.

"Ready?" the referee asks, and the captains answer, "Ready."

But the rule book doesn't say how far a girl can jump. What gives the referee to know how high to toss the ball?

On the bench, Tara and Grace and Sylvestro Avent sway close together, as if to see with one pair of eyes. It's been six days, Grace told me. She is clean, and these girls are brand new. This is a game played in the air. So who's to say how high a girl can jump.

The referee puts the whistle to his mouth. He holds the ball at the very center of the circle—the two tall girls on either side. My daughter is one of these.

I hear the short shrill of the whistle, and then the ball goes spinning up and the two girls loft themselves, their arms stretched straight, long open hands reaching, hair flying.

The ball rides on and on. A cheer rises, then echoes vast all around. I watch, thinking there is no end.

Her fingers strain into the golden light, into the resounding heavens. She reaches through all of creation, soaring for the tap. And I believe we'll never be eliminated. Tomorrow, we'll go on.

There is no end to how high.

ACKNOWLEDGMENTS

I'm deeply grateful to my friends for their encouragement and help with this work: Ginny Snow, Ruth Hall, Dawn Painter, Molly Friedrich, and especially Allan Gurganus. The book was expertly guided to publication by Rebecca Saletan and Denise Roy.

Generous assistance was provided by the staff of the Truckee Agricultural Inspection Station and the California Department of Food and Agriculture. Thanks to Helen Godfrey and the 1991 Tahoe-Truckee High School Girls Varsity Basketball Team. And to Jeff Hamilton, Dick Hamilton, Lisa Abrahams, Pat Hauser, Scott Johnston, Marlene Armsrong, Laurel and Tom Lippert, and Dr. Eugene Glick and staff.

Most of all, my love and thanks to Tom, Jean, Judy and John, Jan and Tom, and Donna and Joe for all the years we've shared as Family.